CLOUDS WILL BREAK

Clouds Will Break

BRENDA HALL

Karingal Books

Dedication

For my clan:
The descendants of
John and Isabella Cameron
and
Alexander and Annie Robertson

Cameron Family Tree

Robertson Family Tree

Alexander Robertson
22 June 1823-30 Apr 1870

Annie Irvine Calder
5 June 1833-9 July 1903

Johnnie
1860-1866

Lily
1861-1946

Frank
1862-1911

Jim
1864-1951

Jeannie
b. 17th
June 1866

William
Ford-
Robertson
1867-1923

Epilogue
By Robert Browning (1812-1889)

At the midnight in the silence of the sleep-time,
  When you set your fancies free,
Will they pass to where—by death, fools think, imprison'd—
Low he lies who once so lov'd you, whom you lov'd so
    —Pity me?

Oh to love so, be so lov'd, yet so mistaken!
  What had I on earth to do
With the slothful, with the mawkish, the unmanly?
Like the aimless, helpless, hopeless did I drivel
    —Being—who?

One who never turn'd his back but march'd breast forward,
  Never doubted clouds would break,
Never dream'd though right were worsted, wrong would triumph,
Held we fall to rise, are baffled to fight better,
    Sleep to wake.

No, at noonday in the bustle of man's work-time
  Greet the unseen with a cheer!
Bid him forward, breast and back as either should be,
'Strive and thrive!' cry 'Speed,—fight on, fare ever
    There as here!'

1892, Wednesday 9th February

Melbourne Royal Botanic Gardens

From his vantage point on a hillside bench in the shade of a large silver gum, William Cameron watched a group of five children all, he supposed, under the age of ten, playing a chasing game by the lake. Their father was lying on a picnic rug, studying a newspaper. A professional, by his clothes, which were of the same cut and hue as William's own black pants and waistcoat. Like William, his white shirt sleeves were rolled up and his neck-tie abandoned on account of the hot weather. Like William he had a neatly trimmed abundance of dark hair, a fine moustache and fashionably long side burns. The children's mother was broadcasting the remains of their picnic lunch to a quickly amassing crowd of black and white swans, wood ducks and teal. When she returned, she combed her fingers lightly through her husband's hair and settled comfortably beside him.

William ached.

The air was humid, its summer heat reduced by a solid cover of grey cloud that promised rain in the late afternoon. Vegetation had rebounded after the heavy rains and dramatic flooding of the Yarra valley in the winter of 1891. The grass was a brilliant green poignantly reminiscent of Edinburgh's Princes Street Gardens, and the many flowers, shrubs and trees planted by the early colonists were growing at a rate that would ensure that Melbourne's Royal Botanic Gardens would soon be on par with the best gardens to be found in Europe.

The happy shouts of the children were interspersed with the twittering of a wealth of small birds—thornbills, wattle birds and reed warblers, to name just a few William could recognise by their call. Along with these pleasing sounds, the gentle breeze carried the fragrance of a medley of flowers, which Jeannie could have identified if she were here. It was their favourite place. He for the birds and the water. She for the flowers and the trees. Together they had talked of children. He had been off-hand, and he sensed her disappointment as the subject slipped away.

Now William gazed upon the very thing he wanted most. He and Jeannie, on a picnic rug stretched in front of a lake. Five children under ten playing chase across a verdant field of grass. His heart's true desire struck him with absolute clarity, now that he knew it to be out of his reach.

If Jeannie became his wife, she would also be denied the prospect of such happiness and for that reason, he must break their engagement. He would have to tell her why, he would have to reveal the extent of his lies, and then he must leave Melbourne and never see her again.

Or ... he heard the admonition in his mother's voice; he remembered the scolding she had given him each time the road ahead had seemed too grim.

He must march breast forward never doubting that clouds will break.

I

1885 - 1888

Chapter 1

William Cameron, M.D.

Saturday 1st August 1885: Graduation Day, Edinburgh University

Back-stage the mood was jubilant. The young men—the nation's educated elite—were waiting impatiently to parade into the hall, sweeping their black graduation gowns over the floor stones, tousling hair and slapping backs. They were primed, ready to take their places, marching Scotland the Brave towards the twentieth century. William revelled in the proud conviction that he belonged in this outstanding cohort. Edinburgh University led the world, in William's opinion, in medical research. It was here, in the university's laboratories and operating theatres, that he and his fellows would discover the cures for the diseases that ravaged mankind; the surgical methods that could repair the human body.

One too many hard slaps caused William to turn away in a sudden fit of coughing. He pulled his handkerchief up to his mouth quickly, but not before some flecks of blood landed on the cuff of his crisp white sleeve. A dark anxiety stained his exuberance. He licked a clean space on his handkerchief, checked that his spittle was clear and scrubbed carefully at his cuff, leaving a dirty smear. He tried to pull his graduation gown down his arm but, being taller than average, the hired robe sat askew on his shoulders. He shrugged it back into place and tucked the cuff of his sleeve in half. That would have to do.

From the stage, William watched his mother's gaze weaving between the rows of identically-clothed graduates; her broad hand out-reaching the more delicate hands that were waving, hoping to make contact. Sweat glistened in the deep furrows of her brow, and the skin around her nose was flushed dark pink from heavy handkerchief use. Her grey eyes were rheumy, and the spider veins born of eleven pregnancies spread in an angry red web over her face, down her throat and across the top of her ample bosom. She was overflowing her seat; cushioning his father with the rounded folds of her body; fanning him with the sheaves of floral cotton that hung from her arm.

His father looked small, beside her, and uncomfortably hot in his formal attire. He was fingering his bowtie; repetitively easing his stiff collar; shuffling his top-hat on his knee. No doubt wishing the event was over. John Cameron was more comfortable in the sawmill, or on the docks in a tweed jacket and flat cap. He was a merchant of corn, potatoes, manure and timber, and he had firm views as to how each of his sons was to gain practical experience in his business.

William's mother, Isabella, had equally firm views about the merit of education.

Their hard-won solution was for William to go to Edinburgh to study forestry. When he begged, at the end of his first year, to switch to medicine, his father was furiously opposed. His mother—invincible on family matters—prevailed.

William hoped, today, that his father would refrain from telling anyone in this venerable hall that medicine was 'quackery'.

After the ceremony, William and his friends gathered on the parade ground, laughing and shouting and throwing their caps;

perfecting the flick of the wrist that would make the mortarboard fly flatter and further. One by one departing members of the group peeled away in the company of their families.

"Och, Willie, you looked so handsome up there! Och aye, I'm so proud of you!" His mother sobbed, dabbing at her tears with an inadequate lace handkerchief. William handed his graduation scroll to his father, and stooped to get his arms as far around her as he could manage.

His father stood close by, reading the certificate. "William Johnstone Cameron, M.B, Ch.M." His bearded face creased into many deep lines, and his pale blue eyes were uncommonly gentle. "Aye, laddie. You've done right."

A professor with many coloured silks adorning his gown emerged from the crowd to put his hand on William's shoulder.

"Mr and Mrs Cameron? I'm Dr Gibson—I supervised William's thesis."

John and Isabella greeted the professor shyly.

"William, I heard you've a place with Dr McDougall?"

"Yes, Sir."

"Excellent! But I want you back in the research lab. When can you spare me the time?"

"Thursdays, Sir," William responded enthusiastically. "I've arranged to work through Wednesday evening so I can be free on Thursday."

"Perfect. As soon as you're ready."

Dr Gibson turned his attention to Isabella.

"You have a very talented son, Mrs Cameron. You've a right to be proud of his achievement. His thesis on contagion in children was truly enlightened. I've often wondered, what *did* you do, to give him such a passion for medicine?"

William cringed. His father looked bemused, and his mother launched into the opening.

"Always, Dr Gibson. Since he was a wee lad. Always asking our Dr Niven questions ... do you know Dr Niven at Newburgh?"

Dr Gibson shook his head, but kept his eyes fixed on Isabella, encouraging her to tell-all.

"And our little Isa, she was not quite four, you see. Willie's favourite. The baby Andrew was sickly, and I had Willie—who was fourteen then—looking after little Isa, and he blamed himself ..."

"Ma," William tried to interrupt, but his mother was unstoppable.

"She fell in the dock drain when they were playing chase, and Willie pulled her out, and she was fine, but the next day she was ill. We told Willie, didn't we John?"

John offered Dr Gibson a wry smile.

"We told Willie—and Dr Niven told Willie—it was the diphtheria from the next village. But he still blamed the drain."

Dr Gibson nodded sympathetically at William. "Hence your interest in Edinburgh's sewerage?"

Isabella continued.

"Then the last baby, Andrew, sickly since birth. Too many babies, you know how it is doctor. He was born too early. His lungs weren't ready. He made it past the first winter, but not the second. He passed only six months after little Isa, and with George in between."

"A third child died?" Dr Gibson probed with genuine medical concern.

"No, George was one of our older boys. He was twenty ..." Isabella stalled momentarily. "Trouble with his lungs. It was asthma, wasn't it dear." She patted John's arm and he scowled at her instead of taking up the story. "At sea," she finished lamely.

William knew his father's customary indictment of the medical profession was imminent. He seized the opportunity to change the conversation.

"My father's in shipping. He owns a quay on the Tay, at Newburgh."

"Indeed?" Dr Gibson turned to John. "And you own ships as well?"

"I have a financial interest in a line of ships that use my quay, and I own the forestry mill and the warehouses alongside. We bring in oilcake and turnips to feed the local stock, and we ship out timber and horticultural produce to ports along the eastern coast as far south as Hull. I'm working on opening trade with brokers in London."

"Fascinating! My brother's also in shipping. You may know him."

To William's relief, his father and Dr Gibson were now engaged in a safe conversation. He turned away to clear his throat. The stringy white phlegm that had been plaguing him caught in his windpipe, pitching him into a fight for breath. He stumbled through the crowd, looking for privacy and when his mother followed him, he waved her away.

"Water," he gasped in explanation, heading for the refreshment table.

He felt her eyes anxiously boring into his back as he hurried to find a glass.

~

John and Isabella Cameron had 14 children: three of them being Isabella's stepchildren, while she had given birth to seven boys and four girls herself. Angus was Isabella's eldest stepson, Bessie her stepdaughter, and George was born two months before his mother, Jane Anderson, died. In August 1860, Isabella was in her second year as the preliminary grade teacher of the Cupar Road School, Newburgh, when the three Cameron children first arrived at the school gate. George, only two years old, was too young to attend, but Angus, five, and Bessie, barely four, held him firmly between them and insisted he stay in class with them.

"He's to stay with us 'cos our Maw's in the ground," Angus self-righteously advised his teacher.

For the first week, the Camerons arrived at school every day, on time, with clean clothes, packed lunches and shoelaces properly tied. But standards slipped rapidly, and by the second week Isabella had gone from teacher to baby-sitter, conducting classes with George on one hip. She hoped to catch Mr. Cameron at the school gate, but every morning Angus led his siblings to school, and every afternoon he led them home. Isabella thought it outrageous. She made inquiries. Why did the man not employ a nursery maid?

Her informants told her, in hushed tones, that Mr. Cameron had been sorely affected by his wife's untimely death. His nursery maid, an honorable woman working at the very limit of her patience due the complete lack of discipline in the house, had vowed that she would stay until the end of the first week of the school year when the baby turned two, and not a moment longer. Mr. Cameron might be proficient at running his business, but he was incapable of running a house. Isabella puzzled over the appropriate course of action. She decided the 'puir motherless bairns' were in need of her love and patience. She would give Mr. Cameron more time.

She had slipped into a workable routine by the winter term. In fact, she'd grown very fond of George. He was an unassuming delight, and the bigger girls were taking it in turns to look after him, which Isabella thought a positive outcome for all. Her aggravation now focused on Angus and Bessie's home lessons, because they were never done. The notes she addressed to their father came back unopened. Eventually, she sent a year six boy home with the children to personally deliver a note demanding Mr. Cameron's attendance at school.

Mr. Cameron was not at all the haughty, unconcerned father she had imagined. He bowed humbly to her, his flat cap nervously flipping from hand to hand. His tweed coat was fastened with just one button over his matching waistcoat. His tie was misplaced, and his shoes muddy because he had walked all the way from Newburgh Quay. His greying hair, sideburns and beard needed a good trim, and he had the palest, saddest blue eyes she had ever seen. Isabella had to study her notes to set in train the bollocking he deserved. He left her schoolroom thoroughly chastised, and promised that the children would arrive every day in good order with their home lessons done. Meanwhile Isabella, contrary to her original intention, had told him that looking after George was no trouble at all.

The next morning, and many mornings after that, John Cameron delivered his children to the school gate himself. Isabella noticed that since her stern words to him, John's hair had been neatly cut, and his beard had been given a professional trim in keeping with the current fashion. If she wasn't already at the school gate when he arrived, he would wait until she went out to greet him. Each time he directed their short conversation so that they learned one new thing about each other. He was 35; she was 23. He left school to work in his father's inn when he was 13. She had gone to work as a domestic servant for her uncle, the Reverend Burnett of Halfmorton, at the same age, and had attended the church school along-side her duties. John's father, attracted to the ale and spirits that flowed plentifully through his public house, drank him-self into the Newburgh graveyard in 1848. Less than two years later John's mother was also interred in the family plot, leaving John, at age 25, in charge of six younger siblings. Bearing a grudge against alcohol, John swiftly disposed of the Newburgh Inn, and invested instead in one of the four quays that serviced the river Tay. Isabella's father, a saddler by trade, died in 1858 and her mother still lived in the family home, 140 miles away in Annan. She and her older sister lived on their joint teaching stipend in the cottage attached to the Cupar Road School.

It came as no surprise to any who had been watching these regular morning meetings at the school gate, when John

Cameron asked if Isabella would take on the burden of himself and his three children.

They were married in Annan, in April 1861. Isabella, now mistress of the grand Cullalo House, did not return to teaching. Her first child, Margaret, was born in May 1862. William was born 15 months later.

Then Jen, Janet, Johnnie, Alexander, James, Robert, Isa, Joseph and finally, in June 1877, Andrew—born three-weeks premature.

Dr Niven had said it was no surprise, that the eleventh baby in sixteen years was born too early. He had firm words with John, that it was time for separate rooms.

Isabella, however, maintained that baby Andrew came early because of her anxiety over George. The shock of the diagnosis. The arguments with George, and with John. Her fear that it would be too late; that George should have left for New Zealand as soon as they knew.

In September 1885, John and Isabella sat once again in the surgery of Edinburgh's leading respiratory specialist, grimly holding hands.

In the seven years since George had died, Dr Wallace told them, there had been considerable progress in understanding the disease phthisis, as consumption was properly called. There was still debate regarding the cause—genetic or infectious transmission—but modern research provided strong evidence for the latter.

"I hope this will be of some comfort for you, Mr Cameron. It is *my* belief that we will soon irrevocably prove Mr Koch's findings regarding the tubercle bacilli. Even though William is the *second* of your sons, so affected, you need *not* be thinking this fate lies in wait for your other children."

John scowled angrily at the specialist, unappeased. "Ye *still* have no cure?"

Dr Wallace shook his head. "Phthisis is the cause of nearly half the deaths that occur in people aged between 20 and 25. It's a terrible toll on our society. Believe me, Mr Cameron, finding the anti-toxin to defeat this disease is our *highest* priority in medicine. We *will* be successful, but the task will not be done in time for William. He must take immediate steps to restore his lungs to health before further damage occurs."

"Meaning?" John growled; his tone laden with suspicion.

"A change of air."

"Hah!"

"I understand that George died on the sea voyage to New Zealand." Dr Wallace spoke with an air of condescending patience. "However, William is at an early stage. I believe he has the opportunity to recover if he spends time in a hot, dry climate."

"My son died at sea, with none to help him. With none of his family by his side. It took us a year—a *year*—to bring his body home to a proper burial!"

William shrank from the outraged grief he heard in his father's voice. He saw his mother take his father's elbow in a firm, steadying grip.

"I do understand your thinking, Mr Cameron. There are now sanatoriums in the European Alps that purport to be of assistance, but the research I follow shows that the lungs are best helped by air that is *hot* and dry. The air in the Alps is rarefied, dry to be sure but cold, and not as effective. Frankly, it seems to me that most of the benefit to be had from those sanatoriums goes to the businessmen who are promoting them as a false hope to the sorely afflicted. If anything, such places create concentrated pockets of infection, and are better avoided."

"The likely progress of William's condition, Doctor?" Isabella steered the discussion. "What will be happening as time goes?"

Dr Wallace looked at William sympathetically. "You will continue to have the sweats and lose weight, William. You must do all you can to eat plenty of good, fresh food to counteract the effect the disease is having." He paused, waiting for William to respond with an obedient nod. "While your sputum is thick and white, it contains the tubercle bacilli Dr Koch has identified. He is certain this is the cause of the contagion. You must take every precaution not to let others come into contact with this."

The doctor turned in his chair. He pulled several facemasks, a bar of red soap and a small black bottle from a cubicle behind his desk. "You must wear the masks to prevent the spread of droplets from your breath when you cough or sneeze. You must wash your masks and handkerchiefs in Lister's carbolic soap and let them dry in the sun. Your hands as well. *Every* precaution, William, to protect those near to you."

"Why does he cough blood, Doctor?" Isabella asked anxiously.

"The lining of the lungs is destroyed by the bacilli. As it breaks down, it bleeds. The portion that has broken down can't be restored, and so there is reduced surface area to exchange oxygen. This in turn increases the risk of asthma, pneumonia, bronchitis and such. He must dry his lungs, and stop his coughing as a matter of urgency. But William, you must clear your lungs of the white phlegm. It's not enough that the bleeding stops."

Dr Wallace placed the unmarked bottle on his desk, and William picked it up. He unscrewed the cap and cautiously sniffed the contents.

"Balsam," he gasped, blinking his eyes rapidly.

"When your chest feels tight you must forestall the coughing."

John groaned. "All this ye tell us ye ken about the disease, and still, all ye have to offer my son is balsam!"

Dr Wallace responded stiffly. "It's a vital help, Mr Cameron, if the airway is blocked."

"Thank-you Doctor," Isabella pushed herself up from her chair to pre-empt further confrontation. "You've been very frank with us, and now we must think on what you've said, and help William in the way he decides."

Dr Wallace placed a restraining hand on William's arm as William followed his parents to the door. "I understand you are employed as an assistant to Dr McDougall."

Their eyes locked momentarily. Dr Wallace lowered his voice.

"I will be obliged to advise Dr McDougall of your results, should I find that you continue in his surgery."

William inclined his head resentfully. "That won't be necessary. I'll give him my resignation in the morning."

Dr Wallace loosened his grip and patted William on the shoulder. "Go to Australia laddie, and God be with you."

William felt tears of self-pity sting his eyes. He turned after his parents, hands clenched on the bottle of balsam and the bar of soap buried deep in his coat pockets.

Wednesday 28th October 1885: Cullalo, Newburgh

It would have been easier, William thought in his darker moments, to countenance imminent death than the uncertainty of a long-term sentence to the Antipodes. Nothing could wound him more than having to leave his family and friends. Nothing could be more punishing than to give up his work in the surgery, and lose his place at the forefront of medical research. He had one consolation, and it came in the form of a new McKellen double pinion, treble patent half plate field camera.

William's passion for the emerging science of photography was well known amongst his friends and associates. In the research laboratory the hat had been passed around, raising almost six pounds. William's old Instanto camera had sold for £1 and Dr McDougall had given him a sympathetic £1 bonus in his severance pay. The president of the university's photography club prevailed on Joshua Billcliff, considered to be England's leading camera manufacturer, to rearrange his order list and send the McKellen camera he had just completed. The camera itself cost William £6.10.2 and he had funds leftover to buy a matching tripod, a pack of pre-sensitized albumen paper and several packs of the latest Lumiere dry-glass plates.

In the joy of assembling his new toy in his bedroom, William forgot his imminent departure for the South Seas. He brushed the smooth Spanish mahogany of the camera box with his fingertips, gingerly felt the supple burgundy leather of the double extension bellows and turned the box at many angles to the light to enjoy the reflections from the brilliant brass slides, knobs and pinions. He attached the Dallmeyer Rapid Rectilinear brass lens and fitted an empty double dark-slide. He practised the movements the camera could make while revolving on its inbuilt tripod turntable: rising front, tilting front, swing back, tilting back—it was nothing short of miraculous, and undoubtedly deserved the gold medal it had won at the Photographic Society exhibition in 1884.

Even more amazing was that the camera folded into a 10-inch square box that was three inches thick and, with the dark-slides, weighed only two and a half pounds. William had discarded several of the sweaters and coats his mother had included in his tin chest, and had arranged the remaining woollens around the sides of the chest to cushion his delicate cargo. The wooden tripod, which compacted to 24 inches, neatly fitted on a cross angle between the corners of the trunk.

William's plan was to ration his dry plates out across all legs of his journey. On his return, he would print and show off the photos he had taken of the fabulous scenery, flora and fauna of the New World. He had allocated one box of plates to the photographs he wanted to take and print before he left home. This morning, on arrival in Newburgh, he had taken the camera to the sawmill to photograph his friends amongst the workmen there. Now he was impatient to use his remaining three plates to take group photos of his family, posed in front of their home, Cullalo. The night, he thought as he admired the camera standing invitingly on its tripod, could not pass quickly enough. Please God, he prayed fervently, the sun would be bright enough tomorrow afternoon to develop his prints before he had to board the overnight train to London.

His mother entered the room, carrying a stack of books in her arms. She unbundled the books on William's bed, and looked disapprovingly into the trunk, which was not as she had left it.

"They won't fit, Ma." William hurriedly pulled his facemask up from his neck.

"Willie," she reproved him, "you'll need the warmth." She picked up one of the jackets he had discarded, and started folding it for re-packing.

"I'm going into the southern summer, Ma. For the *hot* air."

"You'll be freezing as you go round the Cape."

"They'll have jackets on the boat."

"Ach! You don't know what they have on the boat!"

"I need that space for the camera," William insisted firmly.

She looked critically from the trunk to the camera and back.

"That," she said disbelievingly, "fits in there?"

"It does, Ma," Willie said proudly. "It folds up to be that small."

"Books, Willie, you'll be needing books." She looked wistfully at the volumes she had dropped on the bed.

"I can fit two." He moved to the bedside to look at the books while she inspected the camera, walking around it at a respectful distance.

"Maybe you'll have a new job in the New World, Willie. You'll be one of those travelling photographers instead of a doctor."

"I'll always be a doctor, Ma. I'm taking my bag." He pointed to his brown leather medical bag on the floor by the trunk.

"Maybe they'll have need of a doctor on the boat."

William sensed imminent tears in his mother's diminishing voice. "It'll be a grand adventure, Ma," he said cheerfully. "Six months sailing, out on the ocean waves with the albatross following." He handed a tattered book towards her. "You can't give me your Coleridge, Ma. Where will you be without *The Ancient Mariner* to cry over while I'm at sea?"

"I can get another," she sniffed.

"I'll take Robbie Burns, and Browning."

"Tennyson as well, Willie."

"No. I'll have Burnsie committed to memory, but I'll surely be back before I've read *this*." He shook the heavy *Poetical Works of Robert Browning* at her before packing it into the side of his trunk.

"Maybe you'll stay, Willie. Maybe God wants you to help build a better world in Australia than this one here."

"There is no place in the world better than Scotland," William replied vehemently, taking his mother into his arms. "This is my home, and I'll be back before the heather blooms in summer," he promised.

~

The late October sun was hot on William's back, amplified by the glass above him as he worked alone at the bench in the conservatory. His white sleeves were rolled up, his brow was sweaty, and he had discarded his facemask. He processed one print at a time, positioning the glass negative plate on sticky cloth in the centre of his developing frame, and smoothing a sheet of albumen paper over the top. After securing its backing board, he rested the frame on two bricks propped in the doorway on an angle towards the afternoon sun. Hoping he was correctly judging the power of the sun's rays, William waited for six minutes before removing the paper from the frame, and slipping it into a bath of sodium thiosulfate to fix the image.

He had squeezed 17 people into the family photo, including the cook, two parlour maids and Bessie's fiancé, George Anderson. Everyone held perfectly still in front of Cullalo's big bay window, faces grim with posed concentration. After instructing Edward, his best friend from the mill, on setting the shutter for each exposure, William added himself to the group, crouching with his elbow on his father's knee. In the first image recorded on the double dark-slide, he was scowling at the camera, his lips opening to query what was taking so long. The second image was over-exposed.

The parlour maids had disappeared by the time William loaded the second dark-slide into the camera. He rallied his siblings back into position, and took the next pair of photos himself. He varied the f-stop instead of the shutter speed but again, the second photo was over-exposed. He sorely regretted the waste of his plates and paper. He needed time to practise, and he didn't have it.

William used the plate in his last double dark-slide for photos of the house, front and back. These last two, he decided, were the best of all his photos. He was, at least, improving.

His father came into the conservatory as he was cutting his albumen prints into *carte de visite* rectangles.

"It's time to go, laddie. Bessie has the trap waiting."

"Aye. A minute, Da."

His father walked the length of the conservatory and returned aimlessly. "Are these to be in your trunk?" He motioned to the developing tray and chemical bottles.

"No."

"Your trunk is packed complete?"

"It's on the trap."

His father hummed, watching him sort the photos into two neatly aligned piles. "Train tickets?"

"Aye."

"Ye ken *Waimea* will be at *South West* India Docks, taking on timber?"

William nodded.

"Letters for Captain Sinclair? And Aunt Margaret?"

"Aye, both." William picked a small envelope off the table, inserted one of the two sets of photos, and put the envelope in his inside coat pocket. He looked at his facemask with distaste, and crumpled it into his trouser pocket.

"She's a beautiful ship. Barque rigged, 848 tons—not too big; not too small. Fast. Built in Hamburg, 1868. Originally called '*The Dorette*'. The New Zealand Shipping Company bought her in 1874 and changed her name."

"You told me already."

"She'll make New Zealand inside 100 days. Mid-February."

William handed his father the remaining photos. "Copies for you."

His father shuffled the photos absently while William poured the contents of the chemical bath onto the river pebbles that lined the path outside the conservatory. "Send a telegram from Lyttelton. Your Ma would like that."

William smiled and clapped his hand on his father's shoulder.

"Come back to us laddie." His father seized him in an awkward, desperate embrace.

Chapter 2

William's Travel Journal

Monday 2nd November 1885: West India Docks

From the station platform, looking south, the eye beholds a dead forest—hundreds upon hundreds of mast trunks, booms, spars and yards, stretching over acres of lakes sub-divided by reclaimed roads and joined by canals. Ship hulks lie close together, and between them are crammed hundreds of lighters, some laden perilously top-heavy with goods, while others lie flat and empty, touting for work. There seems no room to move, one could veritably step across boat decks from one side of the dock to the other.

Everywhere, there is hustle and cacophony as lightermen claim right of way, and bid to unload cargo. On the roads, teams of horses stand patiently between shafts, while barrels are hoisted onto their drays. Hackney cabs transport businessmen between the ships and the host of warehouses surrounding the quays.

The air is thick with industry. In the distance, obscured by haze, can be seen the shapes of buildings on higher ground beyond the Thames. By my map, the Greenwich Observatory is amongst them, but I can't pick it out, the smoke and dust laying thoroughly over that horizon. The smell is the strangest mix: iron smelting from the Graving Dock; manure and urine from the Cattle Wharf; seaweed from ship hulls; tar from thousands of ropes and, overlaying this nasty concoction, the sweet fragrance of spices, tobacco and rum from the Import Dock.

The physician in me asserts that the men who work here have a dangerous and unhealthy life. The toxic air claws at my throat and burns in my lungs. My eyes sting from the fumes. And yet, there is such excitement here—receiving ships and the stories they bring from far-flung corners of the world; despatching goods that are needed by people who live such an adventurous journey away. The vastness of the enterprise is astounding. That Great Britain should dare to do this—to be at the centre of world-trade; a mighty sea-faring nation. I feel at once proud to be part of it, and daunted because I am such an insignificant part. How does a man carve out for himself a greater role, a more worthy chunk, of such immense human endeavour?

A not insignificant part of this enterprise, is the mob of street urchins who meet every train. I appoint a weedy boy to take my trunk from the goods van to the waiting tram. Something I could easily have done myself, but I know the lad needs my halfpenny. He makes himself out disappointed, but a labourer here makes sixpence a day, so I have paid him exceeding well. At South Dock there is another crowd of ragamuffins jostling for my custom. One sharp rascal says he knows where my ship, *Waimea*, is berthed, but he can't take me straight. He pauses at each ship until I read the name on its bow—and so we go, from ship to ship.

The lad tells me there are over two hundred ships in the docks on any day, and more than four thousand in a year. Ships in the Australia trade come by once a year, if that. They bring in wool, grain and frozen meat. They take back linen, cotton, processed foods, fine timbers, blood livestock, tallow and oils, saltpetre and explosives. He imparts all this, showing such a clever mind that it is clearly fate's wrongdoing that this lad, almost in his teenage years, can't read even the ship names. He tells me he is the eldest son of a lighterman, and he is confident he has the firm prospect of a career in the docks. What need of reading has he?

Waimea floats with her bow to the North Quay of the South West India Dock, fastened to the tenth of twelve jetties. Her handsomely fashioned bowsprit overhangs the quay, and her three masts stand proud, linked to the bowsprit, the deck and the stern by a complex web of stays. Her yards are stripped; her sails in a building nearby, receiving the attention of a seamstress. Hanging from ropes lashed to the deck rail are two men, one below and slightly ahead of the other, scraping barnacles and slime from the hull. A sailor on the deck above attends them, pulling on each rope to bring the man below to another space in need of work. The ship is smartly painted black, with a white stripe along the line of the cabin windows, and the bottom of the hull is also white, revealed as the men scrub. Heavy strips of milled mahogany are raised from a barge by rope and pulley, and lowered into the forward cargo, weighing the ship deeper into the water even as the hull is cleaned. The man with the low-hanging position dips to the shoulder in the foul, cold water.

Noting my distaste, my young helper tells me, with envy, that the man risking himself to these putrid waters is well paid—a shilling, if at the work all day. I advise the boy that he must hold to his inheritance of operating a barge, this water is like to be a cesspool of disease, and the man swinging from the rope alongside us will not be earning his shilling into a fortuitous old age.

The White Horse tavern is where the crew of *Waimea* lodge while the ship is in dock, it being against policy to allow anyone other than pass-holding owners and officers to move about inside the walls of the Isle of Dogs overnight. Any person who can't produce a pass will be fined five pounds.

I have met all the crew, either on ship today or tonight in The White Horse. I am signed on as Sail Trimmer, but have also the unofficial role of ship's doctor.

Captain Sinclair appears the upright, sensible type. I have spent only a little time with him, but he exudes a steady authority and expertise. This is his first command of *Waimea,* but the crew say he has made several journeys to the Antipodes, with only two lives lost amongst his tars, and these at no fault of his own.

I have studied my diagram of *Waimea's* rigging to distraction, reciting the names I must come to recognise at an instant: Martingale guys and back-ropes, the Fore Topgallant mast and its rigging, the Fore Royal yard and lifts—there are 167 index numbers on the diagram, and I contend this task is harder than 'doing my bones' at medical school.

Waimea sails with 12 crew including myself, Captain and an apprentice who was not in the bar, though I did see him following Captain around the ship today. He is a tall, gawky lad of 15, with an abundance of blonde curls, which (if he is still sporting them tomorrow) will prove a mistake because all the tars (and I include myself) have heads and chins close-shaven in preparation for the months at sea. We have time enough, each to learn the other during the voyage, but for now I can say that they seem personable and I may find good friends.

Tuesday 3rd November: SW India Docks to Gravesend

Underway at last! Despite Captain's threats, and the urgency of our supposed departure time of 6am, we did not make way until noon. The delay was due 3 Thoroughbred horses that did not arrive at the customs gate until 9am. The horses—a bay stallion and two mares—are very fine-looking animals, but in way of cooperation they were certainly lacking! Yesterday the sheep and pigs that are for our consumption were easily herded up the gangway. The horses, however, refused to set even one hoof upon the unsteady planks. After some little time, and before the horses became utterly intractable, Captain ordered the hydraulic crane (for which he has to pay). Each horse was strapped into a sturdy rubber sling and hoisted, legs paddling, over the deck rail, and into the hold where their stables are set.

The gangway was then pulled, hawsers let go and a steam tug attached to the bow. Three lighters shepherded *Waimea* out of her berth, through the melee of boats jamming the lock and into Blackwall Reach. That was not the end of our need for the tug, for the Thames in this part is full of shipping. For hours we delicately manoeuvred through all manner of boats, making slow progress towards Greenhithe where we have now paused awaiting the arrival tonight of passengers aboard a steam tender.

I have just come from the navigating bridge where I had the benefit, alongside the apprentice, of watching Captain adjust the ship's compass. By using the Azimuth compass—to which is affixed a small mirror prism that reflects the sun onto the compass card—in connection with published Azimuth Tables that predict the altitude and azimuth of the sun at Greenhithe every 4 minutes of every day, Captain is able to determine the true bearing of the sun. Knowing that, he then adjusts the Mariner's Compass to bring it into exactly the same reading for True North.

Noting my fascination with the compasses, Captain has invited me to join him on the navigation bridge when we are at sea in order to learn the art of celestial navigation, and the use of the sextant.

Wednesday 4th November: Gravesend to the Channel

We were taken in tow at 8am, passengers having come on board last evening, and at 10am Captain ordered us to show sails even though the tug was to remain with us the entire day. It was an exhausting, stressful few hours for me, trying to keep up to the orders of the first mate. He did not spare me, sending me up the Main to loose the sail from the Topgallant yard. Testing me out early for vertigo—better to find out in the Thames than at sea. Vertigo I did not suffer, but the effort of climbing the rigging left me very short of breath.

The wind picked up from the southwest after noon, which allowed us to trim sails and assist the tug in taking us through the estuary. A heavy gale is predicted tonight, so before 4pm we ran the sails down, and will depend on the tug to take us through the Channel overnight.

Passengers have been walking the decks today, admiring the views of the estuary and exploring the environs of the ship. There are nine: a family of six, a young married couple and a single gent. I expect I must look a 'salty tar' to them because they have not deigned to drop a word in my direction.

The passengers (and Captain) take their meals in the dining room at 8am, 1pm and 6pm, and the crew eat in shifts, at other times, so as not to mix. We receive the same food though not in the same degree of freshness! Today's breakfast was steak stew; dinner was soup, roast beef and potatoes; and tea was ship biscuit with raspberry jam. The biscuits are best soaked, else unpleasantly hard on the teeth.

Tonight, when eating with the crew, there was talk of seasickness in anticipation of the gale in the Channel. Second Mate set four large bottles of Lorimer's Coca Jelly on the table, and let us know that if we, or prassengers, suffer from seasickness, we can avail ourselves of his 'medical supply' at a cost of sixpence a tot or two pounds for the bottle. The jelly, a variant of the wine made with Coca leaves sourced from Peru, energises the body allowing one to more easily bear fatigue, the cold, and the wet. We will all need it, he says, on the Southern Ocean. Having some familiarity with the potion, I don't dispute his claims, but one tot will hardly do the trick and his price is extortionate. One of these large bottles can be bought for two shillings at a dispensary—I figure his mark-up to be twenty times!

Friday 6th November: Beechy Head to Plymouth

Yester morn the tug left us off Beechy Head, having towed us overnight through the strait between Dover and Calais. We have made slow progress, beating into a heavy SW wind all day. How glorious though, to be sailing with the rig near full. The canvas stretching magnificent above us; the ship heeling tightly to the wind. First Mate showing his competence at the wheel; Second Mate and I on the sheets.

My muscles are aching with evidence that I am nowhere approaching fitness. Several times in the morning Second Mate was forced to look lively in following instructions I failed to comprehend, but in the afternoon I fared better. We sailed with the English coast in sight all day, and the Isle of Wight to starboard in the afternoon.

Today wind has been light, swinging east to south, making my work easier though likely I have also become more familiar with what needs be done. We are off Plymouth, waiting for a tender to take off the channel pilot and our mail, so I will close this part of my journal here.

From Plymouth, it's a short run down the coast of Devon before we lose sight of England, and commit ourselves to the Atlantic Ocean. Captain does not expect to see land again before we arrive at Lyttelton in New Zealand.

My health is good, and my lungs—which felt ghastly while in the docks—already benefit from the fresh air. I am eating well, and have no seasickness even though the apprentice and all the passengers were taken ill as we weathered the gale in the Channel. I have heard it said that consumptives do not suffer *mal de mer.* Perhaps I have at least that advantage.

Your loving son,
William.

Chapter 3

The Antipodes

Tuesday 17th February 1886: Port Lyttelton, New Zealand

William lent on *Waimea's* deck rail, watching the light at Godley Head hurling beacons of gold towards the pale pink of dawn.

The ship would be towed into Port Lyttelton in a few hours. His feet would be on solid ground for the first time in 106 days, and he was aching for the feel of it. They had been four days becalmed off Akaroa, tantalisingly in sight of land, and with every day his impatience had escalated. He had spent many of the idle hours in angry self-talk, imagining his temper unleashed on his crewmates, to the ruination of the cordial re-lationships he had worked hard to maintain. A few more hours and he would walk away from *Waimea*. Nothing need be said but 'Goodbye'.

In his pocket William carried a letter he had not yet sealed. The second chapter in his travel journal, addressed to his par-ents and ready for posting in Christchurch. There were parts of it he hesitated to include. He didn't want to upset his mother or invite his father's criticism, and yet he had decided not to return to Scotland with *Waimea*. It was the distressing parts of his journal that were his justification.

The second mate, Hutchinson, was the principal cause of William's ire. A big, brutal man who had taken a dislike to him early in the voyage because William dispensed ginger tablets instead of Coca Jelly to seasick passengers. The passengers, appreciative of William's help and recognising him as an educated man, had invited him to a permanent place at the captain's table—a promotion that the crew, led by Hutchinson, took every opportunity to deride.

Hutchinson was further incensed by the captain's favour towards his dandy recruit on the navigation deck. Captain Sinclair had ordered Hutchinson not to send William up the rigging, without giving any reason. Sinclair, aware of William's diagnosis, did not want him shunned out of fear—born of ignorance—that passengers and crew might contract the disease. His advice to William was, 'don't be drawn on the subject'.

The best part of the voyage for William was the Northeast Trades, which he recorded in the ship's log at latitude 24.49N, longitude 22.11W. Even though Captain Sinclair called the winds 'weak', William thought *Waimea's* sails filled magnificently. His measurements showed her making terrific speed. Each day William threw the 'chip log'—which on *Waimea* was a piece of wood in the shape of a quadrant attached to a rope marked off with knots spaced exactly eight fathoms apart—over the stern and counted the knots that passed through his hands during the 28 seconds it took for sand to run through the ship's timing glass. They were making, on average, eight and one-third knots per hour—two hundred and thirty miles a day—and it seemed that New Zealand was in easy reach. William was on deck all his waking hours, scrutinising the set of the sails, and making fine adjustments to achieve the maximum pace.

The winds gave out at 3.46N, 25.23W, and without them the days and nights were suddenly dreadfully hot. The ship languished in the doldrums, making minimal progress, and despite the fact that they had all known to expect this, the temper of crew and passengers alike steadily rose. Passengers came to William complaining of incessant headaches, and all he could prescribe was plenty of fresh water, cool flannel clothing and shade. The greatest irritation of all while they were in the doldrums, was the excessive attention paid to him by the single gentleman passenger, Gordon Meerish.

It began early in the voyage when Gordon came to him with severe seasickness. The young Englishman—the same age as William, but by his manner, William judged, by no means mature—was undoubtedly suffering. His skin was pallid and clammy, his thin brown hair lying lank and wet on his head, his hands fluttering with anxiety and his pulse racing. He could take no food and no rest. Ginger tablets proved no relief. William asked Gordon if he could afford Hutchinson's 'cure'.

Gordon readily confessed that he was in poor circumstances. His was a wealthy family of London merchants, but he had fallen out of his father's favour. His father had paid for his one-way passage to New Zealand, giving him a minimal sum of money and instructions to 'make a man' of himself. He knew no one in New Zealand, he had no trade, and no idea how he was to earn his living after this voyage ended.

William was shocked that a man from a middle-class family like his own could be treated this way. On inquiring after Gordon's mother, he learned that she had died recently, leaving him to his father's unmerciful treatment. Gordon had numerous siblings—he was a middle-child of no consequence to the family dynasty. Indeed, his family found him an embarrassment, and sending him to the Antipodes was their solution.

It was clear to William that developing a taste for Coca Jelly would only add to Gordon's troubles. He advised against Hutchinson's remedy.

Gordon was surprisingly cheerful for the first two days in the doldrums, but then his mood changed to petulant misery. He abused William for not providing better care, and dramatically declared their friendship 'done with'—a denunciation William received with gratitude. Late that night, however, Gordon found William lying on his back on the navigation deck, closely studying the southern stars through Captain's telescope. He tearfully apologised. He confessed to an indulgence in Hutchinson's Coca Jelly. He now owed the second mate a substantial sum, and Hutchinson was threatening violence.

When Gordon asked for money, William's response was an adamant refusal. Gordon begged and clutched at his arm. William lost his temper. Gordon slunk away from the navigation deck, and William pointed his telescope into the night sky, his seething thoughts gradually settling themselves into the countless peaceful points of light.

The next day a breath of wind arrived with a late afternoon downpour, which brought everyone out on deck, dancing with upturned faces and open arms. That night the wind strengthened, bringing them close to the central latitudes where Captain predicted they would pick up the Southeast Trades. At the equator there was a 'bit of fun' to be had—a ritual ceremony where those adult men, including William and the apprentice, who had not crossed the line before, would be called to account for their 'crimes' before a court comprised of the ship's senior crew members. The script varied—it was up to the crew —but generally the men would be dunked and shaved in order to cleanse them of their original hemisphere.

Neptune's court comprised: the captain wearing Neptune's gold crown, his wife Amphitrite (Able Seaman Menzies in voluminous women's clothing), First Mate Stocks wearing a white wig and deploying a gavel, Able Seaman Brown flashing a barber's blade and Second Mate Hutchinson inside the costume of a very large bear.

After suffering the ritual dunking in a tub of refreshing seawater, William was clothed in a white gown, and taken up to the court bench to sit amongst the 'shellbacks' with his medical bag, in anticipation of carnage to the 'pollywogs'. His surgical work, gladly, amounted to no more than swabbing the numerous cuts left on the apprentice's head by the roughly deployed barber's blade.

Of the passengers, Mr Butterworth, a mahogany merchant, was accused of abuse of his wife and children, to which his wife answered kindly in his defence. He was exonerated and presented with his Equatorial Certificate. The fate of Gordon Meerish, who had no one to stand up for him and was intensely disliked by the crew, was in no way so benign.

Gordon was accused of a preference for male company, sodomy and bestiality. He was sentenced to a day and night in the pigpen, where he could satiate his sinful appetites. Instead of receiving a dunking he was dragged away below decks by the bear. He was made, in short, the piaculum—the expiatory sacrifice required to secure safe passage into Neptune's southern domain.

Waimea met the Southeast Trades that afternoon, 3rd December, shortly after crossing the equator. William was kept busy, running out and trimming sails until he was relieved of his duty by the dinner bell. Gordon was not at the captain's table, and no one voiced concern that he was missing. William knocked on Gordon's cabin door after dinner, but there was no answer.

"Looking for your friend?" Able Seaman Menzies caught William with his ear against the cabin door. "He's in the pigpen till midnight. I expect he's in need of a doctor." Menzies slipped a key-chain off his neck and handed it to William. "Not a minute early, mind, or you'll answer to Judge Stocks. Give it back to me in the morning."

At midnight, William took Gordon up to the deserted deck for a sea bath, and brought him fresh clothes. Gordon refused to speak, and would not let William bring any light to bear on his injuries. As soon as he was dressed, Gordon slipped away to his cabin where he remained for the remaining weeks of the voyage.

William spent the dark, early hours of December 4th sitting on a coil of rope as *Waimea* sailed on close reach, heading a few points to the west of south. The moonless night was a canopy of fathomless black satin, pin-pricked by twinkling stars. The horizon could not be sighted, except by taking notice that the stars had been submerged. The whole of the sea and sky hugged the ship, an eternally peaceful, beautiful sphere that lured him to lean into it, and bathe himself clean of the ugliness of humanity.

How he longed to hear the sound of his family's treasured voices. He had never felt so alone, so different from those around him. He had never seen such unbridled, immoral behaviour victimising a helpless human being. He felt guilty. What would have happened if he had stood up in Gordon's defence in Neptune's farcical court? The voyage, and his relationship with that beast, Hutchinson, were irrevocably tainted.

Waimea sailed briskly, almost due south through 22 degrees of latitude. When the winds gave out, Captain again expressed his dissatisfaction—the fast passage that would enhance his reputation was slipping away from him. For many days the ship sailed on a south-easterly heading in light and variable winds. William had little to do apart from watch for birds—cape pigeons and albatross were his favourites. The flying fish that had entertained him greatly the first few times they landed wetly on the deck beside him, were now mundane, but the spotting of a whale was always exciting, as was the sighting of the sails of another vessel, though Captain did not once slow his course in order to be within hailing distance.

William wished he could use his camera to record the beauty of the ocean—its vibrant sunsets, glowing dawns and menacing storm clouds—but he knew it would be a hopeless waste of his plates to attempt a photograph from the ceaselessly rolling deck. Even when becalmed, all it took was one of the beasts below deck to move, and the ship would shudder, ruining the time exposure the plate required. Instead, William focused his passion for mechanical equipment on the ship's navigational instruments.

On 24th December, William recorded that *Waimea* met the Westerlies at 36.17S, 14.49W. That evening Captain Sinclair handed William the telescope and directed his gaze to the line of a volcanic cone intruding on the sky. Queen Mary's Peak, Tristan da Cunha, the most remote, inhabited archipelago in the world.

"Note in the log," Captain paused, peering at the ship's chronometer, "8pm. Barometer?"

"Falling, storm coming in … six hours?" William guessed.

"Four and a half," Captain Sinclair clapped William on the shoulder. "Prepare to meet the Southern Ocean."

At 12.45am William was woken by a violent lurch of the ship. He saw rain and seawater alternately flooding across his porthole as the ship rolled, and he heard a cry taken up along the passageway, "Sails Ho!" He struggled into his oilskin, fending himself off the heaving sides of his small cabin, and ran barefoot to the deck where he was stopped by the hand of First Mate Stocks, laid flat against his chest.

"Cap says you attend sick bay during storm." Stocks shouted, leaning close to William's ear.

The order took William by surprise, but he was glad to be spared the weather. It was a busy night in the sick bay: seasick passengers, a jagged cut in the apprentice's foot, and a probable fracture in the arm of Matthew, Mr Butterworth's youngest son.

At dawn the storm eased, and William took the opportunity to crawl into his bunk for a few hours of sleep until it picked up again mid-morning. The passengers, he learned, had held a Divine Service in the saloon while he was asleep. Christmas dinner had been postponed.

When observations were taken at noon, the captain was exhilarated. They had covered 290 miles in 24 hours.

William's banishment from the sails was made permanent. During the worst of the weather that followed (his noon observation recorded an icy 35 degrees Fahrenheit as they passed to the south of the Crozet Islands on 11th January) he was either working in the sick bay, or sequestered cosily in the saloon by the passenger's fire.

The captain ordered the sailor who also functioned as a butcher and cook, to kill one of the last three sheep in order to provide hearty hot meals to the crew and passengers. William —restless for occupation and not one to condone waste—used the sheep's stomach, liver, heart and tongue to make a haggis, working as closely to his mother's favourite recipe as the ingredients in the ship's pantry allowed. William thought his haggis tasty, but his was the only clean plate at the end of the meal, and the passengers universally recommended that he be kept out of the galley for the rest of the trip.

Neither did the passengers have appetite for the albatross that Mr Butterworth caught with a fishing line baited with bacon. Matthew Butterworth excitedly recounted the catch at the dinner table. His father had hauled the gigantic bird, flapping, over the deck rail, and had killed it by stabbing a blade through its head. The bird's wingspan was ten feet, and it weighed 22 pounds. Clearly, in young Matthew's mind, his father was a dragon-slayer. Mr Butterworth paid the cook to skin and gut the bird, and prepare it as if it were a roast turkey, but several at the table thought it tasted like overcooked fish. The consensus, born of superstition as much as distaste, was that while there were live sheep, pigs and chickens in the hold, there should be no more fishing for albatross.

The Antarctic winds and miserably cold weather caught up with the passengers and crew in mid-January, sending many of them to William to complain of sore throats and fever. There was little William could do to help them. For those with the worst congestion, he prescribed a flannel soaked in mineral turps, wrapped lightly around their neck—at night the fumes would clear their nasal passages and help them sleep. As for himself, he entrenched his reputation as a pitiable wretch, scared of the common cold, because he donned his facemask, and would not take it off except to eat and sleep.

In the midst of the 'flu epidemic', Menzies brought Stocks into the sickbay, suffering from toothache. In the farthest corner of Stocks' mouth, William detected a broken tooth; the gum red and swollen with infection. The tooth would have to be pulled, but it was not an easy extraction, being partly occluded by the tooth alongside. William sent Menzies to get Hutchinson, and a jar full of fresh seawater. While waiting, he gave Stocks a tot of rum, insisting that before swallowing Stocks must swill the rum around his mouth, over the rotten tooth.

William explained to Hutchinson that he had a use for some Coca Jelly.

"Get it Hutch!" Stocks insisted, "I'm dying here!"

Hutchinson reluctantly brought his last half bottle.

William tipped some of the Coca Jelly onto his fingers and smeared it as best he could around Stocks' infected gum.

"Numb?" William asked and Stocks nodded. "Open your mouth wide, and keep it wide." William turned to Hutchinson. "Pin his arms down."

William jammed a cylindrical roll of smooth wood between Stocks' teeth, and held it in place firmly with his left hand while he used a scalpel blade to make swift incisions. Blood streamed freely from Stocks' mouth while William hastily exchanged the scalpel for a pair of long nose pliers.

"Mouth open! Keep holding him!"

Five seconds later it was over. William gripped the stump of the shattered tooth in his pliers. Stocks spat blood and fragments of tooth on the sick bay floor.

"Swill your mouth with salt water till it stops bleeding," William ordered, handing Stocks the jar. "One swill every waking hour for at least a week. Make sure no food remains in the hole. Come back daily so I can check. If your gum starts to hurt, Coca Jelly will make it numb again."

Hutchinson grabbed the bottle of Coca Jelly and held it close to his chest. "Worth a pound," he declared, watching Stocks spit bloody seawater on the floor.

"You fucker," Stocks slurred the words through the working side of his mouth. "You'll give it me for a shilling, not a penny more!"

"Spit into the sea!" William hustled the two men out of the sickbay, and stood at the door, arms-crossed, looking at the bloody floor. A word of thanks, he mused, was evidently too much to expect.

The weather improved, being clear and cool with a fine Westerly making fair work of the distance to Tasmania. At no point did they see the Australian coast, and on February 6th all eyes were fixed on the horizon, straining for a sight of The Snares—the outlying, southernmost territory of New Zealand. The "Land Ho!" came from the seaman on lookout high in the cross-trees, shortly after 2pm.

"Tahi, Rua, Toru, Wha and Rima", Captain recited the names of the stacks of rock—the Maori numbers one to five.

No one left the ship's port rail until The Snares fell out of sight behind them. At the dinner table passengers talked excitedly about their observations of the skerrick of land: hundreds of sooty shearwaters flying overhead; dozens of seals lounging on the rocks; the penguins that, sadly, no one had seen.

With the dawn light on 8th February, they could see the coast of Stewart Island already falling behind, and they were disappointed not to have had a better view. Soon, however, they were crowded at the port bow rail with the mainland in sight, keen to spot habitation. A greater cause of excitement, was the sighting of a steamer that passed between *Waimea* and the coast. Captain, keeping firm hold on his eyeglass, informed his eager audience that it was a coastal steamer showing the livery of the Union Steamship Company, but he was not able to decipher its name.

That night, dinner table talk was an excited buzz of anticipation—not as much about setting foot on land as it was about receiving news from home. There could have been a war. Queen Victoria might have died. Were their friends and loved ones alive and well?

The next day they passed Dunedin and, as they watched steamers turning into Port Chalmers, they wished their journey over. Two days to go.

But off Akaroa, on 11th February, the wind turned to the northeast, coming straight onto Waimea's bow, and making it impossible to head into Port Lyttelton. For four days they waited for the wind to change; the happy excitement of arrival evaporating into the hot summer air, and the frustrations and discontents of the long journey festering.

~

"I've decided I'll not be returning with *Waimea*, sir. I'll be catching the mail coach to Hokitika tomorrow to visit with my father's sister. After that, I want to see Australia, and I'll make my way home from there." William faced Captain Sinclair in the poop cabin. He could feel that his face was flushed, reddened by the mid-morning sun and the excuse he felt compelled to make.

Sinclair studied him for a long moment. "I can't say you surprise me, William. I expect it's for the best. Are you wanting a reference from me?" The captain's tone made it clear the reference would not be forthcoming.

"I'll take a steamer for the return, sir. I'll still get back for summer that way. I know I'm not one to work the sails. I'm sorry I've been a nuisance to you. I hope you find another to go home with you."

Sinclair grunted, slid open a desk drawer, and withdrew two pieces of paper—one blank; one typewritten. "Sit down and copy this out. Write your name and sign at the bottom. It's a deed of release to say I've fulfilled my obligation to you."

While William was completing the document, there was a knock on the door. Stocks showed in a neatly clothed, grey-haired gentleman, introducing him as Port Lyttelton's medical officer. With a very brief conversation the officer confirmed that he had interviewed the crew and passengers and, in the absence of any reportable illness, the ship was free to enter the port. He handed the captain a slip of paper and took his leave. As Stocks was closing the door the captain called to him.

"Stocks, did you organise the disembarkation I ordered?"

"Yes sir," Stocks confirmed.

Sinclair took the paper William had written, and enclosed it, together with the medical officer's slip, in a folder which he dropped into his desk drawer.

"Good luck to you, William. I will say I enjoyed your company on the navigation deck. I have seldom had such an eager student."

"Sir ..." William lingered and the captain looked at him questioningly. "Hutchinson. I have to ask, how can you let that man remain on your crew?"

Sinclair grimaced, considering his reply. "I would love to have the perfect crew, William, but such a one does not exist. Hutchinson and Stocks know everything that's to be known about this ship. I cannot sail it without them." The captain rose from his chair and shepherded William towards the door.

"Mr Meerish ..."

"Is the architect of his own demise." Sinclair opened the cabin door and looked at William sternly. "I see it as my responsibility to your father to advise you to have nothing further to do with that creature."

"Do you not have a responsibility to him, as your passenger?"

"No, William, I do not," Sinclair growled testily. "My responsibility is to uphold the interests of the owners of this ship. Mr Meerish is a person of no consequence, and it's best you say nothing further on the subject."

William said nothing further on the subject to Captain Sinclair, but he did try to find Gordon, initially by knocking on his cabin door, and then by asking among the passengers who were in the saloon for a celebratory drink. He was told Mr Meerish had already left the ship. Mr Butterworth had seen him carry his luggage onto the steam tender that had brought the Lyttelton medical officer.

Thursday 19th February 1886: Hokitika, New Zealand

"Willie! Oh my Lord, it's Willie, you're here!" Maggie Nicol, née Cameron, took William's body fiercely into her possession and sobbed into his shoulder. Over the top of his aunt's head, William looked into the blue eyes of a girl who looked remarkably like his older sister except that she had thicker and darker hair. He watched the initial alarm in those eyes turn to understanding, and then a wide, amused smile. He thought her the most beautiful girl he had ever seen.

"Oh Willie, forgive me, forgive me." His aunt disengaged, patting her apron pockets, and withdrawing a large handkerchief with which she dabbed her eyes. "You're the first, laddie, the first to *ever* get here. I was so excited that George was coming, and it broke my heart, just broke my heart." Maggie blew her nose, and pushed the handkerchief back in her pocket. She took his arms in her hands, and turned his face to the light from the doorway. "Oh, I don't know who you look like! I've forgotten what my family look like. Oh my Lord!" she wailed.

"I have photos," William offered.

"I must see them! I must see them! Willie, I was so scared you wouldn't get here!"

The girl stepped forward, her eyes on William's. "Come to the table, Mum. I'll make us a cup, and Willie can show us the photos."

William felt a twinge of disappointment. His cousin might look like his sister, but she certainly didn't sound the same. Her accent was flat and unpleasant to his ears in comparison to his aunt's familiar Scottish tone.

"Do you remember your cousin Margaret? Do you remember you used to play together?"

"Willie didn't like to play with me, Mum. He liked to play with Euphan and John. They sent *me* to play with Janet and Jen."

"I don't remember that," William laughed lightly, thinking that he certainly wouldn't send her away now. He pulled out his wallet, and laid his family photos on the table.

"Margaret ... my looking glass, and a lamp ... please!"

As he finished his cup of tea, and Maggie was examining his photographs with her magnifying glass, there was a clamorous arrival at the front door.

"Mum, Mum, you'll never guess!"

"Cousin Willie's in Christchurch!"

"And he's coming here!"

Three young girls in white cotton dresses tumbled into the room, all talking at once.

"Meet Cousin Willie, lassies," their mother smiled indulgently at them. "He's arrived on the mail coach today."

The girls were suddenly shy. Their hands fluttered around their dresses, up to their cheerful, tanned faces and over their long brown hair. They stood to attention before him.

"Agnes, Charlotte and Georgina," Maggie named them in order of height.

"Hello," William bowed gracefully to them and they giggled in reply.

"Did you come on a ship?" Georgina, the youngest at nine years old, was bursting with questions.

"I did."

"All the way from Scotland?"

"Aye."

"Were there rats?"

"And chickens and sheep and pigs and horses."

"Was there a cat?"

"I didn't see one."

"Rats can bite and you get sick. You need a cat to eat them. Did you eat the chickens and sheep and pigs and horses?"

William laughed. "Not the horses."

Georgina had sparked the conversation, and now her sisters joined in, mobbing William with their questions about his voyage until the front door banged again, and their father arrived; a shadowy bulk in the front hall, shedding his coat and hat before walking into the warm lamplight of the living room.

"Och Willie, you've grown such legs that you beat the mail!" Robert Nicol extended his hand, and William stood to greet him, surprised to find himself looking down on the uncle he had once thought tall.

"Maggie, I wish I'd been here to see your face when he sassed in that door!"

"She was sobbing all over him, Dad," Margaret weighed into the conversation from the kitchen.

"How long are you here, laddie?" Robert asked.

"Willie can stay as long as he likes, love. He can stay forever if that be his want." Maggie reached out for William's hand and squeezed it in evidence of her sincerity.

~

William stayed for four weeks. Much as he appreciated Maggie's welcoming offer, he was desperately homesick, and keen to be on his homeward path. It was worse, he thought, hearing Scottish accents, and feeling the warmth of family while knowing these people were not his own. It was late summer in New Zealand, but here on the west coast of the South Island, it was cooler than William had expected, and it rained, heavily, for days on end. The district received over 100 inches of rainfall a year. Rivers regularly flooded. Roads, bridges and hillsides were washed away, and the township was isolated for long periods. The coastal scenery was beautiful, but the winds coming across the Tasman from Australia were vicious, and often whipped the waves into frenzied breakers that smashed against the shore, dampening and salting the entire town. The west coast was infamous for shipwrecks, and the Port of Hokitika had the worst reputation of all. A fickle sand bar across the mouth of the Taramakau River had claimed hundreds of vessels over the twenty-one years since the port opened.

In 1870, Maggie and Robert Nicol arrived in Hokitika on the *Argyllshire* with a shipload of immigrants intending to dig wealth from the ground. They were four years too late for the peak of the gold rush, but they fell in love with the wild beauty of Westland and stayed. Robert now made a respectable living as an accountant, and served as the town bailiff. Their younger son, John, who was the same age as William, had not long ago moved to Sydney to try his luck in that energetic colonial city. Margaret was not quite a year older than William, while Euphan, the eldest, was 24. Euphan and his wife occupied two rooms at the rear of the family home in Fitzherbert Street.

Apart from gold, Westland was famous for its greenstone; known and prized by the Maori as *pounamu*. There was a *marae*—a tribal meeting ground—northeast of Hokitika at Arahura, where William attended the *tangihanga*—funeral—of one of Euphan's Maori friends. The *tangi* ran for four days, Friday through Monday. Every day the service started with a *powhiri*—welcome—to guests, and continued all day with friends and family of the deceased climbing onto an elevated stage to speak and sing about their loved one. William was surprised to see that many of the Maori were wearing black woollen trousers and jackets, and when speaking in English their sentiments carried references to the Bible, and to the life hereafter in Christ. Euphan chided him for being disappointed that the Maori were not cannibalistic heathens. Missionaries, he said, had converted most of the Maori in the district in the early 1800's. After Euphan made his speech to the gathering, he took William to a distant corner of the *marae* where they met with a mix of Maori, Scottish, Irish and English men, all in their twenties. A *hāngi* was in progress—a side of mutton had been slow cooking for several hours, laid out in a wire basket on hot rocks in a shallow pit dug into the earth, and covered with strips of bark, leaves and more earth. While waiting for the food to be ready, the Maori threw off their sombre robes, and offered their awesome tattoos for William's close inspection. Then they demonstrated the *haka*—their tribal war dance. They were an impressively strong, energetic and proud people, and their slow-cooked meat was delicious.

Euphan's friend, William discovered to his dismay, had died of consumption—an illness as common among the Maori as it was among Europeans. The *tohunga*—Maori ancestral chiefs—believed that disease was principally a punishment for breaking sacred tribal customs, but they also suspected that some families were prone to certain diseases, and they knew they should isolate victims to prevent others from becoming infected. It was a shrewd but unscientific mix, William thought, of all the options. It was also evidence against New Zealand being a country where consumptives could expect to recover their health.

"The Maori are backward—superstitious—you know," Euphan announced smugly during the buggy ride home. "*We* know, of course, that consumption is genetic—look at you and George, you drew the unlucky card—but you can't convince the Maori that's the whole of it. They still follow their tribal beliefs."

"Euphan, you should know that consumption *is* a transmissible disease," William spoke earnestly. "It *does* run in families, because genetically some people are more susceptible than others, but it *is* spread by airborne droplets of bacilli. If you're close to someone who has the disease, and you breathe in the bacteria they're coughing or sneezing out, you *will* get infected. Vast numbers of people in Europe carry the bacteria around with them all the time. If you have that genetic susceptibility —and you might very well be like me and George—then at some point in the future, if you're weak with some other illness maybe, consumption could take hold of you too."

Euphan drew back from William, and eyed him suspiciously while the horse, taking advantage, slowed to a walk.

"I could get it from you?"

"You'd be more likely to get it from one of the Maori we watched doing the haka. *I* know when I'm infectious. *I* use a facemask, and I make sure I'm not spraying droplets towards you. They don't know if they've got it, and you don't know

... and that's why consumption is so widely spread and so dangerous."

"What should I do?"

"Stand back from anyone who's coughing or sneezing, yelling or spitting. We think the bacilli don't travel far in the open air. Encourage your friends to cover their mouth and nose with a handkerchief when they cough or sneeze. Do the same yourself."

"What about shaking hands?"

"It's best if everyone keeps their hands clean, especially if they have any sort of sickness, but we think that for the bacilli to give rise to consumption, they have to be breathed into the lungs where they settle. Not through the skin, or the blood."

"Kissing?"

"Avoid it while you or your wife have any sort of cough or cold."

Euphan nodded thoughtfully. "You should give this advice to Margaret."

"Why?"

"She's been kissing him that owns the saw mill, James Lincoln. I don't think she minds if he's got a cough." Euphan giggled mischievously, watching for William's reaction.

Margaret was aware, William was certain, of his admiration for her, but throughout his stay she remained cool towards him. It was five days after Euphan's revelation, that Margaret and William visited the Hokitika sawmill where he met James Lincoln. It was when the three of them were on the horse-drawn tramway, heading out to look at the patch James was logging, that William witnessed his companions' mutual affection. Watching them arm in arm his reaction was not jealousy, he concluded, but a deep yearning to have an intimate relationship for himself.

William longed to head home and find a Scottish lass to call his own.

It was not easy, however, to escape the imprisoning clutch of the West Coast. His departure was complicated by torrential rain. The Teremakau river was in flood. The coach road to Christchurch had been washed away and would be impassable for weeks. William booked a ticket to Wellington on the *Kennedy,* but on the day the steamer was due to depart, a fierce storm was flinging the sea water of the Tasman against the flood water of the Teremakau. The mouth of the river was a chaotic wall of froth, raging so high that William could not see past it to the sea. All day the *Kennedy* stayed in port as William anxiously counted the hours. He had passage on *Te Anau* from Wellington on Friday 19th March, bound for Sydney via Auckland, and feared he would miss his connection.

The *Kennedy* left port at dawn. The ship crossed the bar safely, sending spectacular towers of spray up both sides of the bow, and then pushed out into the rolling post-storm swell. With a mile between herself and the coast, the *Kennedy* turned to starboard and ploughed through fearsome waves towards Greymouth, where they stopped to offload mail and take on passengers. At Westport the ship took harbour again, the captain deeming the conditions too dangerous to travel through the night. It took two more days to reach Nelson.

Fortunately for William, there was a family on the *Kennedy* holding first saloon tickets on *Te Anau.* His own steerage ticket would not have earned him any favours, but as it was, on Friday afternoon at the entry to Wellington harbour, *Te Anau* was waiting for them. Passengers and luggage were efficiently transferred, and William was on his way up the eastern coast of the North Island, disappointed that he had seen no more of Wellington than its rugged, almost treeless coastline.

William enjoyed the four days it took *Te Anau* to reach Auckland. The contrast between the weather on the north-eastern side of New Zealand and his experience of the south-west could not have been greater. The seas were relatively calm, the wind a warm north-westerly, and the sky was an opulent blue. *Te Anau* supplemented her single screw steam power with sail, making good speed, which allowed more time in port. He enjoyed several hours in Napier and Gisborne, and had an entire day at leisure in Auckland.

Having expected the worst, William was pleasantly surprised by the value he obtained from his cheap ticket. He was sharing cabin space with a number of men, and the smell was rank, to be sure, but he was able to spend most of his time topside or in the main saloon. The weather was so good that he slept for five consecutive nights in a deck chair.

That all changed, however, as *Te Anau* struck out from Auckland to cross the Tasman Sea. The earliest warning sign was that the stewards packed up the deck chairs. William, personally affronted, demanded to know why.

"We'd lose them all to the sea, sir," the steward said politely.

"This is a sea road as turbulent as any in the world," William confided to his journal, having spent the morning hanging over the ship's rail, vomiting until there was nothing left to expel. "If it be true that consumptives do not get seasick, then I am cured."

Monday 29ᵗʰ March 1886: Sydney, New South Wales

The entrance to Sydney Harbour was naturally wide and deep, facing the rolling swell of the sea with such openness that William could not imagine it a safe anchorage. Soon after passing rugged sandstone cliffs to the north, however, *Te Anau* turned to port around a sharp headland, and steamed into the calm waters of Port Jackson. Here, digging into the rocky coastline were dozens of bays and inlets, some sheltering a single ship, others embracing many vessels of varying size. As the ships became more numerous, so did the houses that dotted the shoreline. The first houses were shacks and farmsteads, but this soon gave way to imposing mansions with fledgling, but handsomely laid out gardens that evidenced high expectations.

It was a fine morning, dry and hot in William's estimation though his fellow passengers told him the day was 'mild'. William could not reconcile the season to 'autumn'—where was the colour? The trees that clung to the steep, rocky sections of the shoreline were a uniform olive green and, where the land was cleared, the sparse cover of grass was the same straw-brown as the dry soil beneath it. The expanse of water, in contrast, was a deep blue, decorated by frothy wakes thrown up by the many slow-moving craft that dotted the harbour. William thought it a scene that would never tire the eye.

With the headland four miles behind, *Te Anau* turned into Sydney Cove where it was able to berth in deep water, and discharge its passengers directly to the town. William was astounded by the convenience of the port, the perfection of the harbour. Could any outpost of empire be so well-situated?

John Nicol shared a semi-detached house with three men in Pyrmont. He had received a letter from his mother, and was happy for William to stay, but if it was longer than a few days, then William would be expected to contribute financially. That was fair, but when William saw the squalid conditions in which the four bachelors—two Irishmen and two Scots—were living, he decided to make alternate arrangements as soon as possible.

The next day, acting on the suggestion of one of John's Irish house-mates, William walked back to Sydney Cove, and did the rounds of the lightermen who were bringing goods to the quay, asking if any of the ocean-going liners needed cargo handlers. The deal, he had been told, was modest pay and the chance of accommodation aboard for a shilling a night deducted from his wages.

The Orient Line's *Liguria* was under heavy guard in Neutral Bay, loading gold bullion. It was due to depart in a fortnight for London via Melbourne, Adelaide and the Suez Canal. Closer to its departure date, it would be loading frozen meats and a consignment of fresh fruit and vegetables destined for the Indian and Colonial Exhibition in London. The ship needed trustworthy cargo handlers, and William demonstrated his suitability by putting 18 pounds on the purser's desk—the price of his third-class ticket.

The cargo work, done by a chain of many hands with an emphasis on the safety of the goods being loaded, was not onerous and positions were rotated regularly. Stacking in the hold proceeded under the scrutiny of the ship's engineer. The load—especially the boxes of bullion—had to be perfectly balanced, fore and aft, starboard and port.

After dark the ship was under curfew, no boats were allowed to approach, and the holds were locked down. There was little opportunity for William to talk to his fellow workers during the day, but in the evenings, he enjoyed the company of the cook and the few stewards who had remained on the *Liguria* instead of taking shore leave. The nights passed pleasantly, chatting or reading in the saloon, standing by the deck rail watching the lights of Sydney sparkle, or lying on his back in the bow, enjoying the vast sweep of the Milky Way against the pitch-black of space.

The *Liguria* departed Sydney on Saturday, April 10th, having moved into the Cove the previous day to receive passengers. The ship's stewards were back from shore leave, and they jealously reserved for themselves the responsibility for all cabin luggage, keen to ingratiate themselves with those most likely to tip generously.

William was glad to be standing shoulder to shoulder with passengers as the gangway was rolled back, and the *Liguria* was tugged away from the Cove. Some passengers were only going as far as Melbourne or Adelaide, but most were on their way home to Europe, and William had caught their excitement. To have stayed behind in Sydney would have been heartbreak for him. He stood at the stern rail, watching the *Liguria's* wake widen across the harbour, feeling only the smallest regret—this city *was* blessed with the *most* extraordinarily beautiful setting.

The same could not be said of Melbourne, William concluded, when the *Liguria* docked at the railway pier at Williamstown. The docklands were heavily industrial, the air laden with smoke from boilers and mineralised dust that irritated his lungs. The wind was blowing cold from the south, and there were low clouds overhead, threatening rain, but then scudding away to unveil a bright sun.

With only one day to explore the city, William stepped onto a cable tram outside Spencer Street Station, and rode it several blocks till he reached the perimeter of the city grid. The cable tram had been brought into service only four months previously. William stood on the running board of the dummy car, asking questions and watching with fascination as the driver manipulated the grip, slowing down for the corner into Flinders Street, and gearing up again on the straight. The driver pointed out the engine house that was powering the cable—a square building of red brick, some thirty feet high with a tall chimney stack, streaming black smoke into the sky. The cables themselves were made up of six strands of seven wires, twisted around a hemp core, lying in tunnels four feet underground. Work was in progress, the driver told William proudly, to ensure that there would be tramlines along every street of the city grid by 1890. William was impressed. Edinburgh did not have any cable trams—the narrow, winding streets were a major impediment. In Melbourne, the streets were wide and straight with only gentle grades. It had the advantage of being a new town, sensibly laid out across spacious, level ground.

The cable tram tracks were only part of the work William saw in progress. There were already many imposing buildings, built with large blocks of bluestone to heights of five or six stories. More were under construction. Everywhere, men were in a hurry, spending the wealth accumulated during the gold rushes of the fifties; riches that powered the city on its mission of self-improvement. Three blocks along Spring Street from the cable tram, a massive construction was in progress— the Victorian House of Parliament. The business of running the colony, William was told, was continuing in the eastern side of the building, while here, on the western side, all was mayhem, quarry dust and noise. William turned his back to the site and continued his walk down Bourke Street, which he had been told was the main shopping precinct.

At the Eastern Market on the corner of Exhibition Street, William marvelled at the range of goods for sale. A colonist need not suffer any lack of tailored clothing, jewellery or tableware. There were long lines of drays topped with crates of fruit and vegetables, as well as carts full of dried fruits and cheeses that had William's mouth-watering. He settled on a stick of bread, an odorous block of cheese cut into wedges at his request, and a paper bag of dried apricots. When the clouds eventually spilled their burden, he took cover under the wide veranda of the Royal Mail Hotel, and stood, chewing on his bread and cheese, while he surveyed the row of carts outside the Cobb & Co Coach office. Drivers hunched nonchalantly under stretched canvas hoods; horses stood with their heads lowered as nearly as possible under the shelter of the cart in front.

The rain showed no sign of stopping. William spent tuppence on a newspaper and continued his walk, holding the paper over his head, and staying close to the building line. Back at Spencer Street Station, he boarded the 'special train' for Orient Line passengers.

The train was packed with wet, steamy bodies there being, in William's estimation, several family members to see off each traveller. The crowds trooped up the gangway behind their ticketed friends, inspected the *Liguria's* two saloons, and wandered the passenger decks at their leisure, giggling with anxious embarrassment and moving on, each time they encountered one of the guards. An hour before departure the stewards moved around the ship, calling out 'Last Ashore', and the exodus began, friends and family stepping gingerly down the wet gangway to line up alongside the dock. Travellers leant over the deck rail, throwing wet paper streamers at their chosen targets. The ship was full, the purser advised William: 90 in the first saloon, 110 in the second and 260 in third class and steerage.

As the grey sky darkened, the *Liguria* was tugged out to Hobson's Bay where it anchored until the late mail from Sydney arrived at midnight. In the morning, when William awoke, the ship was already in Bass Strait, heading for Adelaide with a bitterly cold wind keeping all but its most eager passengers below deck.

The *Liguria* anchored off Adelaide to board the last of its cargo and passengers, affording William just four hours to see that city. He joined a group taken by steamer to Semaphore, and then by rail into the capital. It was an attractive town, William's tour group all agreed. Well laid out, nice gardens, but evidently not as prosperous as Melbourne, and not as scenic as Sydney. It would be a struggle, they concurred, for the colony of South Australia to make its way independently unless new and extensive gold strikes were made. Westralia, one gentleman promised the rest of the group, was where the next, and most lucrative gold fields would be found.

The *Liguria* did not make port in Westralia but nevertheless, by the time they were in the Indian Ocean steaming northwest towards the Gulf of Aden, William was confident he had, through his personal experience and his conversations with passengers, acquired a comprehensive knowledge of all seven of the colonies. He was returning to Scotland, he thought cheerfully, as an Antipodean expert.

Chapter 4

Home

Newburgh, 1886–1888

The town of Newburgh stretches along the south bank of the Firth of Tay, 35 miles from Edinburgh in the far north-western corner of Fife. The train journey from Waverley Station took a little over two hours, and its highlight, for William, had always been the moment the broad sweep of the Tay came suddenly into view, and the township was revealed below the curving rail track. If the tide was low, the tall reeds of Mudgrum Island would be visible from the train window. In line-of-sight between the island and the spire on the Town Hall, stood Cullalo—a handsome, two-story house built of distinctive, dark grey stone, couched between the sawmill, and the warehouses that belonged to John Cameron & Sons.

On Saturday, 29th May, three days after the *Liguria* docked at Plymouth, this view—exactly as he had last seen it—thrilled William more than ever before.

Having left his trunk at the station to be collected later, William walked down the hill towards the town; his kit bag and jacket over one shoulder; his medical bag in hand. The sun was nearing the cloud-flecked horizon, its westerly light throwing a scintillating shaft along the Tay, and spilling from the luxuriantly green leaves of the multitudes of pear trees that graced Newburgh's hillside. Cullalo's orchard was surrounded by a tall stone wall on which hung a sturdy loganberry vine, its branches budding with the promise of delicious picking late in summer. William threaded his free hand through the tangled vine and stroked the underlying stone with an overwhelming sense of gratitude.

To keep the feeling a little longer—to fully experience its intensity—William passed by Cullalo's main entrance, and walked on to the grassy bank that kept the waters of the Tay from Cullalo's back yard. Here he knelt, bent to kiss the ground, and gazed along the sparkling water towards the sun until the dampness in the soil permeated his trousers. He brushed the moisture from his pants and his eyes, and made his way to Cullalo's back gate.

He let himself quietly through the scullery door, glanced into the empty kitchen as he tip-toed along the hallway, and surprised his family in the dining room where they were sitting down to the evening meal.

There were tears and hugs, more tears and laughter, still more tears and then enthusiastic demands for his story, which his mother forestalled by insisting he must eat. An extra plate was filled with fair contribution from each person around the table. William had never before felt such contentment; such certainty of his own well-being. He had beaten his illness and he was home to stay.

~

The only change at Cullalo during the nine months William had been away, was that Bessie now lived with her husband, George Anderson, at Tayview; a walk of less than ten minutes along the river bank. Angus and his wife, Bella, lived even closer at Tayside, which was built on a portion of land John had carved off Cullalo's original estate. Catching up on family news over several cups of tea in the kitchen, William learnt that his mother expected Bessie to announce her first pregnancy any day, and that she thought Bella, still childless after four years of marriage to Angus, must be barren. Dr Clement Gunn had finally come forward to ask for Margaret's hand, and the couple were due to wed in spring. Janet was attracting the eye of many a reputable young man, but Jen had suffered a disappointment, and his mother worried that she had not found a new interest. William's brothers, Johnnie, James, Robert and Joseph, were all set to follow his example, and go adventuring on the high seas if their father would let them. Alexander, however, was a 'home-body'.

"Alex may be one with the Mr. Meerish you wrote about," his mother said thoughtfully. "Not the kind to meet with success. Not the kind to find happiness in a wife and children. Your Da were the worst I've seen him be, about our Alex, but it's settled now. Alex has his place at the bank, and is safe enough there."

William's father was the director of the Newburgh Commercial Savings Bank and yes, William thought ruefully, unlike the fate that surely awaited poor Gordon, Alex would be 'safe' there.

"Is Clement in Newburgh?" William changed the subject.

"Settled in Peebles, where he owns his practice. He oft visits by train though, to see our Margaret. We'll have him with us for a meal. He'll be anxious for our invitation!" His mother giggled, momentarily looking so fresh and happy that William was compelled to lean over and kiss her on the brow.

~

Where William's tete-a-tete with his mother was an enjoyable exploration of family and friendships, his conversation with his father was unpleasantly oriented towards business. A place in the mill, on the quay, or at the bank? His father's scowl deepened with each suggestion William declined.

"What then? Edina? Ye think they won't recall you're consumptive?"

"I'm cured, Da."

"Edina will sicken ye again. It's a den of contagion."

William was, he admitted, in two minds. He felt a reinvigorated attachment to Newburgh and his family, and yet he wanted to return to Edinburgh, to take up the career that had been so rudely interrupted. He had triumphed over phthisis, and there was no reason for anyone to know he had once been diagnosed.

"You're determined then, to be a doctor?"

"It's my calling," William testified firmly. "I didn't study all those years to give it up."

"But who will take ye, lad? How to explain leaving Dr McDougall? What to say of your absence these months past?"

William studied the unadorned, panelled walls of his father's office. He lightly breathed in the smoke that was trailing from his father's pipe and—enjoying the deeply familiar fragrance of the tobacco; exalting in the absence of irritation to his lungs; acknowledging the ineffable aid the pipe was to his father's deliberations—he decided to take up pipe-smoking himself.

"Best talk to Clement," his father concluded. "Maybe he knows a situation."

~

Dr Clement Gunn was a city lad who graduated from Edinburgh University in 1882, sufficiently ahead of William's cohort for William to have heard the name, but not to have met the man. Their first meeting was late in 1884 at Cullalo, when William's mother invited Margaret's paramour, the local doctor's young assistant, to dinner. William had taken an immediate liking to Clement; there was much they had in common. He had enjoyed teasing Margaret about Clement's obvious intentions towards her. He prided himself on having stoked their nascent romance and for knowing, before he left for the Antipodes, that Clement had made his proposal, and Margaret had accepted.

After three years at Newburgh, and wanting to establish his practice before the wedding, Clement had explored possible situations within a two-hour train ride of Edinburgh. He had, only a few months ago, settled on a vacant surgery in the Scottish Border town of Peebles. An interesting situation he had passed up, he told William, was in the small village of Milnathort, a little over 20 miles from Newburgh on the rail line to Edinburgh. The elderly doctor there would be retiring within three years, and wanted an assistant who could buy into the practice. It did not suit *him*, Clement said, because he had already served his apprenticeship. But perhaps the doctor was still looking?

It proved to be an ideal situation. Within reach of both Edinburgh and Newburgh, the only practice in the village, and a picturesque spot, between the Lomond Hills and Loch Leven. Dr Muir had only two interests: William's graduation certificate and John Cameron's financial assets.

Milnathort was a sleepy village, without enough work to keep two doctors occupied. Dr Muir continued to see patients who came to the surgery or lived close-by, while sending William out, on horseback, to more remote locations. William was given the dubious privilege of handling every night call, but these were not many. After his morning duty—making up such pills, ointments, tonics and plasters as were needed to restock the surgery—William was often free to tramp the Lomond Hills or the shores of Loch Leven with his camera. He regularly visited Cullalo for the midday meal, or an overnight stay.

His favourite jaunt that summer was to pile into a coble with his brothers, Johnnie and James, and paddle to one of the fishing banks where the fishermen were netting salmon. There they could pass hours, watching and helping, before they each selected a fish to bring home to Cullalo's kitchen. In autumn, hiking with Angus and Clement, he enjoyed the glorious colours of the woodlands, poking about the 16th Century ruins of Lindores Abbey, and climbing up to the 11th Century remnants of Cross Macduff. He gained a new appreciation for Fife's history from Clement—an unapologetic enthusiast.

In winter he showed Clement a thing or two, taking Margaret in his arms and waltzing her skilfully across the ice of Loch Lindores. Through the Christmas season he settled in the warmth of family, listening to Jen play the piano at home, and the organ in church; enjoying Margaret's lovely contralto as she rehearsed in Cullalo's living room; partaking in a pipe and a dram of whisky with his father in the smoking room to round off a deliciously hot supper.

In March, when the pear blossom was at its most beautiful, Margaret and Clement were married in the garden at Cullalo. William was filled with happiness for them both ... and he was more envious than he had ever been, of anything.

"You could apply yourself better," Clement winked and nudged, "to finding a wife!"

~

With Margaret and Clement gone to Peebles, Newburgh lost much of its appeal. Angus was busy running the sawmill. Johnnie was away in Leith, where he was learning his trade from a timber merchant, and Alex was a pale, unapproachable recluse. He refused William's invitations to row out to Mudgrum; he declined to hike into the Ochils. As far as William could tell the only one who could entice Alex into the open was Jen—he accompanied her to concerts where he stood by the piano, stiff as a lampstand, and turned the pages of her sheet music. Janet, meanwhile, had caught the eye of a tea merchant, John Downie-Morris from Perth, and was rarely at home.

James, 17 this year, was studying agriculture at Edinburgh University, and the thought of that city, its youthful energy and its exciting society, made William keen not as much to visit James, as to renew his friendship with peers from his own university days. It was surely time, in the summer of 1887, to return and take his rightful place.

His health was good; his lungs were clear. He had gained enough weight to be in proportionate measure to his height, and his tailored clothes sat well on him. He was satisfied, whenever he caught his reflection, that he was a fine figure and he knew, for a fact, that some of the evening house-calls he attended at Milnathort were for no reason other than to persuade him to sit down to a meal with a farming family that wanted to display a daughter to him. There were certainly prospects available, but none that sparked his interest. It would be very different, he knew, in Edinburgh.

Dr Muir was dismayed, but in no position to refuse William's resolute proposal that they divide the management of the Milnathort practice such that William could be away in Edinburgh from Thursday morning until Sunday afternoon. The research laboratory at the university welcomed his attendance every Friday, and on Saturdays, as Clement had teasingly suggested, William applied himself to finding a girl who would suit him as a wife.

This pursuit had its ups and downs, and not infrequently William took himself to Peebles instead of Edinburgh—rather more interested in debating the latest research with Clement, or palpating Margaret's expanding uterus.

Winifred Eleanor Gunn was born in January 1888, and as he held his baby niece in his arms for the first time, William fell in love.

"You do know, Willie," Clement nudged and winked, "how to go about getting a bairn of your own?"

The girl who *did* come to interest William, needless to say, was one who evinced no interest in return. This motivated him to turn towards her all the charm he could muster.

William finally prevailed on Hailie to visit Newburgh, and meet his family on the occasion of Janet's wedding to John Downie-Morris in April 1888. His mother initially declared herself 'mightily pleased that our Willie has at last brought a young lady home', but towards the end of the visit William detected a loss of enthusiasm.

"She's a lovely lass, Willie ... maybe young yet. She didn't have much to be speaking of."

"Not every lass got your chance at an education, Ma," William bristled.

"Aye, aye ... give it time ... maybe she'll come out of herself. We'll see."

Despite his mother's effort at tact, William was greatly displeased. Over the next few months, he and Hailie visited Peebles several times, and Newburgh not at all.

They were at Peebles, late in August, when William suffered a severe coughing fit. Clement and Margaret stood over him, mirroring each other; hands on hips and deep concern in their faces.

"You're bleeding, my darling?" Hailie said in surprise.

~

Hailie's father, upon learning of William's condition, was outraged. Blocking William's passage into the house, the eminent man resoundingly rejected the appeal William tried to make. Either phthisis was infectious, in which case William was endangering Hailie's life, or the disease was genetic, in which case he must do the responsible thing and never father children. Most consumptives died within five years of diagnosis, and there was no evidence supporting William's claim that the Australian climate would keep him alive.

"You *knew* you were consumptive, and still you courted my daughter?! You're a disgrace! Be gone to Australia, and may Edina never see your face again!"

William departed from Plymouth on 27th October 1888, comfortably settled in a first-class cabin on the luxurious RMS *Orient,* but nonetheless, unhappily sentenced to Australia for the rest of his natural life.

1892, Wednesday
9th February

Melbourne Royal Botanic Gardens

William, seated miserably on his favourite park bench under the silver gum, knew to expect that Jeannie's mother, when she learnt that he was consumptive, would be no less furious that Hailie's father had been.

Annie Irvine Robertson, a widow who had brought her two daughters from Edinburgh to Australia in 1883, was a force of nature. She had treated William with suspicion from their first meeting, and on discovering that he was courting Jeannie, she had told him forthrightly that she would make inquiries after him in Edinburgh. Inquiries that had not, to date, furnished her his unfortunate medical history. It had taken William three years to again convince himself that he was cured; three years in which he had established a reputable, popular practice as a child specialist in South Yarra. He had saved enough money to offer his intended a comfortable family home. It was eight months ago that William had mustered the courage to ask Annie for Jeannie's hand in marriage.

Annie had kept him waiting, testing his sincerity with her hard, evaluative stare. When he did not look away, she at last replied.

"I don't agree."

His heart turned in his chest. Panic rose in his throat.

"But," Annie continued with no less severity, "Jeannie has her own opinion, and you may ask her."

When William next arrived at Struan, the Robertsons' villa in Cheltenham on the outskirts of Melbourne, he was carrying a large wicker box.

Annie looked at the box with deep suspicion. Jeannie looked at it with puzzlement. William carried it into the hallway, and placed it on the tiled floor where it took on an inner life, thumping and shuffling.

Jeannie fell to her knees, undid the clasp and threw back the lid.

"Willie, Willie, Willie!" Jeannie pulled the Saint Bernard puppy into her arms and held it tightly to her chest.

"Meet Olga, Baroness of Goldenstock." William revelled in Jeannie's astonished excitement.

One of Olga's oversized paws escaped Jeannie's grasp, and swept her woollen cardigan away from her shoulder. Olga gave Jeannie's face a hearty lick, and took a mouthful of Jeannie's long brown hair.

"Olga," Jeannie laughed, "let me go now." As she extricated her hair, her fingers found the small box tied to Olga's collar. She looked questioningly at William who was on one knee beside her, helping restrain the boisterous puppy.

"Open it," William said softly, taking full control of Olga while Jeannie untied the box.

"Will you be my wife, Jeannie?"

"Oh Willie!" Jeannie slipped the white gold and diamond band onto her ring finger. "I thought you'd never ask. A thousand times 'yes', Willie!"

As William lent forward to kiss Jeannie on the cheek, Olga threw a foreleg over his shoulder, and made a determined lunge for freedom. William landed on his back, hauling the puppy into his arms. Jeannie laughed joyfully, and threw herself over the top of William and Olga, to give him a deep kiss on the mouth.

Annie Irvine Robertson demanded a twelve-month engagement. Jeannie negotiated, settling on a wedding in April 1892, when Struan's gardens would be displaying their most vibrant autumn colours.

~

Three years previously, when William and Jeannie had first walked out together, it was to Jeannie's favourite spot—these gardens, on the southern side of the Yarra River, not far from his medical practice in Punt Road. Awkwardly seated on this very park bench, it fell to William to persuade his beautiful, but acutely shy companion, to bless his ears with the gentle, rolling Scottish Borders accent that reminded him of home.

"Will you tell me all about yourself?" he asked.

"There's nothing to tell that you don't know already."

"There's a lot I don't know. I would learn all about you."

Jeannie's usually pale complexion became rosy. She busied her fingers, laying the folds of her dress around her knees.

William deployed a strategy a professor in Edinburgh had recommended—a diversion useful as a patient received their dose of laudanum before surgery.

"Begin with this," he said with a smile, taking one of her hands in his to ensure he had captured all of her attention. "Tell me about your first pet."

II

1873 - 1892

Chapter 5

Jeannie

1873: Sprouston, Scotland: 'Twas Spring, at Nottylees.'

The turnips were sprouting in green tufts, and around the edges of the field that slopes from the farmhouse down to the river there was a sprinkling of delicate colours—white, yellow, blue and orange—but my favourite wildflower was the pink willowherb that grows along the lane all the way from our house, Nottylees, past Haddon and Kerchesters and down to Sprouston. I wanted Lily to paint the willowherb on the sign Ma had asked her to make, but she said she had no pink and I didn't dare go into the studio for Ma's pot. Lily was eleven and I would soon be seven, and even though the sign would look better with the willowherb, Lily wouldn't do what I said because "Jeannie," (she said this with hands on hips), "you're only a wee bairn."

My brothers Frank, who was ten, and Jim, who was eight, were making a planter box to go under the sign from pieces of old wood they found behind the barn. They'd been hammering away, yelling at each other, and they'd started fighting—which is normal. Lily and I were ignoring them as they rolled around on the grass. Ma was not far down the road with Will, who was only five. They were digging up wildflowers to put in the planter box.

I saw three boys approach Ma, carrying picnic baskets. She put her hand in each of the baskets in turn. She smiled and talked to the boys, but she shook her head. Eventually the boys came towards Lily and me. Jim ran through the gate to follow them, and Frank brought up the rear.

The boys were carrying puppies; one fluffy bundle of gold, black and white fur in each basket. We sat on the ground, cuddling them. I got to hold one briefly while Lily put her palette out of the way, and wiped her hands on her apron. Then she pulled the puppy away from me, laying a streak of blue on its fur.

They were Saint Bernard puppies, and the boys were giving them away because their mother was dead. They needed special care, or they wouldn't survive.

Jim said we'd have them, but the boys said Ma had refused, which made me very sad because if Ma says 'no', then that's the end of it.

Ma sent the boys on their way. The puppies were packed into the baskets, and they went off, down the lane. I saw Ma looking after the boys, sort of soft and sad. Jim must have seen it too because, when she was gone, he raced across the corner of the turnip field and down to Redden Burn to catch up with them.

That night we had a Saint Bernard puppy with a streak of blue fur in the house. Everyone wanted it, but Ma said it couldn't belong to Jim because he was disobedient. It couldn't belong to Frank because he already had a dog. It couldn't belong to Lily because she was too disorganised, and it couldn't belong to Will because he was too young. *If* I proved that I could look after the puppy properly, then in summer it would be mine.

I warmed diluted cow's milk over the fire, and fed it to the puppy the way we fed the orphan lambs. I lay on the hearth with it tucked into the bend of my tummy so it didn't miss its mother, and I refused to move at bedtime, lest it get cold without me. During the days, I followed the puppy everywhere, cleaning up its mess and rescuing it from its mischief. Above all, I had to make sure it didn't get into Ma's studio.

After a week, the puppy was twice the size. I shared my porridge with it at breakfast time. Ma said it would be alright now to give it a name, and for that we had to ask Grandpa Calder, who's the best person in the family for stories and names.

Grandpa sat by the fire, holding the puppy's head in his big, wrinkly hands, reading the name written in its eyes. All of us gathered on the floor around him, because we knew he would tell us one of his stories.

"Tamblin," he decided. "Tamblin of Roxburgh, who was rescued from the Queen o' Fairies by Jeannie." Grandpa picked up his pipe and relit it. He gazed into the bowl of glowing tobacco, as he always did—making up a story, while we waited in expectation.

"One day long past, Tamblin, the golden-haired son of the Duke of Roxburgh, was riding through the Cheviot Hills on his superb white stallion. The horse startled suddenly, and Tamblin fell ... right into the snare of the Queen o' Fairies!

"Now, every seven years, on Halloween up there beyond my topmost field, the Queen o' Fairies makes a sacrifice in the hell lands. The Queen o' Fairies put Tamblin under her spell, dooming him to ride his horse back and forth across the hills every day, until she was ready to sacrifice him on a blazing pyre! If he gets off his horse—if he falls and touches the ground—he will die. The only person who can break the spell is Tamblin's one, true love.

"One day, on his endless ride, Tamblin sees Jeannie walking through the hills, picking wildflowers. He falls in love with her bonnie face, her deep brown eyes, and the fall of her long brown hair. He stops her and tells her of his desperate plight. Now, Jeannie is not just a pretty lass; she has a heart full of compassion and Tamblin is a most handsome lad … but is Jeannie Tamblin's one, true love? Will Tamblin take the risk and get off his horse into her arms?

"Tamblin is impetuous. Ye ken what that means Jeannie? He acts before he has thought everything through. He leaps off his white stallion, but Jeannie steps backwards. She's not sure of her feelings yet. She's scared he'll crush the flowers she's holding. In an instant the Queen o' Fairies is there! She lifts her wand to destroy Tamblin, but Jeannie drops her flowers and puts her arms around him. She declares that she *is* Tamblin's one, true love and she will never give him up! The Queen o' Fairies is outraged! She casts a new spell against Tamblin *and* his horse. She mixes them all at once into a squirming, wriggling beast—a puppy with a coat of curly golden hair from the duke, bright white hair from the horse, and black hair stained by the mud of the hell lands. Such a big, boisterous puppy that it will be impossible for Jeannie to hold him! But Jeannie is a *very* determined lassie. Jeannie *does* hold onto Tamblin, she saves him from the Queen o' Fairies, keeps him for herself and loves him forever."

"Grandpa, will Tamblin turn back into a Duke?" I was breathless with awe.

"Maybe …" Grandpa stroked his beard thoughtfully. "Or he might grow as big as a horse."

'Tamblin' was shortened to 'Tam'. He was also called 'Pudding', 'Fats', 'Duke' and 'Roxburgh'. I looked after him as if my life depended on it. Together we roamed the farms of Sprouston, tramped the hedgerow lanes to and from Grandpa's place at Yetholm, and—once I had got over my fear that the Queen of the Fairies would steal him back—we spent every spring searching out fresh, colourful wildflowers in the Cheviot Hills.

The Calders of the Scottish Borders, 1821–1878

Francis Calder had a grand repertoire of exciting stories. He had spent his childhood at Ayton Law, near Eyemouth, on the coast where Berwickshire meets the German Sea. His older brother, Thomas, was employed in the district's most lucrative trade—smuggling. An occupation viewed favourably by the Scots, because the English government charged massive taxes, not just on alcohol but—more insultingly—on tea. As a small boy, Francis earned money keeping lookout for Thomas. As his muscles developed, he naturally graduated to bringing whisky barrels and tea chests from the boats into the coastal caves, and carrying them through secret underground passages to storage lockers under Gunsgreen House.

After Thomas married Jane Hamilton in 1821, he leased the portion of Gunsgreen on the southern side of Eye Water, and built an illegal whisky still. By the time whisky distillation was legalised in 1823, Thomas and Francis had a devoted customer base, which they continued to serve until growing competition reduced their profits. At the height of its production the distillery produced—for tax purposes—25 thousand gallons of fine malt whisky a year.

Francis married Jane's younger sister, Isabella Hamilton in 1828. Five of their nine children, including Annie Irvine Calder, were born at Gunsgreen Cottage; 'Their brains addled by the constant vapours of the aqua', according to Annie's younger sister Margaret.

The distillery was closed in 1837, by which time Thomas and Francis had enough money to buy copyholds on handsome farming properties. Francis took up Yetholm Mains, 650 acres of prime sheep-farming land that stretched from the border with England at Bowmont Water, into the foothills of the Cheviots. His brother stayed on the Berwickshire smugglers' coast, and it was a great treat for Jeannie and her siblings to accompany Grandpa Calder whenever he visited Uncle Thomas at Fairnieside.

While Grandpa and Aunt Margaret sat on a bench on the top of the cliffs, Jim and Frank liked to climb down to the caves. The waves were enormous, crashing on rocks not far from the bottom of the cliffs, and Jeannie watched her older brothers from above, scared they would fall, or be trapped by the incoming tide. Frank always came back first. Jim stayed as long as possible, imagining himself a smuggler; imagining that he could make himself rich enough to buy a farm.

Jeannie and her siblings attended the parish school in Town Yetholm. If there was snow or heavy rain, their mother drove them from Nottylees in the buggy, but in better weather they rode to Yetholm Mains, and walked from there to school. In the afternoon, they walked back to Grandpa's house, and Aunt Margaret would give them tea and scones.

Aunt Margaret had Grandpa's gift for wickedly funny stories, especially those directed against her family members. Their mother Annie, Aunt Margaret told the children, had been chosen by Grandma—bless her soul—to go to Germany for an education. Unlike her sisters, Aunt Agnes and Aunt Isabella (who were both beautiful and were sure to marry rich men), Annie (who had a very prominent nose and a rotten temper) would need a job. In the German school, however, Annie didn't like her classes in music, history and languages. At every opportunity she absconded to the art room. When Annie came home to be governess to Aunt Margaret, Uncle James, Aunt Janet and Aunt Frances, it was a disaster. Annie told them to go away and read their books, while she spent all her time drawing sketches in her journal. Annie, confided Aunt Margaret, may be a very good artist but she was a dreadful governess. Worse still, Annie argued with everyone, all the time ... so Grandpa paid a farmer, Alexander Robertson, to marry her and take her away from Yetholm, all the way to England.

Aunt Margaret was glad, though, that Jeannie's father—bless his soul—decided to move to Scotland when Nottylees came up for lease after Frank was born. It made her very happy that her nieces and nephews went to the Yetholm school, and spent time with her and Grandpa.

When Lily (being 13) no longer went to school, the four remaining Robertson siblings rode to Grandpa's farm on Frigg. Grandpa had cleverly named Frigg after the Norse goddess of fertility and earthly wisdom. Three of Frigg's eight foals still worked at Yetholm Mains, two were at Nottylees, and the rest had been sold to farmers who lived nearby. Jim and Frank would fight over who was going to ride in front, so the rule was: Frank on the way to school and Jim on the way back. Neither boy would let Jeannie hold onto them, so there was a long harness strap around Frigg's big belly, and Jeannie was in-structed to hold onto that, while Will held onto her. Jim tried to get Frigg to go faster, but Frigg knew to walk—all the way to her stable at Yetholm Mains in the morning, and all the way back to Nottylees at night. On safe arrival at Nottylees, their mother would give Frigg a handful of sugar, and a kiss on the top of her nose.

Jeannie and Will missed a week of school in the autumn of 1875, because Grandpa's younger brother, Uncle Turnbull, had died. All the Calders from Yetholm, Buckinghamshire, Kelloe Mains and West Blanerne gathered with all the Calders from Coldstream at Oxenrig to see him buried. At the funeral, Grandpa told a hilarious story about his brother Turnbull, but then, even as his audience was laughing, he started crying, and Aunt Margaret had to help him back to his pew. Jeannie heard him moan, "It shoulda be me; it's nae right that a wee braa'her dies before."

When she found her mother staring out of the window, avoiding the crowd gathered in the farmhouse for the wake, Jeannie thought it could be the right time to ask.

"Why did Uncle Turnbull die?"

Her mother sighed. "He stayed out too long in the wet and cold, and caught a fever. Fevers are dangerous for people who are old. Their lungs fill with sweat and they can't breathe properly. Sometimes they die."

Encouraged, Jeannie went on to the question she really wanted to ask.

"Why did Paw die? He wasn't old."

Her mother's hard stare made Jeannie shrink inside.

"Sometimes it's the brain that fills with sweat, and then *nothing* in the body or mind will work properly."

Jeannie was frightened, near to tears. Her mother softened. "There are many things we don't know about the brain and body. Something caused a fever inside Paw's head, something that doesn't happen to many, and I can't tell you exactly, because no doctor has ever been able to tell *me*. He had terrible head pains, and he was sick for a long, long time."

Jeannie gave this some serious thought. "Does it give you head pain when an angel calls you Home?"

Her mother looked puzzled.

"Lily says, Johnnie called Paw Home."

Johnnie was the first-born Robertson. Lost to the flooded Tweed River, at six years old. Annie had told her children that Johnnie was an angel now, but everything else Jeannie knew about Johnnie had come from Lily.

"Perhaps the head pains were because Paw was trying *not* to go?" Jeannie tried to be helpful.

"Paw didn't want to leave us, Jeannie. He loved Johnnie, but he loved every one of ye just as much. You're right—he tried very hard not to go."

Her mother looked away through the window, and Jeannie knew better than to ask more questions.

"Jeannie," her mother called her back, "don't believe everything Lily says. Lily doesn't know as much as she pretends. Sometimes *you* know better than Lily does."

Jeannie was thrilled to hear that. Certainly, she knew numbers better than Lily did, and she worked it out from the gravestones in the church yard:

- Uncle Turnbull Calder died aged 68
- Alexander Robertson—Paw—died aged 46
- John Francis Henry Robertson—Johnnie—died in 1866 aged 6
- Grandma Isabella Calder was 61 when she died the same year, a month after Jeannie was born.

Grandpa reassured her that he was 124, and was not going to die for years and years. So, Jeannie understood that dying was completely unpredictable.

~

Jeannie's father died on 30th April 1870. Her mother was 36, with five children under the age of nine. Six years later, Jeannie overheard her mother confide to Aunt Agnes, that Frank and Jim were driving her 'to distraction'. Having heard her mother draw an uncharacteristic sniff, and seeing that Aunt Agnes had her arm firmly around Annie's shoulders, Jeannie settled herself behind the lavender hedge, close enough to listen as the sisters sat close together on the garden swing.

Annie called the boys 'wild'. She said she didn't understand them and they needed a father. She said Uncle Adam didn't like Frank, and that Grandpa had said Frank 'didnae ken the beasts', and 'wouldnae make a farmer'. She said she didn't want 'our Will to turn out like Frank and Jim'.

Aunt Agnes was married to William Ford, one of the leading agriculturalists in the Scottish Borders, which was an excellent match (said Aunt Margaret), except that they had been unable to have children. Born after the onset of his father's illness, Will had been given the birth name 'William Ford Robertson', because his best chance in life (said Aunt Margaret) would be to inherit William Ford's fortune.

In 1876, after Annie's disclosure to Aunt Agnes, Frank and Will went to live with Uncle William Ford and Aunt Agnes at Hardengreen, a farm at Lasswade on the Esk Valley train line near to Edinburgh. Frank went to the senior grade school in Dalkeith, while Will attended the Eskbank Academy, which Aunt Margaret said was a very expensive school that only people like Uncle William could afford.

Jim, left behind at Nottylees, was insulted by this preferential arrangement, but it was to Jeannie's advantage during school weeks because she was glad of Jim's company. They rode to school on Frigg, and spent the long summer afternoons tramping in the Cheviots with Tam. On weekends, when the family convened at Hardengreen, Jim ignored Jeannie and spent all his time with Frank and Will, but that didn't worry her because she liked to spend as much time as possible learning piano with Aunt Agnes.

Soon after Frank moved to Hardengreen, Uncle William gave him a pistol and taught him to shoot. Jim and Will were desperate to learn, but Uncle William forbade them to touch the pistol until they turned 14.

Lily was arguing with Annie in the drawing room, and Jeannie was learning some new sewing stitches from Aunt Agnes when they heard a sound like wood breaking in the back garden, and then screaming. Frank shouted "Maw, Maw, Maw" and 'Maw' ran in a way Jeannie had never seen her mother run before.

Will was flat on the grass, with a mangled, bloodied face. His blood spread over Annie's best white dress as she lifted him onto her lap.

"Frank! Go for Dr Felton. Now!" Aunt Agnes gave the order, and Frank was gone to the stables in a flash.

Jim was sitting on the grass nearby, his face very white between splatters of red. The pistol lay in front of him. Aunt Agnes asked if he was hurt, but he didn't speak. He wasn't hurt, at least not the way Will was.

"Lily, take Jeannie into the house," Aunt Agnes called. "Take her into the house!"

But neither Lily nor Jeannie could move.

Aunt Agnes called to her maid, who was also watching. "Beatrice! Warm water, sponge, carbolic and bandages. Quickly!"

Annie sat, gently holding Will's head and rocking, rocking. As fast as Aunt Agnes wiped the blood away, more blood poured out of Will's right eye, and his nose.

Lily knelt on the grass and tugged on Jeannie's sleeve. "What *we* can do is pray."

Uncle William, Aunt Agnes and Annie all went in the doctor's carriage, with Will, to the hospital in Edinburgh. It was dark when Frank finally went out with a lamp to look for Jim. Jeannie was lying frightened in her bed, partly comforted by Lily's embrace, when the boys came back into the house. Frank had found Jim in the hay shed, shivering and blue with cold. Lily warmed some water and washed the blood off him. No one talked about what had happened with the pistol.

The next afternoon, Uncle William took them all to the hospital. Jim was scared to go, but Uncle William grabbed him by his jumper and threw him into the buggy. He sat, crying, penned in like a criminal between Frank and Lily.

"Uncle William." Eventually, as the horses were cantering smoothly along an easy stretch of road, Frank spoke up.

"Hmmm."

"It wasn't Jim's fault. I was showing Jim the pistol. I was showing him how to load it."

"Which *you* didn't have permission to do."

"No, but I was showing him, and we were only part done, and it would have been alright, but Will tried to pull it away.

It was Will who pulled the trigger. It was Jim the bullet would have hit if the percussion cap hadn't backfired."

Some hope came into Jim's eyes. They waited an interminable moment for Uncle William's reply.

"Thank-you for telling me Frank. I'll make sure your mother and Aunt Agnes know what you've said."

The children sat on wooden chairs in the hospital waiting room for a long time before their mother came for them. She hugged Jim, then Frank, then Jeannie and finally Lily. All she said was, "Will is awake now, come along but be very quiet."

Will was half bandage, half head sticking out from under white sheets and a grey wool blanket. He looked at them with one eye, and couldn't turn his lips into a smile.

While they stood around the bed, being very quiet, Uncle William entered the room with an important-looking man in a black coat and top hat. The man picked up the board that was in a box on the end of the bed, and read the card that was clamped onto it.

"William Ford *Robertson?* You're his patron?" He looked at Uncle William, who nodded. "Sign here, and here." Uncle William took the board and wrote on the card. "This is a new operation," the surgeon said grimly. "There's no guarantee the eye will look natural. It's inevitable there will be scars."

Will spent weeks upon weeks in hospital. The empty socket that had been his eye had to heal, and then Dr Coghill (the best surgeon in all of Edinburgh, Aunt Margaret said) sewed a false eye into place. A false eye that was so good that even Will's school friends forgot, once the bruising faded, which eye was the real one. Will became an expert on the hospital, and knew all the doctors and nurses. He made up his mind—he would dedicate himself to his studies, because *he* wanted, in time, to be honoured as Edinburgh's best surgeon.

~

Jim seldom went to Hardengreen after the shooting accident. He preferred to stay behind and help Uncle Adam, Annie's eldest brother, with farm work around Yetholm Mains and Nottylees.

Uncle Adam kept his hunting horses in the barn at Nottylees, and it was Jim's job to feed and water them, and muck out their stalls. Uncle Adam was building a 16-mile steeplechase course from Kerchesters across Haddon and Nottylees to Yetholm Mains. In his money-tin, hidden in the barn, Jim had five shillings that Uncle Adam had paid him for building jumps, plus 3 sixpences saved from Christmas puddings, and all the pennies, halfpennies and farthings that anyone had ever given him. Jim told Jeannie, in secret, that when he had enough money, he was going to get on a ship to Australia where he could buy a farm. If he died before then, he said, she could come and get the tin. She could have the money, because it would be a shame if no one knew, and the money was wasted.

Jim wanted desperately to ride in the hunt with the men, and he regularly practised jumping Uncle Adam's chestnut gelding over obstacles in the paddock behind the barn. He didn't want their mother to know he was building Uncle Adam's jumps because he had overheard her and Uncle Adam fighting about the steeplechase course. Their mother had said that Alexander, their father, would not have allowed it, and Uncle Adam yelled back at her very loudly, "*I* say what happens on Nottylees now and *I'm* building a steeplechase!"

During the October hunt, Jeannie and her mother were in the garden at Nottylees with Tam, when a fox ran across the barley stubble in front of the house, through the hedge and down to Redden Burn. The Duke of Buccleuch's hounds were close behind, and soon the horses came thundering past. They all jumped through the part of the hedge that Jim had cut low. Tam was tremendously excited, and would have run with them, but her mother quickly shut the gate. It took both of them to drag Tam back to where his chain was pegged in the ground.

Uncle Adam rode right up to the front door of the farmhouse that night, and shouted loudly. Jeannie looked out of her bedroom window to see her mother standing on the front step, her hands bristling on her hips; her elbows at their angry angle.

"First brush of the season to Adam Calder!" Uncle Adam lent down from the horse, and waved the bushy fox tail against Annie's nose.

"You're drunk." Annie turned away from him and slammed the door.

In Uncle Adam and Jim's opinion, it was right to hunt foxes because they killed the lambs. It was also right to hunt otters because they ate salmon and ruined the fishing. Jeannie knew that her mother did not agree.

One sunny day in the middle of spring, Lily, Jeannie and their mother had seen an otter in Redden Burn. Annie and Lily were both painting the same picture of the stream, as an exercise for Lily. Tam had disappeared, hunting rabbits, and Jeannie was lying with a book on a grassy patch on the bank when the otter, a little upstream, carried her pup out to the water's edge. The otter dropped the pup into the burn, slipped into the running water herself, and pushed her baby away from the bank.

"She's teaching the pup to swim," Annie whispered.

It was so quiet that they could hear the mewling protests the baby was making. The otter pushed the pup further and further out into the water. After they had floated past and were some distance downstream, the mother swam to the bank, leaving the baby to follow. The otter ran with a bouncy waddle along the shallows until the baby made it onto the gravel, where she grabbed the scruff of its neck, and started carrying it back along the bank. She looked at them in fright, then darted into the woods, still carrying the pup.

When Jeannie looked at the finished paintings, she saw that Annie had drawn the otters, perfectly catching the moment the mother had picked her pup off the gravel bank.

"*Don't* tell *anyone* about the otters. Aye?" Annie entreated Jeannie and Lily, her finger to her lips.

Soon after the otter-day, Annie gave Jeannie a field guide showing beautiful drawings of the animals and birds of The Borders. In Jeannie's scrapbook, her mother pencilled the outline of a fox and added charcoal shadows that made the tail come alive, standing right out from the paper.

"Now Jeannie," Annie instructed, "Do the same, so the rest of the body stands out like that too."

At the top of the title page of the field guide, Jeannie's father had written his name in black ink: '*Alexander Robertson, Year IX*'. Below the title, her mother wrote '*For Jeannie, 1877*'.

~

In 1878, Jim, now 13 years old and desperate to earn money, rejected school in favour of working for Uncle Adam. This led to the biggest argument Jeannie ever witnessed between her mother and her uncle. Not because Jim left school, but because of the sheep wash.

Sheep were normally washed before shearing, and this was done by driving the flock through a shallow section of Bowmont Water. While dogs drove the sheep from behind, one man stood in the river, downstream from the crossing, to catch any sheep that were swept away. Uncle Adam disobeyed Annie's strict order and put Jim in the river.

Usually, it's the smaller shearlings that can't swim well, but that year a full-grown tup with a very heavy fleece washed into Jim, and bowled him over and over under the water. When Jim crawled out of the river, Uncle Adam ranted at him that the tup could have drowned. He made Jim go back in the water, and stand there while the rest of the flock went through.

Jim returned to Nottylees, shaking with cold. He came down with a fever, and within a few days he was so sick Annie had to call the doctor.

Jeannie was in the kitchen with her mother when Uncle Adam came looking for Jim because the stables hadn't been mucked out. In the argument that ensued, many words were said that Jeannie could not bear repeating. Uncle Adam told Annie that Jim had to become a man, and learn the work of running the farm. He said that everything that was wrong with Jim was Annie's fault because she hadn't married again. He accused his sister of pretentious ideas because of her education in Germany. In her turn, Annie spoke rudely about Uncle Adam's friend, Douglas. She swore she would never marry a man like that. Uncle Adam was rude about Alexander, and then Annie slapped him so hard it almost made him fall over.

Lily had heard the shouting, and she arrived in the kitchen in time to see Uncle Adam grab Annie's arms and push her fiercely into the cupboards. While Jeannie was too scared to move, Lily punched Uncle Adam hard in the back. She grabbed a large pot and threatened to hit him.

"Lily, no … NO," Annie called out to stop her and the three of them stood there; Uncle Adam with one hand holding Annie against the cupboards, and the other hand ready to ward off the pot.

"Jeannie's watching, Adam," Annie said breathlessly. Uncle Adam leant forward to say something nasty for only his sister to hear and then let her go. He yanked the pot out of Lily's hand and slammed it on the table.

As he passed Jeannie, he bent down and said, in quite a different voice, "I'm sorry you saw that, Jeannie. Sorry."

Annie was rubbing her arm where Uncle Adam had held her, and Lily was fussing over her. Annie spoke softly just for Lily, but Jeannie still heard the words.

"So, you want a farm boy, Lily?"

"Shhh, Ma."

"He'd have smashed your head with that pot, Lily. You didn't have a chance of hitting him."

"I still stopped him."

"Jeannie stopped him."

Jeannie didn't know how standing in the kitchen corner crying made any difference, but she was glad if it did.

That fight was the 'last straw', Lily told Jeannie some months later.

Uncle Adam got what he wanted. Annie and her family moved to Edinburgh.

Edinburgh, 1878–1883

In the family settlement negotiated by Grandpa Calder, Uncle Adam had the right to farm Nottylees, but he had to pay rent to Annie. That rent was put towards the lease of a large house in Melgund Terrace, not far from the city centre, where she took in four college students as boarders.

Jeannie and Lily loved Edinburgh. The people, the clothes, the shops but the best thing, from Jeannie's perspective, was that the family was reunited.

Will, benefitting from a half scholarship and Uncle William's patronage, was accepted into the distinguished secondary school, George Watson College. Jeannie was enrolled in the George Heriot School, which charged no fees to children who had no father to support them. Jim went into the same grade, though his lessons were in the boy's classrooms. Uncle William made the right introductions to enable Frank to become an apprentice in a law firm.

The worst thing, Jeannie thought, was that she and Tam could no longer go walking in the Cheviot Hills. Most days they walked through the parklands up to Arthur's Seat, but Jeannie could not let Tam off his lead for fear that he would run back to the city, and underneath the wheels of the carts and buggies that crowded the streets. Tam always came with them to visit Yetholm Mains or Hardengreen, but those visits were few because her mother was too busy, running the boarding house.

Jeannie helped her mother by doing the laundry. Annie employed a maid who cleaned the rented rooms, stripped and remade the beds, and put the dirty linen in the boiler to soak. Jeannie's job was to wash the linen, put it through the mangle and hang it out to dry. Jeannie brought the washing in, and Lily was meant to help fold the sheets before stacking them in the linen cupboard ... but Lily could not often be found at the right time.

Lily painted vases and tea sets, which she sold to the shops along Princes Street and on the Royal Mile. Annie sold her own artworks through galleries and by private commission. She often sent Lily, Jim and Jeannie as a group to the city, to deliver a painting, but Lily usually slipped away when they reached Princes Street.

One day, delivering a painting to a customer in Thistle Street at a price of 15 shillings, Jim quoted the price as 16 shillings. The woman paid him that amount without questioning him, and Jeannie, knowing Jim intended to keep the extra shilling, was incensed.

"If *you* don't tell Ma, you got 16 shillings, then *I* will!"

"It doesn't matter. Ma still gets what she wants."

"It *does* matter! You're being *deceitful!*"

Jim admitted to his mother that he had received 16 shillings, and asked if he could keep the extra shilling as his 'commission'. Annie looked at her two children shrewdly.

"You can keep the shilling," Annie surprised them both, "but James, you must *not* charge more than one extra shilling if the price of the painting is 29 shillings or less. You can charge two shillings if the price is 30 shillings or more. Aye?"

Jim was delighted.

Later, folding bed linen, Jeannie asked her mother, "Why doesn't Jim have to give you the money he earns, like Lily does?"

Annie took Jeannie's end of the straightened sheet, folded it twice over her arm, and added it to the stack on the sideboard.

"One day Jim will have to leave us and start a family. He needs money for that. He isn't good at school, and he won't get a job in business like Frank. He must find ways to make money. It's not unreasonable to earn commissions by helping people sell things."

"What about Lily?"

"Lily will be staying with you and me, and *I* make sure we have enough money for the things we need. Also ... Jim saves all his money. If Lily thought the money was hers, she would spend it on clothes in Princes Street before she caught the tram home."

Jeannie knew her mother was right about that.

A few weeks later, Jim came into the art studio when Jeannie was working on a pencil sketch of an owl. On one of the easels Annie had a painting of the Lammermuir Hills, and in the background, standing just apart from the woods, was a finely drawn stag. Jim was very interested in the stag.

"Ma ... would you make a painting like this with the stag much larger, in the front?"

"No."

"If you made a painting like that, I could sell it to the Edinburgh Lodge for twenty pounds," Jim persisted.

Annie looked at him suspiciously. "Who do you know at the Edinburgh Lodge?"

"I was in the gallery on George Street, and Lord Bramley was there wanting to buy a large painting of a stag for the dining room. He offered Mr Ross twenty pounds for the right painting, so I met him outside and I told him I had the perfect one."

"You said you had it *already*?"

"You can do it. Your paintings are *much* better than anything in the gallery. Lord Bramley said he would be two weeks in Balmoral, and I could show him the painting when he returns. Is that long enough?"

Annie chewed her lip.

"If I got twenty pounds, I could keep one pound, could I Ma?" Jim pressed his advantage home.

Lord Bramley loved the painting. He sent Annie an enormous bunch of white roses, and invited her to a hunting awards dinner at the lodge. After that he invited her to join him and his friends for an opera night, but she declined, and the family didn't hear from Lord Bramley again.

Another eminent man from the lodge offered to pay Annie to paint his portrait holding a stag's head, but she refused. Jeannie heard her tell Jim "I *don't* paint people, and I *don't* paint dismembered animal parts."

~

After initial success, sales of Annie's paintings tapered off and Jim, dissatisfied with the content of his money-tin, took all the odd jobs he could find. Before dawn every weekday he drove a milk cart. After school he trimmed hedges in Princes Street Gardens, and on Saturdays he sold garden produce at a market stand. For a week he even emptied night pans because it paid good money, but that disagreeable experience convinced him that it was wise to stay in school.

Frank, meanwhile, thought his education had gained him nothing. His job was boring, he complained to Jeannie. He was in charge of a large stamp, a bucket of red wax, and a box full of short lengths of red ribbon. Having stamped, rolled and tied pieces of parchment, he walked to the court hall to deliver them.

In 1880, in a family reorganisation that took Jeannie by surprise, Lily went to stay with Aunt Agnes and Uncle William at their new farm, Fenton Barns. Aunt Agnes, Annie said, was unwell and needed some help. Jeannie couldn't imagine that Lily would be any help to anyone. Lily was undeniably messy; she never cleaned or tidied the room she shared with Jeannie. Jeannie suspected that their mother wanted Lily to go to Fenton Barns because she couldn't stand another quarrel.

Lily's departure made room for cousin Bella, the daughter of Annie's younger sister, Isabella, who had married Dr Hume and lived at Glen Friars in Jedburgh. Bella was 16 and came to Edinburgh to complete her finishing year. Jeannie thought her a much tidier, more helpful and kinder companion than Lily. Bella would have liked to study science, she told Jeannie, because then she could have been a doctor like her father. Instead, she was learning—as much from Annie as from the college—how to take care of a household business. She would return to Glen Friars to manage her father's surgery.

Bella and Jeannie agreed they did not like Edinburgh in winter. It was dismal; wet and grey. The buildings were black with soot, the roads were always muddy and the drains smelt horrendous. The snow turned to dirty slush, and then refroze into treacherous, invisible black ice. There were dozens of urchins on the streets; thin, dirty children with ragged clothes who grabbed at passers-by, asking for money. Where did they go on a freezing night? At Yetholm, and at Jedburgh, another family would always make room for an orphan.

Jeannie asked her mother if they could let two of the urchins sleep in the scullery at night, but Annie said that if she helped even one of them, a thousand would be clamouring at the door. She said the urchins wouldn't appreciate their kindness, and instead of staying in the scullery they would come into the house and steal the silverware. She said she couldn't run a 'respectable' boarding house if she allowed street urchins inside. She said it wasn't like living in the country; people are different in town.

Which, Jeannie and Bella agreed, was more the pity.

Jeannie and Bella travelled on the train together, sometimes to visit Bella's family in Jedburgh, and sometimes to visit Yetholm where Jeannie had fallen head-over-heals in love with Uncle Adam's baby daughter, Ada Mina Calder.

On one of the trips to Yetholm, Jeannie and Bella found themselves coincidentally seated opposite Benjamin and Henry Mein, two of Annie's boarders who had come to stay at Melgund Terrace through their long association with Yetholm. Ben had been in Jim's grade, and Henry had been in Jeannie's grade at the parish school. Now, Ben was in his second year at the Divinity College, and Henry was apprenticed to a draper in Edinburgh.

On the train, Ben asked Jeannie and Bella how much they *really* understood the Bible, which Jeannie found offensive. Her family attended church every Sunday; she had been taught scripture in school, and her mother had read a story from the Bible most nights. Ben looked at Jeannie sceptically, and challenged her to demonstrate her comprehension. He read a passage, and asked Jeannie for her interpretation. He then told her his own understanding, and made her see the text in quite a different way.

Awestruck, Jeannie asked to learn more and, on return to Melgund Terrace, she and Ben established a spot on the floor by the bookshelves where they would sit together on weeknights, read Bible verses and talk about what the words really meant. Jeannie's mother was against the practice, but she allowed the couple to study the Bible together while she was in her chair nearby, mending clothes. After a while Annie tired of mending and of biblical revelations, and Ben and Jeannie had the drawing room to themselves.

Ben expected to become a minister in the Free Scots Church when he graduated. He could be called to any parish in Scotland, but he was very taken with the work of Henry Drummond, and wanted to join the mission in Africa. Ben gave Jeannie a copy of Henry Drummond's little book, '*The Greatest Thing in the World*', which gave the author's insight into St Paul's letter, 1 Corinthians 13. It made Jeannie think more than ever of the homeless urchins in the city, and that God wanted them to be loved.

> '*It is in the presence of Humanity that we shall be charged … The words which all of us shall one Day hear sound not of theology but of life, not of churches and saints but of the hungry and the poor, not of creeds and doctrines but of shelter and clothing, not of Bibles and prayer-books but of cups of cold water in the name of Christ. Thank God the Christianity of today is coming nearer the world's need. Live to help that on.*'

Ben wanted to go to Africa to 'help that on', but Jeannie argued with him that there was a lot God would want him to do right here in Edinburgh.

~

On discovering Jeannie and Ben's daily habit, Frank and Jim teased her mercilessly, rudely nicknaming Ben 'that *doaty nyaff*'. Jeannie retaliated, claiming that at least Ben would have a meaningful career with the church, while Frank was destined to be a useless bore, and Jim, who had been expelled from school, would never be able to get a decent job. Which approximately equated to words she had overheard her mother say to Aunt Agnes.

Because Jim had been good at driving milk carts, he had been offered a job looking after the horses that pulled trams. He didn't tell their mother about the new job because it meant skipping school classes, but the school eventually sent her an expulsion notice. Annie, infuriated by her son's lies, reacted by insisting Jim had to pay her rent, even though she didn't collect rent from Frank.

Jim's boss on the trams pushed him into more and more work, often without pay. When, inevitably, Jim put his fists up to demand his rights, he lost both his job and the wages owed to him. Then, because the boss of the trams drank at the lodge with the boss of the milk carts, Jim lost the milk cart job too. Luckily for Jim, the Calders at Oxenrig in Coldstream needed help with the harvesting.

Jim spent the summer with Cousin Thomas Calder who had been in Australia for almost 20 years, and had come home to help farm Oxenrig. Cousin Thomas and Cousin Adam travelled to Australia in 1862 to make their fortune picking up the fistfuls of gold that were lying in the rivers in Victoria. Cousin Thomas had returned with enough money to buy a copyhold on a farm. Cousin Adam was still in Melbourne, setting up a mining company that would use steam-powered drills and shovels to extract the gold that lay deeper in the ground. Jim was inspired. If only he could *get* to Australia, he pleaded with his mother, he could make himself rich in Cousin Adam's mining company.

Annie told him he was 'a dafty to thirst after gold'. If he wanted to follow foolish dreams, he must do it using his own money, not hers.

Annie arranged a job for Jim as an apprentice manager with a large department store, and she let him keep his earnings because, as she told Jeannie, he was now learning a trade. But the job came at a price, because Mr Angus, Jim's employer, often called at Melgund Terrace, expecting dinner. Jeannie knew her mother did not want his company because one night, just before letting Mr Angus in the door, she heard her mother ask Frank to stay nearby until Mr Angus left again. Jeannie lingered, listening outside the dining room door after her mother had sent her to bed. Mr Angus stayed and stayed and stayed, but Frank stayed too and eventually he saw Mr Angus out the door.

As they came back along the passage, Jeannie heard Frank say to their mother "Lord's sake Ma, it's better Jim without the job than you having dealings with that *doaty nyaff*."

It surprised her to hear her mother laugh instead of telling Frank not to be so rude

~

Frank finished his apprenticeship that year, 1882, but the law firm replaced him with another apprentice instead of giving him a job. Annie was angry, but Frank didn't care. He said he didn't like the firm or the work. Then Frank tried working at two other firms, but each time there was something wrong and he didn't stay. Annie suggested courses he could do at university, but there was nothing that interested him. He was indeed a useless bore—at least that was Jeannie's judgement until the day Frank surprised them all.

They were together after supper—Lily was home, Bella had gone back to Glen Friars, the boarders had retired to their rooms and Jeannie was about to clear the table—when Frank took a piece of paper out of his pocket and put it down in front of his mother's empty plate.

Annie picked the paper up and looked at it closely. "*Bampot!*" she slammed the table so hard the plates jumped.

Jim's chair fell backwards as he leapt up. He grabbed the piece of paper, and shook it with rage at Frank.

"It's *my* idea!" Jim was actually crying. "*I'm* the one to go!"

Lily sat calmly, folding and re-folding her napkin. Annie glared at her.

Jeannie sidled around the table so she could see what was in Jim's hand.

"It's a ticket on a ship to Australia, Jeannie," Annie said in her frightfully calm, frightfully threatening voice. "Frank means to leave us all."

Jim continued his appeal. "Ma! I've been saving forever. It's what I've always wanted to do. It's not fair!"

Frank plucked the ticket out of Jim's fingers. "It'll be years before you've got enough money to buy one of these." He folded it into his pocket, looking self-righteous. "I'll see what it's like, and when I've got my pot of gold I'll come back. Meantime, you look after Ma and the girls."

Jim looked ready to hit Frank hard, but Annie stood up between them and took Frank's arm. "Come to the drawing room," she commanded. "Lily, Jeannie ... clean up the table." She took Frank out of the room and Jim followed, swinging his tightly clenched fists.

Jeannie looked at Lily in bewilderment. "Can't Jim go too?"

Lily shook her head and gathered the plates. "One has to stay with us. Frank can't get a job here, so he's the one to go."

"Frank didn't ask Ma, did he?"

"She'd have said 'no'."

"She'll stop him, even though he's got a ticket."

"No, Frank's leaving in two weeks no matter what she says."

Lily was right. Frank went by train to Glasgow, and boarded the liner *Wairarapa* there on the 18th July. All of the family (except for Jim) saw him off at Waverley Station. His hair was dark and lank with sweat. His face was very pale and he kept blinking, looking away across the train station. When the train started to move, Annie abruptly turned and walked away with

Will, which was the signal for Frank to shrug his sisters off, and jump on board.

Australia was so far away. Jeannie was distraught, knowing she may never see her brother again.

All that day Jim did not come home. He wasn't at supper.

"He'll be home," Annie said crossly. "He's not one to sleep with the urchins."

The next morning Jeannie went to Jim's room to change the linen. It was obvious he hadn't been home, and when she stripped his bed, she found the note.

Jim promised he would write as soon as he reached Australia.

~

The explanation was in Jim's letter, which arrived three months later.

Because he didn't have enough money, Jim copied Frank's ticket. Jeannie could imagine it. Jim furtively searching through Frank's drawer in their room; pocketing the ticket; sneaking into Ma's studio and taking her stylographic pens and some paper of the right weight; laying out a perfect facsimile of Frank's ticket on the department store's typesetting machine, and then painstakingly copying the handwriting to fill in the details with Ma's pens. Jim, if he put his mind to it, was just as good an artist as the girls in the Robertson family.

Jim *did* have enough money to buy his train ticket, and while the family was seeing Frank off, Jim was sitting in a carriage at the back of the train with a barley sack full of clothes between his feet. At Greenock, Jim stood back amongst the onlookers, watching Frank walk up the gangway. Frank showed his ticket and said a few words to the purser, who listed him on the manifest. At the last minute, in the midst of a crowd of latecomers, Jim boarded the ship and showed the ticket he had forged. The purser didn't remember the names of everyone who had already boarded. He wrote 'Frank Robertson' on the manifest a second time and let Jim through.

Later that night, at sea, Jim knocked on Frank's cabin door. Frank offered to throw Jim overboard, but Jim made himself a bed on the floor, and what could Frank do? Throughout the voyage Frank brought food back to Jim, and they made sure they weren't on deck at the same time. The two of them looked so alike that no one, apart from a few friendly passengers who swore not to tell, even knew Jim was a stowaway.

They both arrived safely in Melbourne in September, a week before Jim's 18th birthday, and the letter said they were on their way to a place called 'Pennyweight Hill' near Ballarat, where Cousin Adam Calder had a gold mine.

~

With Frank and Jim gone, Lily became both Annie's protector (because Mr Angus did not stop calling), and the bane of her existence (because they were always fighting).

Lily and Walter Kerr had been in love for years, but the first time Jeannie caught them together was in August 1882, the day Walter graduated. Annoyed when Lily absconded from what was meant to be a shared outing, Jeannie followed her at a discrete distance and was astonished to see her go into the university.

Many others were passing through the university gate, showing tickets to the two attendants, and Lily, strangely, had a ticket of her own. Jeannie had time to complete the shopping her mother required, and return to the university gate an hour before the time Lily had arranged to meet at the tram.

Lily came out arm-in-arm with Walter, and next to him was his older brother Daniel. The men both looked very handsome in black suits and top hats. Daniel clapped Walter on the back, kissed Lily on the cheek and walked away. Then Jeannie followed Lily and Walter to a nearby park where they sat on a bench together, holding hands and talking.

It seemed to Jeannie that she had always known Walter and Daniel. Their mother died, right after Walter was born, and their father, Reverend Kerr, came to Yetholm regularly to give church services. The community had thought, since they were both bereaved, that Annie should marry Reverend Kerr, but Annie was not of a mind to remarry. She had been cold towards Reverend Kerr for years.

Walter studied at Edinburgh University to become a teacher, while Daniel, two years older, studied medicine. Walter was keen on archaeology, and after their father died, he and Daniel went to Pompeii for a holiday. Daniel sent Jeannie a postcard from the ruins, and Walter sent Lily a long, long letter. It was soon after the Kerr brothers came back from Pompeii that Annie sent Lily to Fenton Barns. Early in 1882, Walter moved to Oxford to study a post-graduate degree in engineering, and Annie allowed Lily to come back home. Jeannie felt like a fool for not realising what was really going on.

Her mother would not be pleased to see Lily and Walter sitting alone together in a park, kissing.

Pretending it was coincidence that she happened to be in the same park at the same time, Jeannie interrupted them.

Walter jumped up, rosy red in the face as he said 'hello'. Lily skewered Jeannie with her most vicious stare.

Walter bent to kiss Lily chastely on each cheek as they said goodbye, but Lily caught his chin in her hand and kissed him on the lips. She said 'Congratulations' and 'I love you', and Walter looked ready to fall dead, right there in the flower bed.

As Walter left the park, Lily grasped Jeannie tightly around the wrist.

"I'm 21, I can do what I like, and don't you *dare* tell Ma!"

"Why not? Why not be honest with her?" Jeannie met Lily's glare, nose-to-nose.

"Because she'll send me away again."

"What's wrong with Walter?"

"*Nothing's wrong with Walter!* It's Ma. She won't let us get married. She says Walter has no father, no property and no prospects. She says she can't provide a dowry. She won't let me marry *anyone.* She wants me to stay home, and look after her when she's old, the way Aunt Margaret looks after Grandpa."

The obvious truth of this made Jeannie more sympathetic. "What will you do then?"

"Walter will finish at Oxford next year, and then he'll get a job teaching in engineering. When he can afford the rent on a house, we'll get married—whether Ma likes it or not!"

"You should be honest with Ma," Jeannie insisted.

"You don't know what it's like. Wait till it's *your* turn. I tried to be honest with Ma and she sent me away to Fenton Barns so I couldn't see him. I won't make that mistake again. We're not doing *anything* wrong; we're waiting until we can afford to get married. I *love* him Jeannie, please don't tell Ma you saw us."

Annie found out anyway, and Jeannie knew it was one of the factors that contributed to her mother's decision. There was also the letter from Frank, saying how wonderful Australia was.

The night after Jeannie's final exams, having sent Will to his bedroom, Annie called her daughters into the drawing room. In retrospect, it was clear she had already talked to Will about her plans, because he sat silently right through supper without looking at anyone and hardly eating.

Annie announced that they were sailing to Australia on the *Iberia*, departing Plymouth in two weeks. Jeannie was thrilled, thinking her mother meant a short visit to see Frank and Jim, but Lily was suspicious.

"How long will we be away?"

"I don't know."

"Are you keeping this house?" Lily's tone pitched-up.

"No, I've found a lovely lady to take over."

"Ma!" Lily was fit to explode.

"What about Tam?" Jeannie asked.

"Tam is going to live at Fenton Barns. He will be very happy there."

"Is Will coming with us?" Lily spat the words.

"No."

"Why does Will get to choose and I don't!" Lily jumped to her feet, shouting.

"Will did *not* get to choose. He is Uncle William's heir and I can't take him away. Uncle William and Aunt Agnes will ensure that Will has everything he needs. You and Jeannie are my responsibility."

"I *won't* go with you!" Lily was in tears. "I'm 21 and you *can't* make me go. I *won't* leave Walter!" Lily turned and shot a furious accusation at Jeannie, "*You* told her!"

"She didn't tell me, Lily." Annie was angry. "I'm not dafty. I know you meet regularly with Walter. You aren't the age to plan a marriage."

"We're not doing *anything* wrong. We're waiting till he has a job and can make a home for us."

"I know Walter's position, Lily. If ye do love each the other, then you'll bide the two years until he has established himself."

"No, Ma! No, no, no, I'm not going!"

"Lily, if Walter is the reputable man, I take him to be, he won't go against my word. *I* say *two years*."

Lily looked wild, her mouth open but speechless, tears streaking her reddened face. She knew Walter would not cross her mother. She made a choking, groaning noise and headed for the door.

"Lily," Annie had a final word to say, "I met with Walter in town this morning. We came to an understanding. *Two years*."

Lily stood at the door, moving her lips like a fish gasping at air. Jeannie was crying too, she felt so sorry for her sister and for Walter. Lily couldn't speak. She turned and ran.

"She'll be alright, Jeannie." Now Lily was gone, Annie's face had crumpled and she was leaning on one hand as if she had a headache. Jeannie didn't know what to say, and it was a few minutes before her mother composed herself.

"It will be grand, will it not, to be with our Frank and Jim again?"

"Aye, Ma," Jeannie nodded to reassure her. What else could she do? The drama over Lily had swept away, unheard, all the protests Jeannie would like to have made.

Jeannie didn't want to leave Edinburgh and her friends. She didn't want to leave Nottylees, the Cheviot Hills, Yetholm, Grandpa, her four-year-old cousin Ada Mina or her new baby cousin, Lockie. She didn't want to leave Will, and even though they were not at all like Lily and Walter—not yet—she hated the thought of leaving Benjamin Mein.

Most of all, Jeannie couldn't bear to leave Tam. It had been ten years since Tam came into her life as a gorgeous, bouncy, hairy puppy. She had loved every day with him. He was an old dog now, and when she came back—if she ever came back—he would no longer be alive.

Chapter 6

William

1889, November: Melbourne Botanic Gardens

Jeannie received the letter from Aunt Agnes, bringing news of Tam's death, in 1886, three years after she arrived in Australia. When she reached this sad ending to the story of her first pet, speaking to William in the Botanic Gardens in the Spring of 1889, there were tears on her cheeks. William was astonished to find himself so moved that he had to blink to relieve the empathetic sting in his own eyes. This was a woman, he realised admiringly, who held an enormous depth of feeling inside.

Three weeks later, sitting on a different park bench, Jeannie again moved them both to tears when she told him how intensely she missed her sister, Lily.

Walter, noble soul that he was, waited for exactly two years before boarding the ship that brought him to Australia. Intent that his savings should remain as intact as possible, he travelled in steerage class and arrived in Melbourne somewhat the worse for wear in September 1885. A few days later, freshly groomed and clothed, he presented himself at the door of Cheltenham House—a many-roomed, 'commodious villa' in

Toorak, a short walk from the South Yarra train station, where Annie offered board and instruction in drawing to lady artists.

Annie did not concede defeat immediately. Walter was put to the test through many dinners with a variety of guests, having to account for his qualifications, his financial standing and his future plans. His faith was scrutinised by the South Yarra Scots Church community and his temperament was tried in Sunday afternoon doubles tennis matches. Annie even laid a trap, allowing Walter to stay late at night after she had retired to bed 'with a headache'. Lily would have been caught out (she told Jeannie to make herself scarce so that she and Walter could have the bedroom to themselves), but Walter was sufficiently wary. To Lily's dismay he said a chaste 'goodnight' to her in the drawing room, and withdrew to his hotel.

Walter proved himself to be perfect, but the insurmountable stumbling block was that both he and Lily wanted to be married in Edinburgh, and live in Scotland.

Annie's permission was, ultimately, extorted from her because Lily published an engagement notice in *The Argus*. What could Annie do but be gracious when South Yarra's closely-knit community offered their hearty congratulations?

Walter Hume Kerr returned to Scotland, steerage class, on a steamer in January, a happy man who wasted no time contracting with his bank to buy a house in Edinburgh, and booking St Giles Church for a wedding service on 25th June 1886. On news of his safe arrival, Lily bought a first-class ticket with the money he had given her and, with no regrets whatsoever, sailed home to Grandpa Calder and their brother Will; back to the beautiful Cheviot Hills; back to Edinburgh and forward to the love of her life.

Jeannie was at once happy for her sister, intensely jealous and desperately forlorn.

~

Jeannie told William the story of Lily and Walter because she had, that day, received a letter written in Lily's flowery, disorganised hand, which announced the birth of Donald Francis Alexander Kerr. Seven pounds, eight ounces. Ten fingers, ten toes.

"He's already eight weeks old, Willie," Jeannie helplessly fingered the flimsy pages of the letter. "I won't see him as a wee bairn. I may never see him at all."

William urgently wanted to repair Jeannie's heartbreak. He wanted to take her home to Scotland. He wanted her to have her own wee bairns, with him.

William had known, since the day Jeannie showed him Lily's letter, that he should make way for another man. Someone who could, without risking his life and her prospects as a mother, take Jeannie home.

But what he *should* have done, he simply could not do. Jeannie figured as the most treasured thought of his every day, the presence he most craved, the person most essential to his happiness. William had intended to enjoy Jeannie's company as a friend. An enticingly shy girl who happened also to be a beautiful asset on his arm at social occasions. He had thought they could walk together through the gardens, and he could pretend, for a while, that he was listening to his sister's voice; he could feel, for a moment, that he was in the warmth of family; he would not be so foolish as to fall in love. He had suffered a sleight of heart, because the real Jeannie, when she opened up to him, had easily skirted his mind's dutiful intentions; his heart had welcomed her in and now, it would not give her up.

Love had come upon William so unexpectedly that it turned his one harmless omission into a massive lie.

Chapter 7

William

Melbourne, 1888–1891

William booked himself on RMS *Orient* to Sydney because, when he had visited both cities in 1885, he found Sydney more beautiful than Melbourne in its setting and more favourable in its climate. In the course of his voyage, however, he read every book and magazine article about Australia that he could find in the *Orient's* library. He talked at length in the dining and smoking saloons with people who had experience of both cities, and he was persuaded that Melbourne was the better city. Melbourne, enriched by Victorian gold, was growing much faster than Sydney, and would soon become the cultural capital of the Southern Hemisphere. Melbourne did not carry the 'convict stain'; its free immigrants were educated, temperate and industrious. It boasted a burgeoning citizenry of Presbyterian Scots, whereas Sydney had an uncomfortably large population of Irish Catholics.

Had he told the ship's doctor he was consumptive, William may have heard the recently compiled statistic that Melbourne's death rate from consumption was higher than Sydney's—in fact, it was as high as Edinburgh's. As it was, William remained aloof from the *Orient's* staff and guests until the ship had passed through the Suez, and his cough had completely cleared. Optimistic on departing Aden that his health was restored, William wholeheartedly embraced the life of the ship, and his new acquaintances readily assumed that he had been confined to quarters by *mal de mer*. Those with whom William forged the closest bonds disembarked in Melbourne, encouraging him to change his mind before the end of the *Orient's* four-day stopover.

On Saturday afternoon, 8th December 1888, in parklands near Melbourne's public library, William was thrilled by the animal and human exploits of Wirth's Grand Circus. In the evening, he was inspired by the demonstration of magnesium flash-lights at the Amateur Photographic Society's annual exhibition. On Sunday, he listened to a worthy sermon at the Scots Church on Collins Street, and during the hot, dry afternoon, he strolled the length of that fine, cosmopolitan avenue admiring its handsome elm trees, galleries and fashionable shops. He spent the entire day on Monday, immersed in the electric machinery annex at the Centennial International Exhibition, delighted by 'the largest electric light installation in the world'. He rode to the parapet of the Exhibition Hall's dome in an electric lift, and gazed down upon the panoramic sweep of 'Marvellous Melbourne'.

William told the purser upon his return to the *Orient* from the exhibition, that he required his luggage brought up from the hold.

~

On 1st February 1889, after a nerve-wracking delay, William's registration was approved by the Victorian Medical Board. He promptly secured the rooms he had been watching—half a house at 112 Punt Road, South Yarra; the other half leased by an obstetrician. On 20th February he attached a shiny brass plate to a pane of weatherboard alongside his front door:

Dr William J. Cameron
Children's Specialist

"As soon as you're settled Willie, introduce yourself to a nearby Church of Scotland," his mother had instructed him.

"It's where you'll make good business contacts," his father added.

"*Friends*," his mother corrected.

For both reasons, William went to the Presbyterian Church in Punt Road, South Yarra, on the Sunday after he had hung out his plate.

The Reverend Maxwell welcomed William with a firm hand-shake as the congregation streamed out of the church after the service.

"Trained in Edinburgh? Wonderful!" The Reverend was en-thusiastic. "We have a great need of skilled practitioners!" He introduced his son, a very tall man who William took to be the same age as himself.

"David, will you take Dr Cameron to the hall for morning tea? He specialises in children's medicine. Be sure to introduce him to our church mothers."

"Are you married, Dr Cameron?" David opened their con-versation.

"I've not been settled enough to make a decent offer, Mr Maxwell."

"Call me David, please."

"William."

"I ask, William, because you may prefer me to introduce you to our single ladies rather than our church mothers." William detected a mischievous nature in David's smile.

"I would be glad of introductions for business and pleasure."

"In that case, we shall meet people in the order in which we find them."

With this David sidled into a circle of middle-aged women, and beckoned William into the gap that opened for him.

"Ladies, ladies! We have a new Scottish doctor in our parish! Please make Dr William Cameron welcome."

The ladies smiled and politely took the calling cards William offered. His qualifications and the location of his surgery met with approval, but he fell short, he knew, of the mothers' scrutiny when he was asked, as a children's specialist, if he had children of his own.

An older woman in one of the groups raised a unique objection to William's qualifications.

"How many years did you study in Edinburgh?"

"Four," William answered confidently, pleased to recognise her accent as originating from the Scottish Borders.

"Is there any good reason that a four-year degree obtained from Edinburgh is considered superior to a three-year degree obtained in America?"

"I have no experience of the American educational system, ma'am. I couldn't say," William replied tactfully.

"Do your colleagues in Scotland object to the American degree?"

"No, we have doctors in Scotland who trained in America."

"How long did it take the Victorian Medical Board to process your registration?"

"More than six weeks, I'm afraid." The line of questioning puzzled William, "I have to make allowance for the Christmas season."

"You would agree that *three years* is an excessively long time for the Board to process someone's registration?" The woman held William's eyes with a fiercely direct stare. She had dark hair, drawn tightly back into a bun underneath her wide-brimmed hat. Her eyes were deep brown, narrowly spaced either side of a nose that was well proportioned in itself, but large for her face, giving her an appearance William considered striking, rather than attractive.

"That's an absurd delay, I quite agree. Did that happen to someone you know?"

"Dr Laura Morgan. Are you aware of her situation?"

William faltered. As an avid reader of the *British Medical Journal*, he was aware of Dr Morgan's situation, and he realised that he had fallen into a very tricky conversation.

"William, I should introduce you properly," David intervened. "This is Mrs Irvine Robertson."

"It's nice to meet you Mrs Robertson."

"*Irvine* Robertson."

"Mrs Irvine Robertson." William hoped he sounded more polite than he felt. He also hoped to change the conversation, but the bothersome woman kept her sharp eyes on him, waiting for his answer.

"I have read something of Dr Laura Morgan," he continued carefully, "but not enough to give an opinion. I think it a most unfortunate circumstance for her."

"And for the patients she supposedly 'illegally' treated, Dr Cameron, of which I am one. Dr Morgan is an *excellent* doctor, well qualified, and she will be returning to America within the month because—after three years of *utter* nonsense—the Victorian Medical Board has rejected her application. They pretend they did this on grounds that she was qualified in America, but in fact *only* because she is *a woman*."

"I'm glad of your testimony to Dr Morgan's excellence, ma'am," William said smoothly. "In my opinion there's no reason a woman who is appropriately trained, and has the necessary skills, should not be admitted to the medical profession. I think our society has a great need for female doctors."

Mrs Irvine Robertson responded with pursed lips, and a hum that William took as scepticism. "Then I hope, Dr Cameron, that when the *next* woman brings an application before the Board, you will remember this conversation and you will make your opinion count."

"On that note," David interrupted cheerfully, tugging on William's sleeve, "I must drag Dr Cameron away."

Mrs Irvine Robertson nodded what William hoped was a respectful farewell.

"Don't worry about that, William," David whispered. "Mrs Irvine Robertson is, well, forthright. She used to live here in South Yarra, but she moved last year to the new villa estate at Cheltenham. You need not fear that you'll see her in your surgery."

"Were other women here illegally treated by Laura Morgan?"

"I would drop the word 'illegal' if I were you. Mrs Irvine Robertson promoted Dr Morgan to the congregation, and many here came to like her so much that they travelled to Collingwood where she worked in the Singleton Medical Centre after her private rooms in St Kilda were closed down. You may well acquire some of her patients."

"Who is this you've brought me, Davy?" A young woman who would be considered tall had she not been measured beside David, obstructed William's path and stretched out her hand to him.

"Dr William Cameron, this is Edie MacMillan. Edie's father is Dr MacMillan, of whom you have probably heard?"

"Indeed," William nodded.

"You should not," David continued sternly as William and Edie shook hands, "take her to be one of the single ladies I previously mentioned. She is promised to *me*, and if you flirt with her, I shall be obliged to *shoot* you."

"If not faced with such a calamitous threat, Edie, I would say I was 'enchanted' to meet you," William bowed gracefully.

"Oooh, he's nice!" Edie told David. "Come on then," she took David by the arm and led him across the hall, leaving William unsure, but supposing he was meant to follow.

Edie stopped David at the refreshment table, took up a glass and tapped it three times on top of the white table cloth to get the attention of a girl who was filling glasses with lemonade.

"Edie, you should be on *this* side of the table," the girl protested in a soft whisper.

"This is for William." Edie grabbed William's sleeve and pulled him to the fore. The girl's eyes stayed on the glass as she poured.

"William Cameron, this is Jeannie Robertson."

"Hello." As William accepted the glass Jeannie held out for him, she graced him with a sliding glance and the slightest of smiles.

"Two more, please, and have one yourself," Edie ordered.

Jeannie rolled her eyes at David and upturned two more glasses. "Take her away Davy. If she won't work behind the table, then don't let her interrupt me, I have too much to do."

"Tell me William," Edie continued imperiously, "where in Scotland do *you* come from?"

"Edinburgh, and Fife—Newburgh actually."

Jeannie looked up and her gentle, brown eyes met William's for a short, inquiring moment.

"The Borders—Yetholm, and Edinburgh," she answered his unspoken question, then turned to Edie. "At least come back to help me clean up, Edie." She moved along the table, jug in hand, to serve another group of thirsty parishioners.

"Ahhh," Edie sighed, "the mistress of the refreshment table speaks. What I came to tell you, Davy, is that it's too hot for tennis," she patted David affectionately on the cheek. "I will see you before next Sunday?"

"Wednesday?" David suggested.

"Perfect." Edie blew kisses off her palm to both men, and walked towards the kitchen.

William and David exchanged an amused nod, and moved back into the crowd in the centre of the hall.

"Does Jeannie have a partner?" William asked with as off-hand a manner as he could deploy.

"No, but she does have a mother." David weighted his words with irony.

"Aye?" William queried.

"That one you encountered before. Mrs Irvine Robertson."

William looked around the room warily, but Mrs Irvine Robertson was nowhere to be seen.

~

Three Sundays later, David invited William to stand-in for their usual mixed-doubles tennis partner who had left town on a visit to Ballarat. William found himself on the losing side of the net with Jeannie.

"William," Edie announced loudly at the end of the first set. "*That* will not do. You must improve your game."

"I'm sorry, Jeannie, I've let you down," William apologised, politely giving way to her as they rounded the net, changing ends.

"Och, Edie and David *could* play to you better instead of being so competitive." Jeannie's complaint was soft, for his ears only.

Edie and David did not cater to his inadequacy, however, and resoundingly won the next three sets. Jeannie played well—quietly, intently, fairly—while Edie and David avoided her, directing their shots to William, targeting him as the weak player in the partnership. It was not till the fourth set that Jeannie came in to the net to intercept the ball instead of letting him miss his shot. Edie, who William had conceptualised as 'flamboyant', adapted by lobbing the ball over Jeannie's head.

"Edie! Be *nice!*" Jeannie objected, loudly this time.

After the end of play, David spread a picnic blanket on the grass beside the court, Jeannie laid out sandwiches and Edie poured lemonade. William learnt (from Edie) that Edie and Jeannie had met in 1885. Jeannie's mother had leased Cheltenham House, which—contrarily—was in South Yarra, adjacent to Edie's house in Toorak Road. It was only recently, at the end of 1888 that Jeannie's brother, Frank, had built his family a home—Struan—on two and a half acres in the newly developed suburb of Cheltenham. Most days, (because there was *no* society on the rural fringe), Jeannie caught the train back to South Yarra to be with her closest friends, (of whom Edie was the very closest). This week Jeannie and Edie had met the *Iberia* (their mutual love-interest) on the steamer's arrival at Sandridge Pier. Edie had immigrated on the *Iberia* with her parents, two brothers and two sisters in 1884. Jeannie had immigrated on the same ship in 1883 with her two brothers, one sister and her mother.

"My brothers came on *Wairarapa* a year earlier," Jeannie corrected.

"And your father?" William asked.

Jeannie studied her sandwich as if she would take a mouthful. She spoke, William thought, only to pre-empt Edie's reply. "He died when I was three, I don't remember him."

William didn't know what to say.

"I have another, younger brother." Jeannie continued, perturbed by Edie's inaccurate report of her family structure. "He stayed in Edinburgh. He's studying medicine, and his name is also 'William'."

William found this an interesting talking point, but his questions about his namesake's studies soon drew a blank. Jeannie did not know who her brother's lecturers were, what subjects he was studying or what area of specialisation he intended.

The 'William' in Jeannie's mind was a fifteen-year-old boy with tears on his cheeks, standing next to Aunt Agnes on Platform 1 at Waverley train station.

"Will your brother come to Australia after graduating?" William asked.

"No, he'll never come."

William wanted to know why, but the sad closure in Jeannie's voice forestalled his question.

"I don't think my sisters will come," William said, "but three of my brothers are very keen, and I hope they'll get here, at least for a visit. The liners are much more comfortable and faster than they were in 1883. My trip on the *Orient* was very pleasant. Your brother may be persuaded to come for a holiday."

"I hope so," Jeannie wiped her lips with a napkin, then surprised him by looking at him directly. "Why did you come by yourself? You could have had a better career in Edinburgh."

William had an answer prepared for questions of this sort.

"There's great opportunity here for a healthier life. I'm interested in public health. I want to explore measures that help people—children in particular—lead healthy lives. Enclosed sewerage systems instead of open drains; a clean, filtered water supply and public vaccination against disease. In Australia we can get these things done before the suburbs are built, while the population is growing. We can keep children healthy, and save them from contracting the diseases that plague the old country."

"Build more tennis courts," Edie interjected.

"Indeed," William laughed. "Playing tennis is very good for fitness."

"*You*," Edie said pointedly, "need to build up your muscles."

"Eye-hand coordination," David added.

"Focus," Jeannie said with a subtlety in her smile that made William wonder if she was mocking him, because his attention had been on her, not the ball.

~

William joined a tennis round-robin competition that was played on Saturday evenings at the South Yarra courts. His tennis improved, but this was to no avail because he did not receive another invitation to partner Jeannie in mixed doubles. Through tennis he extended his circle of acquaintance—business and personal—and was invited to attend other churches and mingle at other events. When the weather cooled in May, he dropped tennis, and joined the Caledonian Society where he played draughts, backgammon and cards with fellow, homesick Scotsmen.

Having tried all the local churches, William returned to become a regular member of the Presbyterian Church in Punt Road. He watched for Jeannie, but whenever he saw her, they exchanged no more than a quick nod of recognition before Jeannie busied herself with some urgent duty. It was evident to William that she was not encouraging him and there were, after all, other girls who found him interesting.

Despite his efforts to socialise, William's practice remained unattended. In desperation, William treated the obstetrician who had rooms next door to an expensive luncheon. His problem, the obstetrician told him authoritatively, was that he was not married. He should advertise himself as a general practitioner, not a children's specialist. It was advice William found irritating, but he persisted in his attempt to solicit the man's help. The obstetrician agreed to refer patients to him, in exchange for a modest fee.

The referrals brought a trickle of customers to William's door, but left him with very little income after his rent and the obstetrician's commission.

William spent his plentiful spare time sitting by his open door, reading the *British Medical Journal*, the *Edinburgh Evening News* and the *Dundee Courier*—all of which offered him a steady flow of absorbing information, infuriatingly six-weeks out of date. For news more pertinent to his current situation, he read Melbourne's leading newspapers: *the Argus, The Herald* and the weekly *Table Talk* magazine, which kept him up to date with Melbourne's social gossip. *Table Talk* was so informative that he spent several evenings in the public library, working his way backwards, issue by issue.

William learnt that, in 1886, Annie Irvine Robertson had opened Cheltenham House for a series of lectures by Dr Laura Morgan. The lady doctor had expounded on the benefits of clean air, sunlight, fresh food and exercise. For too long, she said, mothers had accepted the idea that illness was sent by God. It was time they took personal responsibility for guiding their children in the ways of good health. To that end Dr Morgan had, in her third and final lecture, instructed her audience on the functioning of the heart, the respiratory system and the skin. In her second lecture she dwelt at length on eye health, explaining the eye's anatomy and the causes of various afflictions. In her first lecture she expounded on consumption saying that no disease was 'more easily implanted by the air, or more easily cured in its commencement by change of habits, food, air and sunshine.' Consumption, she was quoted as saying, was inherited 'and yet is often averted by remedial means such as developing the chest and strengthening the constitution'. More people died of consumption 'from breathing bad air than from inheriting the disease.'

William found himself in agreement with most that Dr Morgan was reported to have said, but that did not mean she met the academic standard required by the Victorian Medical Board.

He also learnt from back-issues of the magazine that Mrs Irvine Robertson was a reputable artist who had, between 1883 and 1886, taught many students fine art and china painting, in the Dresden style, at premises in Swanston Street and later in the prestigious Brinsmead Gallery in Collins Street. She had, during the early years, held sketching classes on a weekly basis in Geelong, and week-long drawing retreats in Ballarat. In 1886 some of her work—a hand-painted vase, a watercolour landscape and a decorative cheval screen—was displayed at the Colonial and Indian Exhibition in London. In November of that year, she had held an exhibition of her student's work at Cheltenham House that was received with critical acclaim, her students in landscape painting showing 'a laudable desire to follow Nature as closely as possible'. The critic expressed disappointment that she saw 'so little of Mrs Robertson's and none of Miss Robertson's work in the exhibition', and she concluded her article with the observation that Miss Robertson 'looked well in a gown of black grenadine.'

William imagined Jeannie would look very well indeed and wished he had seen her.

On Thursday 1ˢᵗ August, *The Argus* informed William that *Iberia* was due to arrive in port. Mindful that his diary was devoid of appointments, William recklessly considered hanging out his 'On Rounds' sign, and heading to Sandridge in the hope of a chance meeting. But what would he say? And why was he even thinking such a thing? Only the Saturday before, he had been to the theatre with a perfectly charming young lady—though perhaps, one unlikely to look beautiful in a gown of black grenadine. William slapped *The Argus* on his reception desk, cursed at himself, and went into the dispensary to shuffle bottles and wipe shelves.

~

It was on the last day of that month that his chance meeting occurred.

Closing the surgery after a moderately busy day, he was accosted at the door by an out-of-breath youth. A cart had tipped over. George Ray had been crushed. He must come urgently.

The accident had happened earlier in the day and, in hope that he had not been seriously injured, the six-year-old boy had been carried home. The child had now fallen asleep and could not be roused. William feared the worst.

As he walked into the bedroom, he saw Jeannie by the bed, comforting the child's mother. He nodded to her and went straight to work, checking the child's feeble pulse, shining a light on his unreactive pupils, wiping the blood that trickled from his left ear and feeling the haematoma at the back of the skull. He saw tears in Jeannie's eyes, and realised she already knew his diagnosis.

He knelt beside the child's mother.

"Your son has had a serious head injury. His brain is bleeding."

Mrs. Ray wailed, pulling herself from Jeannie's arms and throwing herself across the boy's body.

"There's nothing I can do. I'm so sorry." William retrieved his bottle of chloroform and a wad of gauze from his medical bag. Jeannie watched him with a level gaze. "He may have fits," he warned her. "His mother may be best to leave."

"She won't go," Jeannie asserted, her eyes on the bottle William had placed on the chest by the bed. "Will you wait, please? Can you stay?"

"Of course."

George Ray died peacefully, not long before 6pm. William was relieved that he did not have to resort to chloroform to end the child's suffering. As he packed his bag and took his leave, he saw Jeannie donning her overcoat.

"You're not staying?"

"The family is best left alone now, and I'm best on my way." William could hear the exhaustion in her voice.

"You're going to Cheltenham?"

"I'll catch the train."

"No, I'll take you in a cab."

Jeannie protested ineffectively as he shepherded her out the door.

In the cab Jeannie was quiet, watching Melbourne's streets slide past the breath-fogged window. William supposed she was crying, and he wanted to put his arms around her, but dared not.

"William," she said eventually.

"Aye?"

"We need to run first-aid classes, and we need an ambulance for the South Yarra police station." She looked at him, dry-eyed and determined. She then insisted he stay at Struan for supper so they could discuss how that was to be achieved.

~

By 'ambulance' Jeannie meant an Ashford litter, which was a light, two-wheeled trolley built to carry a Furley stretcher. Some litter designs included an awning, similar to that used on a child's pram, to provide cover and privacy to the patient. The hinged handles of the litter could be let down to serve as legs while holding the canvas stretcher above the ground. It was lighter to carry, and much more comfortable for the patient than any prior method of emergency transport. Put together the litter, with stretcher, was known as a 'St Johns' after John Furley, and it was from this conveyance, patented in England in 1875, that the 'St John's Ambulance Association' had derived its name.

In June 1889, courtesy of a £100 donation by Lady Clarke, the St John's Ambulance Association of Melbourne purchased five Ashford litters, and placed them at police stations around the city centre.

Jeannie saw the need for at least one Ashford litter closer to hand in South Yarra. William gently informed her that George

Ray would have died from his head injury in hospital, even if an Ashford litter had been used to transport him.

"We need it," she insisted.

In February 1889, a sub-centre of the St John's Ambulance Association had opened at South Yarra. It had, to date, run four first-aid classes—two for men and two for women—through the Anglican Christ Church.

Mrs Ray was one who—admittedly foolishly—would not set foot in an Anglican church, and she was not the only one who held that view. Jeannie saw the need for first-aid classes at the Presbyterian Church, run by Scottish doctors. She had felt woefully inadequate when confronted by the emergency that afternoon, and she wanted—'*without delay*'—to be properly trained.

"You could not have saved George, even with that training," William asserted.

"One day I might save another. As might any woman, or man, who received the training."

William agreed.

"Will you run a first-aid class?"

William would have made some "in principle" qualifications, such as needing approval from St John's, but this point in their conversation was reached in Struan's entrance hall and, just as he was taking Jeannie's coat off her shoulders, Jeannie's mother stepped through a nearby door.

"Dr Cameron, to what do we owe the pleasure?" Annie's tone held no pleasure at all.

"Mrs Irvine Robertson, good evening." William bowed his head, and removed his coat while Jeannie explained the sad circumstance.

"Och," Annie's distress was obvious, "puir wee Georgie, puir Angela. I will call on her. Aye then, Dr Cameron, you must stay to supper. Och, nae!" she pulled a handkerchief from her sleeve and balled it in her fist. "I will tell Maggie." Annie turned abruptly and crossed the hallway to another door.

"Maggie?" William queried.

"Our cook," Jeannie explained. "Come by the fire."

As they stood close together, warming themselves, William observed that Jeannie was taller than average for a woman. The top of her head, when wearing only slightly heeled shoes, reached two inches above his shoulder. She had a tendency to stoop that he had put down to humility, but now wondered if she had a scoliosis in her spine. She was well-boned and yet slightly built—not unlike himself. It occurred to him that she could also be consumptive. At this level of acquaintance, he would not know, any more than she knew it of him. Why had she come to Australia?

William asked the question without considering whether it was a wise subject to broach.

"My brothers came to try their hand at gold-mining. My mother wanted to join them."

"Were they successful at gold-mining?" William asked with a smile—he had not known a man who was.

"No, but now they run a successful business together, supplying lubricating oil to mining and agricultural equipment. The early years were hard, but they've never wanted to go home."

"Do *you* want to go home?"

"I miss Scotland. I miss my sister and brother who live there. Sometimes, I confess, I would prefer their company. Frank ... well ... and Jim rarely comes here—he has a long history of argument with our mother."

Jeannie turned her back to the fire and William followed suit.

"Your mother is a well renowned artist," William focussed on a watercolour landscape hanging on the opposite side of the room.

"She retired when we moved to Struan. We are all independent, and she no longer pays rent, so she can enjoy her leisure."

"And you?"

"I make a modest income drawing—cards mostly—and I paint china, vases—anything a lady wants to have decorated."

"May I see something of yours?"

Jeannie pointed to a small mahogany panel hanging beside the fire place; decorated with a spray of pansies painted in subdued oil colours. "It's a pastime," she said modestly. "It's not good enough to sell."

"It's lovely," William studied the piece appreciatively, then moved to look more closely at the watercolour that had previously attracted his eye.

"My mother's work," Jeannie advised.

"It captures Australia's landscape perfectly," William said admiringly.

"*En plein air,*" Annie announced her arrival.

William's brain scrambled for the meaning.

"Painting in the open air, not in the studio," Annie explained condescendingly. "This scene is in Heidelberg. *Australia*, not Germany. Why would Australians paint European scenes? We at the Heidelberg camp aim to show the landscape realistically, capturing the light and the colour and the vegetation exactly as it is. This is a beautiful continent. The light here is unsurpassed."

"There's a person? Here in the background, gathering flowers by the burn?" William peered closely into the painting.

Jeannie snorted, Annie laughed and William turned, puzzled.

"Mother likes to include a person, or an animal, or both somewhere in her paintings."

William looked again at the person ... or animal.

"Both?" he asked.

"Aye," Annie seemed highly entertained by his interpretation. "Come in to supper now."

"It's a lassie in a blue dress, with the head of a field mouse?" William whispered as he followed Jeannie to the dining room.

"Aye, she has painted her interpretation of me into the middle of an otherwise realistically rendered Australian landscape. That's Mother's sense of humour. Fortunately, few people notice."

As supper was served, Jeannie engaged her mother on the subject of acquiring an ambulance for South Yarra. Annie agreed on the need but when William advised that the litter would cost at least twenty pounds, she disputed its affordability.

"Why could an equivalent vehicle not be made here?" Annie inquired.

"Would Frank know a coach-maker?" Jeannie suggested.

"You should ask, but there will be a cost."

"The Ashford Litter is patented ..."

"Pff," Annie dismissed William's objection and signalled Jeannie to continue. "How do you propose to raise the funds?"

After several fund-raising ideas were discussed and dismissed, Jeannie came to her conclusion.

"A charity dance here at Struan."

Annie held her daughter's stare firmly, as if she had always known that this was where the discussion would lead. "*That* is entirely up to *you* and Frank."

"Is there an expense involved in first-aid classes, William?" Jeannie moved directly to funding for her second ambition. "There will be no charge to use the church hall."

"A modest sum to purchase a medical kit, bandages and the like," William replied.

"Please determine what we need and how much that would cost. We'll add that to the amount we need to raise for the ambulance. Mother, Dr Cameron has agreed to teach the classes."

William detected a wry smile on Annie's lips before she re-arranged them with a dab of her napkin.

"Voluntarily, Dr Cameron?"

"Jeannie is persuasive," William inclined his head with a smile.

"It might bring more customers to your door." It sounded, William thought, as if Annie knew that not many customers were coming to his door.

"I can always hope for that. My practice has been much slower than I imagined."

"Women here want female doctors."

"I do remember our discussion. It's a pity Dr Morgan returned to America, and I hope that the ladies currently studying at Melbourne University will be admitted to practice as soon as possible."

"Are you familiar with the work of Henrietta Dugdale?" Annie challenged him.

The name sounded vaguely familiar to William, but he could not place it. Was she another lady doctor, a medical researcher? Annie's abrupt changes of tack in conversation left him floundering.

"No, please enlighten me," William turned his attention to his food to distract himself from the irritation that was gnawing at him.

"Mrs Dugdale campaigned for the admission of women to Melbourne University, and for married women's property rights. Having been successful in both those areas, she's now our leading advocate for women's suffrage. She argues that women should have the same political rights as men. What say *you* on that subject?"

William had not expected to be dining at Struan, let alone engaging in a debate on women's suffrage, and he was tired of toadying to Jeannie's aggressively opinionated mother. He laid down his cutlery, and raised his napkin to his lips while he gathered his thoughts.

"I think our system of government in Great Britain is the best in the world, and I see no wisdom in experimenting with changes in the colonies. We have, I think, more important things with which to concern ourselves."

"Those 'important things' being decided by men."

"Men who have an expert, practical view of the world and the power to act upon it."

"If you read the paper, Dr Cameron, I expect you would have seen the case recently of a wife who was jailed for 'disorderly conduct'?"

It struck William as another of those sudden switches in the discourse. Jeannie glanced at him with the slight roll of her eyes that he had come to think of as a characteristic substitute for protest. She stood abruptly and moved to clear the plates away.

"A woman was arrested on a night last week," Annie continued, "for being disorderly in the street outside her house. She was 'improperly dressed', she had been heard screaming, and was found lying on the ground, bleeding and severely battered, she said, *by her husband*. The *male* policeman took her back into her house, but *her husband* instructed that he wanted her to go to jail; he wanted her charged with affray—which the policeman did. A *male* doctor examined the injuries on the woman, and found them consistent with the story she gave. He did not treat the injuries, nor did he send her to a hospital. The husband made a statement that the woman had been in a state of hysteria, and had initiated the argument with him. He said he wanted her to spend a week in jail to teach her 'a lesson in obedience'. After that week, the woman was arraigned before a *male* justice of the peace who found her guilty of affray, and ordered her returned to her husband's *care*. The news article, written by a *male* journalist, was titled 'A Sad Case'. What say *you*, Dr Cameron? Might something about this 'Sad Case' be different if women had the same political rights as men? If women had representation?"

"I do remember the news item, now that you've laid out the story," William responded warily because he did not, in fact, have any opinion. He had simply read the story and his thought, if he thought at all, was only to wonder why it had been printed.

"If *you* were called on to examine the woman in jail, what would *you* do? Being 'an expert', being 'practical' and having 'the power to act'?" Annie leant forward on the table, fixing William's eyes with the same challenging stare she had given him in the church yard.

"I would at least want to give the woman a proper, private examination, but you must understand ... like the police, we are constrained by the wishes of the husband."

"My point exactly," Annie leaned back and Jeannie took the opportunity to place a plate of stewed peaches in front of her.

"These are peaches from our garden here at Struan," Jeannie changed the subject. "This area was an orchard before it was divided into villa allotments, and we have more than an acre of fruit trees—peaches, pears, plums, quinces and apples."

"You bottle them yourself?"

"Yes, and we make jam. I expect to have enough jam to raise funds for the church. The garden is the best thing about moving out here, away from South Yarra. There's nothing I like more than being in the garden."

"My mother loves her garden too. We have half an acre of fruit trees—mostly pears—at Cullalo."

William was glad to spend what remained of the evening talking about his family instead of continuing the tortuous argument over women's rights. When his cab returned, he complimented Annie on her lovely house and a delicious supper, and he shrugged on his coat with a great sense of relief. Annie left the hallway without inviting him to call again, and Jeannie stepped—coatless, momentarily—into the cold night air to see him off.

But in that moment, it all began.

She raised herself on her toes, and brushed his cheek lightly with a farewell kiss. Her delicately floral perfume supplanted the oxygen in his brain.

"May I call at your surgery on Monday afternoon to discuss the first-aid classes?"

Of course, she could. Whatever else might have been in his diary was instantly cancelled.

~

On Tuesday nights, for six weeks from late September, William taught first-aid to seven ladies in the Presbyterian Church Hall. Jeannie was his most dedicated student, always attentive, thoughtful, and entirely focussed on learning everything he could teach her about the human body, its repair and maintenance. William was hopeful, each Tuesday, that he might escort her home to Cheltenham after class, but Jeannie, unfailingly, had overnight accommodation arranged with one of her many friends in South Yarra.

On 5th November, the last night of the course, William was surprised to find himself celebrated by a party. On completion of a final run through the bandaging techniques on which the group would be examined by Dr MacMillan the following week, Jeannie disappeared into the church kitchen and emerged carrying plates of sandwiches and sausage rolls.

"Party time!" she announced with a wide smile. "I hope you have nothing else planned, Dr Cameron."

The social event gave the ladies an opportunity to grill William on his personal life: his background in Edinburgh, his family in Newburgh and the progress of his practice in Melbourne. The five mothers in the group consulted each other with consternation when they heard that the practice was barely viable. He was obviously well educated, highly personable, reliable and trustworthy and, while it was regrettable that he was not married, that was surely a situation that would soon be rectified. It was not fair, they agreed, that a doctor should be required to establish himself before making an offer of marriage, and yet he must be married before he could establish his practice. They would bring their children to him, they promised, and they would encourage others to do the same.

"A positive outcome, William," Jeannie spoke softly as the last of the ladies walked down the steps and she locked the door of the church hall. "I'm sure Mrs Ray, Mrs MacGyver and Mrs Argyle will bring their children to you, because they were with Dr Morgan and they haven't found another doctor yet."

"Did *you* enjoy the course?" William asked.

"I did, and I've learnt a great deal. Thank-you. We must make sure more people in the community do this. Would you consider running another course in January? I've already had inquiries."

"I'd be glad to."

"Wonderful, and you're coming to the dance in December?"

"Of course."

Jeannie looked at the ladies clustered mid-way along the darkened path through the church yard. "They're waiting for me."

"Could we meet ... after your examination with Dr MacMillan? I'd like to hear how it went. I'd like to hear your ideas about whether the course covered everything, and what you feel needs improvement."

Jeannie thought for a moment, her eyes still on the group of women. "The gardens are particularly lovely right now. If you meet me at the gate nearest to Dr MacMillan's on Monday afternoon, we could walk."

"Perfect."

"Three o'clock."

"Aye."

"Goodnight."

She did not touch his arm; she did not kiss his cheek; but his spirits soared because he *knew* she would come to the park alone.

It was on that Monday afternoon in the Botanic Gardens, after they had disposed of the insignificant business of the first-aid examination and improvements to the course, that they sat together on the bench and he asked about her first pet.

A week later, without any excuse other than the beauty of the gardens at this time of year, they kept the same rendezvous and compared their ocean-going experiences on the *Orient* and the *Iberia*.

The next week Jeannie asked him why he had chosen medicine and he found himself, quite unexpectedly, telling her about the day his sister, little Isa, had fallen into the drain. He told her about the game of hide-and-seek amongst the crates on the dock, the playful chase along the quay, the putrid mud all over Isa's clothes, and his mother's angry words:

"You'll be the death of this wee lassie, William Cameron!"

When Jeannie took his fist and teased his fingers open, comforting them between her two gentle hands, it was all he could do, not to cry.

The next week Jeannie showed him Lily's letter, and mourned the baby nephew she would never hold.

~

The dance at Struan, raising funds for the purchase of an ambulance, took place on a cool and cloudy Friday evening early in December. On Wednesday, Frank delivered a canvas marquee and the flooring that he regularly deployed at country fairs. On Thursday, David Maxwell commanded a troop of a dozen men from the church, setting up the marquee next to the house. On Friday morning, Jeannie and Edie gathered flowers from neighbourhood gardens.

William arrived at Struan on Friday evening, handsomely (he thought) attired in his best black dress suit, starched neck collar and white cravat. He found himself amongst many similarly aspiring young gentlemen, mingling with a bevy of attractively costumed young women in a large dance hall, festooned with flowers. On a raised platform at the far end of the marquee, was a professional dance band that Jeannie had prevailed upon to offer a discounted concert. At the open end of the marquee Annie Irvine Robertson, dressed in an elegant wine-red gown trimmed with jet, was standing next to a younger, thickset gentleman, welcoming guests.

"Dr Cameron, this is my son Francis Calder Robertson."

"Frank." There was boredom in the man's voice as he revised his mother's introduction; a lack of interest in the handshake. The buttons on his coat, William noticed, were severely strained. Frank was a few inches shorter than William, but at least fifty pounds heavier. His dark hair was thinning, receding in a narrow V on each side of his rounded brow. His brown eyes —the only resemblance William found to Jeannie—slid away rather than engage with his interlocutor.

Until he was able to find Jeannie, William intended to keep his dance card concealed inside his waistcoat pocket, but Edie soon pounced on him and demanded he declare his hand. Expecting to be criticised for his empty card, William was surprised by Edie's approval.

"Excellent. Your second dance will be with me, William, because David must have my first dance." Before he could protest, Edie took the card from his hand, and pencilled her name in the 'Engagements' column alongside the Waltz. She wrote his name into the same position on her card, and then consulted the third dance card that she held in her hand. "You can partner with Jeannie in the fourth dance—that's also a waltz—and in the Highland Schottische—that's the ninth dance. I'm not putting anyone on Jeannie's card after the twelfth dance. Can you waltz?"

"Aye." William's response was an annoyed retort, but Edie disregarded his tone.

"Maybe one of the later waltzes then."

"Edie, I would rather ask ..."

"William, there are 140 people here. What chance do you think the two of you would have if I didn't take Jeannie's card? She's much too kind and you're late. Her card would have been filled already with the *worst* people. But if you'd rather ask, then make sure you ask for dance 14 rather than the last dance. There might not be time to get through all the dances listed, and even if there is, the *last* thing you want is to draw Mrs Irvine Robertson's attention by asking for Jeannie's *last* dance."

William could see, as Edie entered his name, that Jeannie's dance card was almost complete. Perhaps, he conceded to himself, Edie was being helpful. The first engagement, he noticed, had been written in Jeannie's hand, not Edie's, but he could not determine the name.

"Now, William, you should take your card to the group of ladies over there," Edie discretely nodded her head in the direction of a cluster of women, some of whom William had previously met. "I can tell you, confidentially, that there is some interest in you amongst them, and you'll have no trouble filling your card. Harriet—in turquoise—is an excellent dancer, and it would do you no harm at all to make Jeannie a wee bit jealous." With that advice, Edie pressed William's dance card against his chest, turned and eased herself through the crowd in the direction of the band.

The attractive girl in the turquoise gown readily agreed to partner William in both the third and the last dance, while her friend in primrose satin agreed to the polka. William's card was soon filled as he carried it in evidence through the room, and he was still looking for Jeannie when a shrill whistle rang out from the stage.

Frank, two fingers in his mouth, issued a second whistle to silence the remainder of the crowd. He proceeded with stentorian voice, to welcome his guests to Struan and to introduce the coachmaker, Mr Stanley, who was going to build a version of the Ashford Litter.

"For those who don't know what an 'ambulance' is, our Jeannie has drawn a sketch of the vehicle for Mr Stanley's purpose, and we can reveal it to you today." Frank, in showmanship style, walked to an easel that was positioned at the edge of the stage, and threw back its coverall to expose a large blueprint. "If you can't see it in full, you're welcome to come for a closer look. Mr Stanley will be here to answer questions, and I will be here to take pledges towards the funding of not just one, but three of these vehicles to be positioned at the South Yarra, St Kilda and Cheltenham police stations. I will start by pledging that Robertson and Co. will supply Mr Stanley's next monthly order of lubricating oils at cost."

While the crowd politely applauded Frank's generosity, the dance band took up positions on the stage.

"Now," Frank continued, "my mother is disinclined towards so vigorous a dance as the polka. She and I will lead off in an introductory waltz, and then, ladies and gents, please come to the floor with your partners for the first dance."

The crowd ebbed to each side of the room, leaving Annie at the centre front, waiting to take Frank's arm. As guests shuffled towards their partners Frank and Annie elegantly completed one circle of a slow waltz before they stepped apart into the crowd, and Frank signalled that the polka was to start.

William had found his polka partner, and was ready to take the floor, but he held back for a moment expecting that

Jeannie would step out. He was not disappointed. She was in the black grenadine of his imagination, slim and beautiful, with her abundant brown hair only lightly held back, curls falling each side of her face and a gardenia behind each ear. Her partner, flamboyantly dressed in a bright red waistcoat, was slightly taller than her, with brown hair, a moustache shorter than William's own, and darkly tanned skin. William had not seen him before, and he felt a prickle of discontent, noting the easy familiarity of the pair.

The polka is not a dance to take lightly, and William was obliged to pay too much attention to his footsteps to watch Jeannie and her partner on the dance floor, other than to observe that they evidently knew how to dance together. In the latter part of the dance, he saw Jeannie's partner mischievously spin her through three inside turns, and while she kept the line of the dance, she was wrong footed and the man pulled her into his chest for a playful hug. William nearly missed his footing in the promenade as he tried to see Jeannie's reaction.

When Edie claimed him for the second waltz he dared to ask. "Who was Jeannie's first dance?"

"Wouldn't you like to know!" Edie crowed, adding to his irritation by refusing to enlighten him. She pulled him across the floor to where David and Jeannie were standing ready to begin the waltz. "Let's stay near, to be sure Jeannie doesn't flirt with *my* man."

William concentrated hard on the waltz, imagining Jeannie was watching him, intent on impressing Edie with his skill. He stayed close to David, and within two rounds of the floor they fell into competition, with more elaborate turns, faster movements, shoulder and elbow jostling. The dance concluded with slapped backs and breathless laughter.

"Really boys!" Edie exclaimed. She pulled her dance card from her bodice and employed it as a fan. "Jeannie, we need more sensible partners and refreshment. Come."

Jeannie's cheeks were flushed, her dark curls lay wet against her brow, and William thought her eyes gleamed with ... what? He saw the opportunity to suggest they cool off in the garden between dances, but Edie linked her arm through Jeannie's and led her away.

After a cool drink of punch and a smoke with David in the garden, William made his way back into the crowd to find his next partner. The girl in turquoise, Harriet, was indeed a good dancer, and William was more than gratified that he had also engaged her for the last dance. He could do much worse, he realised, than follow Edie's advice, but he did wonder what Edie knew of Jeannie's feelings.

"I do hope Edie was acting on your instructions in filling out your dance card," William said when, finally, he met Jeannie for the fourth dance.

"Edie acts on no-one's instructions," Jeannie laughed.

"Oh." William was crestfallen, but not surprised. "Then I hope you *want* to have this dance with me. I wish Edie had let me ask myself."

"I wish she had. I would have agreed—but Edie is right, if she didn't take my card, I would be obliged to the first sixteen people to ask. I'm the hostess, what else can I do?"

"I didn't recognise your first partner," William ventured.

"I'll introduce you later," Jeannie raised her arms to him as the music started.

She was light on her feet, and followed him easily. Not as showy as Harriet, but certainly a pleasure to have on his arm. As he had grown to expect, she concentrated diligently on her timing, not talking unless he asked her a question, reserving herself entirely for the task in hand. After the dance, he asked her to cool down with him in the garden. Instead of answering she looked away across the room. He followed her gaze to see her mother in conversation with the man in the red waistcoat.

"Will you introduce us now?" William asked.

"No, let's go to the garden."

Jeannie led him not directly towards the garden, but into the crowd and circuitously to the exit where she paused, and again looked in her mother's direction before slipping out the door.

"Edie said I must not attract the attention of your mother, is that your concern?" William asked.

"Edie talks too much."

"Why does your mother dislike me?"

"She doesn't dislike you. She's just ... protective."

"Like she was with Lily?"

"Aye."

William was emboldened. "Does she have reason to think our relationship is like Walter and Lily?"

"No. But she's hasty to conclusions."

"And if she reaches that conclusion? Would I be unacceptable to her?"

"There is no one acceptable to her, Willie." Jeannie stopped, leaning on an ivy-clad stone wall that William was pleased to note was well shadowed.

"May I try? You could coach me in winning her favour." He rested his hand on the stone wall and leant towards her.

She held her palm lightly against his chest and hummed.

"I'm in love with you, Jeannie." It wasn't hard to say. He felt like he was stating the obvious. Something she already knew.

"We hardly know each other," she protested softly.

"Just imagine then, how much I will love you when you have told me everything."

"And you will tell me of yourself?"

"Of course."

Her fingers closed on the rim of his waistcoat and she pulled him to her. Their kiss was light, exploratory and very, very tempting.

"Mondays at the Botanic Gardens then?" William re-settled his waistcoat and cravat.

"That's best. But if it's raining ..."

"Which it often is," William smiled.

"The Cole's Book Arcade."

"Excellent choice."

"We'll be missed," she warned.

"After you." William bowed low over her neck, inhaling her perfume as she stood and pressed herself past him into the light.

"Can you dance the Highland Schottische?" Jeannie asked over her shoulder.

"I doubt it. Do you mind if I make a fool of myself?"

"Not at all, but I was asked by a highlander who was particularly persistent—it's probably the only dance he'll do in the entire night."

"Oh," William felt deflated, "can I trade for another dance?"

"Start beside me for the Lancers, and we'll have the fourteenth dance. That's quite enough to alert my mother."

At the entrance to the marquee, the man in the red waistcoat blocked their way.

"Ah-hah," he said loudly.

Jeannie shushed him, one finger to her lips, her hand pushing him back into the throng.

"Who is this?" the man demanded with a smile.

"Dr William Cameron ... Jim."

"James *Watson* Robertson," Jim imitated his mother's hauteur. "*Very* concerned to be making your acquaintance in this way, sir!" He turned to his sister. "*You* have been missed."

"James! Shush."

"Bit of greenery." He flicked a short strand of ivy from Jeannie's sleeve. "Wouldn't want Ma to think you've been in the bushes. Let me see." Jim clasped Jeannie's shoulder and turned her a full circle, smoothing out her skirt. "All clear," he concluded.

The band struck the call to the fifth dance and Jim grabbed dramatically at the pockets of his waistcoat. "Oh dear! Oh dear! I shall be late!" He threaded his way through the dispersing crowd.

"Is he ... the worse for drink?" William was puzzled; he had not detected alcohol on Jim's breath.

"No, just excitable. Jim loves a party. Never mind. After this dance—the Lancers."

Exchanging a conspiratorial nod, they parted in opposite directions.

~

The Cole's Book Arcade, located between Bourke St and Little Collins, contained over two million new and second-hand books. Patrons were allowed to browse and read all day without compulsion to buy, and as such it was one of Jeannie's favourite places in all of Melbourne. William loved the store for its mechanical devices, which included a wondrous clockwork Symphonion, a hen that clucked and laid eggs when a coin was put in a slot, and two mechanical boys that stood at the entrance cycling through a variety of message boards with wise admonitions such as "Eat Well!" and "Read!" There was a monkey house, a toy land, a mirror maze, an art gallery, a curio shop and a refreshment room—all sheltered under a glass, ornamentally gabled roof. Edward Cole instigated a successful marketing gimmick, dropping tokens around the innermost city streets that were redeemable for purchases in the store—and were capable of persuading the mechanical hen to lay an egg.

The Book Arcade was so popular, however, that it proved not to be a discrete choice for William and Jeannie's clandestine meetings. One wet afternoon late in autumn, while Jeannie was reading to him from the Seventh Book of Saint Augustine's *Confessions,* William looked past her shoulder to see Annie

Irvine Robertson approaching them purposefully. He swiftly disengaged his foot under the table. Jeannie stopped reading and looked at him questioningly.

"Dr Cameron," Annie hailed him imperiously.

"Mrs Irvine Robertson." William bolted to his feet.

"*You said,*" Annie addressed Jeannie, "that you were going to Robertson and Moffat."

"I've been, Mother." William was impressed by Jeannie's smooth, untroubled reply. "I've got some lovely card stock to show you." She reached into the satchel at her feet and withdrew a large paper bag. "Would you like a seat?"

"I'll get another," William hastily offered his chair.

"You're staying?" Annie asked pointedly, leaving William mute, his hand poised on the chair.

"Of course, he is, Mother. We have soup on the way. Would you like to order something?" Jeannie laid a menu beside the paper bag. William looked around for another chair as Annie took his seat and critically examined the card stock.

"This is a regular meeting I take it?" Annie challenged as William positioned his new chair.

"William is well versed in philosophy, Mother, and I find it a great support to discuss my readings with him. Are you having something to eat?"

"I've lunched. Come with me to Foy's, I want cloth to re-upholster Frank's armchair."

"No, I need to finish this reading so I can write my essay tonight," Jeannie declined firmly.

The waitress interrupted their conversation. She positioned pots of soup in front of Jeannie and Annie, and then became confused about William's missing place-setting.

Annie scowled at the soup in front of her, stood up and motioned that William should change seats. "I'm away then. I expect I'll see you at church, Dr Cameron."

"My pleasure, Mrs Irvine Robertson." William stood and bowed politely.

William watched Annie's retreating back, then stretched his foot once again across Jeannie's ankle.

"Finish your meal and leave me," she smiled, dipping her bread in her soup. "I have reading to do."

~

The following wet Monday, Jeannie was not at the Book Arcade. William waited for two hours; certain she would arrive with an excuse. Perhaps the train line had shut down, or her cab had broken an axle. He had seen her at church the day before and she had confirmed their meeting: the usual place, the usual time. Frustrated, he inquired at the sales desk if there were any messages for him, but there were none. He took the tram back to his house where he expected there might be a message, or herself. Surely, she would come to him if she thought she was too late to meet in the city?

William paced the hallway of his empty house; water dripping from the coat and hat he had not yet removed. What if she were ill? What if there had been an accident? How would he know? Could he ask Edie? No, because he knew she was in Geelong visiting a friend. William retrieved his umbrella from the bucket by his door, stamped into the street and hailed a cab.

"Weatherall Road, Cheltenham," he instructed the driver.

Annie met him at Struan's door.

"Dr Cameron, to what do we owe the pleasure?"

William had rehearsed his lines, but he felt his courage drain away.

"Mrs Irvine Robertson, might I come in."

Annie widened the door and gestured towards the hall stand where William deposited his umbrella, coat and hat. There was no sign of Jeannie.

"I was expecting to meet Jeannie this afternoon, and I'm concerned that she did not keep our appointment. Is she well?"

"A 'rendezvous', not an 'appointment', Dr Cameron," Annie corrected him. "Come to the drawing room."

William half-expected to find Jeannie in the drawing room, but it was empty. Annie seated herself and he perched anxiously on the edge of the settee.

"Is she here? Is she well?" he asked again.

"We had guests for our lunch today; an engagement that escaped Jeannie's attention. She left the house as soon as our guests departed. Half an hour ago. If her intention was to find you, then you've missed each other."

William sighed in relief and annoyance. He stood, but Annie waved him down and rang the bell beside her chair. "If you leave now, you'll miss her return. We will have tea. You may take the time to explain yourself to me, since you have not done so before now."

As William sat down again, the realisation struck him that Annie had engineered Jeannie's delay and his presence now, alone in her drawing room. His temper simmered. Maggie looked in the door and took Annie's order for afternoon tea with two scones.

"You know, Dr Cameron, that Jeannie has no father. You must explain yourself to *me*. Some young men seem to think they don't have to do me that courtesy."

"I'm sorry, Mrs Irvine Robertson."

"It displeases me to hear through gossip what should have been openly discussed with me by my daughter, or yourself."

"I do regret that."

"The gossip, or the secrecy?"

"The secrecy was not my idea, ma'am. I'm glad now of the opportunity to tell you I hold a deep and honest affection for your daughter."

"That may be true, and I have no reason to doubt by your appearance that you are a sincere young man, but appearances can deceive. There are many of a scurrilous type who have arrived at this colony with a confected account of themselves. It concerns me that you're without family here. To arrive alone, I have considered, is the mark of a man made of—or made for —misadventure. Is that *you*, Dr Cameron?"

"With all respect, I know many, like myself, who would *not* fit that classification. My circumstances are that I'm not of a mind to follow in the family trade. I've chosen a profession for which I have a deep passion, and I've come to Australia to make my way in a land that needs qualified medical people. I'm deeply fond of my family; I miss them every hour of every day, and I hope that when they come of age one or more of my younger brothers will follow me here."

Annie's downcast lips expressed her scepticism. "You are aware, I expect, that my youngest son is in medical research in Edinburgh."

William nodded.

"He will *not* be coming to Australia because *he* holds a deep passion for the profession that ye have in common. *Every* opportunity in his field, he tells me, is in the United Kingdom. *He* is best placed in Edinburgh and yet ... *you* left. Why?"

William was quick to see his defence in counter-attack. "Are you asking me why I left Edinburgh, or why *your* son will not come to Australia?"

Annie hummed. She averted her eyes and rang her bell impatiently. There was a rush of feet in the hallway, and Maggie arrived with their afternoon tea.

"My daughter is very precious to me, Dr Cameron," Annie continued when Maggie had left the room. "I have been mother and father to her since she was two years old. I have been called on to protect my family from those who would treat us lightly, or would wreak abuse—many times. If you're the person you say, you won't be concerned that I'm going to ask after you in Edinburgh."

Annie gathered a notebook, pencil and eyeglasses from her side-table. Having placed the glasses on her nose, she opened the notebook and looked at him expectantly.

"You can tell me your father's full name, residential address and workplaces."

A tremor ran the length of William's spine. He could not refuse her the information she wanted: his paternal and maternal family names, his professors at Edinburgh university, his graduation date, the doctors for whom he had worked, the name of the ship he had arrived on, the date of his immigration.

If Annie had intended to interrogate him on his personal medical history, she ran out of time before they heard the front door open.

"Mother?"

"In the drawing room."

Annie snapped the notebook closed and placed it on her side-table. William jumped to his feet as the door opened.

"Oh!" Jeannie's gaze fluttered between William and Annie, trying to gauge the situation.

"William was concerned for you, Jeannie. Very keen of him to come all the way to Cheltenham to be asking after you."

"How long have you been here?" Jeannie asked William.

"Not quite long enough for us to cover everything," her mother answered, "but I *am* tired now, so I'll retire." Annie stood, collecting her notebook and glasses. "Dr Cameron ... Maggie has not food enough for you tonight, but please join us for an evening soon, ensuring Frank will be at home. Jeannie will make the arrangements."

William bowed his head to her. "That would be my pleasure."

Annie paused on her way to the door, holding a mutually defiant stare with Jeannie. "Secrecy does not look well on you, lass. If you don't mind your own look, you should at least think what idea of William I might conceive."

The door closed and Annie's footsteps could be heard on the stairs. Jeannie threw herself on the settee and clasped her head in her hands.

"I am *so* angry with her. *So angry!*"

"Shhh," William sat beside her and stroked her hair.

"I was about to leave when she told me the Richardsons were coming for lunch and I *had* to stay. My shopping was not reason enough to leave."

"She did it deliberately."

"Aye. I'm so angry!"

William had been angry himself, but now, seeing Jeannie in this state, his anger morphed to amusement. "I'm glad she knows. I didn't like being secretive. We weren't doing anything we needed to be secretive about."

"What did she say to you?"

"She interrogated me. It's written down in her notebook. My family, my education, my jobs."

"She's going to ask about you in every place you've told her about."

"This has happened before?"

Jeannie waved her hands in an expression of helplessness.

"Often? Am I another beau in a long line? Are you keeping a private detective in business?"

"Of course not! Well ... I don't know where she gets her information."

"Should I be scared?" He traced her cheek with his finger but failed to distract her.

"Did she say you weren't to see me?"

"No, just that she would ask after me in Edinburgh."

"Did she tell you that you aren't worthy?"

"No. Perhaps that will come after she has the results of her queries?"

Jeannie looked into her hands thoughtfully. "No, she's forthright with that. Did you feel that she likes you?"

"I can't say I had that impression, but ... she *has* left us alone now?"

"Yes ..." Jeannie gazed at him earnestly. He raised an eyebrow. "It's been a long time since you kissed me."

William looked deep into her eyes to be sure he understood her suggestion.

"Don't keep me waiting," she insisted.

Late that afternoon, as William sat in his cab clattering through the rain on the corrugated, mud-puddled road that led back to South Yarra, the euphoria with which he had walked out of Struan evaporated. He had no doubt Annie was going to investigate his connections in Scotland. What would she find? Where lay the line that defined him as an honest person? His interview with Annie had felt like a battle for his survival. If he had admitted that he came to Australia as a consumptive, he had no doubt Annie would have wielded his condition as a sword. He hadn't lied; he had a right, had he not, to avoid giving her the weapon with which she would run him through?

~

In September 1890, which William nervously anticipated as the earliest date that results of Annie's inquiries could return by post, news of a different kind brought him tremendous hope. The cure for tuberculosis had been found by the man who had identified the disease as bacterial in origin. Robert Koch introduced 'Koch's Lymph'—later renamed Tuberculin—at the Tenth International Medical Congress in Berlin, surprising his esteemed audience and thrilling the world. At last, the disease that killed one in every seven Germans—the disease that William saw as his personal nemesis—could be defeated.

The vaccine, which had been extensively tested on guinea pigs, had gone directly into use in medical clinics in Europe, and William impatiently awaited its arrival in Australia.

While William was watching the post for his subscription copies of British and German medical journals, Annie, already in possession of much of the detail she had asked for, waited for a further report from a woman in Dundee who was personally acquainted with the Camerons of Newburgh. That information arrived just in time for Annie to give it to Frank to peruse in the cab on their way home to Struan after church on Christmas Day.

Joining the Robertson family for their Christmas turkey, were Annie's cousin, Adam Calder, his wife Mary and their two children: Kathleen, who was not yet two years old and Allan, a baby who had recently learnt to respond with a joyful smile to Jeannie's tickles. During her second pregnancy, Mary had often been unwell and Jeannie had spent weeks at a time at the Calder's house in Armadale, worrying over Mary's health but loving the opportunity to mother Kathleen. When Jeannie met William upon his arrival at Struan on Christmas day, she had Kathleen clinging to her right hip and Allan cradled in her left arm. The image transported William to Cullalo and his own mother, and the nostalgia that had troubled him throughout this Christmas morning bundled itself in his larynx, rendering him speechless.

"I would kiss you but I'm overburdened!" Jeannie whispered cheerfully, leaning as closely towards him as her burdens allowed. "This is Kathleen, and Allan." The children looked at William suspiciously as he cleared his throat and repeated their names.

"The turkey smells wonderful," William commented on the rich aroma that filled the hall.

"Ma is in the kitchen making sure everything is done properly before she lets Maggie go home. Frank and Adam are in the living room waiting for Jim, who is sure to be late. Come through."

Adam Calder, William learnt upon introduction, was Annie's first cousin, son of Turnbull Calder of Oxenrig, Coldstream. He had been lured away from the Scottish Borders, along with his brother Thomas, by reports of the fortune to be made on the goldfields of Ballarat. By the time they arrived in 1862, the surface had been thoroughly picked over, but having brought some pounds with them to invest, they joined a party of tributers—miners who were paid a percentage of the ore they mined—on the *Royal Saxon* alluvial quartz claim. Before that mine bottomed they risked buying two parcels of discounted shares from less persevering miners, and when the reef was found they profited handsomely. Adam broadened his investments and married. Thomas, now a 'spare wheel', cashed in and returned to the Borders where he took up the farm Billie Mains. For some years, as the mining companies in which Adam invested, progressively failed, it looked as if Thomas had made the better decision, but having experienced the thrill of a gold-strike, Adam refused to give up. In 1882, he persuaded a number of Melbourne businessmen to join him in funding The Melbourne Quartz and Alluvial Company, which took up a claim of 100 acres at Pennyweight Hill in Ballarat East. Frank and Jim arrived, looking for work, when the mine was no more than 30 feet deep and profits were years away.

Within a fortnight Jim, convinced of the futility of rock-breaking, moved on to greener pastures that lay further to the west—the land-holding of another of Annie's cousins. Robert Calder emigrated to Victoria in 1851, made his fortune in gold at Mount Alexander and now owned the 3000-acre station Polkemmet near Horsham. Robert helped Jim apply for selection of an adjoining, heavily timbered piece of land, which Jim had the right to farm providing he improved the property with fences and buildings. As the first frosts of 1884 fell on the Western District, Jim moved out of his room at the Polkemmet homestead to occupy the log-hut he had built for himself at Rosebank, realising his life-long dream of farm-ownership. Meanwhile Frank worked on, with little reward, in Adam Calder's Pennyweight mine.

"Eight shillings a day, he paid us!" Frank, sitting in his favourite armchair in the living room with a plate of jam-filled cookies, and a glass of lemonade to tide him through to Christmas dinner, broke into Adam's story.

"That was a fair wage," Adam responded from his armchair, on the other side of the empty fireplace.

"It was slave labour. I hauled tons of rock up from that mine."

"As I did, twenty years before."

"Slave labour," Frank repeated, picking up a cookie.

"You had far better machinery doing the work for you," Adam leant forward, his blue eyes bright with enthusiasm. "On Pennyweight, we had a 13-and-a-half-inch cylinder engine for a 12-head battery—we could have added another eight stampers. We had a 20-inch pumping engine moving up to 4000 gallons of water an hour—magnificent machinery." Adam fell back in his chair, a wry smile on his face.

"What happened to your mine?" William prompted.

"We struck the seam at 130-foot early in May 1885," Adam continued while Frank brushed crumbs from his moustache. "In the second fortnight, we brought up 130 tons of rock and washed it off to give 120 ounces of gold, including 46 ounces of nuggets. We had 4000 feet in our claim along the line of that reef, and the rig could have taken us down to 1000 feet. If we had just been given more time ..."

"Foreclosed," Frank frog-leaped the detail.

"Sixteen thousand pounds invested to that point." Adam was not put off his story. "Two of the partners demanded to be paid out. We couldn't find new shareholders in the time they gave us. We liquidated, thinking we could re-finance within a month, given the rate at which the gold was being washed out, but we hit a bare patch and the creditors sold out on us."

"Nasty business," Frank commented.

"What did you do then, Frank?"

Frank took a sip of his lemonade, preparing himself for a long exposition. "All this working with machinery in the mines, led me to appreciate the critical importance of lubricating oil. Had to be imported. Money to be made in that. I put my profits from the Pennyweight strike into forming Robertson and Company."

"*James* Robertson and Company," Adam corrected.

"James and I ..."

"*James* initially created the business early in 1886 to import lubricating oil for coaches and farm machinery."

Adam explained that Jim's farm land was unproductive. What had sounded to Scottish ears like an extensive land-holding had turned out to be a woefully insufficient acreage given Australia's infertile, dry soil. Without major improvements—all of which cost money—the property was unable to provide Jim with even a basic living wage. The original Polkemmet station had run sheep freely over 26,000 acres, but in parcelling the run out to selectors in the late 1870's, the colonial government made a grievous error in sizing the blocks. Polkemmet itself had been reduced to only the 160 acres around the homestead, and from the moment his ownership of that parcel of land had been determined, Robert Calder had made it his business to buy-back adjoining selections whenever they became available. Meanwhile, the Calder family survived financially by forming a partnership with another western Victorian family. Couch, Calder and Co imported a wide variety of agricultural goods needed in the growing colony, including lubricating oils. Jim's selection was re-absorbed into Polkemmet in exchange for the concession, to the newly formed James Robertson and Co, of the import and sale of lubricating oils.

"I came on board and extended the business to the mining industry. I run the company from rooms in Queen Street and Jim travels as our sales agent."

"That's an amazing story," William complimented Frank, "over just four, five years?"

"Five years, between our arrival on *Wairarapa* and the day Jim and I bought this land at auction."

"And you built this house?"

"I did," Frank confirmed proudly.

"What of you, Adam? Did you continue in mining?"

"He lost his way," Frank inserted.

"My wife, Katie, was ailing. She passed in 1887."

"Only 32, no children." Frank gave a dismal shake of his head.

"I went home, thinking I would re-join the family but for-tuitously, on the voyage, I met Mary. She was returning to her homeland, Ireland, after the death of her husband. We married in Ireland and were both keen to come back to Australia with-out delay—Mary was already carrying Kathleen. Family life now confines me to Melbourne and my desk at the Exchange. I deal in stocks—all commodities, not just mining—and I give advice to investors. Are you interested in owning shares William? Once in a while, tremendous opportunities cross my desk."

"When I have some money to set aside, certainly I would be interested."

"William's father, John Cameron, owns shares in two Scot-tish steamship companies," Frank casually dropped this infor-mation into the conversation, taking William completely by surprise.

"Really?" Adam was impressed. "Which companies William?"

"I ..." William searched his memory, "I'm not sure," he looked questioningly at Frank.

"The New Line Steamship Company, Edinburgh, and the Dundee Shipowning Company," Frank gave a smug smile. "You didn't know?"

"Well ... he owns a quay on the Tay at Newburgh, and I know he has part-ownership in some of the boats there. He ships agricultural products."

"And timber." Frank was enjoying himself. "Cameron owns a sawmill in Perth—used to be in Newburgh, but that burnt down two years ago, and insurance monies paid for its reconstruction handy to the railway in Perth. The company is called 'Cameron Brothers', so I'm supposing William has an interest in the venture?"

William was thoroughly taken aback. Frank even knew about the fire that had destroyed the sawmill and nearly took Cullalo with it, while he was on board the *Orient*.

"My brothers, Angus and John, manage the sawmill, and my younger brother James will be the one to manage John Cameron and Sons, which owns the quay. I don't have an interest in either company myself."

"William's father is also a director and trustee of the Newburgh Savings Bank, and of the Gas Company, and he owns several parcels of land in the district. A man of *considerable* means. I expect William might indeed have some money set aside. You'll be wanting him as a client, Adam."

William clenched his teeth, angered by Frank's conceited air. He wanted to assert his independence from his father, but realised that his quest for Jeannie's hand would be facilitated by Frank's estimation of the Cameron family's wealth.

"That's excellent, William. A very fortunate background," Adam complimented him.

"My priorities at the moment, Adam, are to establish my practice and buy property here in Australia. I might invest in shares in years to come, but right now I think Victoria offers great opportunity in land ownership."

"Land, yes," Adam ruminated, "the great colonial opportunity. There is plenty of it. Where do you have in mind?"

The living room door opened, and Jeannie beckoned them.

"We won't wait for Jim any longer, we best eat while the children sleep. Please come through."

As they passed along the hall and into the dining room, Adam leant towards William to give him some advice. "When you speculate on land, William, follow the railways. The railways will be key. The biggest thing that improves the value of land is access. The next, on this dry continent, is water. A railway line and a river."

In the dining room, Annie was already seated at the head of an elaborately set table loaded with serving dishes of hot turkey, ham and vegetables. She directed Adam to seat himself on her right; William on her left. As Mary moved around the table filling wine glasses, Jeannie slipped into the seat beside William. She arranged her napkin on her lap and discretely took his hand under the table. Frank intoned a lengthy grace, thanking the Lord for the bounty Australia had bestowed on those gathered here, remembering Will and Lily and the rest of their family who would be congregating in Scotland on this Christmas Day and finishing with The Lord's Prayer.

"Pass the plates between ye," Annie instructed, initiating the process by spooning some cauliflower, coated in white sauce, onto her plate and passing the serving dish to William.

"Your table is very elegant, Mrs Irvine Robertson, and the food smells glorious. I have not sat down to a meal like this since I left Scotland." As soon as he said the words he had rehearsed, William worried that he sounded obsequious.

"Does your family celebrate Christmas in the same way, William?"

"The intention is much the same, though with eleven children at the table, it was always a chaotic affair."

"Where is your place in the family?" Annie passed the green beans.

"Upper middle—my oldest brother is now 35, and my youngest brother is 14. Six brothers and four sisters."

"I have heard that one of your older brothers came to the Antipodes before you. What has become of him?"

William was acutely aware of Jeannie's fork, poised over the beans he had passed; her surprised look in his direction. In his self-exposition he had—not without remorse—neglected to mention George.

"My father's sister emigrated to New Zealand with her family—drawn to the gold rush on the West Coast, Hokitika. My brother George travelled to visit them. Tragically, he had an asthma attack and died at sea."

"I expect, then, that it must have been very hard for your mother to see you on the same journey. Was there not a fear that the same could happen to you?" Annie passed the salver of ham, exhibiting no surprise at George's fate.

"By the time I travelled, ships were faster and better equipped—not to mention my capability as a doctor."

"Why did you come to Australia instead of joining the family in New Zealand?"

"I *did* visit with my aunt's family, but the West Coast of New Zealand is a windy, cold frontier, and not to my liking. On the same trip I visited Sydney, Melbourne and Adelaide and I thought Melbourne the most progressive."

"True enough," Adam inserted, "the right choice you've made."

"Indeed," Annie continued, "but after that trip you spent more than two years back in Scotland and it was not until December 1888, that you returned to Melbourne on the *Orient*. Is that true?"

William nodded. He filled his mouth and chewed nervously, waiting for Annie's axe to fall.

"The *Orient,* no less!" Adam was keen to engage with the conversation. "Such a bonnie ship. She would have been my choice, but we would have had to wait a month. Mary and I travelled the very same route, via Colombo, on RMS *Victoria,* arriving in November."

"I've been meaning to ask you, Mary, how *Victoria* compares to *Iberia?*" Jeannie widened the conversation to include Mary, who had been sitting quietly next to her husband. Mary responded with a gentle, unassuming Irish lilt and, much to William's relief, the remainder of the first course was accompanied by comparative discussion of the many ships on the Australian Line and the amazing inventions—not least being the miracle of electric light— that had vastly improved the voyage since 1862.

Jim arrived as Jeannie was slicing the Christmas pudding.

"Why should I feed you, James?" Annie growled, slanting her cheek to his kiss.

"Business to attend betwixt Church and home," Jim excused himself cheerfully.

"You've already eaten?"

"The turkey smells delicious. I'm starving." Jim clapped Adam on the shoulder and shook his hand.

"I'll get your plate," Mary offered.

"No. He's to get it himself," Annie waved Mary back into her seat.

"Back to the 'miracle of electric light' and your enthusiasm for scientific achievement, William," Annie resumed the conversation as Jim walked out to the kitchen. "What do you have to say on the debate between Mr Huxley and Mr Gladstone? Have you been following the arguments?"

One could never relax, William thought as he poured brandy butter over his pudding, into congenial conversation with Annie Irvine Robertson. Her changes of direction seemed random and yet ... William suspected she was laying a trap for him, seeking to elicit an ill-considered reply. Thomas Huxley's writings were highly contentious.

"I have read Mr Huxley's argument against Mr Gladstone and Genesis, and his further—and I think rather more erudite—response to the Reverend Liddon of St Paul's. Is there a more recent exchange?"

"His latest essay is 'The Lights of the Church'."

"'The Lights of the Church *and* The Light of Science'," Jeannie interrupted tersely. "The essay you're talking about Ma, *is* Mr Huxley's response to a sermon given last year by the Chancellor of St Paul's, Reverend Liddon."

"Jeannie is rather on the side of Reverend Liddon, William." Annie scowled, displeased by Jeannie's correction. "She has an orthodox view of the reliability of the Old Testament. She is in the camp of those who Huxley criticises for thinking that if our Lord Jesus Christ *said* that the Old Testament was the Word of God, then it must be exactly so. *You*, however, are a man of science. What is *your* belief?"

"I think the findings of science have demonstrated beyond doubt that much of the Old Testament can't be taken in the literal sense," William replied cautiously, knowing that Annie was setting him in opposition to Jeannie. "I think Mr Huxley, being a man of letters, puts forward a far superior argument against the plausibility of the Noachian Deluge and the Creation story than I could muster."

"You agree then, with Mr Huxley, that if our Lord can't be trusted on the matter of the veracity of the Old Testament, we can't safely trust Him on anything else?"

"With respect, that was not Mr Huxley's claim; it was Reverend Liddon's defence. It's my position—and I expect Mr Huxley's—that when Jesus Christ taught his followers using passages from the Old Testament, he was being neither more nor less trustworthy than modern day teachers reading from Shakespeare."

"You're an 'apologist', then, or are you one of Huxley's agnostics?" There was little doubt, by Annie's tone, that the category 'agnostic' was the worse of the two pejoratives.

"I firmly believe," William responded stiffly, "in the teachings of the Christian Church. I seek to reconcile those teachings with evidence given to us by properly conducted scientific research. I don't believe I need to apologize either for the Bible or for science. If at this point in time we have difficulty reconciling the two, then that can only be because our understanding is incomplete."

"Agnostic then. You excuse the feebleness of your faith by saying that the nature of the Holy Trinity is 'unknowable'. As Jeannie will tell you, the true 'Christian faith' *she* holds is to *know,* to *utterly believe,* that which is 'unknowable', that which our Lord asks her to believe."

William's temper snapped. "May I ask *you* then. What is *your* belief?"

Frank roared with laughter and clapped his hands. As everyone turned in his direction, he wiped his mouth and threw his napkin down beside his empty dessert plate.

"My mother believes in playing the Devil's Advocate. Enough!" Frank pushed his chair back from the table. "William, my doctor says I must exercise after my midday meal. What is your belief on *that*?"

"I agree."

"Then, we shall walk together to the bay." Frank stood. "James, why have you not finished your meal? Come with us. Hurry up. Adam?"

"No, we must go when the children wake." Adam gave Mary an inquiring glance and she murmured her agreement.

James pushed his dinner plate to the side and hurried on to his plum pudding.

"Are you coming?" William asked Jeannie.

"No, Frank did not mean for me to come. I'll clean up here."

William stood and bowed his head to Annie. "That was a truly delicious meal, Mrs Irvine Robertson. Thank-you for inviting me."

Annie nodded curtly in response.

By the time Frank and William had made their farewells to Adam and Mary, Jim had finished his pudding and he followed William and Jeannie to the front door.

"I hope I didn't offend your mother ... or yourself ..." William said softly to Jeannie.

"Don't worry," Jeannie reached up to kiss him on the cheek. "Monday?"

"Aye."

Jim presented himself between them, tapping his cheek. Instead of fulfilling his request for a kiss, Jeannie pushed her brother down the steps.

"She's a lot tougher than she looks, William," Jim said as William joined him. "Don't be fooled. She appears all sweet-ness and light, but there be toughened steel inside. When she sets her mind to something there's no changing her course! Isn't that true, Frank?"

Frank shrugged as the three men fell in step, walking along the side of the wide, dirt road that led towards the beach.

"She has her mind on you, William. What are your feelings in return?" Jim did not hesitate in going straight to the purpose of the walk.

"I would ask for her in marriage, in an instant," William confessed, "but I fear your mother will not allow it."

"Pff," Frank grunted, short of breath despite the level grade of their path.

"Our mother has been against everything any of us has ever done," Jim elaborated. "Ultimately, we must go ahead and do what we will without her permission. Like Frank buying his ticket for Australia."

"Jim, stowing away," Frank puffed.

"Lily, announcing her engagement."

"Will, enrolling at Edinburgh."

"Jeannie's turn," Jim concluded. "She'll break out soon."

"Not before she's 25," Frank said firmly.

"You can't ask for Jeannie's hand before she's 25," Jim explained. "Ma's rule. Same applied for herself, same for Lily."

"In June?" William asked, suddenly so hopeful that he felt his heart would bound from his chest.

The brothers paused their stride and looked at each other questioningly. "June?" Frank asked.

"Aye ... but ..." Jim looked at his fingers, counting. "Lord sakes!"

"Pff!" Frank shrugged and walked on.

~

William wrote to his mother that night. He gave her an account of his Christmas day with the Robertson family, and told her that his conversation with Annie had put him in troubled mind. He wrote of his faith in scientific achievement, and of the great hope that he knew his mother shared with him in Koch's cure for tuberculosis. He confessed that his faith in the Bible—and in those who preached that every word in it was true—had waned as science progressively disproved the Creation Story. Jeannie was one of those who believed in the Bible's literal truth and he worried—was he pure enough in faith to deserve her as his wife? As a woman of deep faith herself, William asked his mother, what was her opinion of her doubting son?

His fourteen-year-old-self had fallen into doubt on Wednesday, 17th July 1878; the day little Isa died.

He had blacked the day out in his diary; right after he told God that he would never be able forgive Him for not answering the most purely heartfelt, the most utterly trustful prayers, he had ever said.

Not long after Isa's death, came the telegram:

'REGRET TO ADVISE, GEORGE A. CAMERON DIED NIGHT
10th AUGUST 1878. CAUSE: CONSUMPTION. ASTHMA.
VESSEL: ST LEONARDS. CAPTAIN: R. TODD.
RECEIVING PORT: WELLINGTON, NEW ZEALAND.'

That night, he had ambushed his mother as she climbed into the bed she had agreed to let him share with her, because Angus needed to be by himself.

"Maw, why does God kill people?"

"God doesn't kill people, laddie. Old age kills people, disease kills people, accidents kill people."

"But God chooses who gets killed."

"No, Willie. It's a science and a chance beyond our ken, I don't believe it's the Will of God."

"I prayed for George, and I prayed for Isa, and God didn't listen."

"God isn't here to serve *us*, Willie. We're here to serve *Him*. We have to learn the ways of nature to better help ourselves. That's what God wants us to do."

"So ... God put contagion in the world because He wants us to learn how to get rid of it?"

"Ach, Willie, it's a strange way to be putting it. That's akin to my thinking, but you can't reduce the mind of God to a simple sentence like that one."

He had pursued a career in medicine. He had made himself a man of science. Jeannie's mother was right. He no longer believed in the Bible. He wasn't even sure about God.

In the morning, William decided not to send the letter. He put the pages into an alcove in his writing bureau where they stayed for three weeks. Upon writing his usual monthly letter to his family, he retrieved his confession and read it again. It expressed his feelings well, he decided. Perhaps his mother would not find it as confronting, as upsetting as he feared and the fact remained—he and Jeannie were avoiding the subject of his doubt versus her faith, and he felt a desperate need for his mother's advice. If only, *if only* he could sit with her in person.

William folded his hope for validation inside his monthly letter and sealed the envelope.

Chapter 8

Isabella's Letter

Cullalo
Newburgh
Fife
18/3/91

My Dear Willie,

I received both your letters and will in this confine myself to the one enclosed. My dear boy I can thoroughly sympathise with you in all those feelings, have I not passed through them all? And do I not know them so fully from my own experience. Ah, Willie, my man, like Tennyson's hero, you are beating your music out. 'Perplext in faith but pure in deeds, at last he beat his music out. There lives more faith in honest doubt, believe me, than in half the creeds.' [1] *I have no patience with those who are so ready, as some are, to take everything upon credit, who are never assailed by a fear or doubt but who simply sail with the tide and, if it goes the right way they go the same and also vice versa. They lead calm and peaceful lives but if ever the tempest or the tornado of passion or of suffering come, they find to their dismay that their home is built upon the sand. I have read much and thought much on religious subjects and my belief is, that in all its great essentials, our Christianity is impregnable. God's book of revelation and his book of nature are both from him and cannot contradict one another, although sometimes they seem to do so. Science with its amazing development and wonderful discoveries, has laid bare truths which cannot be controverted and against which nothing can be said. They are simply truths— proved to be such. Then these truths seem to range themselves against some truths of the Bible which we we're wont to regard as incontrovertible and reasoning from these premises, we say, there is something wrong here, such and such things cannot both be right, and so we are led into fear and doubt and distrust. Not so very long ago, there were other books received into the Canon of Scripture which are not now regarded as belonging to it. I mean the Apocryphal books. These, criticism showed, had not the same credentials as the others and they were removed. Was the Bible therefore less to be depended upon? I think not. I think also that, though some parts are yet proved to have much admixture of man's work, still as Gladstone says, it 'is the impregnable rock of Holy Scripture'. [2] I know that God is truth and believe that none of his truth can be rendered other than clearer by the investigation, either of itself or any other truth. Certainly, truths can never conflict. God's book of nature is receiving investigation from many of the noblest minds in the world. Really to me it is most extraordinary to find what a wonderful thing this nature is and as extraordinary to see how the great minds of the earth have forced it to give up many of its secrets and how they can open its leaves and reach so correctly all its history. How very much the mind of man can achieve, how much he can know of God's power, wisdom and method of working. I feel convinced however we never could have attained to any knowledge of his love, goodness, kindness and tender care without a revelation. That is something altogether beyond the ken of the highest genius of man. There is the 'thus far shalt thou go but no further.' [3] Even the most powerful intellects are forced to confess that there is a limit beyond which they cannot go. This being so and a revelation being before us purporting to come from heaven and accompanied by so many proofs of a divine origin, shall we not receive it? I shall for one. Christ spake as never man spake, his life was a sinless one, passed in the constant exercise of every good work. Surely such a life was a strong proof that the man, who led it, was more than human and such a man's assertions are worthy of belief. He says, he that believeth in me shall never die, he shows what are the feelings of the father towards us and how his mission to earth was undertaken on our behalf, how he was fitted to accomplish it and how in the end he declared 'it is finished'. The work is all done, believe in the Lord Jesus Christ and thou shalt be saved. I think I hear you say, 'I believe all that as well as you, but here is the thing. I cannot understand viz. the incompatibility of our belief with our daily life.' Aye Willie! 'There's the rub.'*

...

Willie, you know as well or better than I do, how much there is in nature that we cannot comprehend and shall we stumble because there is much in grace that we cannot at all understand? This we can all do 'laying aside every weight and the sin that does the more easily beset us, let us run the race that is set before us, looking unto Jesus.' [4]

Paul's weight of testimony is an important one. He was prejudiced against the truth to begin with and knew all sides of the question. He was a very clever man, strong in debate, etc, etc and all his weight of testimony, constantly to the end, is on the side of Christ. In conclusion I can at least subscribe to the Creed, if not to all of the Catechism.

...

Willie, read Tennyson's 'In Memoriam', I think it contains more of God's truth than any other book, the Bible excepted and may God in his mercy illuminate what is dark and help you by your deeds to make men take knowledge of you that you have been with Jesus.

My quotations are all from memory and may not be exact and this is somewhat hurriedly written but it is what I feel on the subject.

We are all well and there is nothing special going on. We have had two very wet days but today the rain has cleared away and the sun shines out. With best love to Jean and yourself. I am your very loving mother.

Isa Cameron. [5]

Chapter 9

William

Melbourne, 1891–1892

The Botanic Gardens were rich with the colours of autumn when William showed Isabella's letter to Jeannie. While she read the letter, he busied himself with that morning's *Argus*.

"I think your mother and I would have much in common, Willie. If only we could meet." Jeannie folded the letter and gave it back to him.

"Have you given the subject much thought? I've taken it that you believe the Bible to be the whole truth."

"Of course I think on it, Willie!" There was an uncommon shade of intemperance in Jeannie's voice. "Do you not think in my Bible study group we examine all the controversy? Do you not think Ma takes pains to discuss every new essay Huxley pens?"

"Your mother favours Huxley?"

"No, she favours discomforting me. She won't give her own opinion. She likes to mention Huxley to test the mettle of any guest at her table. Huxley is her current, intellectual muse."

"I thought she wanted to cause an argument between us."

"You're over-sensitive, Willie," Jeannie reproved him. "She would be happy to cause an argument between us, but the argument could be between any at the table and she would be no less entertained."

"*Is* there an argument between us? Can you abide me as a man of science?"

Jeannie sighed. "I can abide you if you look unto Jesus, as Paul teaches. If by your deeds, you follow Jesus—as your mother writes. I like what your mother says about God's book of nature. This is the book you love; the exciting, wonderful book you study. It's no less God's book than is the book of Revelation. If the two books seem to stand in opposition, then it can only be because we don't understand the work of God, as expressed in one book or the other—and that can hardly be a surprise to us. Who are we to understand?"

Jeannie took his arm and snuggled in to him. "You worry over nothing, Willie. We will read *both* God's books together. We will never reach the end of them, and we will never be bored."

~

On Wednesday 17th June 1891, Jeannie's 25th birthday, William escorted her to a concert given by Sir Charles and Lady Halles at the Melbourne Town Hall. Afterwards, he took her home in a hansom cab and left her with a chaste kiss on the cheek at Struan's door. Later, they laughed about the moment after the door closed. He skipped down the steps in high spirits, nurturing a deliciously exciting secret. She leant her forehead against the door, and closed her eyes in despair.

The following Saturday he returned to Struan's door with a large wicker box, an oversized puppy, and an engagement ring.

~

Then came the rain and the winter wind.

Four and a half inches of rain fell on the weekend of 11th and 12th July. Floodwater rushed down the Yarra, and a south-westerly gale prevented its discharge into Hobson's Bay. The low-lying areas near the mouth of the Yarra were inundated.

River debris damaged pylons, rendering the Victoria Street and Studley Park bridges unsafe. The boat sheds, the Botanic Gardens, and the streets of South Yarra near the river were flooded. A quarter mile of Toorak Road near Chapel Street disappeared under several feet of water. Fortunately, William's surgery on Punt Road was well above the flood line.

Jeannie was safely at home in Cheltenham, but William spent the weekend helping police rescue people by boat from the rooves of their nearly submerged houses. He splinted broken arms and legs; bandaged open wounds and head injuries. Amazingly no lives were lost. More than 200 people were evacuated to the Prahran Town Hall where they lived for weeks, women and children crowded into the chambers above the hall, and men camped on the ground floor. William ministered to their injuries, their coughs and fevers, and their soggy spirits.

When not attending to patients, William spent hours haranguing shire councillors. For months before the flood, he had campaigned for the implementation of enclosed sewerage. The existing nightsoil removal system was a disgrace. Residents did not reliably put out their pans, and council workers did not reliably collect them. Too often, the buckets of human waste were knocked over by roaming animals, leaving the filthy mess lining the streets, washing into drains and from there into the river. A flood, William had warned, would inevitably breed contagion. London had enclosed its sewerage system at extraordinary expense. Edinburgh had done the same. How could this new colony be so backward? Nothing was more important, he vehemently contended, than to enclose drains *underneath* the ground before building above. Comprehensive conversion of the existing suburbs—especially flood-prone areas—was imperative.

The putrid water festered in hundreds of houses in South Yarra for days before it drained away, leaving excrement laden mud over floors and walls. They were lucky, William told Councillor Muntz, that it was winter. If the flooded houses were not thoroughly cleaned before summer, the community could expect outbreaks of cholera, typhoid and tuberculosis. It was Council's responsibility, William reasoned, to clean the houses because it was Council's neglect of the drainage that had caused the problem.

William's arguments were to no effect. The mud putrefied. Malodorous vapours filled the air. His cough started.

William told himself it was a cold. He wore a facemask. He sent a note to Jeannie saying that, because of his exposure to those displaying symptoms of disease, it was best he did not see her for a while.

At the end of August, when his cough worsened, he contacted Dr Springthorpe's secretary.

~

Dr John Springthorpe had begun trials on Tuberculin at Melbourne Hospital in March. In May, Dr Elsner furthered his work, using Tuberculin to treat five consumptive patients at the Alfred Hospital. Together, Springthorpe and Elsner had given Tuberculin their qualified support. 'Qualified', William knew from articles in the medical journal, because the results of trials overseas were mixed. There was some evidence that Tuberculin could be harmful to those in whom the disease was already advanced. Russia had banned Tuberculin because, in their much larger trial, several patients had died after injection of the lymph.

Would those patients have died anyway? Probably, William told himself.

The German pathologist, Rudolf Virchow, claimed to have proved through autopsies that Tuberculin did not kill the bacteria, in fact it appeared to *activate* latent bacteria. Virchow was a known opponent of Koch's germ theory *and* of Darwin's theory of evolution.

Could Virchow's 'proof' be trusted? Probably not, William decided.

Conversely, doctors at the Royal Infirmary in Edinburgh, an institution William revered, were of the opinion that Tuberculin *could* be a useful remedy where no other options existed.

Was Dr Springthorpe accepting patients for further trials? William asked the secretary.

The reply came a few days later. Possibly in October, but the trial would only take patients actively experiencing the disease. There was a high risk that injecting the lymph into someone in remission could cause the tubercles to reactivate.

~

The Botanic Gardens benefitted from the silt and fertilizer dropped by the flood. Dozens of garden lovers, including Jeannie, worked voluntarily to clear away the debris, repair the garden beds and plant new seeds. In spring the gardens looked more lovely than ever, and William did not resist Jeannie's invitation to resume their weekly meetings. His cough had improved, though the mucus in his throat lingered. It had been a cold, he convinced himself, and his sinus cavities needed time to drain. He always wore a facemask while tending to his patients—a hygienic courtesy they appreciated. Jeannie, however, would not tolerate it.

"Am I to expect this shield between us when we're married?" she asked him playfully one day, stroking his facemask; delaying the moment of their farewell at the garden gate.

"It's best I wear it while there are fevers about."

Before he could stop her, she had pulled the mask down to his neck and kissed him on the lips.

"Sweetheart, I will share even your fevers with you."

"I couldn't bear it if I made you ill." A surge of desperation tightened the phlegm in his throat. He swallowed hard.

"Pff!" She kissed him again. "I will see you next week."

~

In his surgery, William inspected his sputum under his microscope. The tubercle bacteria he found there did not grow in any of the petri dishes he tested under varying conditions. He was a carrier, like millions of others, but he was not infectious. He was in remission. He was one of those, as Dr Springthorpe warned, who risked re-activation of the disease if he was injected with Tuberculin.

Surely researchers were close to perfecting a vaccine? William read every news article and medical research report he could find on Tuberculin. Some were positive, some negative. America had approved the treatment. Australia required further trials.

The mucus malingered in William's throat through spring. He told himself it was the pollens in the air. He monitored his sputum with his microscope. His bacterial cultures did not grow ... until January.

His cough worsened. The upper quadrant of his left lung burned as he inhaled. He woke with night sweats. During the day he was breathless and exhausted.

He employed a locum to stand in for him at his surgery while he took a 'summer holiday'. He begged-off his weekly rendezvous with Jeannie.

When William offered himself for a Tuberculin trial, Dr Springthorpe flatly refused. He pushed a copy of *The Argus,* dated 2nd February 1892, across his desk towards William and stubbed the top joint of his index finger on a small article that he had circled with black ink.

The Pharmacy Board of Victoria had moved to have Tuberculin designated as a poison.

There would be no more trials, Dr Springthorpe told William firmly. Tuberculin would never be approved for use in Australia. Koch's 'cure' was an enormous disappointment.

Dr Springthorpe examined William closely. He took blood samples, sputum samples and listened to William's lungs, shaking his head and muttering ominously as he did so. "Come back next Wednesday, my boy. We'll see then, what I've grown in the laboratory. When was your diagnosis?"

"August 1885."

"Amazing."

"Why?"

"You're still alive."

1892, Wednesday 9th February

Melbourne Royal Botanic Gardens

On the morning of 9th February, William re-convened with Dr Springthorpe in the Melbourne Hospital laboratory.

"I estimate you have only half the capacity of your left lung," Dr Springthorpe told him. "Your right lung is at seventy-five percent. It was probably the influenza you suffered in August, but now the tubercles have reactivated. I ran our Tuberculin test in my laboratory with the usual result we see in advanced patients: it irritated the tubercles into even greater action. It is emphatically not a cure for you. It would likely kill you within months, weeks even." Dr Springthorpe organised some papers on his desk while William, speechless, absorbed the devastating news.

"Another influenza is likely the end of you, William," Dr Springthorpe continued. "Melbourne has as high an incidence of tuberculosis as Edinburgh. Did you not know?" Dr Springthorpe detected William's surprise. "You must have hot and *dry* air, and you are best well away from crowded, urban populations. That you are still with us today is remarkable, but it will *not* last. Go to sea again, or better still, the desert."

"How long, Doctor?" William asked.

Dr Springthorpe shrugged, but his voice carried no doubt. "Could be the coming influenza season, or the winter after that. Could be an asthma attack in spring. I give you three years at most. I'm sorry."

~

The children by the lake had finished their game of chase. The oldest boy was now standing on a bench, the lake at his back and his family audience sitting on the picnic rug in front of him as he dramatically recited lines from a play, or a poem that William could not hear.

What William could hear, internally, was his mother's voice, inciting him with the words of Robert Browning's *Epilogue*:

> *One who never turned his back but marched breast forward,*
> *Never doubted clouds would break,*
> *Never dreamed, though right were worsted, wrong would triumph,*
> *Held we fall to rise, are baffled to fight better,*
> *Sleep to wake.*
> *No, at noonday in the bustle of man's work-time*
> *Greet the unseen with a cheer!*
> *Bid him forward, breast and back as either should be,*
> *'Strive and thrive!' cry 'Speed—fight on, fare ever*
> *There as here!'*

He must rise and fight better. He must don his armour, breast and back, and fight on.

William stood abruptly, rolled down his sleeves and fastened his cufflinks. He threw his coat over his shoulder and tucked his folded copy of *The Argus* under his arm. He then strode purposefully to the gate on the city-side of the gardens, where he hailed a hansom cab and told the driver to take him to the office of Thomas Cook and Sons, on Swanston Street.

III

1892 - 1893

Chapter 10

William

Tuesday 23rd February 1892

William was leaning backwards, confidently mid-shuffle, when *The Pearl* hit Cowana Reef. His spindly chair dumped him instantly, and 52 cards sprayed across the varnished floorboards.

Swear words burst from the wheelhouse. The tri-level paddle steamer shuddered as deck hands rushed the steps; it groaned as the stern waterwheel ploughed into reverse. Dark shapes fussed in the glow of the solitary electric light that was fixed to the underside of the second deck. A long shaft of wood materialised, and one end disappeared into the black water of the Murray River. The men grunted as they pitched themselves against the sand bank. Another pole arrived, and more men, but *The Pearl* remained deeply wedged, and the paddle wheel sighed into motionless respite.

Captain Willy Mier abandoned his post and stomped downstairs. Mrs Roberts, who had ventured timorously out of her cabin, hastily retreated, closing herself away from the expletives that were boiling in Mier's wake.

"She's dry, Cap."

"We ain't gettin' through, Cap."

"River's too low, Cap."

"Cowana Reef, Cap."

"I know it's bloody Cowana Reef, get outta the bloody way!" Captain Mier seized a pole and prodded it into the water around the bow until, apparently resigned to the end of the boat's passage, he tossed the pole into the dark interior of the cargo deck. He peered towards the starboard, Victorian river-bank, and then moved to the other side of the stranded boat to evaluate the greater distance to New South Wales.

"You're in the right spot, Cap."

"Of course, I'm in the bloody right spot!" Mier retorted, his face briefly illuminated by a portable kerosene lamp carried by Warner, the deck hand who had verified his course. "Shallow draught stern wheeler, my ass. Guaranteed to ply the Murray all seasons. Bloody ass Geo Chaffey! This river ain't the Mississippi!"

Mier and the lamp disappeared into the cargo space. William heard him call to the engine hand below, "Say again Jones!"

"Still dry, Cap," Jones reassured.

Maitland, William's whist partner, pressed a bundle of cards against William's bare arm. "I hope you didn't need to be in Mildura tonight, mate."

William frowned, tapping the cards on the table, squaring the pack. It had been a week since he left Melbourne on a steamer for Adelaide. He had boarded *The Pearl* at the river port of Morgan on Saturday morning after travelling for several hours by train. While he stayed in Mildura, *The Pearl* would travel down to Morgan and back again. It would be a week before he boarded the paddle steamer for his return journey. Would the river be too low for navigation? Was his schedule in jeopardy?

He had already spent a regrettably long 'summer holiday' away from his practice.

~

William tamped the third and final layer of tobacco into his pipe, lit a long match, and charred the surface of the leaves, moving the match in a slow circle as he drew on the pipe with several short puffs. After tamping again, he reapplied the match and drew deeply, holding the match steady until he was satisfied that the tobacco was properly alight. He noted with satisfaction that the deep breaths he was taking did not make him cough. This was not the only respect in which the steady, deliberative process of lighting his pipe gladdened him—it narrowed the great physical distance he felt, between himself and his father, the man who had taught him the method.

What would he write to his father about this river? How to compare Australia's Murray to their beloved Tay? William leaned back in his chair—hesitating momentarily as he remembered his ungraceful fall of less than an hour ago—and settled the heels of his bare feet on *The Pearl's* deck rail.

The Tay—rising in Ben Lui in the Scottish Highlands and travelling 117 miles to enter the German Sea near Dundee—was Scotland's longest river, with what William had previously thought was an impressive water catchment of 1920 square miles. The Murray, in comparison, was said to be over 1500 miles long, and the area of its catchment, when combined with its main tributary, the Darling, was over 410 thousand square miles—a single inland water basin, more than five times the size of Scotland and England combined.

The Tay at Newburgh rose and fell nearly 12 feet each day. The Murray's rise and fall was seasonal, not tidal. Droughts could reduce it to a trickle; floods had gouged striations in cliffs at 30 feet above the river floor.

The Tay was reliably navigable from the sea all the way to Perth for vessels drawing 14 feet of water. It was only at the breaking-up of winter that the river might close, due to dangerous masses of ice floating with the current. Ice was unthinkable on the Murray, but the trip William had taken between Morgan and Mildura, was nevertheless imperilled by fallen trees that, like icebergs, were a greater danger for what was hidden below the surface than what was showing above.

The Tay was slate grey, brightening towards blue under a strong sun. The Murray was the tawny colour of dry grass, and in the evening, it took on the olive-grey of the gums that over-shadowed its banks. Where tree roots dangled into the water, they instantly disappeared, painted over in solid colour. The Tay had translucency enough see the shape of a snag, or the shade of a sandbank that was two feet below. Fall into the Murray, the deck hands warned, and your clothes would be found hanging on a snag during the next drought.

The Tay was the best salmon fishing river in Scotland, or so those who lived along its upper reaches maintained. The Murray, in keeping with its other muscular attributes, boasted a much bigger, meatier fish—the Murray Cod—which, by the time it reached its natural average of 50 years old, had likely eaten the flesh out of several sets of snagged clothes. It was a fish to be reckoned with, William conceded, having seen what Maitland described as a '30-pound tiddler' hauled onto the boat near Renmark.

The Aboriginals in the South Australian leg of the river, below Renmark, told a Creation Story about a giant Murray Cod they called *'Ponde'*. As the fish fled from Ngurunderi, a great ancestral hunter, the thrashing of *Ponde's* tail formed the innumerable bends and billabongs in the river. Ngurunderi speared the fish at Lake Alexandrina, near the river's outlet to the Southern Ocean. He cut it into pieces that he threw back into the water. Each piece became the ancestor of one of the many species of fish that inhabited the river.

William stared towards the woodlands that lay across the water, wondering if there were any Aboriginals there now. It was so dark he could barely make out the shoreline. There was no sign of anything beyond; not a single light to frame a silhouette; no sound further away than the frogs that called from the tangle of tree roots that laced the riverbank. He had heard that the Aboriginals had long since relocated to more remote parts of the country, leaving behind a vast and empty river land that was waiting not for him, William mused, but for someone—or some multitude—much more ambitious than he.

People like the owners of *The Pearl,* George and William Chaffey—Canadian brothers who had pioneered irrigation settlement in California and had, only four years ago, taken up colonial government grants of 250,000 acres at Renmark, and another 250,000 acres at Mildura. The Chaffeys were in the business of turning what had been harsh, unviable land into the profitable irrigated smallholdings he had come to inspect.

~

"Ahoy *Pearl*!" Chaffeys' man waved his hat, beating back the dust that caught up, and over-curled the drag as it creaked to a standstill behind a team of four heavyweight horses.

"Thought as would find you here, Cap!" he called when Captain Mier stepped out of the wheelhouse. "Ha-ha bloody ha, I say!"

"Mick! You tell George he can take his bloody Mississippi showboat back!" Mier retorted.

"Nah, you love her pretty looks!"

Mier lent on *The Pearl's* railing. "What does George want to take off?"

"Them crates for the old homestead, and we'll sit his house guests and Mrs Roberts on top."

While the nominated passengers prepared for disembarkation, Warner and another deck hand paddled a large, square raft to a patch of sand on the Victorian river bank. The two men set about rigging a running line, connecting the raft at one end by a pulley to *The Pearl*, and at the other by a pulley to the roots of a large redgum. Pulling hand-over-hand on one side of the line, Warner sent the raft and the deck hand safely back to *The Pearl.*

William and his fellow travellers gathered in the shade under the top deck, watching several rafts of produce transferred to the large wooden tray of the drag. The hour had not yet reached nine, but already the sun was baking hot and the day breathless. Mrs Roberts fanned her perspiring face under her wide-brimmed hat. The armpits of Maitland's white shirt darkened with sweat, and William felt his own shirt clinging wetly to his back as they waited for their turn to board the raft.

Clambering up a gully carved into the high, red-earth riverbank, William heard *The Pearl's* engine sputter into action. He stopped gratefully for a rest, and watched the stern paddle-wheel gear itself into a thrashing, white-water reverse. With a loud slurp, *The Pearl* eased backwards, and the opaque brown water in front of the bow slumped into a deep crevice that was immediately re-filled. The paddle slowed, biting effectively into the water. Warner unhooked the running line and jumped onto the raft. The passengers cheered and clapped from scattered vantage points on the bank.

"Ta-Ta Cap!" Mick waved. "See you at Ranfurley's."

Mier saluted from the wheelhouse, and turned to concentrate on his reverse course.

Mrs Roberts fixed Mick with a disdainful glare as she approached the steps that hung from the rear of the drag.

Mick tipped his hat to her. "Apologies ma'am," he said unapologetically, offering his dirt encrusted hand to assist her onto the tray.

"Dr Cameron will help me," Mrs Roberts surprised William more than Mick with her blunt announcement.

"*Doctor* Cameron, pleased to make your acquaintance, sir." Mick stood aside to let William hand Mrs Roberts up the steps to Maitland who had prepared a crate for her to sit on. "To be sure, we need the likes of you, sir. My wife's expecting in just three months, and I'd be mighty pleased to know you were attending!"

"Well thank-you, Mick ...?"

"Gallagher, sir. I'll be taking you and five others," Mick paused to look over the passengers seated in the drag, "on a tour of the settlement today. Any questions you have, you'll be asking me. It's my job to make sure you learn all the wonders of our town, and make up your mind in the positive direction."

"I'm just here to look, Mr Gallagher."

"Of course, Dr Cameron. But every smart cove as comes here sees the opportunity, and I think you'll be one of those. We've already lost the largest bit of our morning. Best away."

~

The idea of visiting Mildura had come to William from several directions. In a conversation after the last meeting of the Victorian Medical Association for 1891, Dr Warren of Studley Park had enthused about the prospects of the new irrigation settlement. The acreage in which Dr Warren had invested less than a year earlier, had now been irrigated and planted with orange, peach, and apricot trees. It was already valued at twice his outlay. So good was the investment opportunity that he intended to buy another 20 acres.

Mr Staughton, to whom William had been introduced by Adam Calder, had told a similar story. Staughton had been an early investor in the settlement, buying up a number of urban blocks, some of which he was now re-selling at multiples of the price he had originally paid.

These were, to William, personal testimonies of the merit in a promise that was being widely advertised in newspapers in Australia as well as overseas. Investment in the irrigation colony of Mildura was a no-fail proposition: settlers would be rewarded with valuable property and plentiful work; medical staff were in high demand for the proposed hospital; the young township was in urgent need of qualified general practitioners.

On the afternoon of Wednesday 24th February, Mick Gallagher's tour group of six prospective investors—all men—called first at the building site of the Mildura Cottage Hospital where William met the man who was, at once, Mildura's only doctor, apothecary and public health officer. Dr Abramowski, who William estimated to be in his early thirties, was a small man with prematurely greying hair that was most prominently featured in a broad moustache overlaying a goatee beard. His tailored pants and crumpled white shirt hung loosely from his narrow frame, leading William to diagnose a careless nature. He spoke in a thick accent that William struggled to decipher, but by listening intently and making occasional requests for repetition, William learnt that Abramowski was a graduate of Berlin University, and had spent several years as a surgeon in the Prussian army. He had served in the Franco-Prussian war before coming to Australia with his wife and two children in 1884. He had found in Mildura, he told William confidently, the perfect climate in which to erect a sanatorium for consumptives—something he intended to do once the Cottage Hospital (which he had personally designed), was constructed, fully staffed, and running independently of him. While he was an apothecary, he believed that the health of the population relied not upon the powders and tonics he was trained to concoct, but rather upon the God-given, natural ingredients that Mildura had in abundance—fresh air, sunshine, nuts and fruit.

It was clear that Mick Gallagher, who had stayed with the drag while George Chaffey's guests surveyed the hospital site, was not one of Dr Abramowski's faithful adherents.

"Folks here would prefer a Scotsman, Dr Cameron," he murmured confidentially as William stepped up into the drag. "A proper surgeon, graduated from Edinburgh rather than one who learnt his trade in the Prussian army. Dr A. couldn't save his own wife who died in childbirth not a year past. You've qualified in the business of child birthing, Dr Cameron?"

"I have," William replied.

"It's in May my wife's due, Doctor."

Mick took the driver's seat, and turned to his tour group, reins in hand. "Now gents, having seen the beginnings of Mildura's modern medical facility, we'll take a gander at the educational establishments."

Mildura was to be well-served with educational establishments, William learnt. Not far from the site of the hospital, there was a well-built, brick primary school that was already attended by more than four hundred children, and as part of their contract with the Victorian government, the Chaffeys would shortly commence work on an agricultural college. Here, Mick said, waving expansively towards an empty paddock, would be built a modern college that taught all matters of horticulture and the science of farming. *His* sons, Mick told the group, would not have to leave home for an education. Indeed, others would send *their* sons to Mildura to study the latest methods of agriculture.

Everybody's religious preference could be satisfied here, Mick boasted as he piloted the drag past the Congregational, Wesleyan and Anglican churches. Pulling the horses up alongside the Presbyterian church, Mick made a point of telling William that the modest, weatherboard building situated on a dry patch of dirt, was soon to be rebuilt as a grand, brick church with a magnificent spire. The new St Andrews would be surrounded by pretty rose gardens and green, irrigated lawns, lovingly cared for by the strong Scots community that lived in Mildura.

The streets of the township were laid out in a grid of wide avenues crossed by streets numbered in the American fashion —the cottage hospital was on 13th street; the primary school and the Presbyterian church were on 11th. Some of the outer avenues had names reminiscent of California—San Mateo; Etiwanda—while many were named after the trees that were to be grown here—Walnut; Lime. The central avenues were named for prominent men connected with the formation of the irrigation colony—Langtree, the Secretary of Water Supply; Dow the Minister of Lands and Agriculture. The main street was called Deakin Avenue because it was the chief secretary of the colony, Alfred Deakin, who had visited California and, impressed by the wonders he saw there, had persuaded the Chaffey brothers to develop an irrigation settlement on the Murray.

William thought Deakin Avenue most impressive. It was a wide and well-surfaced divided road with space set aside for a tramline between two rows of sapling gums in the centre, and young peppercorn trees lining the outer kerbs. Substantial gutters protected the raised footpaths from the dirt and, presumably, the water run-off in the street. It was hard to visualize the effect of rain on the avenue. Indeed, it looked like it hadn't rained here in years. The road surface was hard-baked red clay, covered with a layer of fine-grained dust that swirled and resettled each time a cart or buggy clattered past.

There were many shops along the central avenues doing a prosperous trade, and many more were under construction. Most buildings in the township were made of weatherboard, with corrugated iron rooves and wide verandas supported by locally hewn redgum posts. Promisingly, the township boasted a brick factory which put the local red clay to excellent use, with current production turning out over 20,000 bricks a day. There were already several handsome brick buildings including the primary school, the post office, and the Coffee Palace hotel where Mick Gallagher set his tour group down, inviting them to partake of tea in the dining room before he drove them back to their lodgings at the Old Homestead.

~

The next morning, the group convened at the Chaffey Brothers' office to meet with George Chaffey.

George was of medium, stocky build with a handsomely full beard and deep set, hazel eyes. The hair on the top of his head was a light, sandy brown, thinning and receding deeply at the temples such that William guessed him near to fifty years of age. He wore a well-fitted suit, a crisply starched white collar, and he exuded the air of a prosperous man. He apologised, in a deeply intoned North American accent, for not meeting his guests at the Old Homestead the previous morning—he had been unable to adapt his schedule to their delayed arrival. This morning, however, he would accompany them to the pumping plants at Psyche Bend and Nichols Point, and the engineering workshops on the riverfront.

George, William surmised during the drive, was an energetic, innovative businessman who had brought with him to the new settlement a wealth of expertise in all things engineering. Not only had he specified the shallow-draft sternwheeler that had brought William up river, he also designed the two powerful triple expansion steam engines that drove the pumps used to raise water into the irrigation channels. The engine on the river bank at Psyche Bend was capable of lifting water from the Murray into King's Billabong at a rate of 120,000 gallons a minute. The second engine, located a mile away on the shore of the billabong, worked three pumps lifting 30,000 gallons of water per minute into the channels that distributed water around the settlement. The smooth, 1000 horsepower purr of that second steam engine filled its capacious pump house and resonated thrillingly through William's body.

In just four years, the Chaffeys and their settlers had cultivated 7,500 acres, watered by 150 miles of irrigation channel. The current demand, with all irrigationists actively watering, was 25,000 gallons per minute. The engine at the billabong had abundant capacity for extra pumps as the area under cultivation expanded.

Having inspected the billabong, an irrigation channel, and one of the supplementary, smaller lifting mechanisms used to overcome gradations in the landscape, the group of men were driven back to town along the river bank via Risby's sawmills and Chaffeys' workshops. Steam engines were running, and men were working industriously at both venues. The sawmill was turning out weatherboard planks for house construction. Chaffeys' carpentry shed was framing glass windows and making furniture; the foundry was shaping corrugated iron; the engineering shed was building and servicing pumps. Everywhere there was industry—it was little wonder the settlement had progressed so rapidly.

When William inquired about the single-wire telegraph line that connected the engineering workshop to Chaffeys' office and the Old Mildura Homestead, he learnt that it was George Chaffey who established the first trunk line telephones in California. From telephones it was only a small segue to one of William's favourite subjects, electric power. William was delighted to learn that George, as president and joint engineer of the Los Angeles Electricity Company, had implemented in that city the most extensive lighting in the United States. Mildura's town plan, George assured his audience, provided for connection of all urban residences to electric power and, in the not-too-distant future, telephone.

George Chaffey, William concluded, was eminently capable of transforming Mildura into a Garden of Eden served by all modern conveniences. He was not surprised to learn that the Chaffey brothers, while born in Canada, were of Scottish heritage.

William was disappointed in his hopes of talking further with George. That night, for tea at the Old Homestead, their host was Chaffeys' manager, Mr Waddingham, who talked exhaustingly of soil type, water rights, orchard yields, and years to profitability. William's mind wandered away from the figures as he studied photographs of the irrigation settlement the Chaffeys had established in California. Acre upon acre of fruit-bearing trees, green grass, and colourful flower beds.

Jeannie would love that.

~

In the morning, William dipped into the large 'Red Book' he had been too tired to read the night before. He opened *The Australian Irrigation Colonies on the River Murray* at a page he did not remember having dog-eared, and he read, or re-read, the remarks made by the Hon. A. Deakin, M.P. to the Royal Commission on Water Supply. A small, established farm growing a variety of fruits could be expected to profit by £40 to £50 pounds per acre, per annum. Twenty acres was as much as a hard-working man could attend by himself, but Deakin estimated that ten acres, under frugal management, was sufficient to maintain a man and his family. Importantly, the labour of women and children could be utilised in picking, packing, and processing the fruit, which provided the family with a healthy and productive livelihood. The 'chief secret of success', Deakin had said, was to farm a variety of products.

> *'On a ten-acre farm there will be a plot of Lucerne, maintaining a horse and head or two of stock, an acre or so of vines, another acre or two of mixed fruit trees, with perhaps an acre of some special kind of orange or apricot, an acre of grain or root crops, and a great brood of chickens. From these sources a family largely supplies its own wants in the way of food, and by the sale of its products provides clothing and comforts, and still lays something by, or more probably invests in permanent improvements.'*

William enhanced the image in his head. His children picking apricots; feeding the horse a wad of Lucerne hay; collecting eggs from the hen coop. Jeannie, peacefully sitting in a wicker chair on a shaded veranda laced with a leafy grapevine; sewing the children's clothes with Olga faithfully settled at her side. Himself, seeing a grateful patient off at the gate; pausing for a cool glass of lemonade with his wife before the next appointment.

Surely it could be?

~

After breakfast, Mick Gallagher collected the group and drove them miles out of town, past recently planted orchards and an expanse of tangled mallee scrub to *Chateau Mildura,* Chaffeys' vineyard at Irymple. George's brother William—locally known as 'W.B.'—had planted 150 acres of vines imported from South Australia. The first vintage had recently been crushed, and the community had high expectations. Mildura's rich red loam and Californian climate were, the experts agreed, perfect for wine production.

William thought it ironic, as he surveyed the rows of young vines, that Mildura—widely advertised as a 'temperance colony'—should be developing a wine industry.

Mick laughed at him. "W.B. knows opportunity when he sees it. We ain't got no pubs in Mildura, nowhere to go after work to socialise and drink, more's the pity, but we can drink all we like at home."

"But if you can't buy the alcohol ...?"

"Regular deliveries by punt from New South Wales. As long as the purchase is done on the other side of the river." Mick accompanied his sly advice with a wink.

"I recall the Red Book saying that the settlement attracted 'the right sort'—temperate, industrious, good-living people," William said sardonically.

"It does, it does, and we work so hard in this hot, dry place that it's a real pleasure to have a quiet drink at home with the missus. That's good-living. Are you a teetotaller then, Dr Cameron?"

William shrugged. "I don't forgo a whisky, but I've seen men ruined because they didn't know they've had too many."

"That's the truth," Mick nodded sagely. "The Chaffeys don't entice the drunkard, but they don't afront a man's personal liberty in his own house. That's the best way of it, to be sure."

That evening the investors sampled 'the future of Mildura's wine industry' in the form of Californian wines in the glass conservatory at Rio Vista, the imposing two-story brick mansion recently built by W.B. Mr Waddingham presided over the wine tasting, apologising for his inability to invite the investors to dine in the house with the Chaffeys.

"A new arrival is imminent," Waddingham explained, "Mrs W.B. is expected to deliver her first child any day, and disturbance must be kept to a minimum. You may, gentleman, wonder at this if you know W.B. already has a number of children. Tragically, his wife died shortly after giving birth in 1889, and the babe was lost as well. Now W.B. has married again, and it's his *second* wife that is near her term. I'm sure you can sympathize with the anxiety in the house at the present time. W.B. has asked me to walk you through the gardens to show you what may be done here with the irrigation."

What had been done with the garden impressed William more than the taste of the wine. The carriageway entered the house yard through an avenue of young date palms, curved through attractive green lawns, and circled back around a grand fountain and flower beds that, while evidently recently planted, were growing abundantly. In years to come Rio Vista would be the equivalent, William thought, of the grand houses that dotted South Yarra.

~

On Saturday morning the Chaffeys' guests, now well-versed in the glowing prospects of the settlement, were taken to inspect the horticultural land that was being offered for sale. Mick handed each investor a pencil and the subdivision plan for 'Block F', where unimproved ten-acre lots were priced from £20 to £25 per acre.

"Two and a half percent discount for cash, or finance over 10 years. Work the land yourself, or if you're the investor-type let Chaffeys do the clearing and planting according to the schedule of fees, printed right there on the back of your plan. Either way, as Mr Waddingham said, you'll have your expenses returned, and your ten-acre orchard will be a nice little earner before seven years. Mark on your plan the blocks that take your fancy. Say the word, and I'll drive back for a second look."

William marked Section 122, lots 9 and 10 on his plan. Either would do nicely, he thought. For his house and surgery, however, he needed a two-and-a-half-acre villa block close to the hospital, the school, and town. Section 74, in Block D between San Mateo and Etiwanda Avenue, was ideally located.

"Block D has been sold, Dr Cameron." The masterplan of Block F overflowed Mr Waddingham's large desk in Chaffeys' sales office. "It's the horticultural lots on Block F you toured today. Do you have your copy of Block F there?"

"I may be interested in buying a horticultural block for investment purposes, but *only* if I can also buy a villa block for my *residence.* If I'm to run a surgery from my home, my residence needs to be closer to town."

Waddingham looked at William with new-found respect. "Certainly, certainly. Let me look at which villa blocks we might have available." He turned to the architect drawers behind his desk.

"I'm *only* interested in Section 74, Block D."

Waddingham unrolled the plan for Block D over the plan for Block F, and shifted his four glass paperweights onto the corners of the top plan. William saw the name 'Staughton' written across Section 74.

"All lots there and in the adjoining sections have been sold, sir. The only villa blocks left," he tapped the plan with a well-manicured finger, "are in Sections 19 and 47, and they remain in anticipation of the rail corridor. Unless you suppose that a location near the railway line is suitable for your surgery?"

"No," William stroked his moustache thoughtfully, examining the plan. "I understand Mr Staughton is selling some of his blocks. Must I make arrangements with him directly?"

"I may be able to take care of that for you," Waddingham said shrewdly. "Did you have a specific block in mind?"

William pointed to the villa block closest to the township. "Corner San Mateo and 10th."

"You understand, it's Mr Staughton who sets the resale price?"

"Of course."

"And his agent will charge you commission?"

"Aye."

"However, if you sign a contract on a horticultural block *today*, Dr Cameron, Chaffey Brothers will handle the purchase of the villa block for you, commission-free. Does that sound like an arrangement you would like to make?" Waddingham picked up his fountain pen and scribbled on a pad of paper.

William watched Waddingham suspiciously. It *did* sound like a good arrangement, but could he be sure he was buying at a fair price?

"*This* block, at the right price."

Waddingham moved his paper weights and the plan rolled itself up, brushing past William's finger.

"Which lot do you prefer on Plan F?"

"Section 122, Lot Nine or Ten."

Waddingham located the lots on his plan. "These?" William nodded and Waddingham made a note on his pad. "Lots Nine and Ten. *Very* good choice, perfect for fruit trees. You won't be the only one with an eye on those blocks."

"Only one of them," William clarified. "I don't mind, either nine *or* ten."

"Hmm," Waddingham didn't amend his note. "It's a *very* nice parcel, the two blocks together. Tell me, do you plan to work the blocks yourself, or will you be asking Chaffey Brothers to clear and cultivate?"

"I'm returning to Melbourne. I had in mind organising labour to do the work here."

"You've seen the services Chaffey Brothers offer? On the back of your paper?"

"Aye."

"*Best* prices in the district and the work is guaranteed. I can tell you, it's hard for absentee landlords to regulate contract labour. If investors go that route to begin with, they invariably come to us within six months, asking for help. Not that we can always be of service at a later time, mind, because our first commitment is to those who make a combined contract with us. Guaranteed results."

William inclined his head; it made sense to employ labourers through Chaffey Brothers. It was in their interest, after all, to ensure that those who purchased from them developed successful orchards.

"Now if you're purchasing *two* horticultural blocks, *and* you're contracting with us to develop those blocks, we can offer you a tidy discount off the second block."

William pursed his lips. "How much?"

"Cash or finance?"

"It won't all be cash."

"The proportion?"

"Only if I get the villa block at the right price."

"How much do you have to spend, Dr Cameron?"

"We're going in circles, Mr Waddingham. *Tell me* what you know about the block on the corner of 10th and San Mateo."

Waddingham studied his note pad. "Two hundred and twenty pounds."

"I have five hundred to spend. That villa block, lots 9 and 10, and I'll sign the servicing contract according to the schedule of charges."

"Dr Cameron! The land purchase comes to six hundred and twenty pounds!" Waddingham over-dramatized his horror.

"Then it will be lot 9 only. I'll take your two and a half percent discount for cash and offer you four hundred pounds even."

Waddingham looked uncomfortable. Clearly, he did not like to leave any money in a customer's wallet.

"I have to move on, Dr Cameron." Waddingham gestured towards the other prospective buyers, waiting in the sales office. "Will you pay six hundred cash for lots 9 and 10, and the villa block?"

"No."

"Your best offer?"

"Five hundred; cash."

"Then I will have to see whether any of our other guests have a fancy for Lots 9 or 10. You understand you may lose your preference?" William nodded firmly. "Very well, please take a seat. My man will get the contract for the villa block."

As William moved away, Waddingham summoned a boy who had been sitting idly by the door. He whispered in the boy's ear and handed him a page from the note pad. Clutching the piece of paper to his chest, the boy scampered away through a door at the back of the office. William settled himself for the wait, gritting his teeth and doubting the wisdom of his bargain. He had come to look, not buy. Was he being suckered into an impulsive purchase?

"You're in luck, Dr Cameron," Waddingham said heartily when William resumed his seat at the sales desk. "I managed to divert a buyer away from your lots 9 and 10 to another section. Another expressed an interest, but has put off his decision until the morrow. The opportunity to buy both lots is still here for you. I also have the contract for the villa block." Waddingham pushed the document across the desk. "You *truly are* fortunate because it's still available at the price I had in my recollection. *Two* parties have made offers on the property and, having been rejected, they're considering increasing their bids. Two hundred and twenty pounds will secure that block for you today. I'll come back to the *discounted* price I gave you before—six hundred pounds in cash."

Waddingham waited in silence while William scanned the contract.

Eventually William sighed, placed the contract on the table and met Waddingham's stare. "Five hundred."

"You have to give me *something*, Dr Cameron. Five hundred and eighty."

"I'm giving your irrigation colony a general practice and a fully qualified surgeon, Mr Waddingham," William said boldly.

Waddingham blinked. He sat back in his chair. The door at the back of the office opened and George Chaffey walked into the room.

"Dr Cameron!" Chaffey shook William's hand heartily. "Buying into our venture? Wonderful!" He leant over the desk and made a show of reading Waddingham's note pad before turning to look at William directly. "Your *best* offer, Dr Cameron?"

"Five hundred," William held Chaffey's stare until Chaffey laughed.

"Make it work, Mr Waddingham, make it work." Chaffey took William's hand into another vigorous shake. "Great to have you on board, Doctor. I look forward to sharing a meal with you!"

George Chaffey moved to the centre of the office, and raised his arms in the air to gather any attention that was not already granted to him. "That goes for all of you smart folk who have signed up with us today! Congratulations on joining the magnificent venture that is Mildura. I look forward to getting to know you all. Best wishes for your onward travels." With that, Chaffey barrelled on, through the front door and into the street.

William turned back to find Waddingham offering him a fountain pen.

~

That night, in his room at the Old Mildura Homestead, William lay awake and worried. He had a £500 line-of-credit, which his father had specified was, if he used it, his inheritance. William's practice had been profitable for several months now, he had been frugal with his expenditure, and had accumulated £750 in a savings bank in Melbourne to put towards a house for himself and Jeannie, after their marriage. He had now spent his inheritance on land, and would still need to use his savings to build a house and cultivate the horticultural blocks. Clearing, fencing, and planting the blocks was going to cost him £30 per acre—£675 pounds he had committed to pay Chaffey Brothers over the next 12 months. Beyond that, there was a house to build, and William had no idea how much that would cost him in this remote part of the world.

William was confident about the purchase of the villa block. He could build a comfortable home there with a large, irrigated garden to rival the garden Jeannie loved at Struan. He had chosen a corner block because it afforded dual access—a public entry for the surgery; a separate private entry for the residence. It was a brisk walk to the hospital; an even shorter walk to the school. As Staughton had originally understood, it was in a prime position and would, William had no doubt, increase further in value as Mildura prospered.

But why had he bought the horticultural blocks? Had he pursued the deal just to score against Waddingham? Had he won the bargain, or had he fallen prey to the sales pitch? What did he know about fruit farming or irrigation? He had put himself completely in the hands of Chaffey Brothers, trusting that they would coax the dry land he had bought into profitability.

There was another reason he had invested his entire inheritance. One that dwelled firmly, but unhappily in William's mind.

When he died—and he knew it would be 'when'—Jeannie would be able to sell all the properties at a substantially improved value. She would return to Melbourne a wealthy widow. This security was the least he could offer her.

Chapter 11

Jeannie

Monday 7th March 1892

Autumn was creeping across the Botanic Gardens: a chill amongst the perfumes of wilting flowers; a smattering of deciduous leaves crisping on the ground; green giving way to red, orange and yellow in the canopy overhead. Oak trees turning papery brown; elm trees sickly yellow; liquid ambers vibrant orange and red. Amidst all this wonderful colour, Australia's gumtrees remained stoically ever-grey-green, knowing that here, shorter days did not presage snow.

Jeannie missed snow. The crunch of it under her boots. The softness of a new fall. The transparent surface crystals that glistened on a sunny morning. The white pleats that spreadeagled, and the lacy curtains that drooped from the bare boughs of winter. It had been nine years since she had seen snow, and in the autumn of every one of those years, as the last leaves fell from the European trees that lined the paths she walked, she had conjured up for those trees (and for herself) the deep, white sleep of winter. Scotland's winter gave time to be still, to rest, reflect and prepare for the burst of life that would come when the snow melted. Scotland's winter brought such joy to spring.

Now, with spring awakening Yetholm Mains, the snow would still be blanketing the fields that stretched up towards the Cheviot Hills. It would have melted along the laneways, unsmothering dark pockets of wet soil that were rich with the seeds sown by wildflowers last summer. The ice would be gone from Redden Burn and there too, along the banks, wildflower seeds would be stirring. The salmon would be running; the otters would be fishing; there would be new pups to feed.

Ada Mina Calder would be 13 years old. Did she walk in the Cheviots picking wildflowers? Grandpa Calder would be 90. Did he tell Ada fabulous stories?

Jeannie stopped at the edge of the lake, looking into the green depths of the water. Were there fish today? Frogs to be seen amongst the lily pads? The ducks—that Ada would surely love to feed—gathered expectantly, muddying the water, fighting for space near her feet.

Jeannie chastised herself. Her nostalgia was not unusual, but today she was over-indulging. An uncertainty was weighing on her. William had not been himself for many weeks and Jeannie sensed that today's rendezvous, after their month-long separation, held some portent. Most likely, he was anxious about his investment plans and whether he had enough money to support them both. She knew he had talked to Cousin Adam Calder; she knew he had gone to Mildura to look at investment properties and quite probably he wanted to measure up to Adam and Frank's expectations. She hoped he hadn't overstretched himself. Whatever it was, she intended to talk to him and get it over with. William, she thought, troubled himself unnecessarily. He made 'mountains out of molehills', as Grandpa Calder was fond of saying. He worried too much about what others thought of him. He leapt mentally at worst possible outcomes instead of trusting in God's plan.

Jeannie sent a small-thanks to God on seeing that William, walking down the slope towards her, was not wearing a mask.

She supposed his trepidation about the flu had evaporated in Mildura's hot wind. When she took him into her arms and kissed him, he did not try to hide his face from her.

"I missed you, *so* much," she kissed him again.

"Aye, but I missed you more." William's reply lacked its usual levity.

Jeannie pulled back to gaze into his face. He looked, and sounded, like a child about to cry.

She took his chin in both hands and stroked the side of his moustache with one finger. "You must tell me all of it, William," she instructed firmly. "No talking around it now. I know you've been sorely troubled, and I see the time away hasn't fixed you."

William meekly submitted to her pull on his arm, sitting down with her on the ground near the water's edge. The ducks responded with excitement, two of them brave enough to paddle their dripping webbed feet onto the grass, approaching in the hope of bread crusts.

"Not today," Jeannie waved them away.

William was staring at his hands as if spiders were erupting from his skin.

"Speak," she commanded him.

"I don't want to lose you Jeannie. I don't want to lose you," the words came out in a long sob.

Jeannie felt the creeping chill of dread enter her chest.

~

She told him she loved him. She forgave him. She reassured him he would not lose her. She told him she needed time by herself to think about the ramifications; she needed time to pray.

William's mountain, she realised, had always been a mountain. She hadn't recognised it because up till now, in her own life, she had only faced molehills.

He had not presented his death sentence as a death sentence. He had presented Mildura as the cure. Hot, dry air and a rural way of life. But Jeannie had drawn the nuance out of the diagnosis he quoted. *If* he relocated now, he *might* have three years to live. Minor provocation could collapse his lungs —influenza in winter, pollens in spring, miasma in summer, mould in autumn. Jeannie initially thought the trauma of his diagnosis new, but as he talked the realisation grew on her.

"*When* were you diagnosed?"

He bent his head low. He gave the answer to his upraised knees. If she had opened her mouth, sputtering horror would have escaped. Instead, she closed her eyes and exhorted herself to understand the reasons he gave for deceiving her. She traced the story she knew of him—twice the reluctant immigrant from Scotland to Melbourne—and she saw the black thread that had always been there; the flaw on which her mother's critical attention had focussed. She herself had seen orange in William. The colour of determination and optimism; strength and endurance. If the black had caught her eye at all, it was only as a charcoal shadow line, a depth.

"There wasn't a right time," he excused himself for the three years of pretence she perceived. In his optimism, he had let himself believe he was cured. He had hoped never to admit to his condition. Never to speak his fears. Never to cause her any worry. Never to lose her.

"I could have prayed for you, William! *All this time*!"

William lost his voice momentarily. Then he whispered, "I wanted you to love me, not pray for me."

"I can do both," she asserted.

"I can't offer myself as a fit husband and father," William mourned.

"I will be the judge of that."

"Your mother ..."

"No."

"She will refuse me and with good reason."

"It is *not* my mother you ask to marry."

They would face Annie's wrath together, Jeannie promised. In a few days; after she had time to think. Time to pray: about Mildura; about the plans William had set in train without any consultation with her; about the radically different shape he had suddenly wrought of her future.

To face her mother, Jeannie needed all the self-assurance, all the certainty and positivism she could muster.

~

Frank was impressed with William's investment in Mildura. The size of it. That William had an inheritance to spend. He chuckled as he poured a celebratory whisky. He professed that he knew William 'had it hidden' in him, by which he meant 'money in the bank' rather than 'merit worthy character'.

Jeannie studied the image of herself that hung on Struan's drawing room wall—the girl standing irresolute by the river bank. She had accompanied her mother, two years after their immigration, on an excursion with the Heidelberg Camp, purportedly to receive instruction in sketching the Antipodean landscape. Bored, she had wandered along the rocky bank of the stream, looking for the wildflowers and burrowing animals that were not there. Annie had painted her with an empty basket; her face having the shape, the whiskers and the expression of a disappointed field mouse.

Annie did not paint people, she had told a much younger Jeannie, because if she did, she would not be able to resist caricature. Her subjects would not like the portraits she drew because they were too honest. They would not like to see themselves revealed, and that was true of this picture, Jeannie thought. She did not like the diminutive field mouse in the blue painting smock. It was a mockery. It showed her out of place, empty handed, a meek and forlorn character.

And yet, Annie had also explained why she would not paint portraits of wild animals. The stag that hung in the dining hall of the Edinburgh Lodge was an exception—she had been unable to resist the money offered. The men in the dining hall prized the life-size image, flattering themselves with delusions of conquest and domination. They hoped to hang the antlered head of one of these majestic beasts on their own wall. But wild animals shouldn't belong to people, and Annie would never again paint a portrait that suggested they could. She drew wild animals in the background—where Jeannie the field mouse could be spotted—because they belonged to the natural world.

Older now, with a better understanding of her mother's complexity, Jeannie saw that the field mouse was drawn with only a little mockery, and a greater part of love for one of nature's timid creatures.

Because of Jeannie the field mouse, the painting had not been sold. Annie's other *en plein air* landscapes had paid the rent, put food on the table and afforded the materials with which she had sewn clothes that suited her family's new Antipodean life. Her regional drawing classes had paid for trips to Ballarat to visit Frank; Horsham in the hope of catching up with Jim; Geelong and Tasmania to refresh friendships they had made on *Iberia*. Money had always been tight. Frank had ambitions for their lifestyle, especially when building Struan, that led to an excess of red ink in his ledger columns. He found William's investment—in cash—an exciting assurance from a man soon to be kin.

Which was why Jeannie had ensured that Frank would be at Struan that afternoon, and that William's investments would be their opening gambit.

While Frank enthused, and William grew in confidence, Jeannie waited for the moment her mother would choose to enter play. Annie sat in her usual chair, listening intently, her sharp eyes sometimes on William, sometimes on the back of Jeannie's head. Jeannie could feel her mother willing her to turn around.

"Who is going to live in this house ye build?" Having heard enough, Annie selected the central, structural pillar.

Jeannie turned around. "We will, Ma," she said firmly.

Frank's mouth fell open, revealing a crushed mass of short-bread biscuit.

"I see. If ye wanted to be away from us, I expected it would be to Scotland." Annie's tone was accusatory.

William examined the floor, exploring the edge of the woollen hearth rug with his toe.

"Within the year the train line is to be all the way to Mildura, Ma. As you've heard in all Willie has said, there's great opportunity there, and we will be but a day away by rail, not six weeks across the ocean."

"You thought Horsham an ugly, empty wilderness, lass. How do you think you will fare in the mallee? You could not be at more remove from the scenes you love. Do you know what little is there?"

Jeannie looked at William, an acknowledgement that she was trusting the description he had given her. "Irrigation is turning the land into a garden paradise. Here in Melbourne, we could at most afford to add a room to Willie's surgery. In Mildura we can have a garden the size of Struan. I will grow vegetables and fruit trees of all sorts. I will have rose gardens, grape vines and green lawns. I will seed wildflowers between the trees in our orchards."

"Who is going to look after Ma?" Frank had finished his mouthful.

"Pff!" Annie snorted.

"I run a business. I can't be here all the time," Frank objected.

"We will see what needs to be done, when it needs to be done," Jeannie replied evenly.

"I have looked after myself—and you—for twenty-two years," Annie growled.

"There will be extra bedrooms in the house. You can come to visit," Jeannie added.

Annie fixed her stare on William. "You've painted Jeannie a pretty picture, William. She has a wish to believe you and will take no heed of my concerns. Your income?"

"The township needs a qualified general practitioner," William found his voice, but did not meet Annie's gaze. "The house will have a surgery attached. Two blocks away there is a new hospital, where I will operate. I am assured of a good income from my practice alone. The produce from our villa block and the profits, over time, from the orchards will all provide an independent income for Jeannie."

Jeannie worried that with the word 'independent' William had opened a crack in their story. Annie's eyes narrowed, but only in suspicion that William was pandering to her. It was Annie's oft-argued view, after all, that women should not be made chattels of their husbands.

"An income of £50 per acre, per annum, you said?" Frank had his mind on the money.

"After five years, yes," William confirmed.

"£1000 from the orchard each year for Jeannie."

"It's a tidy sum for her, yes. My surgery, of course, can be expected to earn several times that amount."

"Excellent!" Frank, Jeannie thought uncharitably, was salivating. He took a swig of his whisky, a finger raised to express the fact that he was not finished speaking. "As you say," he motioned his glass towards Jeannie, nodding to himself, "we will see what needs to be done."

He had realised, Jeannie mused, that Annie could—when it needed to be done—move to Mildura.

"So," Frank continued cheerfully, "what needs then, to be done for the wedding? Are the invitations sent?"

As they walked to the entrance hall, long after Annie had retired to her room, William shook his head at Jeannie.

"I'm uncomfortable with this," he said mournfully.

"Step by step."

"We should tell her everything."

"We haven't lied."

"You're not giving her the chance to call off the wedding."

"We're not going to call off the wedding."

"She has the right to tell you that you mustn't marry me."

"I *am* going to marry you."

"It would be her position. She won't have you a widow like herself."

"You aren't going to die."

"Jeannie ..."

She took his worried face in both hands and quoted from the Bible:

> *"Entreat me not to leave you, Or to turn back from following after you; For wherever you go, I will go; And wherever you lodge, I will lodge; ... Where you die, I will die, And there will I be buried. The Lord do so to me, and more also, If anything but death parts you and me.'"* [6]

~

Jeannie and William tied the knot on the morning of Thursday 28th April, 1892. She wore a full-length dress of white, slightly wrinkled surah twill—a painstaking, two-month sewing project—over the cream silk petticoat her mother had worn in 1858. Covering her head was a veil borrowed from Mary Calder, and fastened to the collar of her dress was a sapphire broach given to her by William. She walked to him, trailing an abundant flounce of fabric, through Struan's rose garden, arms linked with Frank on her right and Jim on her left. Jim offered William a large handkerchief on account of the tears in William's eyes. Frank scowled and kicked Jim's foot, after which the brothers managed to confirm in compatible unison that it was they, who were giving Jeannie away in marriage.

Reverend Maxwell, wearing a full-length black robe and a white beard of truly Biblical proportion, spoke sternly to the gathering on God's purpose in marriage before facing Jeannie and William to perform the traditional Scottish Handfast Ceremony. He bound William's right hand to Jeannie's with a broad swatch of entwined Robertson and Cameron tartan, while asking him for his vow.

"Do you, William Johnstone Cameron,
take Jean Bolton Emily Robertson to be your wife?
To be her constant friend,
her partner in life, and her true love?
To love her without reservation,
honour and respect her,
protect her from harm,
comfort her in times of distress,
and to grow with her in mind and spirit?"

William sniffed and swallowed. Jeannie thought him unable to speak, but he succeeded in making his two words audible, at least to her.

Reverend Maxwell faced Jeannie, skilfully tying the cloth into a slip knot as he asked her the same question.

"I do," she said firmly.

On cue, William and Jeannie drew their hands apart and the entwined tartans pulled into a perfect reef knot. Holding each end of the cloth, they turned to face the wedding guests as Reverend Maxwell intoned the final blessing of the ceremony.

"Now ye are bound one to the other
With a tie not easy to break.
Take the time of binding
Before the final vows are made
To learn what ye need to know -
To grow in wisdom and love.
That your marriage will be strong
That your love will last
In this life and beyond."

Jeannie handed the knotted tartan to Edie. David handed William the ring. As William slipped the white gold band on her finger, Jeannie promised him:

"I take ye my heart
At the rising of the moon
And the setting of the stars.
To love and to honour
Through all that may come."

William completed the blessing of the ring—bravely, she thought:

"Through all our lives together,
In all our lives,
May we be reborn
That we may meet and know
And love again,
And remember."

Edie had observed the solemnity of the occasion for as long as she could bear. As soon as Jeannie and William had sealed their union with a kiss, she dropped a handful of confetti over their heads and hooted her approval, scooping Jeannie into a hug. Reverend Maxwell frowned at Edie; then at his son. David shrugged his shoulders in reply, and shook William's hand.

After a brief, congratulatory mingling with the guests, they followed Reverend Maxwell into the marquee where they signed the marriage register before returning to the garden for photos. Edie ushered the guests into a compact rectangle on a floor rug that had been placed in front of the canvas marquee wall. She fussed over the hem of Jeannie's dress, trying to keep the train on the rug without standing on it as she positioned herself behind Jeannie's chair. William was seated on Jeannie's left and next to him, Annie, sitting primly in her magnificently embroidered, apricot silk skirt and bodice. Frank and Jim were behind Annie, casually hatless and barely distinguishable from each other, wearing black wool waistcoats with white-tied collars. David, his top hat at a precarious angle, towered darkly over them all from the back corner.

The rug was not big enough; the guests overflowed and William had to move his field camera back a few yards. The assemblage waited uncomfortably while he hurriedly reset the focus and returned to his chair. One of the waiters who was to serve the luncheon inside the marquee, pressed the camera's shutter on William's count of three.

~

Two days later, when William developed the photos in the sun on the back step of the surgery cottage he now shared with Jeannie, he was harshly critical. He struggled with the contrast on the dark slide of the family group, using several of his precious photographic papers at different exposures before deciding he could not reach perfection. The second slide was a close-up photograph of the four in the wedding party. Edie was blurred—she must have moved; David was in perfect focus but wore the grim expression of an avenging angel. William and Jeannie, in the foreground, were in soft focus with sombre 'why is it taking this long' faces.

Jeannie understood William's disappointment; these photos were for his family in Scotland. He wanted to capture the event perfectly, which was something, in her opinion, these flat, black and white, still-life images could not do. She had a use for the photos though, she mused as she watched William write names in tiny print on a card filled with circles representing the position of each person. They could be the prompt for a cartoon. Each person could be drawn as a caricature; a pencil sketch that had movement and character and story. It would say more about the event, and the people who had attended, than the artificial pose the camera had captured. She would draw the cartoon, she decided, but only for William's eyes. People loved to see others in caricature, but seldom themselves.

The same could be said for photographs. It was very odd, seeing herself arrested in time. She had only seen one other photograph of herself, which William had taken after a formally-attired picnic outing two summers ago. He had explained the wonders of his camera at length, and had instructed her on its use so that she could take a corresponding photo of him. Thankfully, he had been pleased with the results and now, sitting at the dining table, he compared that photo of himself favourably to the new ones. By posing in the wedding photo with Jeannie on his right hand, he complained, he had presented his wrong side to the camera. His brow receded in a deep triangle to the part in his hair on the left side of his head, and did his face really look so gaunt?

Jeannie leant a hand on his shoulder and kissed the smooth corner of his pate. "I will fatten you soon," she said provocatively.

She had been shocked, on their first night, to feel his naked body, under the bedclothes, in the dark. The long, exposed bones of his arms and legs; the rectangular frame of his shoulders; the sharp angles of his elbows and knees. His well-tailored clothes had hidden his emaciation well. He was heavy, as he carefully laid his weight on her, but much lighter than she had anticipated. He was strong, as he lifted her and held her, but gentler than she had been told men usually were. As he lay beside her, his breathing returning to normal, she bumped her finger wonderingly across the corrugations of his ribcage.

"I'm sorry," he said, which she took to be an apology for the weight loss caused by his illness.

"I will fatten you soon," she said.

"You've fattened me already, my love. Do you want to do it again right away?"

"Ha!" she was shocked, but entertained. "Is that possible?"

"If you give me a wee while. Are you alright? I've not hurt you?"

It had hurt a little, but not as much as she had been led to expect.

He stretched an arm under her and rolled her on top of him. "Kiss me, then do as I do," he instructed.

He pushed his tongue between her lips, so she did the same to him and their mutual exploration soon became an energetic duel. When she needed her breath back, he bit her neck, so she did the same to him. When he moved his body beneath her, and she moved hers on top of him, she could indeed feel him fattening. When he rolled over her and pinned her arms to the bed, she had neither the strength nor the will to roll him back.

~

William did gain weight, much to Jeannie's satisfaction and largely thanks to the copy of Ma Beaton's Book of Household

Management that her mother had given her. The book was 1644 pages long, and it covered everything from Jeannie's new duties as mistress of the house to rules regarding vaccination of children; from the utensils required to operate a kitchen to the legalities of evicting a tenant; from pictorial identification of herbs to the exact mix of bismuth and soda with which to treat dyspepsia. Having grown up in a household that always employed a cook, Jeannie's experience was sorely lacking, but now she studied Ma Beaton's guide, consulted with William, and tried her hand at the recipes on which they agreed. He liked the baked whiting, *loved* the haricot of mutton but vetoed the stewed kidneys. Deserts were how she was going to put weight on him: raspberry jam omelette, tapioca, sago, bread and butter puddings—he loved everything that was sweet.

For tea on Friday 17th June—her birthday—Jeannie planned a menu of his favourites: oxtail soup, roast sirloin of beef with Yorkshire pudding, and a jam tart. She had allowed ample time for his return from his rounds and yet, by the time she heard him at the door, the Yorkshire pudding was deflating, and the succulent roast was drying on the top of the stove. He wasn't alone. She could hear David's voice as well, and her initial response was an irritable assumption that William was surprising her with uncatered-for company.

It soon became clear, by the thumps, scrapes, and excitable voices that the two men were manoeuvring something awkward through the hallway and into the living room. She moved the gravy pot off the stove and went to investigate.

"Happy birthday!" William flung the dust sheet that covered his purchase onto the floor, revealing a beautiful, five-drawer ladies' writing desk.

Jeannie gasped. "Willie! It's mahogany?" She touched the warm, polished wood with reverence.

"Mahogany," William confirmed proudly. "Regency, look at the legs."

Jeannie ran her fingers down the finely carved legs to the small brass rollers on which the desk was delicately perched. "Where did you get it? It must have cost a fortune!" She opened the slim drawers, revelling in each perfectly smooth slide.

"Beauchamps. They're selling a deceased estate. Made in England in 1820."

"It's perfect, Willie. Just perfect!" she wrapped her arms around his waist.

"I'm off," David announced.

"You won't stay for dinner?" Jeannie offered.

"No, I was ordered to do the heavy-lifting and then make myself scarce. I will seek recompense another evening." David swept an imaginary hat across his chest and bowed low. "Happy birthday," he kissed her on each cheek and left.

"It took longer than I expected," William apologised.

"Aye, our Yorkshire pudding will be as digestible as the sole of a slipper." Jeannie spread her hands on the top of the writing desk, delaying her return to the kitchen. "I've never owned a piece of furniture before," she said wonderingly. "Not something I could call my own. This is so beautiful."

William hugged her from behind and nuzzled her shoulder with his chin. "Next, I must find you the right chair."

~

Together they frequented furniture auctions, and rejected many chairs that did not match the desk. Instead, they brought home a hallstand for their coats, hats, and umbrellas; a valet-stand over which William was to fold his clothes instead of dropping them on the floor; shelving to hold the ornaments with which Jeannie brightened his hitherto spartan accommodation. Still looking for the right chair, they found a set of six which, together with the mahogany, one-leaf extension dining table, were an irresistible bargain.

"We don't have room for it," Jeannie worried, sliding her fingers around the bevelled edge of the table top, checking for damage.

"It will fit," William assured her as he wound the augur handle, closing down the extension.

It didn't fit. Not allowing for the hearth-space, the two arm-chairs and her writing desk.

"We need a dining room now," she said, as they pushed one side of the table against the wall, creating sufficient passage between the hearth and the hallway.

William tucked one of the chairs into the niche in the writing desk. He hummed in dissatisfaction, wondering where to put the sixth chair.

"Behind the reception desk," Jeannie suggested, "then you can sit with me while we wait for patients."

These days, however, the patients were waiting for William. His business had picked up gradually over the first three years, but the increase in patronage since his marriage had been extraordinary. William was making a substantial income, which was just as well given their mutually expensive taste in furniture and the budget over-run that was imperilling the completion of their house in Mildura. The bank, more than satisfied with his business account, had allowed William a sizeable overdraft. It would take only a few extra months in Melbourne, he assured Jeannie, to clear the debt.

Jeannie was blissfully contented in Melbourne. She was near to her friends, her family, her church, the city, and the gardens. William's one-bedroom cottage behind the surgery was cramped—she looked forward to having a larger house and a garden of her own—but she also loved the intimacy of this space that only fitted the two of them. Her major regret was that there was no yard for Olga but, in the interim, Olga was good company for her mother at Struan.

In July, when William told her that he had rented their newly completed house in Mildura for six months, Jeannie was in one part pleased, but in another part anxious. What of his illness?

He was fine, he assured her. Since his trip to Mildura his lungs had been clear. No night sweats, no expectorating cough. He regularly examined what sputum he could cough up under a microscope, and there had been no active tubercles. Standing in the warmth of the fire, he pulled up his shirt and placed her hand upon his not-so-prominent ribs.

"I'm getting fat!"

~

Influenza cut short the lives of several elderly people in South Yarra in August. William's cough started in September.

"We have to go," Jeannie said.

"The house is rented till December," he replied.

William's cough was worse in October. He donned a mask; he hired a locum to run his practice.

"We have to go NOW!" Jeannie begged.

William ordered her back to Struan; for a week or two.

"What is it that's brought you home, lass?" Annie demanded on seeing the suitcase.

"William's ill. He won't let me stay with him for fear I'll catch his complaint."

Annie cast her acutely perceptive gaze over the slim waist, the straight fall of Jeannie's dress.

"Are you with child?" Jeannie heard doubt in her mother's voice, but also a trace of excitement.

"No." She would like to have been, but William would not allow it.

"Then are you to be sent to me whenever there's a flu instead of being by your husband's side?"

There was a scratching at the scullery door. Olga's throaty bark rang through the hallway. Glad of the excuse, Jeannie turned away from her mother and headed towards the sound.

"Muddy paws!" Annie warned.

Jeannie fought Olga backwards. She shut herself and her exuberant dog into the scullery.

Annie came across her later, sitting on a garden bench with her face buried in Olga's soft fur.

"You must tell me, lass. Be straight. What's amiss?" Annie sat down and waited.

"It's not the flu."

"I gather. What then?"

"Consumption."

Jeannie heard her mother's intake of breath, then brooding silence while she digested the news.

"And you? Are you safe from it?"

"Willie takes every care." Jeannie combed her fingers through the thick ruff on Olga's neck, listening to the cogs turning in her mother's mind, waiting for the punitive questions she knew would be forming there.

Instead, Annie put her arm around Jeannie's shoulders and gave a light squeeze. They sat together, stroking Olga, until Annie broke the silence to announce that fortunately Maggie had not found another full-time position and could come back to be their cook.

"We don't need that now, Ma," Jeannie sniffed. "*I* can cook."

~

The argument came the next morning after breakfast. Annie put down her empty tea cup and went directly to her central question.

"When was William first diagnosed with consumption?"

"1885." There was no point in avoiding the truth. Jeannie was glad that the dispute was to happen now, without William.

Her mother drew a sharp breath.

"He thought he was cured," Jeannie offered weakly.

"They can't be cured."

"The sea voyage made him well."

"Until the next time he was struck down."

"He immigrated, and he was well here."

"Until the next time. And when was it *you* knew about this?"

Jeannie hesitated.

"Before the wedding?" Annie accused.

"Aye."

"Before the engagement?"

Jeannie did not reply.

"It's unconscionable!" Annie thumped her fist on the table with such force that the breakfast plates jumped.

"He thought he was cured!"

"Consumptives are *never* cured. The disease is carried in the family line."

"The *predisposition* only."

"The contagion spreads to those intimately connected."

"We take ample precaution."

"There is no vaccine."

"There *will* be."

"In whose lifetime? How long is William expected to live?"

Jeannie did not reply.

"I will have the marriage annulled."

"You will do *no* such thing." Jeannie growled emphatically.

"You will not have children." It was an order.

Jeannie stared doggedly at her empty plate.

"I will *not* have you a widow raising children. I *know* of what I speak!"

"He is *not* going to die."

"Hah! You think your prayers have such power? You think *I* did not pray?"

Jeannie looked up and saw that the tears she had heard in her mother's voice were also in her eyes. She looked away, embarrassed.

Annie scraped her chair back from the table and stamped out of the room.

~

That afternoon, as Jeannie was making a mulligatawny soup, her mother came into the kitchen and sat at the preparation bench.

"Will ye be off to Mildura now?"

"Aye."

She had not spoken with enough certainty. Her mother pounced. "Why not?"

"The house is rented till December."

"Pff!"

"We can't just throw them out."

"Yes. You can."

"William won't."

Jeannie tipped a tray full of sliced carrots and turnips into a large pot that was heating on the stove. She deposited the tray in the sink and selected curry powder, salt and pepper from the spice rack.

"Do I remember correctly that the house is rented to Cousin Adam's acquaintance, Mr Staughton?"

"Ma, don't interfere," Jeannie stood poised over the pot, a quantity of curry powder cupped in her hand, scowling at her mother.

"Twice as much curry," Annie instructed. "Yes, *twice* as much. And a stick of rhubarb. I have some in the garden."

Annie promptly left the kitchen. Jeannie thought her mother was going to bring back the rhubarb, but that didn't happen.

~

The next morning Jeannie carried a jug of the mulligatawny soup to William at the surgery.

"You shouldn't be here," he wheezed.

"I have soup for you," she stood uncertainly at the bedroom door and hefted her basket towards him.

William nodded his thanks and quickly turned his face away from her, seized by a coughing fit.

"I'll be on the reception desk," she said to his back.

Cousin Adam walked into the surgery's empty waiting room early in the afternoon.

"That was quick," Jeannie greeted him.

"Your mother was very insistent," Adam smiled. "Can I see him?"

"No, he's unwell. He would be most distressed if he knew Ma had spoken to you."

"Is there a true need then, for what your mother wants? Do you need my help with arrangements?"

"We must go to Mildura as soon as possible. If you could ascertain Mr Staughton's position? Perhaps he could make another arrangement—either for himself or for our accommodation—until the end of his lease."

Adam looked thoughtful. "I'm sure something can be done. It may take a week or so. Will you be taking your household goods?"

Jeannie made up her mind on the spot. "Yes."

"And Olga?"

Jeannie nodded.

"Then you need to be quick about it and book the goods on the train with some weeks' notice. From Swan Hill you book the goods by paddle steamer and yourselves on a coach."

Jeannie thought this sounded overly complex. "Why on the coach?"

"What's a dog like Olga to do on a boat for three days? The coach stops every two hours to rest the horses."

Jeannie gave that some thought. There was so much she would need to arrange. If only she and William had used the last few months more wisely. "How do I book the train?"

Adam shook his head and clucked his tongue at her. "Ahh lassie. You have not the faintest idea of it, have you. Is he too ill to do any of this himself?"

Jeannie opened a drawer in the reception desk. She pulled out a copy of *The Mildura Cultivator*. "Will it be in here?"

They looked through the paper together until Adam pointed to a large advertisement.

"Call on this company. Settle a sum at which they'll do the packing and carting as well. Don't forget to ask for a crate to carry Olga on the train, she won't be allowed in the carriage with you. It won't be a small sum. Do you have the funds?"

Jeannie had no idea, but she nodded.

Adam looked at her sceptically. "I can't go in to see him?"

"No."

"Is he well enough then, to even take the journey?"

He would be, Jeannie tried to calm her anxiety. He had to be.

"Be discrete in speaking with Mr Staughton, please Adam," she asked as she saw Adam to the door.

Adam acknowledged her request by tipping his hat, and walked towards his waiting cab.

In the evening, Jeanie looked into William's room to say goodbye before she headed back to Struan. He was lying quietly, looking at the ceiling.

"I'll be back in the morning, sweetheart. Will you be alright?"

"Jen?" he spoke firmly.

"Aye?"

"Will you bath Isa? She fell. In the drain."

Jeannie stepped up to his bedside and felt the sweaty heat of his forehead with the back of her hand. She went into the surgery to collect a facemask for herself; then into the bathroom for carbolic soap, a basin of water and a face washer. She was not going back to Struan after all.

As she swabbed his face through the night, Jeannie told William the plan. She talked about the train and the coach ride, their furniture, their luggage and Olga. She talked about the rooms in their new house; where the furniture would go. Then she planned the garden. She straightened the future out in her head. She eventually fell silent, thinking he was asleep, and was surprised when he spoke.

"George, read another one? Please George. One more story. Help me sleep."

Jeannie panicked. She roughly turned William towards her and dragged him up, back against the wall.

"George," William protested.

"It's not George. It's Jeannie. William!" She shook him hard.

"George?"

"You're with *me*, William. It's *Jeannie*." She slapped him.

He scowled at her and worked his jaw.

"Drink this, or I'll hit you again." She offered him a glass of water.

He took a long sip, eyeing her suspiciously.

"I told you, don't come."

"Well, I'm here and there's nothing you can do about it. Drink it all."

Friday 19th November 1892

Frank and Jim, Edie and David, William and Jeannie stood together on the northbound platform at Spencer Street station, watching luggage handlers load the last of William and Jeannie's furniture into a goods van. Olga lay quietly in a large wooden crate in their midst, her soft, wet nose pressed between the floor and the lowest slat, as near to Jim's boots as she could reach.

"The length of this train," David remarked lightly, casting his eyes slowly from the engine that was venting steam at the northern end of the platform to the last goods van visible at the southern extremity, "is due to the amount of furniture the Camerons carry with them. I hope the load will not sink the paddle steamer on its trip down the Murray."

He looked to Edie for her usual repartee, but she was unable to oblige. She and Jeannie were holding hands, preparing for the end of the world.

"Dog to the guard's van, sir," one of the luggage handlers spoke to Jim.

The luggage handler tried to pick up the crate by himself, and dropped one end heavily back to the ground as Olga shifted her considerable bulk.

"I've got this end." Jim angrily waved the boy towards the handle at the other end of the crate, and together they awkwardly carried Olga away.

"She'll be scared," Jeannie whimpered.

"She'll be okay." Edie was wringing all the blood from Jeannie's left hand.

"We must go to your carriage," Frank said.

"Jim ..." Jeannie protested.

"Will catch up." Frank shepherded the group towards the head of the train. The crowd on the platform was thinning as travellers boarded the train and well-wishers stood back.

"I'll help you," David said to William, taking his elbow.

"I'm alright," William muttered through his mask, turning the elbow clasp into a hand shake and back-pat. He shook Frank's hand gruffly, grasped the handrail, and pulled himself up the steps.

Jeannie anxiously watched him go and looked along the empty platform for Jim.

"You can come back," Frank whispered into her ear as he held her for a kiss. "I'll take care of it. Just send word."

David kissed her playfully on each cheek. "Letters. Lots of them."

Edie clung to her, sobbing and showed no signs of letting go when the train whistle resounded through the station.

"Look out!" Jim, short of breath after his run along the platform, forcefully disentangled Edie and lifted Jeannie in a hug, setting her down on the steps of the carriage. "Get my room ready," he called to her back. "Garden views!"

As she walked along the corridor of the train looking for her cabin, Jim shadowed her on the platform. She found William leaning sideways on the green leather seat, resting his head against the window. Jim punched the glass and William jerked back in surprise.

"Good luck!" Jeannie knew, from the movement of his lips, what Jim said to William, but the rattle of the window, the clank of the couplers and the knocking shunt of the wheels as the engine strained forward, made it impossible to hear.

Jeannie had booked a private cabin. William could lie down, knees bent across a seat normally reserved for three. He could cough and clutch his ribs without concerning other passengers. She pulled a plump cushion from her hand luggage and passed it to him.

"Sorry," he mumbled.

"It's a bonnie carriage. New, I think." Jeannie admired the polished woodwork; the brass fittings; the clear glass sliding windows.

The train was rolling more quietly now that it was underway, and clear of the echoing confines of the station. Jeannie watched the backyards of suburban Melbourne pass by, giving way to green fields enclosed by dry-stone fences with steel gates that opened to muddy tracks leading to clusters of wooden farm buildings.

William had been exhausted by the effort—emotional and physical—of handing over his surgery to the new doctor, packing up their furniture and household goods, and taking leave of their friends. She was glad when the comfort of his cushion and the steady rocking motion of the train sent him to sleep. She watched over him warily, hoping he would not wake as the train jolted into and out of short stoppages at Creswick, Clunes and Talbot. At Maryborough, however, she encouraged him to walk to the refreshment hall with her.

"Impressive," William commented as he stepped down from the train, looking each way along the extended platform. Together they examined the wide roof that sheltered the refreshment and booking halls. A continuous panel of glass ran either side of the hip of the roof and a broad cantilever stretched towards the train. Large signs were hung on chains from the iron roof supports. Instead of heading directly towards the 'Refreshments' entrance, William walked along the station tapping each of the cast iron ribbed columns that held up the canopy.

"What are you doing?" Jeannie asked when she caught up with him.

"There's a drain pipe inside. The columns must channel the water that falls on the roof into water tanks under the station. Very clever."

Jeannie welcomed the return of William's enthusiasm for things-engineering. For her part, she was impressed by the tessellated tiles on the floor of the capacious dining room; the carved ticket boxes and the high, wood panelled ceiling of the booking hall.

William had sparked-up. Between Maryborough and Bendigo, he regaled her with facts and figures about Victoria's golden era; he recounted the wonders of the modern steam-powered machinery that had replaced the early diggers and spoke of the promise of wealth hidden beneath the barren, scarred land that Jeannie saw outside the train window. Jeannie was not as ignorant about the workings of the gold fields as William supposed, and she did not share his optimistic view, but she encouraged his chatter and kept her thoughts to herself.

In Bendigo the train stopped for their overnight rest. While Jeannie and William dined in the Railway Hotel, Olga fretted, linked by a long chain to a stake in the back yard. Jeannie, making her last trip to the outdoor toilet before bedtime, spent a long time sitting on the dog crate, comforting Olga ... and herself.

~

The next day was an early start and a long haul to Swan Hill. As they returned Olga to the guard's van, they saw that several stock cars had been added to the end of the train. Jeannie could hear cattle bellowing in protest and she could see the thin, tufty legs of sheep angled worrisomely through the lower side slats. The stench of the animal's crowded confinement was gruesomely offensive. What would poor Olga think of these terrifying sounds and smells? William patted her arm and led her away.

Jeannie watched the land wither as the miles passed slowly. Was the train travelling at a leisurely pace for the comfort of the stock in the rear carriages? Or was their speed through this interminable, featureless landscape deceptive? William thought the latter. He immersed himself in the latest edition of the *British Medical Journal*. Jeannie read *The Woodlanders*, which impressed her, by its fourth chapter, as the best of all Thomas Hardy's novels to date.

It was dusk by the time the train reached Swan Hill. Having rescued an overjoyed Olga from the guard's van, Jeannie thought they should retire directly to their hotel. William, however, insisted on seeing *The Pearl* which was lying at the wharf, the white cabins on its upper and middle decks brilliantly illuminated by electric light. The paddle steamer looked handsome and very welcoming as they watched a number of train passengers transfer to the boat. Not for the first time,

Jeannie questioned Cousin Adam's advice to travel on by coach. William had agreed with Adam, citing his experience of the variability of the river; the possibility that it could become unnavigable by the date of their journey.

Outside the range of the electric light Jeannie could not see much of the river, but she could tell that it was not the 'mighty Murray' of her imagination. The water level was far below the top of the bank where she walked with Olga, and she wondered at its capacity to float the large paddle steamer. The dog moved uncertainly, swinging her large head from side to side to take in the sights and smells, startling whenever loud noises reverberated from the wharf. The night was warm, the air motionless and the mouldy odour of mud that rose from the river made the edge of the bank dangerously appealing to Olga.

Loading of cargo and baggage was to continue through to midnight, so they did not stay long at the wharf. By 8pm they were eating a light supper in their hotel room, both drained by their inactive day.

"It's a long way," Jeannie commented.

"We're only half way there," William replied—morosely, she thought, but it was hard to tell his tone of voice through his mask.

~

Their red Royal Mail Line coach was not ready for boarding at the appointed hour of 5am. Four strongly-boned horses were harnessed, ready to go, but the heavy canvas mailbags were still on the ground, inside the dimly lit livery stable, next to the rear coach wheel. A man Jeannie took to be the coach driver, was sitting on one of the mailbags, idly chewing a piece of hay.

Jeannie, William and Olga stood with three other passengers, watching a boy on the top of the coach arranging bundles of newspapers inside the luggage rails. The boy signalled his readiness with an 'Oi!' and the man on the ground picked up a mail bag and threw it, followed by several more, up to the roof of the coach as easily as if they had contained pillows instead of letters and parcels. After all the mail bags had been stowed, the man signalled for the coach passengers to bring their personal luggage to him. This he stacked on a narrow platform at the rear of the coach, before dropping a canvas tarpaulin over the pile and tying it securely. Having finished his own knots, the man checked those tied by the boy above him, making some adjustments before he waved the boy down.

"On ya get," the man finally announced. "I'm ya driver. Me name's Thomas."

Jeannie showed Olga the high, narrow step of the coach, but she refused to mount.

"You get on," William suggested.

"Come on Olga," Jeannie entreated from inside the coach, but to no avail. In Olga's mind the step was not for climbing, not even when William placed her front paws on it. She squirmed away from his attempt to boost her from behind.

Thomas watched with amusement. He caught Olga by the collar, bunched her legs up with a wide sweep of his arm and threw her into the coach. The passengers, two men and a woman, shifted their feet awkwardly, worried by the frightened, angry snarl Olga addressed to the man who had treated her so rudely.

"I'm sorry," Jeannie apologised. "She won't hurt anyone, she's very friendly." She stroked Olga's head reassuringly, embarrassed by the censure on the faces of the three on the opposite seat.

By virtue of being last to take their seats, William and Jeannie travelled backwards. The coach bumped, bounced and clattered over the deeply rutted and pot-holed dirt track and Olga fidgeted in protest, trying to stand. William lifted his legs over her back and bent his knees around her, tucking her into the base of their seat and holding her down.

The noise inside the coach made conversation difficult, and the lurching, backwards motion made reading impossible. William pulled a triangular bandana over his nose and mouth, and closed his eyes. Jeannie looked out the window, peering through the red dust that flew from the horse's hooves and increasingly obscured her view. Despite the closed windows and doors, the dust soon invaded the cabin and settled onto every interior surface. It crept inside her collar, caught in her eyelashes, and assaulted her nose.

The mallee was devoid of grass, populated by salt bush and scrubby eucalypts that straggled inelegantly on multiple stems from an underground root. Often branches of this mallee scrub lay brokenly across the coach track, causing Thomas to slow the horses. Sometimes Thomas turned the coach out of the wheel ruts and bashed a new course around the debris. Sometimes he stopped and moved the twisted mess out of the way. With the coach at a standstill Jeannie had the chance to take a better look at the scenery, and what she saw was frightening. The land stretched interminably, dry and scrubby, to a flat horizon. In the distance on the right-hand side of the track a dense line of gum trees marked the course of the river. At times the trees disappeared from view, and each time Jeannie prayed silently for their return.

Some twenty-five miles from Swan Hill, the coach made its first stop at Pyangil where the horses were changed while the driver and passengers ate breakfast at a small hotel. Here the Murray River made a tight loop, its sluggish brown water coming to meet the track at a gently sloping sand bar before turning away again into the trees. There were several horses and a few cows grazing on the riverside flats, penned in by fences made of stacked mallee roots. A barn built from roughly slotted slabs of wood stood on higher ground, near to the track. Olga drank gratefully from a bowl placed underneath the tap of the hotel's galvanised iron water tank. The passengers quenched their thirsts with tea, and Thomas ordered a beer even though it was not yet 9am. When they were due to depart, William was quick to lift Olga into the coach rather than risk an incident between the dog and Thomas.

Three hours later they stopped for the next change of horses at Narrung, where they lunched and drank tea. Thomas downed several beers before he took up the reins for the ongoing journey. Jeannie looked to her fellow passengers to object, but they settled into their seats, unconcerned.

The horses had been walking steadily for half an hour, and William was snoring lightly, when the two men opposite Jeannie briefly conferred. The man who had earlier introduced himself as 'Richard', opened the cabin door and leant out.

"Asleep!" he announced before jumping out of the moving coach, running forward and scaling the driver's steps. The horses stopped momentarily as Richard shoved Thomas to the side and took up the reins. The coach restarted and they continued at a brisk pace to their afternoon tea at Wyrong Station.

Thomas was in control again when they pulled into Euston at last light. He untied the dust-caked tarpaulin and handed out their luggage as if nothing untoward had taken place.

Over dinner, sitting with Richard and fellow coach passengers John and Sarah, Jeannie learned that Thomas lived in Mildura and that his inebriated behaviour was nothing unusual. He had moved to the temperance colony two years ago, on his wife's insistence. Thomas, Richard asserted, was making a serious attempt to reform his drunken ways. There were no public drinking houses in Mildura and his wife would not allow alcohol at home. Thomas had taken the job of coach driver in order to satisfy his thirst during his weekly trip to Swan Hill.

"The horses know the way," Richard laughed, "but they're too slow by their own device. We wouldn't have got here till midnight!"

Jeannie worried that there would be more drunken-driving the next day.

"No," John smiled knowingly at his wife, "he'll be sober when we arrive in Mildura. She's got an iron rule over him, that woman!"

"Doesn't anyone tell his wife about his drinking on the road?" Jeannie asked, looking at Sarah.

All three shook their heads. "She's a hard woman to talk to," Sarah explained.

Jeannie and William saw Thomas again as they left the dining hall. He gave a slurred 'goodnight' before resuming his deep conversation with the local men who were clustered at the bar.

~

There was no sign of Thomas when the coach was due to depart the next morning. Richard and John packed all the bags onto the luggage rack and lashed the tarpaulin. Richard re-tied the ropes that lay loosely over the depleted stack of mail bags on the roof, and checked the harness with which the livery boy had attached the four horses to the coach shafts. By the time Thomas wandered into the stable, tousled and yawning, the coach was ready to go.

"Always a pleasure to have you, aboard Ricky." Thomas patted Richard on the back in thanks. "On ya get!" he instructed his passengers.

At lunch, after another bone-jarring, dusty drive, Jeannie asked her travel companions why they had chosen to travel by coach instead of paddle steamer.

Richard, she learnt, was a bank clerk come postal worker who was responsible for personally escorting documents and money orders between the bank at Mildura and points along the road to Swan Hill. While the most sensitive financial instruments were in the satchel he kept with him at all times, he was also tasked with ensuring that the larger mail-bags were safely transported. There had been trouble in the past—not robberies, Richard reassured them, just foolishness. Loose ropes, burst bags, letters wafting over miles of mallee wasteland.

John and Sarah were travelling to Mildura on short notice because John's father was seriously ill and the paddle steamer was fully booked. They agreed it would be best, if the river was running—and it should be running at least until January—for Jeannie to make an early booking for her mother on the paddle steamer. It was a much more comfortable trip.

A couple of hours later, Jeannie woke from her uncomfortable doze when the coach stopped rolling and heaved sideways. She peered through the dust-caked window to see Thomas pulling a wire gate to the side.

"Oi!" He slapped a harness strap against the flank of the leading horse and the coach started forward, passing through the gate.

Jeannie observed that all the passengers were inside the coach, which presumably meant that while Thomas was holding the gate, no one was holding the reins.

When the coach was clear of the gate Thomas tugged the rear luggage rail and the horses stopped, waiting patiently while he secured the wire and stamped it into a trench dug below ground level.

"Rabbit proof," Richard noticed her mystification. "All the way round the settlement. Thomas won't lose his job for drinking, but he *will* lose it if he doesn't close that fence properly. You can see Mildura now. Sit on this side. I'll go up on top."

Richard shook the cabin door, and let the resulting shower of dust clear before stepping out. He scraped the persistent red-earth rim from the window frame, and smiled at her through the smeared glass.

Jeannie looked hesitantly at William who showed no interest in the scenery. He gave an indecipherable mumble through his dust-creased bandana and motioned her to move. Olga was more attentive. She sat up and pressed her nose expectantly to the window.

The horizon ahead and to the river side of the coach was an incongruously green line. They were approaching an oasis, Jeannie fancied, like an Arabian sheik, with a camel train. Inside the rabbit proof fence, the rough track widened into a road with gutters formed on each side. The horses cantered, the coach rolled comparatively smoothly and soon they reached fields where men were working, clearing the land. Jeannie watched two traction engines, hauling a massive log across the ground, ripping the mallee trees that were in the log's path out of the soil. Two men, roughly clad in khaki shorts and shirts, followed the log, just out of range of the settling dust, gathering the tangled scrub into heaps. Far across the cleared corner of the field, Jeannie could see smoke trails rising from similar piles. In between there were more men, working with crowbars and shovels to extract the dense roots that had defied the rolling log. Jeannie's heart went out to these strangers, engaged in such gruelling work in this oppressive heat and dust. Their pioneering effort, to turn barren land into productive fields, was extraordinary. In truth, she did not understand why men felt compelled to do such a thing, even though she admired their enterprising spirit.

The first buildings the coach passed were little more than lean-to iron sheds—the rough habitations of the workers who were clearing the land. Nearer the town, they passed numerous houses under construction, each attended by labourers who were fixing weatherboard slats to timber frames or hauling iron sheets onto the triangular trusses of a new roof. As the men worked, their draught horses dozed, heads nodding, tails constantly switching at flies.

There was no shade, Jeannie realised with dismay. No trees to give the horses shelter. If there had once been taller gums, they had been cleared with the hated mallee and salt bush and now, readied for fruit tree planting, the land stood bare. It was an alien, apocalyptic landscape. Could anything be further removed from the beautiful, wooded valleys of the Cheviots?

The first vines, while small, were a most welcome sight. Wire climbing frames were strung in straight rows high above the young plants in expectation of future growth. In the shallow valleys between the rows Jeannie could see a variety of vegetable crops. Nearer to the town, the recent plantings gave way to established vines and, when the coach stopped at a cross road allowing John and Sarah to alight, Jeannie was able to look closely at a mature patch. The vines bore a glorious abundance of healthy leaves shaded all colours of green, from light-apple through dark-iron, sprinkled with a gorgeous burgundy. This, Jeannie thought, she would love to see in her garden.

Arriving in the township, Jeannie looked keenly at the shops scattered along the road, committing their location to memory. She was alarmed by the rickety weatherboard edifices of the National Bank and the Bowring and Jacka grocery store, but soon they came upon more substantial buildings. The white ironwork gables on the two-story Williams and Yule drapery store impressed her, as did the newly constructed red-brick post office, where Richard jumped from the coach and bid a cheerful farewell.

The central avenue of the town was the widest street she had ever seen. Two carriage-widths of hard-packed earth in each direction, bordering a strip of luxurious grass implanted with colourful flower beds. Handsome peppercorn and gum trees lined the footpaths on each side. At the end of the avenue the coach turned left, and Jeannie looked past several imposing gum trees, down a gentle, grassy slope towards the Murray River—Mildura's artery; the fertilising water of this little community's astonishingly grand dreams.

"Cawfee Palace, Mildura!" Thomas opened the coach door.

Jeannie grabbed the end of Olga's leash and stamped her foot against the door frame as the dog leapt to the ground. Olga took one enormous bound towards the river and flipped backwards, caught by the suddenly taut rope. Jeannie tied the leash to the handrail by the door, arranged her dress and hat, and stepped down from the coach with as much dignity as she could muster.

As Jeannie waited for William to compose himself, a scrap of a boy came to stand hesitatingly beside her; one of her cases under each arm and one in each hand.

"This is Walter," Thomas announced. "He'll take your luggage to your room."

Leaning heavily on Jeannie's shoulder, William climbed down from the coach and shook out his clothes and his hat. Jeannie watched him anxiously, half-expecting him to faint.

"Welcome to Mildura." He waved his hat at the river before planting it on his head. "A stroll? Along the wee burn?"

"I think you need to lie down."

"Cup of tea."

"Yes, tea and a lie down." Jeannie pulled William's arm over her shoulders and turned him towards the hotel. Olga jumped to follow, and tumbled over her lead.

"Walter, could you please take Olga to a piece of grass, and then bring her in when you bring the luggage?"

Walter jettisoned the cases and readily took the leash Jeannie offered him. Olga stood miserably, watching her beloved owners walk unsteadily up the steps and into the Coffee Palace.

~

It was not till Wednesday morning that William was strong enough to walk with her, through the township to San Mateo Avenue. When they reached their house, he was outraged to see that the Mildura Fruit Preserving Company had constructed a canning factory on the adjoining block.

"This is preposterous! These are residential blocks. *Residential!* They can't build that here!"

Jeannie watched a team of horses hauling what looked like a boiler, into the enormous wooden shed. There was at least fifty yards between the shed and the border fence. Another fifty to the southern wall of their house, where the surgery was under construction. She could hear the workers shouting to each other. How much noise, she wondered, would reach their house from the factory?

"I'll have words with Waddingham about this!" William sputtered.

Their house—a small weatherboard dwelling with an iron roof—stood starkly exposed in a barren paddock, surrounded by a shiny, wire fence that stood almost to her shoulder. Sufficiently high and well enough made, she thought gladly, to keep roaming livestock out, and Olga in. She wished she could go through the wooden gate, but Mr Staughton was in residence until 17th December. She would not be able to start on her garden until the summer heat had passed.

The earth under her feet was parched and unyielding; its colour dramatic. *'Cinnabar red,'* she imagined writing to Lily, *'ranging from Persian orange where dry to dark carnelian where damp.'* It was not like any soil she had seen before. Her fingers felt solid brick under the thin powder of transient dust. How could anything grow in it?

Jeannie took note of the gardens they passed on their walk back into town, and with every garden, her dismay increased. Were the conditions on this side of the settlement different to the wonderful gardens she had seen alongside the river? How could the promise 'just add water', possibly be true?

"I'll put it to Waddingham," William declared, from the steps of the Chaffey Brothers' office. "We bought an 'irrigated, *residential* villa block'. I'll insist on it!"

Jeannie didn't want to witness William's confrontation with Waddingham. While he went into Chaffeys' office, she browsed the shops on Langtree Avenue.

She was acutely aware, everywhere she walked, of the eyes that turned to watch her. It was not, she knew, because she had a unique appearance. It was because she was a stranger. It was uncomfortable, but it would pass—once she met the right women; once they knew she was the doctor's wife.

That turned out to be as easy as walking into Shillidays, a general grocery and drapery store.

"Can I help you find something?"

Mary Shilliday was, Jeannie judged, only a few years older than herself. A few inches shorter and a few pounds heavier, with golden blonde curls, inquiring blue eyes and heavy red lipstick. She wore her storekeeper's apron with a crisp, busy air and she left, in her wake, the homely aroma of lavender.

"Mrs *Doctor* Cameron," Mary gushed after their introduction was made, "we have *so* anticipated your arrival! There's an appointment list as long as my arm, waiting to see your husband. We are *so* pleased to have an Edinburgh-trained doctor. Have you taken up your rooms at Riverbank yet?"

Jeannie's confusion must have shown on her face, because Mary rushed into an explanation.

"No, of course not. You just arrived and you needed a day to recover from that terrible coach ride. Mr Waddingham will be speaking with your husband. He's offering you the western wing of his house on Cureton Avenue, opposite Rio Vista. It's a lovely, roomy bungalow set in a *perfect* garden. Hattie—that's Mrs W.B. Chaffey—insisted on it. She is, of course, at the top of Dr Cameron's wait list."

In hushed, sorrowful tones, Mary described Hattie Chaffey's bereavement. Her first child, lost to 'goodness-knows-what ailment', when only months old. Hattie was 'the *second* Mrs W.B.'.

There was prior tragedy. W.B. had older children. Mary went on to share with Jeannie all she knew about the Chaffey family.

"Now, have you seen your own house yet?"

"From the front gate. We also saw the fruit preserving factory next door." Jeannie kept her tone neutral.

"George Proudfoot's factory. There's another thing the town's been eagerly anticipating!"

Jeannie learnt that the Proudfoot family had, along with the Shillidays, been early settlers in the irrigation colony. The brothers owned the town's largest produce store, and now George, responding to Mildura's desperate need, had branched out to build the settlement an on-site fruit preserving facility. It would be ready to handle some of the late summer harvest instead of having to transport all the crop to Melbourne. In winter, Mary boasted, she would have Mildura's produce on her shelves instead of importing 'inferior foodstuffs' from Melbourne and Adelaide.

In the light of Mary's enthusiasm, Jeannie did not voice her concerns about the proximity of the canning factory. Aware that another customer was in the store and her time with Mary was running short, Jeannie changed the subject by asking about church services.

Mary, as Jeannie had already identified by her accent, was English, and her husband, John Shilliday, was Irish. They had settled their religious differences (Mary laughed roundly in saying this), by establishing the St Andrews Presbyterian church. Surely Dr and Mrs Cameron were with the Scots church?

"Aye," Jeannie confirmed.

"Then we will see you both on Sunday at 11a.m. I'll wait for you at the door, and after the service I'll introduce you."

When she found him, later that afternoon, in the reading room at the Coffee Palace, William brushed over the issue of the Proudfoot's factory. Waddingham had shown him the zoning permit for block D. 'Residential' villa blocks permitted the establishment of family businesses—his own surgery, for instance. More importantly, William hurried on, Waddingham had offered them use of the bungalow opposite Rio Vista and William had confirmed they would move in immediately. He had agreed to open his general practice at Riverbank on Friday.

"Waddingham says Riverbank has a lovely garden," William said.

"I know," Jeannie smiled. "I walked past on my way back from the shops. It's a beautiful setting, truly beautiful."

"I've received a card from Abramowski." William showed her the invitation, hand-written on a poor quality, un-embossed piece of bond paper. "You're to join us for lunch here, on Monday. After Abramowski introduces me at the hospital."

She had heard enough about Dr Abramowski from William to interpret the disgruntlement in William's voice. It was a pity, she mused, that Dr Abramowski was a widower. A lunch that included a 'Mrs Abramowski' as well as herself, could have helped foster a more congenial relationship.

~

St Andrews Church was a modest wooden building with an iron roof, set on a block that had no trees or garden worthy of the name. There was no church hall, and no shade to give shelter to the sixty or more members of the congregation that gathered outside after the Sunday morning service. Inside the church the heat was stifling, and Jeannie's sympathy settled on Mary Shilliday's one year old daughter, who was volubly discontent with the confines of her pram. With Mary's permission, Jeannie rescued the poor child and kept her quietly entertained with bounces and tickles throughout Reverend W.P. Matthew's sermon, much of which laboured on the evils of alcohol. On Saturday night there had been a ruckus at a spot on the river called 'Pinkie Bend', where sly-groggers had landed alcohol by boat. The congregation, said the reverend, should pressure the local constabulary to enforce the law. This would be difficult, Mary confirmed after the service, because the constabulary had but one member, Sergeant Carter, and the drinkers at Pinkie Bend had numbered over 100!

As promised, Mary introduced Jeannie and William to a great many people, most of whom Jeannie could not name five minutes later. The next step of their path into Mildura's Scottish society was forged, however, with an invitation to a musical evening the following Saturday.

The Findlays of Craigieburn, as Jeannie wrote that night to Lily, were several years older than she and William, but she thought Ellen 'entirely charming', while Gilbert was, 'every bit the Scot'. She was very much looking forward to Saturday's outing, and she was hopeful that Gilbert and William would be good friends.

Jeannie crowded words onto the slither of paper remaining at the bottom of the page.

> *"Mary's bairn, Bessie, is the cutest wee thing, of an age with your Lilian Anne. I held her during the service and all the while I was thinking how dearly I wish to hold my niece. I will wish it all the days we are apart.*
> *Love JBEC"*

~

Otto Abramowski's head was disproportionately large in relation to his short, angular body. His trouser-legs bunched around his ankles; his jacket sagged off his shoulders. His goatee beard and sideburns were streaked with white. His handlebar moustache, the spiky eyebrows above his deep-set hazel eyes and the thinning hair on his head were uniformly russet-blonde. The skin on his face and hands was dry and roughened, burnt red in irregular patches by the sun. Jeannie thought him 'wizened', which surprised her, given that she knew, from William, that he was only 40 years old. His startling bodily composition lent itself to caricature. She imagined him in the rear of his apothecary, grinding a pestle against seeds, an aromatic brew bubbling on the stove to one side, a book of spells lying open on the other. Perhaps the dried residue of a sheep's foetus hanging from the door frame? No ... that would be amusing, but would not fit the man.

Otto described himself, over lunch, as a 'fruitologist'. He did not consume meat and he did not use animal products in the medicines he mixed. He preferred traditional herbalism to modern chemistry, but even herbal remedies, he argued, could be avoided by the pure practice of a diet of fruit, vegetables, nuts, and clean filtered water. Sunlight and fresh air were essential, and contagious diseases could be cured by fasting, with the intake of only fruit juice and water. Otto had chosen Mildura as the ideal location to test his radical ideas. On arrival in 1887, he had planted olive trees and now, as they were coming to bear, he had established a factory to press the olives. Their oil, he told Jeannie earnestly as he handed her a sample bottle, should always be used in the kitchen to replace unhealthy animal fats such as butter and lard. He intended to open a sanatorium in Mildura, but he had, to date, only been able to elicit support in building the hospital.

When Jeannie inquired after the origin of his ideas, Otto was vague. He had studied chemistry in the university of Konigsburg, but the knowledge given him there fell far short of the remedies he learnt from his mother in his hometown, Osterode in East Prussia. During the eight years he had spent with the Prussian army, he relied constantly on remedies he could concoct from the field and forest. He had found strong evidence in favour of a fruit and vegetable diet. He had observed greatly improved surgical outcomes in patients who had not eaten meat for two weeks prior to an operation.

"Have you published your research?" William broke into the conversation testily.

"This is not possible in war." Otto spoke with a thick accent. Jeannie excused his brusque manner on account of his limited English vocabulary.

William hummed, and Otto scowled.

The lunch was not going well, Jeannie thought. That she was an eager audience and that Otto was keen to hold the stage, displeased William.

"Dafty!" William growled as they walked down the steps of the Coffee Place.

Jeannie shushed him, linking her arm with his and pulling him close.

"I can't believe any but a gipsy would take him for a doctor."

"You've come here for sunshine and fresh air yourself, Willie."

"Aye, but not a diet with no protein to speak of. He intends to treat typhoid patients with two weeks of nothing but fruit juice. It's reckless!"

"Perhaps it's worth trying?"

"Would *you* have me subject Jim or Frank to such a trial? The man has no evidence. Did he have his poor late wife fasting on fruit juice before she gave birth? Did she have not a joule of energy for the labour? Was the baby starved of the nourishment it needed to grow a healthy brain?"

"Willie! You shouldn't say such things!"

"I warrant his experiments have been on his family and the results are proved."

They walked a block in silence, broken only by William's occasional throat-clearing grumbles.

"I can't believe he has the run of the hospital." When he spoke again, William's tone was edged with despair.

"You can't work beside him?"

"No!" William turned sharply to the side and coughed into his elbow. "There's no pay," he resumed indignantly. "He's an 'Honorary Surgeon' and offers me the same. The only salaried surgeon is Dr Hill, who has taken the position originally commended to me. Two nurses receive a wage. The rest are volunteers. The hospital depends on community fundraising. Patients are asked to donate what they can afford. Abramowski himself says most can't afford a penny. I can't believe what I saw this morning! The hospital is woefully ill-equipped for surgery. I refuse to work under those conditions."

"Can we get by without pay from the hospital?"

"Aye," William cleared his throat, then continued more firmly. "Already I have seen three in my surgery who were previously attended by Abramowski."

"Will he be angry you take his patients?"

"Och, that's the way of it. I have the better qualification. Abramowski is an apothecary and an olive-grower. Let him stick with that."

~

In the early afternoon on Saturday, Jeannie was selecting a small, multi-coloured bouquet of flowers from the Waddingham's garden when William arrived with a gig he had hired from Jones' Livery Stable.

"I haven't driven one of these since I left Scotland!" He called to her excitedly from the high-seat. "Och, it's grand to drive again!"

Jeannie tied the flower stems with a strip of cotton, and dipped them into an old dish she had placed in the garden as a watering-place for bees. She shook the excess droplets off the bouquet, and laid it on the top of the present she had wrapped for Ellen Findlay, before handing her basket to William.

"I shall buy one, Jeannie," William continued as she climbed up into the gig, "as soon as we have lucerne on our field. A horse and a buggy! I'll extend my rounds, and use it to transport patients. We'll visit our friends anywhere in the settlement, and you can come and go easily from your orchard."

Jeannie was glad of his enthusiasm. She took it as evidence his health was improving.

"Can you drive a buggy?" It was his sudden afterthought.

"No, I never have."

"Then I must teach you!" William offered her the reins.

"When we get our own, sweetheart. You drive today."

"It's not hard," he urged.

"I'm in my best, Willie." Jeannie declined firmly. She checked that her hat was securely tied, and placed her basket on top of the clean tea-towel she had laid across her skirt. "Let's be on our way."

They had allowed time on their way to Craigieburn, to visit their landholding in section F. It was Jeannie's first visit and, having counselled herself against over-expectation, she was pleasantly surprised to see the progress of their orchard.

Their twenty acres had been cleared and the perimeter fenced with wire. Along the short edges of the rectangular field lay the main irrigation channels, which Jeannie estimated to be two feet wide. Smaller channels, eight inches in width, ran the full length of the block, breaking it into regular strips. The block looked perfectly flat, but William assured her that there was a slight fall from the irrigation channel where he had stationed the gig, down towards the river. There was no water flowing, but she could see that the ground in the channels was damp. William explained that the main irrigation pumps at the Billabong Plant were turned on in the early morning to supply the water quota with least evaporation.

Between the narrow channels, dotting the field at intervals of two yards, were fresh plantings—tiny saplings only twenty-four inches high, supporting a small crown of glossy leaves.

"Where do we get in?" Jeannie asked urgently.

"You're in your best," William reminded her with a smile as she hurried to climb down from the gig.

"Can't be helped," she retorted, lifting the hem of her dress off the dirt and bunching folds of cloth into her hands.

He pulled the wire gate far enough from its holding post to allow her to pass through without catching her skirt. She tiptoed across the wooden planks that bridged the irrigation channel and took the leaves of the nearest sapling into one hand.

"It's an apricot, Willie," she said approvingly.

"Roly-poly pudding, yum." William trailed behind her as she headed away from the gate, crossing row after row of fledgling trees.

"Figs." She caressed the waxy, dark green foliage.

"I like fig jam."

"Peaches."

"You'll need preserving jars."

"Not fresh peach crumble? With clotted cream?"

"Preserving jars, so I can have peach crumble *all* year round."

She laughed at him, and raised her hand against the lowering sun to scan the field.

"Where are my citrus trees?"

William waved towards the far corner of the field. "We can drive around."

He wrapped his arms around her waist, his fingers pressing firmly through her dress to flex against her ribs. "Happy?"

"I love it, Willie! I can see the orchard, full grown. I can see it already. It can't be mine? All this?"

"It *is* yours. For the chance you take. Coming here with me."

"You didn't have to pay me to come, Willie. I came because I love you." She turned in his arms and made to kiss him, but he pulled back, a finger defending his lips.

"Arrgghh," she issued a long groan. "Keep your hands from me, then." She pushed past him and headed back towards the gate.

"Not much longer, I can feel it." He drummed his chest to prove the action would not make him cough.

"Take me to my oranges," she ordered.

~

Ellen Findlay made soft, cooing noises as she lifted the small jug from its protective folds of parchment paper. The creases of her smile spread from her vividly blue eyes to the stray silver strands of her black hair.

"Is it hand-painted?"

"Aye," Jeannie replied. "You said you're from Dalavich?"

"Aye, and these are the bluebells of Loch Awe." Ellen traced one of the finely drawn flowers with a rough-edged finger nail. "Did you paint this?"

Jeannie nodded.

"Och! What a talent!"

"No, it's my mother and my sister who have the talent. I draw for the love of flowers."

"It makes a charming gift, thank-you *so* much." Ellen gave Jeannie a light kiss on the cheek and laid an arm across her back. "Come through."

Jeannie resisted. "Perhaps we could see your garden, Mrs Findlay, before the light fades."

"Of course, but you must call me Ellen. Aye?"

"Aye."

"Gilbert, William might like to see the pumphouse," Ellen threw the suggestion over her shoulder as she exchanged her house shoes for a pair of rubber boots.

The hour spent with Ellen, in her garden, was a revelation to Jeannie. Her mind was packed with ideas by the time they returned to the house to prepare tea. They had started with the best flowers for the garden beds—no bluebells, of course, the air was much too dry; no snowdrops, the winter was not nearly cold enough. Iris, daffodils and dahlia could all be grown and roses would thrive with plenty of water and manure. Vegetables were ideally grown along the small irrigation channels in a newly planted orchard. Peas, beans and tomatoes needed shade in the hottest months. Pumpkins and all sorts of melons thrived where there was ample space. Potatoes, carrots and peanuts grew well, easily cultivated in the mounds pushed up at the side of the water channels.

Chickens were an essential component in any garden, though their territory must be managed to ensure they picked over weeds, offcuts and vegetable remainders rather than the succulent seedlings. Their manure was especially useful where the vegetables grew. Unfortunately, chickens did not eat the paspalum that clogged the irrigation channels. Weeding paspalum was the worst of all seasonal chores, Ellen warned Jeannie, and the task could not be assigned to goats because goats were a menace amongst young trees in an orchard. In fact, Ellen added, goats were a menace at *all* times and in *every* place. She did not keep them and thought any serious gardener would agree with her.

Turkeys could also be a nuisance, but it was worth growing one brood each year for mid-winter meals. A breeding pair of pigs provided for waste removal, and their offspring were easily fattened with unprocessed grain soaked for 24 hours in curdling milk.

A house cow, of course, for milk, cream and butter. One would be enough, at first, but as Jeannie's family grew, she would find it useful to have two to ensure a continuous supply. The Findlays ran a dairy herd at Craigieburn, supplying milk to the township. For a small fee, those on villa blocks could paddock their cow annually with Craigieburn's bull.

An acre of lucerne on their villa block would feed two cows and a horse. They should set aside half the acreage by rotation to cut for hay in December so that there was feed in the winter months. There were chaff-cutters in Irymple who could be contracted to do the work, and the same men had a set of harrows, which were used to spread the manure and aerate the soil twice a year.

Did Jeannie know how to make butter?

Standing in Craigieburn's kitchen, looking at the butter churn, Jeannie was ashamed to admit that she did not. She remembered milking the cow at Yetholm, and knew she had watched Aunt Margaret Calder separate the cream and make butter, but she could not say now how it had been done. In the Robertson household there had always been a cook, and in South Yarra she had bought their needs from the dairy.

"It's an easy thing," Ellen assured her. "I'll show you, when you have your cow. I bring our produce into town on the road past your house—Tuesday, Thursday and Sunday before church. You may buy your eggs, dairy and vegetables direct from me until you've established your own ways. Would you like a turkey for your Christmas dinner? I'll keep one aside— there'll be none in the butcher. Och, here they come now to disturb us!"

Gilbert and William walked into the kitchen, faces ener- vated, talking enthusiastically about steam engines and the design of a punt that would cross the river to collect much- needed firewood from the heavily-treed banks on the New South Wales side.

William thought a steam engine should be designed to run the punt pulley instead of a horse turning a cog-wheel.

"Why burn wood to collect wood? Dafty." Gilbert advanced on the stove and lifted the lid of a large cast iron pot, releas- ing a mouth-watering burst of lamb and rosemary fragrance into the room. He issued a guttural expression of appreciation, his accent still thoroughly rooted in the Scottish Highlands, twenty years after immigration. William stepped forward to take a look inside the pot.

"Hot," Gilbert warned unnecessarily.

"Steam is more efficient," William resumed their argument.

"Not necessarily." Gilbert shook his thick mane of prematurely grey hair. "A steam engine needs hours to warm to the right temperature. The engine would be running all day, with only a chance that a cutter would arrive with a dray full of logs. We don't have wood to spare."

The men moved away from the heat of the stove to the preparation table, where they inspected the plates that Ellen and Jeannie were filling with vegetables. Gilbert picked up a carrot, freshly peeled, and bit it in half. Encouraged, William stopped opposite Jeannie and helped himself to a handful of shelled peas.

"The firemen at Billabong," Gilbert continued, munching the second half of the carrot, "start feeding wood to the boiler before midnight to be ready for irrigation at dawn. Four irrigations a year, 30 to 35 days in duration. The pumping system— all of it together—uses 3000 tons of box wood and red gum *each* irrigation."

"Lot of wood," William responded agreeably.

"Not so much needed in early days. We had a roster amongst the blockies, to cut wood and supply boilers. Plenty here then. Thick with box on flats at Psyche bend. Gone now. Mallee roots for house fires and stoves—they're gone too. Now we have wood cutters, contracted to Risby, supplying all the wood. Risby has total control. He's holding the Irrigation Company to ransom."

"Och, you're not going to talk about Risby again," Ellen protested.

"He stood down the woodcutters and seized the firewood."

"He never!" Ellen looked at her husband in alarm, holding up knife and carrot, mid-peel.

"Aye. Pumps won't run tomorrow."

"Why for?"

"He can't pay woodcutters because the Irrigation Company hasn't paid him. Which," Gilbert added for William's benefit, "is because the company can't collect water rates."

"Which is because the rates are supposed to be six shillings and instead, they're twenty," Ellen added.

"Why are the rates so high?" William asked.

"Because Chaffeys don't pay their share," Gilbert replied.

Ellen slammed her knife onto the wooden table top. "We need the water!"

"Risby says Chaffeys should pay rates for their acres, same as the rest of us," Gilbert explained to William.

"Why don't they?" William asked.

"They built all the works. The government gave them the water."

"The pumps are on *Crown* land," Ellen retorted, "and it's *Crown* water. Mr Deakin didn't *give* Chaffeys the water. Every block came with a water *right* and a share in the Mildura Irrigation Company, which is a co-operative—it isn't run by Chaffeys, it's run by *us,* the irrigators. The rates we pay are set by the Irrigation Company to cover the cost of running the pumps."

"Actually," Gilbert interrupted, "New South Wales says the river and therefore the water belongs to *them,* and we should be paying *them* for it."

"Ridiculous! There's none farming that side. Without us the water would be wasted to the sea." Ellen carried her pot to the stove and poured boiling water over the carrots.

"Done?" she asked Jeannie.

Jeannie sped up, splitting the succulent green pods between her thumbs and scooping peas out with her forefinger.

"Chaffeys have to pay their rates," Ellen continued.

"Which is what Risby says," Gilbert pointed out.

"I don't agree with him shutting down the pumps and bringing us all to ruin—which he will, if this goes on!" Ellen drew breath, glaring at her husband across the cluttered preparation table.

"He's making a point, love," Gilbert placated her. "We'll get the water back soon."

"Go away with ye, I *told* you not to talk of that troublemaker to me. You've put me all in a fluster, and in front of our guests. Talk irrigation with William in the drawing room if you must." Ellen shooed her husband away with an oven mitt.

William hovered his fingers over the bowl of peas, enticing Jeannie to push his hand away. They exchanged a smile before William followed Gilbert out of the kitchen.

"Ye have a sweet fondness," Ellen observed.

Jeannie blushed. "A bucket for these pods?" she asked.

~

That evening at the Findlays' house was Jeannie and William's introduction to Mildura's busy musical scene. Their fellow guests were Timothy and Christina Campbell who lived nearby at Fairholme in Nichols Point. With their five musically gifted children in attendance, the Campbells made a complete ensemble and, after tea, Jeannie was delighted to be entertained with violin, cello, piano and voice.

Timothy Campbell had recently formed the Mildura Harmonic Society and on the following Tuesday night Jeannie and William enjoyed front row seats at their inaugural concert, *The Pilgrim Fathers*, at the Institute Hall. The performance of over 50 voices was of an excellence that Jeannie had not expected to hear outside Melbourne. The event was a fund-raiser for the hospital, and William and Jeannie had a busy evening of introductions, before and after the concert.

It was their second consecutive outing. The night before they had joined Mary and John Shilliday on a moonlight trip on *The Pearl*. The Mildura Brass Band entertained a crowd of more than 300 people as the paddle steamer travelled 12 miles upstream from the wharf and back again. That musical performance was also excellent, and the introductions were extensive and encouraging.

The busy round of social engagements was good, Jeannie knew, for William's business, but not for his health. On Tuesday night, after the choral concert, she found him in a faint, lying in the Waddingham's garden near the outhouse. Despite her insistence, he refused to close his surgery for even a single day.

Saturday 17th December 1892

"Stand there, to the left of the gate post, with Olga."

Jeannie positioned herself and Olga according to William's instructions. She brushed dust and dog hair from her navy skirt, and spread its folds beyond her shoes. As she placed a steadying hand on top of the dog's head, more white hair wafted in her direction. Olga was moulting in swathes. Jeannie sighed, squared her shoulders and posed for the camera, slightly side-on.

"Be still now," William ordered unnecessarily, standing to the side of the camera and pressing the shutter.

He was creating the memory of their first day in their first house; the moment before they walked in the gate to take occupation; the starting point. The garden would grow from here. In years to come she would look back at the barren block, the bare walls of the house, the stark veranda and marvel at the change they had wrought, turning this characterless place into their home. She would be reminded of the freshly hewn fence posts, the crisp silver wire netting and the robust construction of the wide, wooden gate. She would be reminded of Olga. Photographs made time stand still. Drawings did not make her feel the same way, they had a timeless motion. Was it because they were imprecise? Because they carried the artist's interpretation? Photographs had a utility, but Jeannie did not like them. She particularly disliked them when she was the subject but, on occasion, she was obliged to indulge William in his favourite hobby.

The photograph was done. William swept the legs of his tripod together and, cradling the body of the camera in his hands, carried the whole apparatus towards her. She opened the gate for him and ushered Olga inside.

"Are you going to take a second photo?" she asked as he laid the camera and tripod carefully on the veranda.

"From the back," he said.

"We'll go in first?" she asked hopefully.

"Wait," he released the door latch and turned to her.

"William, you can't, I'm too heavy!"

He picked her up, staggering, and carried her across the threshold. She paused him for a moment, picking Olga's hairs off his black vest while he regained his breath. Then they walked from room to empty room, with Olga padding in front of them, reading the past life of the house through her acute sense of smell.

In the kitchen, Jeannie examined the stove. It was one of the latest Wilson cooking ranges and William was keen to impress upon her how miraculous it was. By means of an ingenious invention called a 'baffle plate', the air that was super-heated in the fire box comingled with the smoke and gases produced by the fire, effecting near perfect combustion. This made the stove extremely efficient in its use of wood, while it output more heat and very little soot. Water could be heated more rapidly by this range than *any* other, William told her proudly, because the heat travelled all the way along the base and up the sides of the wrought iron high pressure boiler *before* going under the hot plates and around the two ovens—very little heat was wasted up the chimney.

While William explained all this, Jeannie investigated the two ovens to confirm they had been left satisfactorily clean by the tenant. She removed the top centre hot plate cover, checked the fit of the heavy circular grill that was used for cooking chops and steaks and, satisfied, returned the grill to the warming rack. She picked up the rectangular toasting grill, tested its light weight and its measure across the hotplates. She was pleased to see that there were two irons resting at the back of the stove, both of them as-new.

"It's wonderful, Willie. It has everything I need. Do we have any coals?"

"Maybe out the back."

They moved on to the scullery where Jeannie paused to inspect the washing and wringing machine.

"Bradford's 'Vowel Y' combined washer and wringer," William informed her. "You said you liked the one at Struan."

Jeannie lifted the lid of the wooden wash box and peered inside. With her left hand she turned the geared cog wheel, pleased with its smooth action as it rotated the inner washing drum. Moving to the right-hand side of the machine she tested the wringer, lifting the upper roller, reseating it and turning the handle.

William, less interested in the mechanics of the washer, had gone out the scullery door.

"Some coal here," he called, "we'll need to buy more." She heard a metallic clang as William dropped the lid of the coal can back into place.

Jeannie stepped out the back door and was immediately struck by a crushing pain in her chest and rising panic in her throat. She gripped the door frame for support.

There was nothing out there.

She searched the tawny land that stretched drearily to the eastern horizon. Her eyes desperately fixed on a scrap of dull green that marked a planting. Here and there, plumes of dust indicated that something was moving.

It wasn't *nothing*, she told herself firmly, trying to deflate her anxiety. She reminded herself of the fruit preserving factory that stood out of sight, on the other side of the house. She studied the solidity of the two concrete steps; the shape of the coal bucket that sat by the first stone of the path. William had gone that way, to the right, where the outhouse stood, exposed and forlorn. He had closed himself inside.

Jeannie turned back into the scullery and leaned against the wall, her hand pressed to her heartbeat, willing it to slow down. She would be alright, she promised herself. She was not going to have a panic attack whenever she stepped out the door to go to the toilet, or hang out the washing. She would get used to it.

No—she would *change* it.

At Nottylees, the scullery door opened onto a gently sloping crescent of lush green grass, embraced by a thick hawthorn hedge that had stretched solidly above her childhood head-height. A discrete pocket in the hedge hid the outhouse, discernible only by the path that led towards it. Beyond the hedge, overhanging, were large rowan, ash and oak trees. A willow stood to the right-hand side of the lawn, its waterfall of soft leaf separating the back garden from the front. Hanging from a strong, horizontal bough was a swing with thick ropes and a well-worn wooden seat. Jeannie's seat, in times of distress. Legs forward, legs back, legs forward, legs back in a soothing, steady rhythm, hidden under the willow's cloak. She still went there, in her mind, when she needed.

"There you are," William came through the house, carrying his camera and tripod. "I'll take the second slide. Will you stand on the back step?"

"Enough of me," Jeannie refused. She squeezed past him, into the house.

~

Hansen and Co. brought their furniture and boxes from Chaffeys' storage depot near the wharf, arriving on schedule at 9am. Gilbert Findlay and his eldest son, Stuart, were on hand, helping to lift and lug, positioning furniture according to Jeannie's instructions; carrying boxes to the rooms she indicated. Ellen was not with them. Saturday was a working morning—milking, butter-making, vegetable picking and packing ready for transport to town early on Sunday morning. Tomorrow, at about 9am, Gilbert told Jeannie, he and Ellen would drop in a welcome-crate of dairy and garden produce on their way past. At 11am, they would all meet up at church.

Jeannie was unsure William would make it to church, though she did not say so. He was not standing aside to let the others do the heavy work. He refused to show any weakness and she knew he would suffer from his pretence.

The moving was done, as intended, before the heat of midday, and Gilbert and Stuart headed home. William stood in the midst of a stack of boxes in the living room, his fingers interlocked on the top of his head, his elbows sharply angular, his arms skeletal below his rolled up, grubby white sleeves. He had shed his vest, and his shirt clung wetly to his ribs, betraying the flail in his chest as one lung worked hard, compensating for the other, in his struggle for adequate breath. The blue tinge to the skin around his lips and nose worried her.

"I'll make up the bed," she told him. "I'll find the box with the sheets. You must rest this afternoon."

He scowled, dissatisfied with himself, but did not object. He sat on a tea-chest and watched her through the bedroom door.

She levered the lid off a box, pulled out the sheets, and spread them on the mattress.

"Pillows?" she asked herself, looking among the boxes.

He came into the room and stepped out of his shoes, leaning heavily on the bedstead for balance. The wheeze in his breath was evident as he sat down, leaning forward over his knees. She hurried; clumsy as she used a claw hammer to grapple with the lid of the tea-chest she had picked out.

"Balsam?" he asked as she plumped four pillows against the bedhead, shaping them to support his shoulders. Breathing was much harder for him, when lying flat.

"You had it in a pocket?"

"Vest." His tone was urgent. He was unable to say more than one word at a time.

"Where did you leave the vest?"

Was he thinking or unable to speak?

"Kitchen?" she suggested.

"Porch."

Jeannie found the vest discarded by the post nearest the front door. The bottle of balsam and a handkerchief were in the inside pocket. She opened the bottle, and saturated the handkerchief as she rushed back to the bedroom.

William pressed the handkerchief to his mouth and nose, and inhaled deeply; coughing, and inhaling again until the coughing eased. He looked at her over the rim of the handkerchief, eyes watering.

"Go," he croaked.

"Willie ..."

"Unpack. Go. I'm. Alright."

~

The following Monday, when Jeannie and William arrived at the wharf, the members of Mildura's brass band were milling around, issuing desultory, un-orchestrated strains of music from various instruments. Neither William nor Jeannie knew why the band was there, but they were amused to envision the scene as a reception party for Jeannie's mother.

When *The Pearl's* whistle signalled its imminent arrival, the band speedily assembled. As the boat drew up, many bodies materialised from the dusk and crowded together under the wharf's electric lighting. Mooring ropes were thrown and fastened to bollards, and a wide gang plank was put out from the paddle steamer's top deck.

The band, disappointingly, remained silent as Annie stepped carefully, holding her hem clear of her ankles, across the bridge onto the wharf. She looked dignified; tidy but tired, Jeannie thought. It was a long journey, five days travel from Melbourne in the mid-summer heat, and her mother was neither young nor in robust health. Jeannie's tears were loosened by the vulnerability of welcome, the thought of the effort her mother had gone to on her behalf, and the knowledge that this visit could not often be repeated.

They hugged, speech rendered pointless as the band struck up, gathering from a ragged start into a cacophony. Mother and daughter separated and looked at the figure at the top of the gang plank, his hat held high in a wave to his welcoming committee.

"Who is that?" Jeannie threw her voice above the noise to William.

"Mr George Risby," Annie answered when William looked nonplussed. "Shall we move away?"

"Is this all your luggage?" William asked, pointing to the small case Annie had set on the ground by her feet.

Annie raised a mocking eyebrow and handed him four luggage tags. She picked up the case, offered her elbow to Jeannie, and together they walked to the waiting hall, leaving William scanning the wharf, looking for baggage handlers.

"Why is Mr Risby being met with a brass band?" Jeannie asked as soon as they were sufficiently sheltered from the noise.

"He has been arguing the case of the irrigationists to Parliament in Melbourne. Presumably his followers see him as a hero. Others see a villain."

"You follow the case?"

"It's been an interesting trip."

There was a burst of noise as the waiting hall doors swung open and closed again behind the burly figure Jeannie recognised as W.B. Chaffey.

"Annie!" W.B. boomed in greeting. "What a noise, eh? What a palaver! Poor Risby, I don't think he expected that!"

"You assured me the brass band was well talented, W.B. I am put to doubt!"

"Thrown together at the last minute. Unrehearsed!" W.B. laughed heartily. "Mrs Cameron, lovely to see you. How do you find your new house?"

"It's very well, thank-you." Jeannie was struck shy by this bold, authoritative man.

"Your mother has been a *most* invigorating travel companion." Jeannie was astonished to see W.B. wink at her mother, who inclined her head, smiling demurely in reply. "I swear I'd like to see her on the board of the Irrigation Company!" W.B. laughed at his own preposterous suggestion. Jeannie blushed and Annie looked indifferently at the people who were passing through the waiting room, carrying luggage out into the darkness beyond.

"Before you leave, Annie, you must all come to dinner," W.B. continued smoothly. "Hattie will arrange it with you, Mrs Cameron."

"That's very kind, Mr Chaffey," Jeannie murmured.

"Not at all, I should be paying your mother a consultancy fee! But no talk of irrigation at our dinner table," W.B. wagged a thickset finger at Annie. "Hattie detests politics. She will want to hear of Melbourne, of society and of art—especially art."

W.B. turned in the direction of Annie's gaze and saw William entering the hall, his long arms wrapped around four cases.

"I offered your mother my jinker, Mrs Cameron?"

"Thank-you, Mr Chaffey, very kind, but my husband has made arrangements."

"Very well, I must let you go then. I hope to see you again soon." W.B. lent forward and gave Annie a kiss on the cheek.

"That was very *familiar*," Jeannie murmured to her mother, askance, as they walked out of the hall, towards the cab William had hired.

"Americans," Annie replied nonchalantly, as if that were sufficient explanation. "He and Mr Risby are at odds with each other. Not satisfied with their exchange in the Parliament, their debate continued, inexhaustibly, on the paddle steamer."

"Encouraged by *you*, I suppose?"

"I read the papers for news pertaining to Mildura. I'm well across the developments. Are *you*?" Annie challenged.

Jeannie pursed her lips and clenched her jaw rather than retort. She had only a vague idea of the dispute between Risby and the Chaffeys. The irrigation water had come back on a few days after their visit to the Findlays. She assumed the issue had been resolved. It would be typical of her mother, Jeannie thought, to stir the pot of any dissension. In contrast—or perhaps in consequence—Jeannie craved peace and harmony. She felt her enthusiasm for her mother's month-long visit wane— and they had not yet left the wharf.

~

William, thankfully, was well across 'the developments.' While Jeannie had been moving furniture, unpacking crates and setting up house with minimal time to be ready for her mother's arrival, he had been confined to his favourite wicker chair on the veranda, struggling for breath, inhaling balsam and absorbing every newspaper that arrived at the door: *The Mildura Cultivator* twice weekly; *The Irrigationist* on Saturday; *The Argus* from Melbourne—five days old when it reached Mildura by the mail coach on a Monday afternoon.

The Cultivator and *The Irrigationist* had quite different accounts of the reception that met George Risby at the Mildura Wharf. *The Cultivator* reported a meagre assembly that must have been an embarrassment to the returning trouble-maker. *The Irrigationist* reported a handsome welcome, fit to make the settlement's hero proud.

On Saturday morning, William read *The Cultivator* while Annie read *The Irrigationist.* Then they swapped papers and kept reading while Jeannie deployed a wet cloth, waging her never-ending war against the dust that invaded the house and threatened William's compromised lungs. William, accustomed to both papers, read easily past the discrepancy in the reporting, but Annie slammed *The Cultivator* onto the table that separated them.

"Unmitigated bias!" she declared.

"Best to read *The Argus* for news," William agreed. "Mildura's papers are good for horticultural advice and local advertisements."

"The Chaffeys own *The Cultivator?*"

"No, but it's undeniably pro-Chaffey, and *The Irrigationist* takes the opposing stand. Reading both arrives at a balance."

"What *is* your balanced opinion, William?"

"I'm a doctor, not a horticulturalist, and we are recently arrived," William replied equably.

"You have irrigated fields. It's in your interest," Annie told him impatiently.

"We're feeling our way."

"This 'Mildura Difficulty' as the press name it, stands to bring the settlement down. Do you not see that?"

"The Chaffeys—and the government—won't let that happen. It will be resolved."

"None from Melbourne want to buy land in Mildura now, William. Indeed, many are trying to sell. The word is that the grand experiment has failed; that the Yankees have swindled the government. People like *you*," she stabbed a finger at him, "have been misled."

William scowled and shifted in his seat. Jeannie, dusting the nearby window ledge for a second time, thought it prudent to intervene.

"Chaffeys have paid the wood cutters, the pumps are working again. It was no more than a short disruption," she said amiably. "Will I bring tea now?"

"The Irrigation Company should function in such a way as to cover the ongoing cost of running the pumps. It must raise enough revenue to cover its expenditure," Annie lectured.

"You're quoting W.B.," William growled.

"You think I don't understand the principle?" Annie growled back.

"The irrigation farmers can't afford the high rates the company set," William explained.

"Which means that it costs too much to run an irrigation scheme, on this scale, in this remote, unsuitable place."

"Did W.B. say that?" Jeannie asked anxiously.

"Of course not!" Annie retorted.

"People writing in *The Argus* have said it," William attributed Annie's economic wisdom to its source. "They are nay-sayers, is all."

"They are nay-sayers with influence. Land sales have stopped. Without the sale of land, the Chaffeys have no funds to continue development, and the irrigation company can't receive water rates from undeveloped land."

"The Chaffeys have no funds?" Jeannie knew of the gossip, but hearing it from her mother was startling.

"The Chaffeys didn't bring with them the funds Mr Deakin trusted them to have. At every turn they've relied upon sale of the land the government *gave* them, to fund the development of the settlement. They see nothing wrong in this. It's the way business is done in the Americas, but here they've over-reached themselves."

"They have not 'swindled' the government," William said testily.

"Perhaps too strong a word, but it is used, nonetheless. The success of the Chaffey enterprise has depended entirely upon the showmanship that convinced people to come to Mildura, buy the land, and pay the Chaffeys' contractors to work it up. With papers like *The Irrigationist* and people like Mr Risby tarnishing Mildura's image, the grand plan is near to ruin. The man may be speaking the truth, but he anticipates not what the consequences be."

Annie and William stared at each other across the table, their mouths set in grim, antagonistic lines.

Jeannie felt dread slinking into her chest. "I'll bring tea," she murmured.

~

Christmas day went well. Everyone was dressed for the occasion and Annie appreciated the sermon given by Reverend Matthew—at least, she did not contest his assertions. Annie cast a critical eye over the weatherboard church on their arrival, no doubt judging it to be flimsy, but made no remark. She fanned herself briskly throughout the service, and she warily separated her skirt from the roughly hewn pew each time she stood to sing a hymn but in words, if not mannerisms, Jeannie thought, her mother was remarkably tolerant.

"You came here for heat, and you certainly have it," Annie commented as they sheltered in the shade of a large square of canvas that had been tied between the church and two young trees.

"It's an easier, drier heat than in Melbourne. We are becoming accustomed, and Willie feels the benefit already."

"I have my doubt about the dust." Annie nodded towards the road, where the dust raised by each passing buggy gathered in a red cloud before the hot north-westerly wind dispersed it in their direction.

"We must keep Willie apart from it," Jeannie agreed.

"Will there be rain?"

"We don't expect it before autumn."

William returned from the refreshment table, two glasses of lemonade in hand.

Mary and John Shilliday arrived with their baby, Bessie, who was sleeping comfortably, loosely wrapped in a cotton sheet and shaded by the large, black hood of her pram. While Jeannie leant over the pram, struggling against the overwhelming temptation to wake Bessie up, the conversation around her delved into the world of grocery stores and drapery. *Everything* could be supplied in Mildura, Mary assured Annie, it may not be on display in the windows, but with only a short wait it could be brought into their store.

When Ellen and Gilbert Findlay joined the group, talk turned to the abundant local produce available in the Shillidays' store, much of it supplied by the Findlays—there was fresh cream available even on Christmas morning. Melbourne couldn't compete with that, they laughed.

Neither could Melbourne compete with Mildura for community, friendships, the bonds formed in the creation of the settlement, the memories they had made and were still making. Mildura's Harmonic Society, Gilbert said, may not play in such glamorous halls, but it met with a much warmer reception amongst friends than was to be had in the city. He would never go back, Gilbert declared, and Ellen nodded her enthusiastic agreement. Mildura was their home now.

Were conditions not difficult—financially? Annie inquired politely. To which the Shillidays looked uncomfortable and John replied that they did not extend credit. Gilbert agreed that cash on delivery was essential, but Ellen modified his assertion—with dairy, fruit and vegetable produce, there was often barter. She would exchange an over-supply of peas, for example, for a like quantity of potatoes.

Annie wondered aloud, how that worked for William.

"Jeannie has been most innovative with rabbit and apricots," William responded lightly, but Jeannie, alert to the drift of the discussion, knew he was angered by her mother's effrontery.

"As are we all!" Ellen laughed. "We won't starve in Mildura, thanks to the endless supply of rabbit and apricots!"

"Seriously, William, you must not extend credit," John Shilliday cut in.

"I'm obliged by the Hippocratic Oath, John. I must work to the benefit of the sick and I can't turn a patient away if they're in need," William replied earnestly.

"It's dafty, Doctor, you need to be paid," Gilbert said gruffly.

"We have an excellent harvest on the trees and vines this year," Ellen intervened cheerfully. "An abundance of oranges, apricots, peaches, nectarines and figs. People are a bit short today, but at the end of the summer picking the bills will be paid. People here are very honest."

It was true, Jeannie thought happily. The established orchards and vineyards looked wonderful, with fruit hanging heavily from handsome, healthy trees. She had heard optimism similar to Ellen's from every patient who asked to defer their bill. She had checked with William, and he had agreed without hesitation. It would help establish his practice if he gave the horticulturalists credit pending their harvest. It worried Jeannie, hearing John and Gilbert speak, but she pushed their stern advice to the side, preferring Ellen's hopeful promise.

"You will see, my dear," Ellen continued, attracting Jeannie's attention with a light tap on the forearm, "how busy the blocks become. The first pickers arrive in a week. There will be tents all along the river; every wagon in town will be hauling crates and it will be all we can do to keep up the supply of milk, butter and bread to the camps. We're expecting such a harvest that we've asked that the school holidays be extended. We have much work for the children to do."

Annie raised an eyebrow in disapproval. "The children miss school to work?"

"They love the harvest," Ellen placated her. "It's an exciting time and they earn pocket money. The winter term will be extended. There's no loss to their learning."

"That's right," Mary nodded her head in agreement. "The School Advice Board will agree. Oh!" Mary laid her hand on Ellen's arm in suddenly remembered angst. "Isn't it shocking about Bella Leslie! William ..." she turned to him, "you attended?"

William inclined his head and kept his mouth firmly closed. The Hippocratic Oath also obliged him not to discuss his patients.

"Oh, and you couldn't save her! The river, it claims so many lives! You would have been called much too late. I do understand. Shocking. Bella was just 11, such a sweet lass, and Alec, only nine but so brave. He nearly drowned himself, trying to save her. What on earth were they doing down on the river flat alone?"

"Minding their father's horses," Gilbert inserted.

"But why would the lass go into the river to swim? How often do we tell the children the danger of the river?"

"Who was first to find her?" Jeannie inquired.

"Mr Leslie. Beside himself, poor man. Nothing he could do, when he pulled Bella from the water," Ellen replied.

"Is there no first-aid training in the settlement?"

Ellen and Mary looked blank.

"We must do something about that," Jeannie said with a purposeful glance towards William.

~

Boxing Day was celebrated with a river excursion on *The Pearl*, followed by sports and games at the woolshed, and finally a ball at the Institute Hall. Jeannie had bought tickets to the ball for all of them, but Annie declared she did not have the energy to continue into the evening; she would stay quietly at home with Olga. William and Jeannie gladly stepped out without her.

The Institute Hall rocked to the brass band until midnight, and for the first time in many months William agreed to dance. Indeed, to Jeannie's delight, he enthusiastically led her to the floor. They completed several dances and, after parting from their friends, he still had the energy to suggest a walk along the river bank.

Out of sight of the town, Jeannie leant against him, wrapping her arm around his waist and untucking his damp shirt so she could rest her hand on his bare skin. He shortened his stride and they walked comfortably together in the embrace.

"You're feeling much better, sweetheart," she commented.

"Aye. Good tonight." He had fallen into the habit, even when breathing adequately, of clipping his sentences.

"Then it's time," she pulled him to a stop and turned herself against his chest. She placed a hand momentarily on his cheek, giving him the opportunity to refuse, and then stretched to kiss him. Lightly at first; deeply when he responded. All too soon, he pulled away, bent at the waist and sucked air into his lungs. She breathed in disappointment and concern, but he straightened and pulled her back for a second round. When he stopped and bent over again, gasping, she laughed.

"Don't. Make. Me. Laugh," he spluttered.

She gave him a playful push and he landed on his hands and knees.

"Dust," he objected.

He was right, the river bank was dry, covered with twigs and leaves. Definitely unsuitable for sitting or lying down without a rug. She helped him up and slid both hands under his dishevelled shirt, exploring the all too prominent vertebrae in his spine as they kissed again.

"Intimidated," he said, dusting the knees of his black pants while he was next bent over, wheezing.

Had she misheard?

"Mother."

"Oh." She thought. "You don't want to go home."

"No."

"The surgery?" she suggested. It wasn't much further along the river bank.

He straightened and smiled.

~

"I *want* to have your bairn, Willie," she spoke as he tightened the strings of her petticoat around her waist. She was distressed that he had withdrawn from her just when she thought she had secured his climax.

"I don't want you burdened. You must be free to marry again."

"You won't die."

"Then we wait. Until I don't die," he said flippantly.

"I want *your* bairn."

"Arms."

She obediently raised her arms into her sleeves and he dropped her light cotton dress over her head.

"This?" He held out her corset.

"A bag?"

While he searched the surgery store for a bag, she studied herself critically in a mirror. Her hair was admittedly a mess but it was not obvious, she thought with satisfaction, that she had shed her corset.

"You're much better, Willie." She took the paper bag from him and wrapped it in the cardigan she would not need to wear during the walk home, even though it was the coolest pre-dawn hour.

"We agreed."

"You wouldn't marry me if I didn't."

"We agreed," he repeated firmly.

"It's cruel to me, Willie. It's cruel to me," she sniffed.

He kissed her tenderly on the forehead and wrapped her tightly in his arms. "For all Creation, I would not be cruel to you. It's for the best."

She shook her head vehemently against his shoulder. "No," was her muffled reply.

"You've mussed your face."

"Arghh," she growled at their joint image, took a shuddering breath and padded barefoot to the store shelves, where she found some muslin to use as a face cloth.

She helped him spread and smooth the cotton sheet over the mattress he had repositioned on the surgery trolley, then sat down to slip on her shoes.

"How long till you know you haven't died?"

"Don't start."

"I pray for you night and day, Willie. You. Won't. Die," she loaded her voice with the utmost conviction.

"Ask God to speak to me. So I may believe, as you do."

"God doubtless speaks to you often, but you don't listen, same as you don't listen to me. You're fixed in your own ideas."

"Ready?" William offered his hand and pulled her out of the chair into a light hug before shepherding her towards the surgery door.

~

The next morning, as Jeannie squared the stubby wooden pegs and straightened the string that marked out a new section of her vegetable garden, Annie engaged Jeannie's workman on the subject of crayfish.

"Way to cook 'em, missus, is over a steamin' pot. Five minutes is all. Till shell turns orange. Then part tail from body like so." As he demonstrated imaginatively with his empty hands, the labourer's shovel fell away from his elbow. "Oops!" He stooped to collect the shovel and continued. "Flesh comes out easy. Only a tit-bit, mind, but tasty and there's thousands in main ditch. Protein. Just as well God gives it us, free to eat, eh? We'd be starvin' at camp without it."

"The crayfish are undermining the banks of the channels, are they not?" Annie brought the workman's attention back to her original query.

The man gave the word 'undermining' some thought. "We get them out of burrows just below the water line. A bit o' fishin' line and a tit-bit o' rabbit—they're sure to grab at rabbit. A tug on the line and they're straight out."

"Does the water leak out of the channels through the burrows?" Annie persisted.

"Water leaks any ways, ma'am. Burrows or not. Channels need cementin', like Lord Ranfurley did. Chaffeys don't stump up for that."

"Should this channel have cement lining?" Jeannie asked.

"Too late up here, missus. This is a tit-bit stream for your garden. It's the channels from the pump house to the blocks that's the trouble."

"How much water is being lost?"

"Can't rightly say, missus. Seems a lot to me. People say they lose the half of it, but I dunno. Reckon Chaffeys got it wrong. New blocks are too far from river. No one buys, and there's no work to be had clearin' now. Mighty glad you got me for this job, missus. I got nothin' else payin' me way."

Jeannie felt a twinge of guilt. She had engaged this particular man to repay his debt to the surgery. His son had been treated for a broken leg after a fall from a horse. She would have to find another reason to pay him in coin, once his debt was extinguished. It would be better, however, if he spent less time chatting and more time using his shovel.

"We'll let you get on then. You can finish before the heat of the day." Jeannie took her mother's elbow and steered her forward.

"Lord Ranfurley?" Annie inquired.

"He has a large landholding down the river, with a separate pumping system. It's independent of the Chaffey's business."

"He has fared better by your man's account?"

"Perhaps Chaffeys *should* cement the channels," Jeannie pondered.

"They don't have the funds," Annie replied with smug certainty.

"Of course, you were rude enough to ask W.B. his affairs," Jeannie retorted.

"You should ask more questions yourself, lass."

"Alright. What vegetables are best grown in this garden bed with tomatoes?" Jeannie stopped and spread her arms wide to encompass a patch of land that had been roughly turned over. "This is where the dung is going."

"Don't plant corn, potatoes or cabbage. Melons grow well with tomatoes. Cucumbers too. Carrots and radishes do well." Annie gave this advice without hesitation, drawing on decades of folk wisdom. "Plant the cabbage and leafy vegetables in the new moon," she continued. "Corn, tomatoes and melon when the moon is waxing; carrots and radishes at the full moon. Nothing when the moon is waning."

Jeannie recalled last night's moon as a semi-circle shining on the western horizon—waxing gibbous. She could plant her tomatoes and corn as soon as the manure that William was collecting from Craigieburn was dug into the soil.

"Your man should turn the dung in tomorrow," Annie vocalised Jeannie's exact thoughts.

Jeannie looked past the proposed vegetable patch to the dust cloud that signalled an approaching wagon. "This will be Willie," she said. "You should come out of the sun, Ma."

By the time the two women reached the house the wagon was turning in the front gate, but it wasn't William driving, it was Gilbert Findlay.

"Gilbert?" Jeannie queried in surprise. Then she saw William curled in the back of the wagon and rushed to undo the tail-gate.

Gilbert promptly arrived to help her. "He went to coughing, Jeannie," he told her urgently. "He dropped that bottle he sniffs. It broke on cobbles."

"Help me, Gilbert."

William was shuddering as he struggled to breathe. He was blue to his cheekbones, unable to speak and, while he took some weight on his feet, he would have fallen if Gilbert and Jeannie had not supported him, one under each arm as they dragged him past Annie, into the house.

"He said you had another bottle." Gilbert blustered on, clearly frightened. "While he could still speak, he said that."

"On his bed, back against the wall!" Jeannie instructed, leaving Gilbert to drag William the rest of the way while she darted into the kitchen, and grabbed the spare bottle of balsam from a cupboard.

William fought the handkerchief Jeannie had soaked with balsam away from his nose. He was unable to take a breath, indeed, he seemed to be *holding* his breath, unable to let it out. It was a danger he had taught her about, in a first-aid class on asthma.

"One, two, three …" Jeannie yelled into William's face, and as she finished with "BREATHE!" she thrust her hands against his rib cage and slammed him against the wall with a violence that made Gilbert step backwards in alarm.

William coughed, desperately sucked at the air and then his breathing jammed again. Jeannie repeated the manoeuvre five times before William was able to exhale without her help. He pressed the handkerchief she gave him against his nose and collapsed sideways, his chest heaving as he replenished his lungs.

It was Annie who eventually broke the sound of William's wracking breaths. "I'll show you where to empty the dung, Gilbert."

~

It was not long after Gilbert's departure that Mrs Proudfoot arrived, carrying a wicker basket, its contents hidden under a faded tea-towel. Annie graciously invited Jeannie's neighbour to take a seat on the front porch while she investigated whether her daughter had finished 'her rest'.

Jeannie was lying on the bed, her arms wrapped around William, her chin against his shoulder and her eyes watching the door. She nodded assent to her mother and, when Annie had closed the door, she stood and composed herself in front of the bedroom mirror.

William—who had been quiet for a while now—made a sobbing sound through his pillow.

"Shush," she told him softly and, when he was quiet, she opened the door and slipped outside.

Mrs Proudfoot had brought two pots of jam—apricot and fig—and two cans that were labelled 'Mallee Apricots'. A small offer of compensation, she said, for the additional traffic Jeannie would have noticed since the preserving factory opened on Boxing Day. It wouldn't always be this busy—there was pent-up demand, hundreds of cases of apricots and figs waiting to be processed. The first cases of fresh fruit sent to Melbourne and Ballarat had not arrived in the best condition, and now the horticulturalists were keen to take the price the Mildura Fruit Preserving Company had offered. The plant had been set up to can 15 hundredweights of fruit each day, and to process an equivalent amount into jam. They had plans, Mrs Proudfoot confided, for their 'Mallee' brand to expand into canned vegetables and they would be glad to purchase any over-abundance of seasonal vegetables that Jeannie had in her garden.

"It will be a while," Jeannie responded with a wry smile as she poured three cups of tea, "before my garden produces anything."

"Of course, dear. We all know how much work it is to get started," Mrs Proudfoot replied kindly.

"Is there not supposed to be a railway to take the fruit to Melbourne?" Annie blew lightly on her hot tea, then sipped.

"Oh, this is a miserable subject amongst us!" Mrs Proudfoot exclaimed. "The railway! We were promised it would be built by now, but no. The men visit and they talk and they make promises but nothing happens. Another harvest arrives, and we have no option but to send the fruit by boat to Swan Hill to meet the railway there. It takes too long. The fruit spoils."

"Were the Chaffeys not meant to build a preserving factory?" Annie asked.

"My George has beaten them to it. There was such a need. This harvest is the settlement's biggest yet. George foresaw there would be tons of fruit that could not get to the city in time. Indeed, we have not enough vats to handle all the orchardists want to sell."

"He'll be lowering the price he pays then," Annie observed.

Mrs Proudfoot drew her lips into a thin, disapproving line.

"I'm intending to put all the land to the east of the house into cultivation," Jeannie redirected the conversation. "We're starting late this year, but next year I hope to have a much larger area. Mostly for our own consumption, of course, but there may be extra vegetables in season."

"Well, no point preserving them yourself, my dear. We can do the job for you easily, right next door."

"I've been told sultana grapes are becoming popular?"

"Indeed. They can be dried before transport, which is much to their advantage."

"I thought I could divide my garden into small sections, and protect it from the summer wind with lengths of grape vine."

Mrs Proudfoot nodded in agreement. "Allow a space for drying racks. We don't handle sultanas ourselves. There's a packing shed that takes in dried fruit."

The conversation paused as the women watched a four-horse dray trundle past, raising a low wave of red dust that spilt through the wire of the front fence.

"I have told the drivers they must *walk* their horses along San Mateo Avenue, my dear. But perhaps a hedge ..."

"I have hawthorn bushes on order from Skene's," Jeannie smiled. "They should be here in autumn."

"That's lovely. Hawthorns grow well." Mrs Proudfoot bent to pick up her basket and pushed back her chair. "*Do* give my regards to Dr Cameron. I'm sorry I missed him today."

Mrs Proudfoot left with a smile for Jeannie and a chilly frown for Annie.

"You embarrass me, Ma," Jeannie complained as she gathered the cups. "Would you not talk to my visitors in such a way."

"Your visitor was talking business throughout, why should I not?"

"Perhaps she simply came to say 'welcome' and to give me some produce."

"*That* was an effort to forestall you in complaining about the traffic on your road." Annie followed Jeannie into the house.

"Perhaps you could take this to the kitchen." Jeannie turned, thrust the tea-tray into her mother's hands and darted back into William's bedroom.

~

Jeannie brought her mother's late-night pot of tea to the veranda where Annie was sitting in semi-darkness, her powdered face lit by the silver half-light of the moon. The cream cotton shawl that was draped over her back and arms was warmly illumed by the orange glow of the kerosene lamp that hung by the door. A thin plume of manure-smoke rose from the smouldering contents of a used kerosene tin that was placed under the table near Annie's feet. The aroma was mildly unpleasant, but it was a commonly accepted shield against pesky mosquitos.

"Sit with me," Annie ordered, seeing only one cup on the tray.

Jeannie sighed and sat.

"Is he better now?"

"Aye." William had eaten the evening meal with them and had retired to bed early. He had recovered his breath, Jeannie knew, but not his pride.

"Have you had to do that before?"

Jeannie considered querying her mother's meaning, but there was no point, it would annoy, and in no way divert her.

"No, but he has practised it with me."

"He expects it, then, this ..." Annie couldn't find the right word. "This stoppage in his breath?"

"He says his lungs, being weak, may close on the air. When he can't breathe out, I must help him."

"And if this happens when you're not at hand?"

It was a question that worried Jeannie dreadfully. Now it hung in the air between herself and her mother, unanswered.

"Why today?" Annie resumed.

"The work of shovelling dung. He shouldn't do such things."

"Your man could have gone."

"I told Willie that. But Gilbert put out the invitation and Willie wouldn't send someone else. He doesn't want to appear either lordly or weak."

"He has shown his weakness today."

"Aye, he has that and he's furious in himself. I almost think he'd rather ..."

"You hadn't saved him?" Annie finished the sentence.

Jeannie turned away and pulled a handkerchief from the short, puffed sleeve of her dress.

"He hasn't thanked you, I suppose," Annie continued.

Jeannie waved a hand.

Annie drank her tea and waited.

"It's that ... he waits for the blade to fall," Jeannie explained, turning back to the table. "That specialist gave him a death sentence and he waits for it. Each day, he thinks ... He gets so broken down in himself that he wants it over with, rather than keep waiting. He won't fight."

Annie put her hand over Jeannie's bare forearm and squeezed. "He thinks not of the burden on you."

"He *does* think of me," Jeannie protested sharply, "and it makes it worse. I wish he would just let me have what I choose without ..." She waved her hand again, dismissing the remainder of her thought.

"Ye argue over a bairn?"

Jeannie gave a throttled groan. She knew her mother's opinion aligned with William's on this matter, and she did not welcome the lecture she thought forthcoming.

"Is there no friend you talk to?" Annie made one of her surprising conversational turns.

"Willie ... *We* think no one should know. It would keep people from coming to his surgery. They don't understand the disease. He's not infectious. Not now."

"This is the burden I speak of. You're a woman. You need to share your troubles with another woman. Can you confide in your friend, Ellen Findlay?"

Jeannie shrugged. Her mother was right, she would very much like to be able to air her woes in person to a friend, but she did not yet know the people of Mildura well enough to trust them. If only Lily was here. Or Edie.

"Who did *you* talk to, Ma?" It was a daring question.

Her mother blinked.

"Aunt Agnes?"

Annie drained her cup and mopped her lips with her napkin.

"The villagers didn't understand your father's trouble," Annie spoke slowly, choosing her words. "Some were to say the devil had taken a person, if they were to watch or hear tell of a convulsion. It was best kept out of sight. Your Aunt Margaret and Uncle Adam couldn't be trusted to keep their tongues. Aunt Agnes was a blessing."

"But you had a doctor?"

"Aye. Doctors take an oath of secrecy. With good reason given the spite the ignorant of the village speak."

"Your priest?"

"Some priests would agree it was the devil's work. It strengthened their position."

"What caused his death? You've never told me."

"Because I don't know. To be sure, it wasn't the devil."

"Convulsions?"

"In the last. Long before, he oft had a bad head, his eyes went poorly and on a turn he couldn't find his words or ken his place. Some days, he was perfectly himself. Doctor thought it something he ate, but we couldn't see sense in it. It was not akin to the thing they call 'brain apoplexy' today, that leaves an old man disfigured on one side of the face, with no strength of muscle and brainless in manner. Your father was young, and he was strong before the fits wore him down. He was the same as William, in the end. He knew he couldn't win, and he wanted the fight done with."

"You were with him?"

"Aye."

"Where were we?"

"I sent ye into Aunt Margaret's care, in the last days."

"You knew it was nigh?"

"Aye."

They were silent for a time, both studying the moon. Eventually Jeannie moved to pick up the tray and Annie stayed her arm.

"It pains me deeply to see you treading this path, lass."

Jeannie nodded, mute in acknowledgement of her mother's rare admission. She took the tray away, leaving Annie settled in the chair, watching the night.

~

Annie, due to her habit of reading through an hour of midnight wakefulness, was reliably a late-riser. Long before she appeared from her room the next morning, William had eaten his breakfast and, professing himself perfectly well, had left to open his surgery. Soon after he pedalled away on his bike, Ellen Findlay arrived on the doorstep, holding out a crate of produce and asking after William's health.

Jeannie walked back with Ellen to the wagon where Gilbert was sitting, reins slack over one knee and a foot on the seat. He tipped his hat to her.

"William is well, Gilbert," Jeannie looked up at him, shading her eyes against the bright sun.

"Glad to hear," he said awkwardly.

"Thank-you, for what you did."

Gilbert grunted. "Gave me a fright."

"It was an asthma attack, Gilbert. A bad one because he couldn't sniff his balsam."

"Aye."

"We'd like you not to speak of it," Jeannie looked between Gilbert and Ellen. "It doesn't look well with patients if the doctor is ill. I hope you understand."

Gilbert nodded and Ellen squeezed Jeannie's arm in reassurance before climbing up onto the seat beside her husband.

"And Gilbert, William shouldn't do hard physical work, like digging the manure. It starts the asthma, but he's too proud to tell you. Can you stop him if he tries it again? He won't listen to me."

"Aye, he's to stay with his doctoring and employ a man for digging."

"That's right."

"Jeannie," Gilbert's lips curved into a sly smile as he gathered up the reins. "Did you break his ribs?"

"No, but he *is* a wee bit sore this morning," she grinned.

"You've got a braw punch in that skinny frame." With this Gilbert angled a provocative elbow into the abundant flesh that lay around his wife's ribs and Ellen slapped his shoulder in return. "I've a job for you, shoving our cows into bale."

Jeannie laughed. "Get away with you, Gilbert."

Gilbert tipped his hat again and slapped the reins against the horse's back.

Had she been on her own, Jeannie could have caught a lift into town with Gilbert and Ellen, but as it was, she waited for her mother and together they walked the distance to Shillidays, each deploying a parasol as a shield against the blistering sun. Annie eagerly availed herself of a glass of water from the jug Mary Shilliday kept on the counter.

"Where do you buy ice?" Annie asked between sips, judging the water insufficiently refreshing.

"There's an ice-maker at the engineering works, by the river," Mary replied cheerfully as she examined Jeannie's shopping list. "Mostly there's enough for the town, but with Christmas and all, they're hard put. We have to save the ice for the ice-box." She looked at Jeannie and pointed to an item on the list. "We don't have any browning, Jeannie, but you can make it yourself. Chopped onion fried a dark, dark brown in butter in the pan before making the sauce. You can strain the onion out later."

"Pity there's no red wine to help the colour," Annie observed.

"Oh," Mary looked around the store and lowered her voice, "we sell wine to our preferred customers for use at home. I'll add a pot to the basket, Jeannie. I just ask that you bring the empty pot back."

Jeannie shook her head, "No, I don't ..."

"Please add a pot," Annie overruled.

Mary nodded and picked up Jeannie's basket, moving along the shelves behind the counter to select the various items that were on the list. She went through a door at the back of the store and returned shortly with the contents of the basket covered with a tea-towel.

"I'm so glad you don't trouble me for credit, Jeannie," Mary confided as Jeannie opened her purse. "Mrs Wallis asked me this morning. Can you believe it? A proud English woman like herself? Their apricots didn't get the asking price in Melbourne, and now she wants me to wait till their oranges are bought. What could I say? You've heard how particular John is."

Jeannie counted out silver coins and Mary handed back pennies.

As they left the shop Annie muttered, "Don't tell that one your secrets."

"She's a shopkeeper, Ma. It's her way of letting us all know the shame that follows if we dare ask. As I recall, in Edinburgh you had similar means of ensuring the parents of our boarders paid their rent."

Annie hummed. "Who else are you calling on?"

Dr Abramowski's chemist shop was on the corner of Langtree Avenue and 9th Street, two blocks from Shillidays. A bay window occupied two thirds of the veranda, leaving a narrow step in front of the door.

As Jeannie entered the shop and rang the bell on the counter, Annie inspected the window display. "Olive oil," she called out approvingly, reading the label on a green bottle, "from local trees?"

"Dr Abramowski planted olive trees and built a factory to press the oil," Jeannie confirmed.

Annie picked up a black wooden box and sniffed at it, unconvinced by the label. "He sells tar for foot rot?"

"He's the town veterinary," Jeannie whispered.

"Insecticides?" Annie picked a sachet of powder from a box on which was drawn the outlines of a rat, a cockroach and a spider.

"Pest exterminator," Jeannie smiled.

"Seeds!" These interested Annie more. She rifled through the box, holding the small packets at arm's length to interpret the writing that was scrawled on them. "Asparagus!" she said enthusiastically, holding a packet towards Jeannie.

"We don't need them in our garden, Ma. Dr Abramowski has sown them for free-picking along several irrigation channels."

Annie looked impressed and returned the packet to its box.

A woman Jeannie did not know, emerged from the surgery behind the shop, closely followed by Otto Abramowski who was carrying a pestle in one hand and a spoon in the other.

"Mrs Cameron. I will help in a moment." Abramowski cast a curious glance at Annie before turning his attention to a drawer behind the counter from which he extracted a small jar. He spooned the dark cream from his pestle into the jar, covered it with a lid and handed it to his customer. The woman gave him a slight curtsey and hurried from the shop.

"You are together?" Abramowski inquired.

"Aye, Dr Abramowski, this is my mother, Mrs Irvine Robertson."

Abramowski bowed respectfully.

"You are come from Melbourne then. How is your travel?"

"Very long," Annie replied. "You are Prussian?"

"I am. I remember your daughter to say you studied in my country."

"In Germany."

"Ah. I think now we are the one country, with the one King."

Abramowski appeared cheerfully ready to hold a skirmish with Annie on matters of history, but another customer entered his shop, necessitating efficiency.

"Mrs Cameron?" he inquired.

"Do you carry balsam, Doctor?"

"Of course." He turned and walked the breadth of this shop, holding a finger up to an array of small bottles on a high, narrow shelf. His finger stopped and snatched at a dark brown bottle, not unlike the supply William had brought with him from Melbourne.

"Do you mind?" she asked politely, her fingers encircling the bottle-top. He inclined his head in consent. She sniffed the vapour and drew back, blinking hard.

"Your husband knows how to take it?" When Jeannie looked surprised Abramowski continued. "I hear the wheeze of his speech."

"Do you sell paint pigments, Dr Abramowski?" Annie interrupted loudly from across the shop.

"If it be ground from nut, seed or stone, then I can make to your request. What colour do you seek?"

"Did you know my daughter is an artist?"

"No," Dr Abramowski looked at Jeannie with admiration. She felt heat rising in her cheeks, and looked down to her purse.

"The price?" she inquired.

"She has brought her needs with her," Annie continued, "but it's good to know you can keep her supplied."

"A shilling, Mrs Cameron."

Jeannie handed over the coin and ushered her mother towards the door.

"You're an endless embarrassment to me, Ma. I don't know why I thought to ask you to come today," Jeannie burst out irritably as they walked away from the shop.

"You've done no painting since you left the city," Annie accused.

"I've had much else to do."

"I know you don't think yourself an artist, but you do fine work and I want you to have the pigments to hand. You've not the idea, lass. I didn't paint for the money alone. It's been a great comfort to me, all the years."

Jeannie made no reply. Annie judged her case won and switched the subject.

"Does William not have balsam at his surgery?"

"This is for my purse," Jeannie replied tersely.

"In case he drops his again?"

"Aye."

"I won't mention then, that I met the very versatile Dr Abramowski today?"

Jeannie hummed.

~

The next morning William and Annie were reading papers, ignoring each other when William called out. "Jeannie! You wouldn't credit this!"

She came to the door, dusting cloth in hand.

"Abramowski. He's been elected to a committee to design a replacement scheme for the Irrigation Company!" William consulted the paper again. "With Risby!"

"He might have some ideas," Jeannie ventured.

"What about the hospital? Can the man not concentrate on one thing at a time? We have no funds to run the hospital and he's dilly-dallying with the Irrigation Company!"

"Perhaps if the Irrigation Company is set to rights there *would* be money for the hospital," Annie suggested demurely.

"Pff!" William dismissed her argument. "Let Chaffeys get on with their work and put this Risby nonsense aside."

"I heard Abramowski served on the Progress Committee," Jeannie continued. "He saw to it that the new wharf was built."

"That's exactly my meaning. He has his oar in everything. The chair of the board of the hospital should have the *hospital* as his priority."

Jeannie had no rejoinder. She looked nervously at her mother.

"It's a very handsome wharf," Annie said thoughtfully. "This apothecary sounds like an interesting man. Is there any chance he will be dining with us at Rio Vista tonight?"

~

"Dinner is half an hour away," W.B. told them, at the front door. "Would you like a tour of the house?"

Annie was quick to agree.

As they followed him through the hall and up the stairs, W.B. cheerfully detailed the construction of the building. The floor of the expansive entrance was inlaid with Italian tiles of multiple colours and various patterns. The wallpaper was the best English Lincrusta embossed with a pattern of soft green, brown and beige hue, and the walls were lined to the height of Jeannie's hip with wainscotting carved from a lustrous, russet-brown wood W.B. called 'Westralian kauri'. The elaborately carved ceiling panels were of Murray pine; the floor boards on the stairs were of Westralian jarrah and the solid handrail was a lovely, long piece of blackwood. The fireplace mantles were of dark Italian marble and in every room, there were pieces of furniture that William and Jeannie silently pointed out to each other, unable to resist a brief touch to feel the warmth and texture of the wood. William's eyes lingered long over the very handsome desk in W.B.'s office. Jeannie looked closely at the furnishings in the nursery and was embarrassed to find Hattie Chaffey watching her from the doorway after the others had moved on to the next room.

"You will have more children?" Jeannie said gently, half compassion, half question.

"We mean to," Hattie replied with a wan smile. "Yourself?"

Jeannie nodded.

"Then our children will grow up together." Hattie's smile warmed and she held her elbow out to Jeannie. "Let's keep up."

George Chaffey and his wife, Annette, were W.B.'s dinner guests, and also Mr Staughton, the recent tenant of William and Jeannie's house, who had, W.B. declared as entrées were laid on the table, expressly asked to meet the 'renowned' Mrs Irvine Robertson. Mr Staughton explained that his wife had, years ago, taken an art class in Melbourne with Annie, and that revelation led to a debate between Mr Staughton and W.B., ably moderated by Annie, in which were contended the names of the worthiest, collectible Australian artists.

William and George fell deeply into a discussion about electricity while Jeannie, who had been intentionally seated between Hattie and Annette, found herself the subject of interrogation as to her experiences with St John's Ambulance. There was a desperate need, the two women asserted.

"Bella Leslie—drowned."

"The Roberts boy—snake bite."

"Young Oswald—burnt in the fire."

"Mary Shilliday speaks highly of your experience."

Mary Shilliday knew not the first thing, Jeannie mused, about her 'experience'. Nonetheless, she had already decided to conduct first-aid classes. It was only her modesty that kept her quiet while Annette and Hattie persuaded her.

"I'm not in Mildura often, Jeannie, but you may use my name as patroness. I will ensure George makes funds available," Annette offered.

"I would like to be in your first class," Hattie said.

"That gets us off to a very good start." Jeannie finally gave her agreement. "I will have to apply to St John's in Melbourne to open a branch here."

"Excellent!" Annette and Hattie spoke as one and raised their wine glasses. "To Mildura's branch of St John's Ambulance!"

Jeannie looked at her own wine glass reluctantly, before taking a small sip in solidarity.

After dinner the group adjourned to the lounge on W.B.'s insistence that he would like to hear the ladies play piano. This was a flattery, Jeannie realised, to Hattie who showed herself to be very talented. Annette was not Hattie's equal, but she was competent. Jeannie tried to decline on the basis that it had been so long since she had lived with a piano in the house, but W.B. insisted, teasingly, upon her contribution. She played an easy piece, and infuriated herself with two nervous mistakes.

Annie, as Jeannie expected, relied on her seniority and responded to the invitation to play with a dismissive wave of her hand. She then indicated that W.B. could include her as he offered a tumbler of whisky to Mr Staughton. W.B. chuckled appreciatively, passed over the glass he had in hand and poured another for the older man.

"Not for you, Jeannie?" W.B. checked with a smile.

Jeannie shook her head.

William and Annie were both in good humour in the cab on the way home. Miraculously, they were in agreement on all topics. Electricity was a great boon to civilisation, and the effort should be made to ensure every shop and every home in Mildura was supplied as soon as possible. Annie pondered the expense of transition, but William convinced her that existing kerosene light fittings could be readily adapted to hold incandescent light bulbs and, in the longer term, the supply of electricity would be cheaper than importing kerosene. There would one day be a telegraph line into every house, William added, and a handset like the one they had seen in W.B.'s office, to receive voice calls. They debated the location of the handset and agreed on placing it in the hallway, near the front door, where a conversation could be carried on privately.

Half asleep, against William's shoulder, Jeannie imagined herself standing in the hallway, with a telegraph line connection to the St John's office in Melbourne. She could make arrangements immediately, to set up a Mildura branch. What a different world that would be.

As it was, it took almost four months for final approval to be granted. Head office replied, at the end of February, with questions and requirements. Jeannie could act as secretary, but the president must be a man. Mary Shilliday introduced her to the most likely candidate. Mr Blackmore was reticent but, on the basis that all he had to do was chair the annual general meeting, he agreed. Jeannie sent a letter confirming arrangements and when, a month later, she had received no reply she sent a third letter repeating every detail given in the previous two. A fortnight later she received an apology, there had been a change of secretary, her earlier correspondence had been lost. Early in May 1893 she received a letter telling her she could go ahead. A registry book, three rule books, information pamphlets, printed certificates and a stamp made up in the name of the Mildura Branch would follow in a separate parcel.

By then, much had changed.

~

Annie left Mildura on 26th January, fortunate to have passage on the last upstream riverboat of the season. The Murray was so low that travellers had to catch *The Nellie*, as far as the ingloriously named 'Bitch and Pups' sand bar, before transferring to *The Ruby* to voyage onwards to Swan Hill. There were, it was said, several boats linked to barges stacked with fruit crates, stranded on the sand bar. *The Nellie* would tow the barges back to Mildura's wharf, where the crates would join the hundreds of fruit boxes that were stacked there, waiting for alternative transport. The paddle steamers themselves would stay put, wedged in the mud till the river rose again, late in autumn.

Every dray was booked, carting Mildura's abundant harvest to Swan Hill by road, but the fruit arrived bruised and unmarketable.

The carpenters at the packing shed made drying racks and, instead of packing, the packers halved and pipped the stone fruit before laying it out to dry.

The Shillidays wrangled over cash payments towards a large back-log of orders for preserving jars, muslin and sugar.

The Mildura Fruit Preserving Company operated day and night, and Jeannie found herself endlessly dusting.

It had been sad, but a wonderful relief to see her mother go. Even as *The Nellie* steamed out of sight around the river bend, William caught Jeannie tightly around the waist, and bit her teasingly on the bare curve of flesh between her neck and shoulder.

"Hurrah," he whispered, and she was glad for him.

~

The 25th of January was a crucial day in William's annual calendar. In an unthinkable departure from tradition, he had deferred his celebration of 'Burns Night' by 24 hours. After seeing *The Nellie* off, they hurried home to prepare for a party with the Findlays.

"We've named our house," Jeannie announced on Ellen and Gilbert's arrival, pointing to the new sign she had hung at the front door.

"The Nest," Ellen read. "That's lovely, did you paint it?"

Jeannie nodded. Beneath the words on the wooden plaque, she had drawn a shallow basin of twigs intertwined with flowers, a delicate blue wren on one side and a robin red-breast on the other.

"I have the Cullen Skink," Ellen lifted the tea-towel to reveal the cast iron pot and a knob of crusty bread in her basket. "It's warm."

"It can go on the stove for five minutes before we serve." Jeannie led the way to the kitchen. Hearing William laugh, she looked over her shoulder to see Gilbert carrying a bottle of whisky as the two men walked into the living room.

Murray cod, all around the dining table agreed, was a meaty, useful fish, but it did not have the pungent flavour of the smoked North Sea haddock that was the true basis of Cullen Skink. Nevertheless, the soup was delicious. Ellen had mashed her potatoes with cream, butter and sauteed onion before adding them to the fish, which made for a much smoother chowder than the chunky-potato recipe William and Jeannie both knew.

The Murray cod was caught, Gilbert told them, by boys from New South Wales who fished the river below Wentworth. It was possible to place an order with the entrepreneurial lads through a woodsman who regularly came upriver to Risby's mill. Apart from specifying the approximate size of the fish, a buyer could ask for a supply of 'sauce'. The quality of the 'sauce', Gilbert laughed, was a matter of chance, but for today's consumption he was delighted to have received a Glenfiddich single malt.

William and Gilbert wasted no time sampling the whisky before the meal, and William was in good form when Jeannie placed the haggis and a carving knife in front of him on a large, wooden board. William stood, rapped the handle of the knife on the table demanding silence, then burst into a full-throated rendition of Robbie Burns' *Address to the Haggis*.

Jeannie marvelled at the strength William found in his voice and the drama he affected in his mannerisms, but she barely understood a word of the poem. Her family had been closer to the traditions of Northumberland than those of the Scottish Highlands. She remembered her mother refusing to eat haggis, declaring that it was a food endured by impoverished highland clans who 'couldn't afford a decent cut of lamb'. Jeannie had been dismayed by the ingredients William had instructed her to buy, and affronted by the aroma in her kitchen as the haggis cooked. She was even less impressed when, during the course of the recital, William stabbed the tight skin of the haggis, slit it lengthways and flicked some of the sloppy, gritty contents over the table cloth.

Gilbert and Ellen, however, roared with delight and applauded roundly at the end of the poem.

"*Slàinte mhath*," Gilbert offered the Gaelic toast, pronouncing it as 'Slanj-a-va'.

"*Slàinte mhath!*" William roared back at him, and they downed their next tot of whisky.

Jeannie picked lightly at the haggis William doled onto her plate, and filled up instead with servings of neeps and tatties.

Inspired by the haggis, Gilbert and Ellen talked of Robbie Burns' nights past, of family and friends they had left behind, and of wild places in the highlands that William had visited, but Jeannie expected she would never see. Ellen confessed that she had not set foot in the part of Scotland that was south of Edinburgh, and she listened attentively to Jeannie's description of the Cheviot Hills, the colourful wildflowers and the woolly-white sheep that dotted the fertile green fields near the Tweed. The evening was spent in nostalgia; Gilbert and Jeannie were both, at different times and with differing sentiments, moved to tears.

"Your oatmeal shortbread is perfect," William told Jeannie, taking the remaining piece from a plate that had been cleared away to the kitchen sideboard.

Ellen had helped her wash all the dishes and pans, and the kitchen was tidy except for the last side plates and whisky tumblers she had brought back from the drawing room after Gilbert and Ellen had left. Jeannie plugged the sink and lifted the kettle from the stove, but William reached around her back, catching her arm and making her set the kettle down.

"Leave it," he said, gathering her to his chest and stepping her backwards, out of the kitchen as he kissed her.

He was clumsy, stepping on her feet, so she paused him momentarily and kicked off her shoes before eagerly resuming their embraced two-step to the bedroom.

Whether it was the whisky or his relief that her mother had finally gone, Jeannie did not care. What mattered most was that he took her at her word and made love to her without reservation.

~

For a fortnight she was thrillingly confident, and then came disappointment. It turned out she had told William the truth after all. Returning from the outhouse, she went to her bedroom and selected one of the thickly folded, narrow rectangles of cotton she kept on the right-hand side of the top drawer of her cedar chest. She pulled out a pair of bloomers and placed the pad of cotton on the gusset, securing it beneath the thin bands of satin that were sewn there. She replaced her soiled underpants with the padded bloomers and went to the scullery. Her tears drizzled miserably into the wash tub as she scrubbed the underpants with a bar of soap and cold water.

The near miss did, however, secure in William's mind a different idea of her monthly cycle and she took care—even though it meant working in the garden while her stomach ached—to keep up appearances.

In the meantime, Jeannie used the excuse of impending first-aid classes to make contact with Mrs Mitchell, an English woman who served the settlement as a midwife. Apart from persuading Mrs Mitchell to make herself available for a lecture on the topic of home births, she teased from the woman's extensive knowledge all she could learn about how to become pregnant, avoid a miscarriage and grow a healthy baby. When William frowned at the leafy green vegetables on his plate, she told him she was looking after his health and insisted he adapt his diet. If he noticed the increase in her consumption of milk and cheese, he did not comment, and as for the fruit juices that largely replaced tea-drinking—she could not give up her first and last cups of the day—not only was a cool drink more refreshing, but she was obliged, she told him, to use the cases of fruit that were presented to her in lieu of payment of surgery accounts.

Immediately after Annie's departure, William relocated his practice from Riverbank to the rooms Annie had occupied on the southern side of The Nest. The new surgery was not busy but the problem was not, William assured Jeannie, their location on San Mateo Avenue. Many people stayed away, nursing their injuries and illnesses, risking a prolonged and imperfect recovery, rather than face the embarrassment of being unable to pay the doctor. Others had learnt that William would not refuse them help, and took advantage. It had been William's intention to build his patient register by allowing credit, but it had become a position that was impossible to reverse.

Fortunately, Jeannie had heavy work to be done building her garden, and William was not the man to do it. She found a steady stream of work for those who owed money, to the extent that she wondered if there weren't pretenders who came to the surgery with obscure stomach complaints in order to be added to her list of workmen.

Jeannie was proud of her house-keeping. She successfully bartered most of her needs and kept tight watch over her expenditure. When she expressed her concern about the parlous state of the settlers, and its possible effect on themselves, William dismissed her airily. He had ample funds, he boasted, to withstand what would be only a temporary shortfall.

Through to the end of March the river remained unnavigable, and the weather exceedingly hot and interminably dry. Losses of water through seepage and evaporation were frightening in the face of what had been declared a drought in Victoria. Could the level of the Murray fall below the irrigation water intakes? The debate over how to effectively run the Irrigation Company raged on, with the pumps frequently held hostage.

The dry weather suited William. Dust and strenuous exercise were the enemy, and he had learnt to avoid both. Jeannie sewed a supply of cotton scarves he could easily pull up over his nose if he found himself in a willy-willy or a dust storm; events that had become more frequent as the drought persisted. She dusted with a wet cloth; the house and the surgery, morning, noon and night. The little bottle of balsam in her purse remained unused. She noticed, happily, that William was becoming more optimistic.

In March he was so impressed by a demonstration of Edison's latest phonograph at the Institute Hall, that he persuaded Timothy Campbell to bring his violin to the Hall for a personal trial of 'this amazing electrical machine'. As Timothy played, William bent closely over the machine, watching the sharp needle vibrating against the revolving wax drum, carving music that could be replayed by simply turning the drum back to the starting point and letting it roll forward again. With this device, he assured Timothy, the musical performances of the Harmonic Society could be recorded and played back, time and time again. Timothy, while admitting that the technology was astonishing, was unimpressed by the sound quality and saw no reason to become part of the consortium William proposed to buy one of the expensive devices. "Speeches maybe, but not music," Timothy said firmly

William was disappointed, but his enthusiasm was not dimmed. Sound quality would surely improve with the next model.

"One day," he told Jeannie, "we will have an electric phonograph. On a stand in our living room. We will relax in our armchairs and listen to music recorded by the finest orchestras in Edinburgh."

Whether or not his trust in Edison's invention was warranted, Jeannie did not care. What mattered to her, was that he was projecting the 'we will' of their lives so far into the future.

There was no phonograph playing at the fete held in the gardens of Rio Vista on the evening of 2nd April, Easter Sunday. The Mildura Brass Band, Jeannie had agreed with Hattie Chaffey, was a better source of musical entertainment. In the early evening the band played on the central grass lawns in front of the fountain, with fundraising stalls arranged inside the semicircle of the drive. The lawn was damp underfoot, clouds were threatening overhead, and the mood was celebratory. The drought was over, the river would soon be open, the price of stock feed would normalise and seasonal planting would get underway. The crowd and the stall-holders were generous in their contributions towards the hospital fund. Jeannie sold the 100 velvet bookmarks on which she had hand painted various orchard fruits, within the first hour of the fete, and wished she had made more.

While Jeannie was selling her bookmarks, William disappeared with W.B. and by the time he returned to her, the clouds had broken and the setting sun was bright on the horizon, its rays colouring the underside of the clouds with spectacular streaks of pink, gold and crimson. W.B. had led a number of gents on a tour of the stables and, by the smell of William's breath, Jeannie understood that the tour had included a sampling of W.B.'s wines.

The band moved to the tennis court, where the cleanly-swept surface served as a useful dance floor for the ticketed guests. William was a willing partner and together he and Jeannie enjoyed an exhilarating evening of dance. As they walked away from the tennis court, across the lawns towards the gate, Jeannie pulled William to a stop and swung him to look towards the house, which was wreathed with multi-coloured lights and Chinese lanterns.

"Isn't it lovely, Willie?"

William stood with her, admiring the reflection of the lights in the splashing water of the fountain.

Jeannie dipped her hand into the pond and spooned a shower of water across one of the light beams. She watched the droplets separate and sparkle.

William cupped water into his hand and drained it down her back, inside her dress.

"Arghh!" Jeannie shook her wet collar away from her neck. "You've wet my dress!"

"Come home now, and I'll take it off you," he whispered promisingly.

Later, while Jeannie was curled silent and content inside his arms, remembering every detail of her baby cousin, Ada Mina Calder—the tiny toes, the curling fingers, the pudgy bulges of arms and legs—William enthused about W.B.'s wine cellar.

"One day," he assured her, "Mildura will be a great wine producing region. We'll export wine to Europe. Even the French will buy our wine."

Jeannie's thinking graduated from Ada Mina to little Kathleen Calder; the milky-baby smell of her.

"We should turn two acres over to grapes. The peaches aren't yielding. Blockers are pulling them up. Planting grapes instead."

Jeannie wondered if Lily's younger child, Lilian Anne, might look very similar to Bessie Shilliday.

"I like W.B.," William announced after some quiet deliberation. "He's a good man. He wants the best for Mildura. He's not a 'Yankee swindler'. He's going to get us through this."

"Through what?" Jeannie murmured sleepily into his chest.

"The depression. The rain's here now. Planting will go ahead. By next harvest ... a train line. More settlers will come."

"Hattie enjoyed today," Jeannie thought to tell William. "She says we can hold another fete in spring. Will that fix the hospital funding?"

William laughed at her hopeful suggestion.

"A few accounts. Not wages."

"Oh," Jeannie was partly crestfallen, mostly asleep.

"Never mind," he gave her a comforting squeeze. "Won't be long now. We've enough in the bank."

~

When *The Mildura Cultivator* reported on 8th April 1893 that the Commercial Bank in Melbourne had closed its doors, William explained to Jeannie that the bank was 'restructuring'. He read to her the paragraph that said 'no depositor would cease to get interest for a single day'.

A week later the paper reported that the E.S. and A.C. bank had also closed its doors, 'owing to the steady withdrawal of deposits'.

"'No alarm is felt in Melbourne'," William read aloud, "'at the suspension of the two banks, as it is simply looked upon as a stoppage to enable these institutes to reopen with such constitutions that they will be practically impregnable, and for the future beyond all danger of a run by depositors.'"

On 29th April, *The Cultivator* reported that the London Chartered Bank of Australia had suspended payments to prevent the 'exhaustion of coin in the colony to the detriment of British depositors.' Apparently, William chuckled, some locals had taken their money across the road to the Post Office Bank, and the same day the postmaster brought it back to deposit again with The National, the only bank left in Mildura. There was a postscript to the article, promising that 'the position of the bank's account is most satisfactory.'

On the morning of Monday 1st May, Mildura's National Bank placed a notice of temporary suspension of payments on its closed door. The manager, Mr Kelly, said he was unable to give the town any information. Mary Shilliday animatedly told Jeannie the bank had closed because depositors had withdrawn all the money. What cash there was in the town was now hidden in kitchen cans on high shelves, seed envelopes in garden sheds, and sleeves of cotton sewn inside mattresses.

When Jeannie anxiously reported this to William, he beckoned her into his surgery and picked a long, polished box off a shelf. He opened the hinged lid, revealing a glistening set of glass test tubes. With a fingernail, he levered the thin board to which the tubes were fastened out of the box, and showed her a wad of one, two and five-pound notes.

"We'll be alright," he said with a self-confident smile. "This banking trouble will be sorted out soon."

Mary Shilliday was less confident about the settlement's future. One good thing, she told Jeannie, was that while Shillidays was in a strong position thanks to her husband's firm policy regarding cash payment, their competition was shrinking. Two stores had closed their doors permanently in the last week, and John had been able to pick up their leftover stock at remarkably cheap prices. There was some cloth of just the sort Jeannie might like to buy.

What particularly worried her, Mary continued after Jeannie politely declined, was the Chinese hawkers who were increasingly deserting the bigger, depressed cities of Bendigo, Ballarat and Castlemaine, and were bringing their many vices with them into outlying towns.

"They are a *most* undesirable class, Jeannie," Mary insisted as she packed groceries into Jeannie's basket. "And not only because they're selling poor quality fruit and vegetables. They've brought their game of Fantan, and are enticing gambling and opium amongst the working men. There is consumption of spirits of all sorts in their sly grog shops. As if those men can afford that behaviour, when they can't even put food on the table for their children! Sergeant Carter has laid forty charges—*forty*! It's a shocking influence on the town. Many think it better if the working men have a legitimate club to drink in. It would prevent their fall into such bad ways."

"The temperance colony isn't working very well, is it," Jeannie concurred as Mary checked the shopping list one last time.

"To be sure, it is not. What about poor Helena Roach? She was tricked into selling beer to that excise detective *twice* and now they've put her in gaol for *eight* months—*with hard labour*—because she can't pay the fine."

Jeannie murmured reassurance. "They wouldn't do that to you, Mary."

"They would not dare!" Mary snorted, "Imagine how many names I could mention! Think how many would go thirsty! On that subject—anything else for you?"

Jeannie laughed and shook her head.

"Oh Jeannie, I almost forgot!" Jeannie turned back at the door to see Mary rummaging under some papers on her counter. "Two more ladies signing up for first-aid classes."

Jeannie took the piece of paper Mary offered her. "That makes 15. We need 5 more."

"An advertisement in *The Cultivator*? No … ask Mr McKay to mention it in the Local News section. He won't charge for that."

"Thank-you Mary," Jeannie said brightly, "I'll do that."

Saturday 27th May 1893

Jeannie leaned over William at the breakfast table and asked him to turn to the local news. She scanned the item and read out the paragraph the editor had inserted for her.

> *"'Mrs. Cameron, wife of Dr. Cameron, is interesting herself in the formation of a sub-centre of the St. John Ambulance Association. Fifteen ladies have already promised to take an interest in the commendable movement, and when five more signify their willingness to identify themselves with the proposed organisation, twenty being the minimum number, the series of lectures will be commenced.'"*

"That should help," William commented.

"It sounds pompous," Jeannie complained, "I should have written it myself."

"The river is up three feet." William read on. "Open to Swan Hill next month."

"Dr Hill has been appointed a Justice of the Peace?" Jeannie summarised the next paragraph.

"Aye," William confirmed. "I was thinking," he put down the paper, "I might offer myself as a J.P. next year."

Jeannie looked at him with surprised approval. "You would be well suited."

"Aye," he ruminated, "I think so."

He was, she thought, in a most positive, forward-thinking mood.

"William ..."

Her voice stalled. He looked at her expectantly.

"If we start classes in July, we'll finish before the end of September."

"Time to run another group before Christmas?"

"No. I have ... plans."

William interleaved his fingers on top of the paper and waited for an explanation. The anxiety that had been building in her for weeks came to a peak.

"Don't be angry with me," she procrastinated.

"You want to go to Melbourne?" he suggested.

"I'm pregnant."

William stared at her, beyond words. She reached across the table and prised his hands apart, clasping them with her own.

"Tell me you're happy."

He looked distinctly unhappy.

"This is the most life-affirming thing I can do, sweetheart. I *need* to do this," she pleaded.

William pulled her around the table to stand before him. He rested his hands on her waist and stared at her belly as if trying to see inside.

"How long?" he muttered.

"Two months."

"End of December," he calculated.

"Aye," she confirmed, directing his right hand to the top of her abdomen, where she was certain she could feel a slight bulge. "I'm so happy, Willie," she said softly. "Tell me you feel the same."

"I'm terrified," William replied.

"So am I, but tell me," Jeannie entreated.

William stood and pulled her into his arms. "I am also happy," he said, lowering his mouth to hers. She felt desperation in his kiss, and tears on his cheeks.

Chapter 12

William

Saturday 3rd June 1893

William was rugged up in woollen trousers, woollen jumper and knitted wool cap, wrapped in a blanket and enjoying his Saturday morning paper in the cold sunlight on the veranda when an open buggy approached at breakneck speed along 10th Street.

"Jeannie!" He disentangled himself from his rug.

By the time she arrived he had pulled on his boots and picked his hat and overcoat off the hall stand. The buggy came to a jolting stop at the gate and William made a salutary wave acknowledging the driver's shout.

He picked up his medical bag and kissed Jeannie on the cheek. "Sorry," he apologised, in respect of the lunch they had planned.

"Mr Oakley, sir. Real bad." The driver and the horse were both blowing hard as William climbed into the buggy.

"Vomiting blood, sir." The lad turned the horse in a tight semi-circle, slapped the reins, and sent the animal straight into a canter back the way they had come.

William pressed his hat to his head, held his bag against the footrest with one foot, and clutched the seat rail with one hand.

"Blood, not food?" William shouted above the clatter of the fast-moving cart.

"Blood. Gobs of it, bright red and frothy."

William asked no more questions. He wanted the lad to concentrate on his driving. Mrs Oakley, a passably attractive young woman as he recalled, had been in the surgery recently for confirmation of her first pregnancy. She had come to Mildura two years ago in the domestic service of one of the wealthier settlers and had married nine months ago. She had described her husband as a blocker, in fine health.

As the buggy stopped, the Oakley's house seemed peaceful. Then William's ears caught a soft, keening wail coming from the side-veranda and he strode towards the sound.

Mrs Oakley was sitting cross-legged on the decking, holding her husband's head, rocking and crying. The dead man's eyes bulged open. His face was puffed and blue from asphyxiation, blood congealing around his mouth and nose. The veranda was splattered with drying blood, as was Mrs Oakley's apron and the sleeves of her beige cardigan.

William grabbed at the veranda post, suddenly nauseated and faint. He sat down, dumping his bag on the ground beside his feet. The driver of the buggy stood beside him, watching in horrified silence.

"Are there any relatives here?" William found his voice.

"She's out from England. No one, as I know it."

William thought. "Do they know the Findlays?"

"We all know the Findlays, sir."

"Fetch Ellen Findlay and come straight back with her please. I also need Gilbert or another strong man from the farm to bring their dray. We must take Mr Oakley's body to the hospital."

The lad was clearly relieved to be given a task. He rushed back to the buggy.

William rubbed Mrs Oakley's back with a light, circular motion until her sobs eased.

"Was he consumptive?"

Mrs Oakley nodded and drew a deep, shuddering breath.

"I prayed," she sobbed.

William rubbed her back firmly and sat with her in silent sympathy.

~

At the hospital late that afternoon, in the room used for autopsies, William stood in a full-length white cotton gown, cloth mask covering his mouth and nose, and rubber gloves on his hands, scowling at Mr Oakley's ugly, scarred lungs. Extensive necrosis with severe cavitation in the apex of the left lung. The cavitation, he knew, increased the risk of the spread of infection. The semi-liquid necrotic material that gathered in the cavity would be discharged, during coughing fits, into the bronchial tree from whence it would seed infection in other parts of the lung leading to bronchopneumonia. It would mix into the sputum that surged into the throat. If swallowed it could lead to infection of the intestinal tract.

Mr Oakley had bled from a branch of the pulmonary artery, which confirmed to William that the cause of death was pulmonary tuberculosis. Not ulcerative bronchitis, where bleeding was from the bronchial system; not pneumonia, which involved veins rather than arteries.

Pulmonary tuberculosis. The disease *he* carried.

William pressed thin cross-sections from each quadrant of the revolting, damaged lungs into four glass slides. He spent several minutes examining the slides through a microscope.

Finished with the lungs, William made a slide with a drop of the bloodied sputum he had drawn from Mr Oakley's throat.

When he detected live tubercles, he drew back from the microscope in dismay.

Mr Oakley had been living in Mildura for three years.

Was nowhere safe?

William wrapped the lungs in muslin and packed them and the slides into a box alongside the ten test tubes he had filled with blood and sputum.

Then he stitched Mr Oakley back together, washed and dried him, and finally covered him head-to-toe with a crisply starched sheet. He spent an hour wiping down the autopsy room and all the equipment he had used with a powerful mix of carbolic acid and water. He discarded his gown, gloves, and mask in the infectious materials bin, and bathed himself in the surgeon's bathroom before dressing again.

The last light from the sun was a pale glow on the horizon as William stepped out of the hospital, box under his left arm and medical bag in his right hand. Instead of taking the direct route home, he headed along 13th Street into the gathering darkness, his mind churning.

Was it God's doing? This graphic vision of his future? Was it a portent? A warning? A wake-up call?

Of course not, the rational part of William's mind retorted, and it was insulting to the memory of the man, Mr Oakley, to think that his death was intended to serve such a purpose.

All the same, William was badly shaken. As he walked, he saw Mr Oakley's distended head, the ravaged lungs and the tubercles under the microscope. He contemplated Jeannie in her apron, blood on her hands, crying over his dead body. It was all too foreseeable. He didn't want Jeannie to suffer the way Mrs Oakley was suffering.

They too, had a baby to think of.

Something had to be done. William walked the block in dark contemplation.

It was late when he returned to The Nest. Jeannie brought his meal out of the oven, but he waved the plate away and went to his writing bureau where he kept a bottle of whisky and his favourite tumbler.

She sat with him by the fire while he sipped his drink, and asked him to share his thoughts with her.

"You know I can't say, darling. What news of Mrs Oakley?"

"She's spending the night at Craigieburn."

"Good. Send her an appointment card. She must come soon."

"She's pregnant, Willie. Their first bairn."

"I know."

"It's so sad," Jeannie took his spare hand in both of hers.

They both stared into the fire, neither wanting to take the subject further.

~

William was surprised by how cold Mildura became, as winter crept into the settlement. The days were fine, but the sun had little power to warm him after nights where the temperature fell below zero. Many were the mornings when frost coated the ground in a sparkling, brittle white. It felt cold enough to snow, but there was no moisture in the air. It had never snowed in Mildura. The Aboriginals who had been here before the settlers came, didn't know what snow was—or so he had been told.

The raw, early morning air filled William's lungs with myriad icicle daggers. He kept his mouth and nose wrapped in a cashmere scarf, adding the warmth and humidity of the air he breathed out to the air he breathed in, while dangerously diluting his oxygen intake. He had no body-fat to insulate him. Jeannie did not feel the cold in nearly the same way. William knew that he was struggling due the deterioration of his body mass; the loss of his energy reserve.

Afternoons were better; the sun having gained supremacy over the frost. On his rounds, peddling his bike, William would be dressed-down to his shirt sleeves; his coat, scarf, and vest rolled up in the basket hanging from the handlebars. On some longer rides between houses, he even worked-up a sweat. It felt good to warm up his body; to feel it working as it should. In the afternoons he could think himself well.

The Nest was cosy. To ensure he was warm enough, Jeannie kept both the kitchen stove and the living room fire burning day and night. She lit the surgery pot belly early on working mornings. Every week a man from the clearing camp arrived with a cart full of mallee wood—supplies of coal, it had turned out, were intermittent.

Jeannie also kept hot soup and a slow-cooking stew on the stove every day, ready to warm him from the inside. He had surprisingly little appetite, but he made himself eat six times a day. Hot, energy-rich food. Protein, carbohydrates, sugars. Apricots were best served cooked in a sweet roly-poly with plenty of cream. A mutton or brisket stew felt like Christmas, but it was rabbit, unfortunately, that was the staple fare.

Rabbits, skinned and gutted, were frequently offered in lieu of payment. To find live ones, William had to strike a contract with a rabbit catcher. Which was, of course, strictly illegal. The inspector with the Vermin Board, William was warned, was a perceptive man, not easily deceived.

Money, and assurances of secrecy, resolved William's problem. Over a fortnight he collected eight live rabbits, bringing them back to The Nest in a closed wooden box concealed under his overcoat in the basket on the front of his bike. One of Jeannie's workmen built a shed in a discrete section of the garden, and it was here that William housed his rabbits, two by two in large newspaper-lined slat boxes with a constant supply of water and raw vegetables. Following the peculiar law of rabbit-averages, three of the four boxes soon had babies. William kept his breeding pairs together, and separated their young.

Meanwhile, using samples originally drawn from Mr Oakley's lungs, William diligently cultivated tubercle bacilli in the surgery store room. This required much greater care and concentration than propagating rabbits. He used sterilized glycerol agar as the medium, seeded it with positive samples of sputum, and capped the glass test tubes with paraffin-soaked cotton. A major problem was maintaining the bacilli at incubation temperature—the very warm equivalent of the human body, 97 to 99 degrees Fahrenheit. For this he had no alternative but to place his box of test tubes discretely near to Jeannie's kitchen stove. It wasn't the perfect temperature, but it was the closest he could find.

As soon as he put the box down against the wall, to the left of the stove, he knew his wish for secrecy was hopeless. If Jeannie picked the box up (and she would find it, he knew), the first thing she would do would be to shake it (he would), and that would be the end of his cultures. He had to tell her not to touch the box.

"I'm growing culture samples in test tubes." He held the closed box forward for her inspection. "They must stay warm. You mustn't touch the box or a sample may touch the wax stopper and it will be contaminated. You mustn't even nudge it with the broom."

Jeannie looked suitably impressed by his tone. She watched as he set the box down on the floor with exaggerated care.

"What are you cultivating?" she asked the obvious question.

"Bacteria. My hobby. My research lab. Sorry it has to be in your kitchen."

She looked at the box quizzically, but seemed to accept his explanation.

The shed, of course, was in *her* garden and within fifteen minutes of the arrival of the first rabbit, Olga had raised the alarm. William was obliged to show Jeannie the new occupant.

"Live rabbits?" Jeannie was shocked.

"The shed will be locked. They won't get out."

"The pest inspector ..."

"Won't find them."

"What if someone tells him?"

"None will know."

"They'll make a noise. Olga knew."

"They'll be quiet, happy rabbits."

"Will I feed it?" She softened, peering between slats at the bundle of fur cowering in the far corner of its box.

"No, I'll do that."

"I can feed them from the garden."

"No, you'll grow fond of them."

She looked at him with cold suspicion. "What are you going to do to them?"

"*You* are to have *nothing* to do with the rabbits," he said emphatically, nudging her back through the door of the shed and locking it. "Wild rabbits carry viruses in their saliva that can be dangerous to the foetus. Don't touch them. Don't even enter the shed."

She stepped back, looking at the shed as if it contained the plague. Which, he thought with satisfaction, was the response he wanted.

That evening, when he was by the fireside under the kerosene lamp, scanning an old journal for research references, Jeannie settled herself in the armchair opposite him.

"William."

It didn't bode well that she had used his proper name. He looked at Olga as the dog padded into the room and faithfully laid her big paws and head across Jeannie's slippered feet.

"You are growing tubercle bacilli and you intend to experiment with it on the rabbits," she announced.

"Aye." There was no point denying her assessment.

"You could have told me that," she reproved him.

William hummed and looked back to his journal.

"What do you think you can achieve here that has not already been done better in a proper laboratory?"

"You're pregnant," he replied.

Her hands moved to her stomach. "I'm aware," she retorted. "I have to do *something*."

He said it with a desperate intent that surprised them both. Olga lifted her head and looked at him, then at Jeannie as if debating which of them she needed to comfort. She took the lazy option and dropped her head onto Jeannie's lap.

"You've been much the better, Willie ..." Her voice trailed off as she fondled Olga's ears.

This time William hummed because he didn't trust himself to speak. He had words he didn't want to send out into the world. Negativity that could not be allowed to escape lest it manifest itself. He was embarrassed by his near brush with emotion. He turned a page of the research journal and feigned concentration.

Olga kept one paw raised in indecision as she watched Jeannie leave the room. Was her mistress going to the kitchen? No. The dog padded across the hearth and sat next to William, inviting him with big, soulful eyes, to comfort his hand with her fur.

~

Since leaving Melbourne, William had maintained a regular correspondence with Dr Springthorpe. In return for providing the lung specialist with weekly data of the number and appearance of his sputum's tubercle bacilli per microscopic field, William received a summary of the most interesting, novel research ideas that had caught Dr Springthorpe's attention. By agreement, Dr Springthorpe sent him information specifically about anti-toxins. While the testing of animal serum was receiving intense attention from researchers, the development of a vaccine would be too late for those who. like William, already suffered from advanced pulmonary tuberculosis. As was the case with Tuberculin, it was apparent that vaccination with any sort of serum drawn from animals infected with tuberculosis could reactivate his existing bacilli. The answer for William was an anti-toxin.

The powerful antiseptic, creosote carbonate, was the latest subject of experimentation but it was said, Dr Springthorpe wrote in his letter dated June 7th, to have resulted in dreadful damage to body tissue. If ingested, there was unacceptable corrosion of the oesophagus and stomach lining—testing animals invariably died. Sub-cutaneous or intra-muscular injection was ineffective—the antiseptic was metabolised, injuriously, before it reached the site of the infection. Intravenous injection was the only hope of an antiseptic reaching the lungs, and there was some evidence that before that happened the body reacted to the poison in a manner that, while it did suppress, actually seemed to protect the bacilli. Upon halting the course of injections, the bacilli multiplied with frightening rapidity. There were some benefits from inhalation, in disinfection of sputum, but it could not be tolerated in sufficient strength to reach the lungs. It was a symptomatic aid, not a cure. Experiments were continuing with creosote derived from the wood tar of various trees, mixed with varying dilutions of distilled water, saline, mucilage, ether, and such, but Dr Springthorpe was not hopeful that any creosote-based anti-toxin would kill the tubercle bacilli without killing the host.

William was studying a slide of his sputum through the microscope, when the bell on the waiting room door jangled. He found Otto Abramowski at reception, passing his hat from hand-to-hand with the attitude of someone who did not intend to stay long.

"Dr Hill," Abramowski said abruptly.

"Has he turned for the worse?" William asked anxiously. There were cases of typhoid in the settlement and Dr Hill, the head surgeon at Mildura hospital, had the misfortune of treating the first case, before they knew precautions were necessary.

"No, but he takes leave. For recovery."

"Sensible." William nodded.

"I have taken his place."

William failed to keep his surprise from his face. Abramowski hurried into an explanation.

"The hospital has no money for a locum. I could not ask you."

"I would not have asked for money," William bristled.

"And your wife, she is pregnant. You cannot risk."

"I see." William was angry, even though he knew Abramowski had made the right decision..

"I have ordered much formalin." Abramowski continued. "It arrives in three days. You must disinfect between every patient. It is cheaper for you from my shipment."

"Are you advising me as Mildura's chemist or ordering me as the Public Health Officer?"

Abramowski grimaced. "I hardly need to order you ..."

"No, you don't," William snapped. "I always disinfect my surgery between patients."

"With formalin?"

"Carbolic."

"Formaldehyde is natural in the living cell. It converts to formic acid. Then carbon dioxide and water. Dissipation is quick. It is less harmful."

"Thank-you for the chemistry lesson," William growled.

Abramowski bowed slightly and turned for the door.

"What price for your formalin?" William called him back, on an afterthought.

Abramowski pulled a slip of paper from his pocket and laid it hopefully on the reception desk.

Formalin, William knew, was a 40% stabilised solution of formaldehyde and water. He made a quick, mental calculation. "I'll have a gallon."

"Cash?"

"Of course."

"I will have the flagon dropped here?" Abramowski indicated the surgery's 'welcome' door mat.

"Thank-you kindly."

As the door closed behind Abramowski, William drew the letter he had already composed to Dr Springthorpe out of his desk drawer. After re-reading the page, he added a tightly-scrawled postscript.

"What research using formaldehyde?"

That night, as he watched Jeannie serve his desert from an oven dish, he challenged her. "How is it that Abramowski knows you're pregnant?"

Jeannie looked at him, serving spoon mid-air. "Does he?"

"Aye."

She shrugged and returned her attention to the peach strudel, scraping the crusty side of the dish and shaking the proceeds from the spoon onto his plate.

"Are you taking a tonic from him?" William growled suspiciously.

"I haven't been in his shop for months."

"You won't take *any* concoction without me knowing it," he ordered.

"He doesn't make tonics for pregnancy. He recommends fresh fruit, fresh vegetables and fresh air. Everything to be as natural as possible."

"You did talk to him?"

"No. Mary Shilliday."

William was relieved. "When did you tell Mary Shilliday?"

Jeannie put his desert in front of him, laid her arms in a cross over his shoulders, and kissed him on the neck. "Yester morn. No, the morning before. None knew before you."

"You shouldn't be in such a hurry to tell. There's much can go wrong in the first months."

"I can't keep it in, sweetheart. I'm so happy, I had to tell. And *I* know a secret you will soon enough learn yourself."

William turned to look at her with a suspicious scowl.

"Mary is in the same condition."

~

Ten days later, William was obliged to call on Abramowski for surgical assistance at the hospital. Harper, a twenty-year old man from the clearing camp, had been brought to him with severe abdominal cramps, vomiting and diarrhoea. William could feel a swollen mass inside the lower, right quadrant of Harper's abdomen and diagnosed the life-threatening condition of acute appendicitis. William had performed the operation, recently named an 'appendectomy', on a cadaver in Edinburgh. He hadn't removed an infected appendix from a living person, but he was confident he had the skill required. He told the driver of the wagon to travel on to the hospital, with instructions for the matron: Harper was to be prepared for emergency surgery at 4pm, and could she kindly ask Dr Abramowski to attend.

Upon arrival at the hospital, having read an account of an appendectomy in the latest edition of the *British Medical Journal*, William felt well prepared. What he was not ready for, was Abramowski's contention that the operation should not be performed at all.

Abramowski wanted to put the boy on a juice fast for 7 to 14 days, and keep him under observation.

It was unacceptable. Harper had a dangerous fever. Infection was spreading from what was probably a perforated appendix, throughout his body. The man on whose cadaver William had performed his one appendectomy, had died from that infection. William had held the diseased organ in his hands. He *knew* the importance of quick surgical intervention.

Abramowski had performed abdominal surgery many times during the war in Prussia. He had removed a score of body parts and projectiles. His observation was that patients who had surgical interventions died more often than not, and he was convinced it was due to their 'internal impurity'. Abramowski worked hard, in his limited English, to make it clear to William that, in the case of abdominal or rectal surgery, the bowel of those who ate meat, was in a septic condition; it must be cleaned out by juice fasting *before* such an operation. It was entirely possible, Abramowski asserted, that a juice fast would relieve the man's symptoms and surgery would not be required at all. By permanently following a diet of fruit, vegetables, and nuts, the man would avoid any recurrence of his unfortunate condition.

William could not believe what he was hearing from the man who was standing in as head surgeon of the hospital. Did Abramowski not believe in *any* surgical intervention?

Yes, Abramowski conceded, sometimes surgery would be needed. If done when there *was* internal purity, there was no need for the commonly used antiseptics that, in his opinion, *poisoned* the wound. Providing antiseptic procedures were correctly followed to sterilise equipment prior to surgery, sterilised water would be sufficient to cleanse the wound—a 'pure' body had all it needed to heal itself.

William had heard enough. He was outraged. Abramowski was contesting decades of the finest medical science without a shred of research evidence.

"I am going to operate on this young man," William growled, checking his watch, "at 4pm today. Will you assist or do I have to ask the matron?"

Abramowski was quiet for a moment, weighing up the authority with which William had delivered his ultimatum. He inclined his head and shrugged his narrow shoulders. "He is your patient."

"Then let us *both* follow our most thorough antiseptic procedure." William led the way into the hospital scrub room.

The operation went well. The appendix had ruptured, but with only a small tear and the infectious fluids had not yet spread. William was confident he had cleaned out the infection with his squares of formalin-impregnated muslin. He kept careful count of the swabs, and removed them all before replacing the section of the intestine he had moved aside. There was scant blood loss and he was able to stitch into healthy, strong tissue to repair the wound.

Abramowski proved an able assistant. He had surgical skill even if he was disinclined to use it. They had little to say to each other during the operation, and even less afterwards as they peeled off their gowns and washed up.

William visited his patient in the hospital ward the next day. Harper was reclining in bed reading a copy of *The Irrigationist*. He had a "helluva stomach-ache", but his temperature was only slightly above normal, and his skin colour and heart rate were much improved.

The matron, however, took William aside to express her concerns. Dr Abramowski was encouraging—no, 'enforcing' was the better word—his 'fruitarian' diet on the hospital's patients. Not Harper, she told William, rather the patients who were isolated in the typhoid ward. The matron was worried. It was a significant departure from the norm. Dr Abramowski was treating the typhoid cluster as an experiment—a proving ground for his radical theory. She had no authority to question him.

William was sympathetic.

"I have no authority either, Matron. In Dr Hill's absence, these are Abramowski's patients. Where Harper is concerned, we will introduce solid foods slowly, as usual and within his tolerance, from day three of his recovery."

The matron nodded.

"Do you have Dr Hill's forwarding address?"

"Yes Doctor."

"Then your best course of action, is to write your concerns to him. He may be able to exert some influence."

"Yes Doctor." She shuffled away with an air of defeat.

William regretted that he could not alleviate the matron's worry, but one could not interfere with the treatment another doctor prescribed for his patients. It was a confounding breach of that sacrosanct etiquette that Abramowski had questioned *him* before Harper's operation. He would not respond with a like transgression.

When Harper recovered, he was added to the list of Jeannie's indebted work-force. He was an adept kangaroo hunter, and she appointed him her principal supplier of meat for Olga.

~

During their next lunch at The Mildura club, William queried W.B. about the impoverishment of the men at the clearing camp. In part, he wanted to be sure his patients were not taking advantage and, suspecting that was not the case, he wanted to press W.B. on the financial state of the settlement. It was rumoured that Victoria was in depression, and could be for years ahead. While he would admit it to no one, least of all Jeannie, William was anxious about his financial position.

"We pay well if there *is* work, Doc." W.B. assured him. "But since the ruckus over the water rates, our sales have fallen away. We couldn't ship the harvest and now men are walking off their orchards, almost giving them away. Why would anyone buy an uncleared block? I have no work for these men and won't have for many months."

"Till the end of 'The Depression'?"

"Don't use that term. No surer way to cause a depression than to talk as if we're in one. We have to be positive or the house of cards falls down."

"House of cards?" William hadn't heard the phrase before.

"We borrow money to create a splendid irrigation scheme and a beautiful city. We sell blocks to pay the bank's charges and the workmen. The working men, the settlers and their families spend their money in the town, buying goods, creating a robust economy—all of which encourages more people to buy our blocks. Any enterprise like this depends on confidence. Take away that confidence and everything stacked upon it falls down." As he spoke W.B. demonstrated the construction of a house of cards with his hands. Finally, he swept his hand sideways, knocking the imaginary structure down.

"Is the Chaffey house of cards falling?"

W.B. sighed and lifted his glass of wine from the dining table. "Let's hope not."

"Is there any sign of the bank reopening?" William expected W.B. to have advance knowledge of this, and he was not disappointed.

"Next Monday."

"Excellent."

"However," W.B. lowered his voice, "it may not be as customers expect."

William raised an eyebrow.

"Depositors will be offered a mix of preference shares and deposit receipts payable in a number of years."

"Years? No one will get their money out for *years*?"

"Those with a balance of less than five pounds will be able to claim their money, and some might be able to take a loan against their deposit receipts, but in the main, it will be at least five years. Interest will be payable on the deposits. The bank guarantees that."

"The bank," William growled, "guaranteed all depositors ready access to their money."

"You got your money out before it closed, didn't you?"

"Aye, thank-you."

"Well, regardless of what you hear in the next few weeks about the bank's restructure, *don't* put any money back in."

There was a pause in their conversation while a waiter deferentially cleared their plates and took an order for their dessert. W.B. had circumvented the town's temperance regulations when he created, in The Mildura Club, a venue where the professional gentlemen of the town could dine together and be served alcohol at their tables. William enjoyed the status that being W.B.'s dining partner afforded him. What he did *not* enjoy was the frequent interruptions by people who wanted to capture W.B.'s attention for themselves. He had several questions in mind to put to W.B., but lost the opportunity when Abramowski approached their table and queued behind the waiter for an opportunity to speak.

"Gladly I catch the two of you together," Abramowski began. "I have Councillor Williams. We would like to speak of the unhealthy condition of the town water."

If W.B. was reluctant, he concealed it well. He looked across to the table where Councillor John Williams was sitting—presumably it had not been the councillor's idea to interrupt W.B.'s lunch—and beckoned him over.

Abramowski, in his capacity as Mildura's Public Health Officer, was keen to conscript William's help in convincing the councillor and W.B. that it was the town's unhygienic water supply that was the cause of the growing typhoid cluster. The councillor looked bored while Abramowski repeated his case.

During the summer months the frequent turning off and on of the irrigation pumps had left air in the pipes. Frogs, lizards and such had crawled in; they died and decayed. Small quantities of water lay stagnant; heating and festering. Diseases such as typhoid and cholera flourished in such conditions. Regardless of the cost of the water, the pipes needed to be flushed clean—immediately, and on a regular basis. Furthermore, the intake pipe must be moved upstream, above the engineering sheds and the washing facilities. He had made these recommendations in response to the typhoid outbreak last November. He had raised them again in March and still, nothing had been done.

This was a subject on which William was in firm agreement, and he did not hesitate to add his weight to Abramowski's recommendations.

"The flushing of the pipes is a matter for the Irrigation Company," W.B. responded irritably.

"It is not done and now Council must insist it is done," Abramowski declared.

"The intake pipe was placed well clear of the settlement," Councillor Williams, one of Mildura's early settlers, defended the historical decision.

"Now the settlement is grown beyond. Council should *not* have allowed." Abramowski's voice became squeaky, his pitch varying erratically as his emotions heightened.

"*You* pushed for the location of the new wharf," Councillor Williams pointed out.

"It is agreed. Engineers would move the intake," Abramowski snapped.

"Where is that written down?" W.B. queried smoothly.

William felt unexpected sympathy for Abramowski. He guessed that W.B. already knew all the facts regarding the intake pipe and had Chaffeys' defence solidly pre-formed. It would not be Chaffey Brothers spending money to relocate the pipe, and did Council have *any* money? Money, that is, not locked up in the bank for at least 5 years?

"It's an unfortunate appearance, W.B.," William interrupted Abramowski's angry sputter, "when the healthful benefits of Mildura have been widely advertised, to have people dying of typhoid in our hospital. It hardly promotes *confidence* in the settlement."

W.B. gave him a wry smile.

"John," W.B. addressed Councillor Williams, "put it on the agenda for the next Council meeting. Now, let us get on with our meal." He nodded in the direction of the waiter who was hovering behind Abramowski, two dessert plates in hand.

When they were alone again, William posed his new question. "Is Council's money caught up in the bank restructure?"

W.B. nodded. "They'll have a loan account, against their deposit receipts. They can operate, but there will be limits."

"Will they be able to pay their staff?"

"There will be some ..." W.B. looked for the right word "consolidation."

"Sackings," William substituted.

W.B. did not reply, so William continued with increased fervour. "People are *dying*. The town water pipes *must* be flushed. The intake pipe *must* be moved. The open drains are filthy; they should have been enclosed from the start. Council's contractor doesn't empty the sanitary pans often enough. People throw their muck into the nearest drain. Should I go on?"

"No Doc," W.B.'s voice was suddenly weary, "let us enjoy our pudding. There was a point—and it was years ago—where Council was obliged to take responsibility for the ongoing maintenance of the town. George and I cannot do everything. They must learn not to bicker amongst themselves. They must find out for themselves how to be effective. If you want to influence the situation, become a councillor."

"I could think of nothing worse," William laughed.

"Personally," W.B. replied, raising his glass and tipping it towards William, "*I* would rather make wine."

~

It was Abramowski who became a councillor in order to influence the situation. He was elected on 24th August and the next day, at closing time, he dropped into William's surgery. He would walk with William, he said, to the state school for their evening first-aid class.

As William (groaning internally) gathered his hat and coat, Abramowski confessed that he needed to devolve some of his responsibilities. (William could not agree more.) Would William consider taking on the role of Public Health Officer? The officer was required to make quarterly reports to Council, and the annual stipend was ten pounds.

William was surprised, and pleased by the sum. It wasn't much, he reminded himself lest he seem too enthusiastic, but it was much better than another crate of dried apricots. The job was within his field of interest, and he knew himself to be the Health Officer the town needed, right now. He allowed himself to be persuaded.

"Wonderful," Abramowski gushed, pumping William's hand. "A formality only. Council will accept you at the next meeting. Monday."

Abramowski had been voted off the board of the Irrigation Company in April having achieved, in William's view and apparently that of the majority of the company's shareholders, nothing towards resolution of the ongoing dispute over water rates. He had filled his newly found time by joining the committee of the Mildura and Wentworth Railway League, which had the impossible task, given the parlous state of the colony's finances, of persuading the Victorian government to complete the promised railway line. He was also on the School Board of Advice; a committee member of the Horticultural Society; and a director of the First Mildura Building Society. In July, he had agreed with Jeannie that he would conduct the men's first-aid classes.

"Why did you ask *him*?" William had blurted out his surprise when Jeannie showed him the article, she had written for *The Mildura Cultivator.*

"Because you're taking the women's classes, sweetheart. Would you prefer it the other way around?"

William definitely didn't prefer it the other way around. He worried about Abramowski's influence on the women of the town. He was suspicious that his own wife was paying the herbalist too much heed. He would like to have found a reason to forbid, or at least forestall Jeannie's arrangements, but he knew the determination with which his wife approached what she called her 'job' and he did not dare countermand her.

This particular Friday was the fourth of five weekly lectures in Jeannie's first-aid program. There was to be a review held at The Nest, and then an examination at the end of September, by which time Jeannie hoped Dr Hill would be back from his convalescence in Bendigo. The lectures were held at the state school, with the women in one classroom and the men in another. The three-hour lecture William was to give that evening was set out in his diary, in Jeannie's hand:

> *"First aid to those suffering collapse from injury, to those stunned, to the apoplectic, inebriate, epileptic, fainting, poisoning (including snakebite); burns, scalds, etc. The immediate treatment of the drowning."*

William and Abramowski began their two-block walk from The Nest to the school by sharing their mutual concern about the state of Mildura's sanitary facilities. In proposing the solution, William pointed to the proven success of the enclosure of London's sewerage system. Abramowski agreed, proper sanitation reduced the prevalence of disease, but it was certain, he asserted, that dietary habit was of the most significance in the way disease impacted the human body.

"It is evident," Abramowski told William earnestly, "that man is the fruit eater. Anatomically, we are with the fruit-eating animals. Free-living, fruit and nut-eating animals know no disease. Their life is one of constant health, unto death."

William raised his eyebrows, invisible under the brim of his hat, and watched his forward foot-falls.

"Man too," Abramowski continued, "would know no sickness if he ate only fruit and nuts. Such a diet would make the normal life of man 150 years."

"Now *that's* an exaggeration!" William could not suppress his disagreement.

"Listen," Abramowski exhorted. "Even if only once in the year. Four to six weeks, purification by eating only fresh fruit. This would bring great benefit to the body. We should build a sanitorium for this. It is better for the body and soul of the man, to undergo the fruit purification regime, than take a holiday at the seaside."

"You won't convince people of that," William snorted.

"And the children," Abramowski continued, gesticulating as his state of enthusiasm reached its crescendo. "Children who eat only fruit and nuts. They will be healthy and strong, and not just this. They will be gentle and kind. They will be free from vice and unnatural propensities. It is the consumption of meat that brings the aggression. We see the nature of the carnivores. It is man's invention of fire that gives us the cooking of meat. It is not the natural food. It is the salty seasoning of the meat that makes men take alcohol for their thirst."

Abramowski caught William by the elbow and dragged him to a halt in order to reinforce the delivery of the central message of his rant.

"Our children in Mildura have the unique opportunity to grow in purity. It is the public health imperative, William, to encourage the mothers in this."

"I cannot agree with you, Otto. I will not ..."

"Listen!" Abramowski wagged his forefinger vehemently. "We *must* start with the children. We will have the healthier citizens. We will have the less transmission of disease. We will have the happy, prosperous settlement."

William walked on, lengthening his stride, increasingly annoyed.

"*These* are the goals of the public health." Abramowski trotted after him, failing to catch up. "We will *not* achieve this by having the poisonous substances put in our bodies to cure or prevent disease. No! Serums and anti-toxins must not be used. Listen! These substances, they increase the impurity of the body. Natural fruit juices. Pure water. The freshest of air. These are our tools."

William took the steps into the school two at a time. He turned to Abramowski and tipped his hat. "Good evening, Otto."

"We will discuss later?" Abramowski asked hopefully.

"Not tonight." William turned his back and strode angrily along the veranda to the classroom Jeannie had allocated to him.

Jeannie attended all the classes herself. Not because she needed to review her skills, but because she enjoyed the company. She always brought a basket-full of finger foods, which she arranged, along with contributions she had solicited from five of the female participants, on the teacher's table at the front of the school room. There were thirty women on the course, and each had their turn at bringing food for one of the six classes. Half-way through the evening the group took a twenty-minute break and the men's class joined them to share the food. William judged this the best part of the night—he relished the baking done by different women; he enjoyed complimenting them and asking for their 'magic ingredients'.

As they walked home from the state school, hatted, scarved, and overcoated against the cold night air, William and Jeannie discussed coconut. Jeannie hadn't seen any in Shillidays but, having tasted it in a home-baked cookie that evening, William asserted it must be available in the settlement. Were there coconuts on the palm trees the Chaffeys had planted?

"They're date palms, silly," she said smugly.

"Ask Mary to order coconut for us."

"Maybe the chemist."

Jeannie's oblique reference to Abramowski reminded William to tell her about the role of Public Health Officer. She was excited—not about the money, she said, but because he would be making a contribution to the future wellbeing of the town.

"What worries you?" She detected the reservation in his voice.

"Abramowski. He's already pressuring me to promote his fruitarian diet as a public health issue, and I will *not*."

"There's some sense in what he says," Jeannie's tone was reasonable, but her accommodation of Abramowski's madness irritated William.

"That meat-eating leads to bad temper and alcohol consumption? That a man can live to be 150 years old if he eats only fruit and nuts?"

"150? Does he say that?"

"Aye, he said precisely that to me today. He's dafty. I don't want mothers paying him any mind. It takes a varied diet, including meat, to grow a strong baby." William pulled his hand out of the warmth of his pocket and laid it on the small shelf that had formed on the top of her belly. She responded by snuggling in to his hug and matching her pace to his.

~

On Monday 28th August, at the council meeting, William's appointment as Public Health Officer was announced by the new Shire President, John Williams. W.B., who had initially expressed surprise to see him, nudged him in the ribs.

"You dark horse!"

William shrugged. "Someone has to get that intake pipe moved."

"If you *ever* bring up my 'responsibility' for Mildura's public health, that's the end of our lunches at the club!" W.B. laughed and William laughed with him.

"You're coming tomorrow night?" W.B. asked as they were leaving the Institute Hall.

"Tomorrow?"

"The inaugural meeting of the Mildura and Wentworth Federation and Intercolonial Freetrade League. It's George's doing. He's invited your newfound political friends. He wants all our professional business men on board. The excise is crippling trade. The different regulations between New South Wales and Victoria and South Australia are ridiculous, and who has more interest than we who live on the Murray River! We have everything to gain by throwing our weight behind federation. We've talked about this haven't we? You support federation?"

William *did* support federation. He considered that the union of the colonies would not have much impact on him personally, but he had taken an interest in the debate and was steadfastly aligned with the proponents. He was confident he could bring an intelligent interpretation to the legal and prudential matters involved.

He listened attentively, the next night, to the proceedings of the federation meeting, but he refused nomination for a position on the committee. He was unyielding despite the shortage of nominees, and did not explain his reticence. Abramowski had accepted a nomination, and there was no way, William told himself, that he could serve on the same committee as that man.

"I can't see that they'll be effective," he told Jeannie tersely. "It's another rendering of the Railway League. It will go the same way. They confer often and at length about how wonderful it will be to have the railway. How marvellous the benefits of federation. But there's no plan to make it come about. All that was done today, apart from electing the committee, was agree to talk to other committees. I couldn't stand it."

"You'll have enough to do as Public Health Officer, *and* ..." Jeannie paused to be sure of his attention, "I *do* want to fit in another set of first-aid lectures. I have several women who missed out on the first course and I could easily find ten more if you're prepared to take the classes—you're *very* popular with the ladies, sweetheart."

William was not swayed by her tongue-in-cheek flattery. He knew that if he didn't agree, she would ask Abramowski. There was no point reminding her how close to term she would be by the end of the course; she had already made up her mind.

Jeannie placed his supper cup of tea and a cookie on the kitchen table in front of him. She stroked his neck, waiting while he took a bite.

He looked at the freshly baked biscuit with appreciation while he chewed.

"Coconut?" he asked.

"Aye," she said proudly. "Dr Abramowski uses it in his remedies. He says it is very rich in micronutrients."

~

By the end of September, William had more than thirty, two-month-old rabbits in his garden shed. He also had a growing supply of tubercle bacilli with which he had infected half the rabbits. In his laboratory, he had introduced minute concentrations of formalin to bacilli with satisfyingly deadly results. He was impatient to start experimentation on the rabbits with differing methods of treatment—inhalation, ingestion and injection—but he had to wait for the disease to take hold.

Meanwhile, Dr Springthorpe had replied to his letter. Formalin had been mentioned as one of the antiseptics that could be trialled in the search for a tubercle anti-toxin, but he was not aware of any research program.

Dr Hill returned to duty as Head Surgeon. He adopted the use of formalin as the hospital's disinfectant but, to William's relief and Abramowski's distress, he ordered the return of normal dietary practice for public in-patients.

Thursday 4th October 1893

In October's first mail delivery, a letter came from his mother that at once thrilled William and sent him into despair.

Two of his younger brothers, John and Robert, would be with him for Christmas.

John had been diagnosed with phthisis.

The letter despaired Jeannie too, but for a different and, in William's opinion, comparatively trivial reason. She had arranged that her mother would come to stay for the birth of the baby. How could she accommodate everyone in their small house?

William offered her no solution. In the surgery storeroom he stared through tears of rage and frustration at his hopelessly inadequate mini-laboratory. He must make faster progress. He must find a cure. This hateful disease had his entire family in its sights, and it was up to *him* to find a way to stop it.

That night, William forced a compressed pellet of formaldehyde down the throat of the biggest of his three-month-old infected rabbits. He enclosed another of the rabbits in a tin box he had fitted with a glass lid and a rubber tube, plugged through a hole in one side. He waxed the lid and the tube to the tin to make an enclosed gas chamber, before attaching the tube to a bottle of gaseous formaldehyde. He opened the valve for five seconds. He took a third infected rabbit and struggled with the squirming bundle of fur and legs, trying to find a vein into which to inject his formalin solution. He failed, with the result that that rabbit became the experimental subject of a subcutaneous injection. He knocked the fourth rabbit out, temporarily, with a whiff of chloroform. This allowed him time to find one of the tiny veins and complete an intravenous injection. He watched anxiously as the little rabbit recovered from its sedation, and resumed its usual, timid attitude, sitting at the back of its crate. In the red, hard-backed journal he had reserved for recording his experiments, William made detailed notes of the age and weight of each rabbit, the mechanism of delivery and the dosage each of his experimental subjects received. He opened his home-made gas chamber exactly an hour after he had enclosed the rabbit, noting that he could not smell any traces of the gaseous formalin, and he returned the rabbit, seemingly unaffected, to its box.

He barely slept overnight and, in the morning, when he entered his rabbit-shed he was only partly disappointed to see all the tested rabbits sitting in their boxes, as if nothing had happened. He had a baseline of small dosages at which no harm was done.

He selected four different rabbits for a much larger dose.

A fortnight later William received a telegram from his father, telling him that 200 pounds had been added to his line of credit. He was to assist John and Robert in establishing themselves in Mildura. He was thrilled. He had admitted it to no one, but his financial situation was tenuous; he could not spare any money to help his brothers.

William scoured the advertisements in *The Mildura Culti-vator* and *The Irrigationist*. It was a buyer's market. Gold had been discovered in Coolgardie, and disgruntled horticultural-ists were leaving for Westralia, in search of easier money. He snapped up two horses and a good quality jinker at an excellent price. He bought wire from the Proudfoot's produce store, fence posts and a gate from Risby's sawmill and he contracted Jeannie's workmen to fence in the acre they had sown to lucerne in autumn. The horses were kept hobbled while their paddock fence was built around them, and Olga watched with fascination, from a respectful distance.

By mid-November, a block in F section, not far from Jeannie's orchard, had come to William's attention. The owner was unable to meet his water rates payment; he was deeply in debt, his orchard failing due lack of care. William offered to rent the house on the block for three months while the man tried his luck in Coolgardie; with an option to buy the property and all its farming equipment if the man chose not to return. The price William offered was substantially less than he had paid for their own, undeveloped blocks twenty months earlier but nevertheless, the embattled owner was glad to accept.

William was greatly heartened by the deal. His brothers were coming, and he would make sure they had reason to stay.

Jeannie was relieved.

William and Jeannie normally slept separately in the two bedrooms of their five-room house. It was a rule William had regretfully imposed from the beginning of their relationship; one of the most important things they had to do, he told her, to protect her from infection. It was at night, mostly, that he suffered short fevers, turned restlessly and coughed frequently to clear the phlegm in his throat.

For Annie's first visit, before he started his practice at The Nest, he had turned the newly constructed surgery waiting room over to her as a bedroom. He had intended to add two bedrooms to the northern end of the house, but he hadn't reckoned on the depression, the bank crash, and a register of patients where more than three quarters simply could not pay.

Now, not only was Annie coming to stay for several weeks, but there would be a baby in the house, and no nursery. On seeing him buy the horses, the jinker, and the fencing materials, Jeannie asked if they could get the house extended. He regretted his gruff refusal, but what could he do? It was not his money. It was for John, and Robert. It was already a stretch, buying the horses and the jinker with the practical intent of common use.

"Will it be *so* bad to share a bed with me?" he growled at her accusingly rather than explain his complex financial concerns.

She looked dismayed, then affronted. "It's *your* rule, William. Not mine. And will you want to share also with the bairn?"

They had begun quarrelling, William thought angrily, before his mother-in-law had even started her journey from Melbourne.

Jeannie didn't raise the subject again. One day, late in November, he was surprised to look into her bedroom and see a crib positioned against the wall. It was dressed in an embroidered white ruffle, and inside was a woollen mattress wrapped in a crisp cotton sheet with a small pillow, decorated in one corner with a brilliantly blue wren. Draped over one end of the crib was a quilt, with six panels, each showing the same blue wren, in different attitudes—flying, or sitting nearby a nest so finely sewn that he could see each individual twig, blade of dry grass, and horsehair.

"Where did this come from?" he asked as Jeannie came into the room.

"Mrs Proudfoot gave me the crib and the mattress. I sewed the ruffle and the quilt." Jeannie tied a string to the rail that hung over the crib and let drop a short, stiff piece of fencing wire to which were attached several pieces of paper, cut and coloured in the guise of various animals. The shapes fluttered lightly and he reached out to turn each one to his gaze: a fox, a deer, an otter, a salmon, a badger, and a hedgehog—wild animals from the Scottish Borders.

"When did you do all this?" he wondered aloud.

"You've been preoccupied, William." Her tone was short. She had been calling him 'William' a lot lately.

"You're not moving into my room?"

"No."

"Where's your mother going to sleep?"

"She'll be in your room, and you can sleep in the surgery."

William made to speak but thought better of it. There was a determined finality in her manner. She looked at him as if challenging him to object, and when he remained silent, she left the room.

He had intended to tell her how beautiful the embroidery was, how stunned he was by her talent, but somehow, in the chill there was between them, he had missed his moment.

That Jeannie had heard the screams of the dying rabbit had not helped. It was the second ingestion-rabbit; the one he had given four compressed formalin tablets. He could not put it out of its misery, as she had demanded. For the purpose of his experiment, he had to let the impact of the formalin run its course. When he opened the rabbit up, he could see the extensive scarring in the oesophagus and the stomach. When he looked at the blood he had drawn after the animal died, he could see the tubercle bacilli; defiantly alive in his microscopic field.

One rabbit had to die this horrible death to prove the futility of further experiments with ingestion. Only one, but Jeannie took little comfort in his argument. She could not fathom how *any* of his experiments on the rabbits would be able to prove the safety and efficacy of the anti-toxin in a human being.

The second inhalation-rabbit also died, but it was a peaceful death, and Jeannie did not know about that one. He had watched, with grim satisfaction, as the last remaining bacilli on the slide withered under his microscope, but what was the use? Through inhalation, the subject died before the bacilli. William knew this was in keeping with experiments done using other antiseptics.

The rabbits receiving subcutaneous injections developed nasty skin irritations, with no reduction in the number of tubercle bacilli. Again, much as he expected.

The intravenous injections were difficult to give; there were skin irritations that implied he had not successfully delivered the desired titration into the vein; there appeared to be a reduction in the bacilli, but it was an inconsistent effect when charted against weights and dosage. The rabbits survived their injections apparently unharmed and, upon cutting them open, he found no evidence of organ damage.

William focussed his efforts on intravenous injection, increasing the dosages and trying to get accurate, repeatable results. More and more, he felt that Jeannie was right. He was not achieving anything that would give him the confidence to move on, from rabbits to himself.

Summer hit Mildura in earnest on December 4th, with ten successive days of temperatures over 90° Fahrenheit. On 5th December when the mercury first touched 91° in the shade, William thought, too late, to check on his rabbits. The galvanised iron shed had become an oven; every rabbit was dead. He was stunned that it had happened so suddenly. He gathered the bodies into a sack and buried them in a pit beyond the garden perimeter, where Jeannie never trod. He stood beside the freshly dug earth, muttering a miserable apology even though (he corrected his thinking) this death was likely a more merciful end than the one he had planned. He dragged a sheet of iron over the mass-grave, and weighted it with rocks to make sure Olga would not exhume the corpses. He told Jeannie his rabbit experiments had finished, and she looked up from her sewing briefly.

"Good," was all she said.

~

On Annie's first day on *The Ellen* from Swan Hill, the temperature hit 99°F, and on her second day it reached 100°. She arrived soon after 7pm on Monday 11th December, when the temperature had dropped to a stifling 87°. William was called onto the boat to collect her from her cabin.

His sharp-witted, forthright mother-in-law was not her usual self. She was dressed in a light cotton shift; her multiple undergarments abandoned. It was less apparel than William had ever seen her wear. She was pale, sweating heavily, and complained to him of abdominal cramps, nausea and a general weakness. She was by no means the first case of heat exhaustion he had seen that week. He hurried her off the boat, into the jinker, and straight home to The Nest where he sat her down with a cool drink in her hand and her feet in a bucket of melting ice. Jeannie sponged cold water over her mother's hair, brow and bare shoulders.

Jeannie, heavily pregnant, was not in much better condition herself, which is why William had been first in line for ice at the engineering workshop at 6am that morning.

The cool change came, at last, on the evening of December 14th while Council was deliberating inside the Institute Hall. There were three new cases of typhoid at the Kings Billabong camp and William exercised his powers for the first time, issuing a Public Health Order that the camp be cleared immediately. With Dr Hill and Abramowski both serving as councillors, it was an easy win. No-one cared where the ousted workers went, as long as they did not continue to drink and bathe in the fetid water of the billabong.

December 18th was a relatively pleasant evening—only 70° inside the Institute Hall as certificates were handed out to the graduates of the second St John's First-Aid program. Jeannie clambered up the steps, leaning on William's arm, to receive a certificate of appreciation, a large bouquet of flowers and a kiss on each cheek from the class examiner, Dr Hill.

William was pleased with his own reward—a pouch of fine pipe tobacco—but he was dismayed, on coming down from the stage, when Abramowski was ushered into the seat next to him. As the school children arranged themselves on stage to give their end of year concert, Abramowski launched into his predictable rant about the treatment of typhoid, and William was relieved when, between items, Jeannie touched his arm.

"I need to go, Willie. I'm too uncomfortable."

It was hardly surprising; on the hard, wooden chairs. William jumped up and helped her out of her seat.

"I'm sorry Otto," she apologised as she waddled past.

She was barely able to climb into the jinker, so William helped with a shoulder under her buttocks. The livery boy who was in charge of the buggies parked outside the hall, snorted and clapped his hand over his mouth to throttle the rest of his laughter. William winked and handed over a penny.

"I can't do this anymore, Willie." Jeannie held her belly firmly as they bumped over the roads on their short trip home. "I want this baby out. I can't stretch any further."

William tied the horse to the hitching rail outside the surgery entrance and helped Jeannie down. Annie, he knew, would be sitting on the front veranda, taking in the air that was, at this time of night, much cooler outside the house. He wanted to avoid his mother-in-law; she had come on the premise that she would help Jeannie in these last weeks, but with the heat affecting her badly, she had instead been a worrisome burden.

He led Jeannie into the surgery waiting room, and left her to undress and lie down on the couch he had been using for a bed.

By the time he had unhitched the horse and let it go in the paddock, she had made up his bed and was lying naked and drowsy under the top sheet. She had been restless for many nights now, he knew, exhausted by the heat but unable to sleep. He roused her by palpating her stomach. Then he checked her cervix.

"Who would marry a doctor?" she mumbled in protest.

"His head has engaged. He'll be early. Not tonight, but soon."

"She. *She'll* be early."

"It's a boy," he said earnestly. "He's active, strong and you're carrying him well out front." William stroked her tightly stretched stomach. He fingered her protruding belly button.

"But I hear her voice, Willie. I *feel* her," Jeannie countered with utmost certainty.

He was envious, William realised. For all the discomfort she had been suffering, Jeannie was experiencing a wonder that he himself could never know. A life growing inside her. A tiny person with whom she had already established some sort of communication. He had not previously thought of this, despite the many women he had helped through pregnancy and birthing. Rather, he had pitied them for their ordeal; he had been glad he wouldn't have to go through such inconvenience and pain. But this was different. *This* life, inside Jeannie, belonged to him too. He wanted to *feel* it.

Friday 22nd December 1893

It was 87°F, just after ten in the morning when Jeannie informed him of her first contraction. The day's maximum temperature was reached at 2pm with the gauge on William's surgery wall showing 98° as Jeannie, both hands pressed hard against the small of her back, paused to read the thermometer on her circuit through the waiting room, the surgery and back through the connecting door into the house where Annie was sitting, feet in the bucket of ice water, fanning herself wearily.

William had kept the surgery open during his usual morning hours, but received no customers. Those with appointments failed to appear, as was normal in times of extreme weather. Patients expected *him* to travel to them, he knew, regardless of what weather might beset his afternoon rounds but for once, on *this* afternoon, he was going to disappoint them. At mid-day he sent his errand-boy, Douglas, off on a bicycle with several envelopes, each containing a note to say Doctor was unable to attend because Mrs Cameron was in labour and could they make a new appointment after December 26th.

Douglas pedalled back through the gate as William was tying a notice— *'Surgery Closed, Reopening December 27th'*—over the top of the 'Surgery Hours' sign that was fixed to the gate-post. William noticed, with concern, that the lad's hair was wet, as were the creases in his cotton shorts and shirt.

"Douglas!" he called as the boy propped his bicycle against the veranda. "You've been swimming?"

"It's bleedin' hot, sir!" Douglas defended himself.

"Did you swim in an irrigation channel?"

Douglas looked guilty. "Maw says I'm not allowed in the river by myself."

"You're not allowed in the irrigation channels either. There's typhoid about."

"I wasn't out by Kings Billabong. I went in just here." Douglas swept his arm vaguely towards San Mateo Avenue.

"You're not allowed in *any* of the channels. If you're hot, get a bucket of house water and tip it over your head. There's a tap on the tank behind the surgery."

"Yes sir. What do you want me to do now, sir?"

"Wait in the surgery, I put some books out for you. It might be a few hours yet, but I'll be asking you to fetch the midwife."

"Mrs Mitchell has gone to Mrs Walker at Irymple, sir. Mrs Shilliday was worried about Mrs Cameron. She says Mrs Mitchell will be away this night."

"You spoke to Mrs Shilliday?"

"She knew I was on your business. She gave me an ice drink."

"Did Mrs Shilliday have anything else she wanted you to tell me?"

Douglas thought for a moment. "She said they're busy at the hospital, sir. She said there's people from Billabong crowding in. Not 'cos they've got the typhoid, she said, but 'cos they got nowhere cool to go, and they're pretending they're sick."

William could imagine it. The hospital, with its high ceilings, ventilated hallways, and abundant supply of ice water was the coolest place in town. He had considered booking Jeannie a room there, but he knew the hospital facilities were stretched and he was anxious about the inpatients. They seldom admitted to close contact with a typhoid victim. Add to that the influx of refugees from Kings Billabong and he was certain he had made the right decision in keeping Jeannie at home.

"Well then, Douglas," William patted the boy on the back and ushered him into the surgery waiting room, "fortunately, I have a certificate of midwifery myself."

"You, sir?" Douglas clearly thought all midwives were women.

"Essential knowledge for a surgeon from Edinburgh. We are not, however, trained in delivering babies on days as hot as this. I don't presume to compete with Mrs Mitchell."

"Could I use one of them house water buckets now, sir?"

William motioned Douglas to follow and walked through the surgery to the scullery of the main house, then out the back door where, to the lad's mortification, they found Jeannie soaking herself in the iron tub William had put there as a plunge pool. She was wearing her undergarments, William saw with amusement, but their wet adherence to her body revealed much more than they concealed.

Uncharacteristically—though in keeping with William's observations of other women in labour—Jeannie was not the least concerned for her modesty. As poor Douglas ducked back into the house, she moaned an acknowledgement of William's presence.

"Help me out."

She flopped an arm out of the tub towards him and he pulled her to her feet.

"Arghh!" she grimaced and clamped her arms around his neck, sucking air through her teeth.

He held his pocket watch behind her wet shoulder and pushed the start button on the lap timer.

"I. Want. This. Bairn. Out," she gasped as the contraction subsided.

He laughed.

"Not funny."

He helped her step out of the bath and climb up to the veranda. They sat together while her clothes dried, evaporatively cooling her skin. Olga lay prostrate beside them.

"Do you think she's alright?" Jeannie watched the dog meditatively.

William felt for Olga's pulse, and Olga jerked her paw away without opening her eyes.

"Good reaction time," he concluded cheerfully. He rubbed Jeannie's back firmly.

"Aye. Keep doing that," Jeannie nodded appreciatively and lent forward.

When she straightened, stiffened and gasped in pain, he consulted his watch again.

"You've got a while yet," he confirmed.

An hour later Miss Bailey, one of the new first-aid graduates, knocked at the front door and walked into the house, calling "Anyone home?" William heard her apologise to Annie, who had woken in surprise.

He looked out from the kitchen, where he had been making himself a sandwich.

"Mrs Shilliday said you might need some help." The girl gave him a wide, cheerful smile.

At ten o'clock that night, the lively Miss Bailey, still waiting for a call to action, was playing rummy with a greatly revitalised Annie. Douglas had gone home to bed. Jeannie was lying on the couch in the surgery waiting room and William was seated beside her, his finger on her pulse and his pocket watch in his hand. It was the hour he had set for himself. The time he had to make a decision.

Her cervix was well dilated. Her contractions had, for a short time, been distanced at three minutes, but now they had weakened, as had her heart beat and the baby's. He could still hear both beats distinctly, but they were enfeebled, slow and irregular. She was exhausted; sweating even though it was cooler now, and her skin had taken on a sallow pallor that he had seen too often. She refused to get up and walk with him; she barely sipped at the sugared water he tried to make her drink.

His decision was the hardest he had ever had to make.

He had led birthing surgery before. Twice on cadavers at the university. He had assisted in three live operations. Once to separate a premature baby from a dying mother, so that it could be baptised before it died. Twice more in an attempt to save mother and child and he was proud of the fact that one of those operations had been successful. Much had been learned about the operation since then and many things had changed —its name, for one. Now it was called a 'caesarean section', and modern thinking was that it was better to operate early, before the mother was exhausted and the foetus in distress.

Apart from leaving the operation too late, sepsis was the biggest killer of women who were given a caesarean section. William was confident in his antisepsis procedure and he had made sure in advance that he had everything he needed in his surgery. He even had a box of the fine silver wire that had only recently become available in Victoria for use in making the internal uterine stitches that greatly improved the operation's success rate.

When William had operated at the university, before the research that proved the success of silver wire, surgeons favoured performing a hysterectomy at the same time as the caesarean operation. It was shown to have a much higher success rate in saving the mother because it limited blood loss while avoiding the infection that normally attended any attempt at internal stitching, but being unable to have more children was a devastating price to pay. William had decided that, if it became necessary to perform a caesarean on Jeannie, he would not repeat the operation he knew; he would use the new silver wire and stitch the internal wound. He had taken the opportunity to practise his sewing on one of his mother rabbits.

Still, it could not be denied that the operation was a dire risk. Even if he performed a perfect caesarean, Jeannie would have a more difficult recovery and there was a high probability of uterine prolapse in future pregnancies.

If only he could give her more energy. Something to restart the contractions. He had read of research involving the synthesis of hormones made by the adrenal glands, but it was not yet proved and there was nothing of that kind in his medical kit.

She was falling asleep instead of drinking the sugar-water.

He shook her into confused wakefulness and sat her upright against the wall.

"Don't sleep!" He closed her fingers around the glass. "You *must* drink this. I'll be back in a moment."

He interrupted the card game, beckoning Miss Bailey to follow him. He had not intended to include Annie, but when she also followed, he directed her to sit with Jeannie and make sure she drank all the water. She needed it not just for energy, but to help maintain blood volume during the operation.

In the surgery, he told Miss Bailey what he was going to do. He showed her the equipment he had laid out on the bench and made her repeat the name of each item. He pointed to the surgical gown, gloves and mask that were for her use, and told her to start scrubbing herself with the carbolic soap that sat beside the water basin. She nodded, pale with fright.

Back in the waiting room, he knelt before Jeannie and told her he was going to operate. She made no objection; beyond caring. Annie looked at him with sharp eyes and a firmly set, sceptical mouth. She followed them through to the surgery and watched anxiously as he helped Jeannie onto the operating trolley.

"You must leave, Annie," William told her as he tied his gown.

When he turned back from the bench with a tube full of chloroform in one hand and a square cotton pad in the other, Annie was still there, holding Jeannie's hand.

"Are you sure?" she said in an uncharacteristically small voice.

"Yes," he said with a certainty he did not feel.

Annie held Jeannie's hand up to her lips, then bent to kiss her daughter's brow.

"God be with you," she murmured.

"And with you," Jeannie replied, by rote.

After Annie had closed the door, William bowed low over Jeannie. He kissed her skin below her belly button, and then her lips.

"I love you both. I will keep you *both*," he promised her.

"I love you, Willie."

"Sleep now."

She closed her eyes as soon as he lowered the chloroform pad, and within seconds she was away, loose under his touch.

Miss Bailey looked at him with wide eyes.

"Formalin pad," he instructed.

With the scalpel, he was less decisive. He paused for a moment, sterilised blade in hand, mindful that he was silently praying as fervently as he had prayed for his sister Isa, so many years ago. He had prayed then because he was a child, and there was nothing he could do but place his hope in a God who had not answered him. There had been a falling-out between himself and God. He had determined that he would do for himself and others, what God had not cared sufficiently to do. He was now a skilled surgeon but, with his wife and un-born child under his imperfect hand, he felt a desperate need for God's grace.

He pushed God and Jeannie from his mind. He projected himself into the operating theatre at Edinburgh University; a female body on the table. He was required to make a transverse incision in the lower segment of the uterus.

~

His daughter did not cry when he lifted her out of Jeannie's body. Like her mother, she was floppy. Where Jeannie's skin was white, the baby was a purple-blue.

"Towel," he instructed and Miss Bailey obliged. He balanced the baby on Jeannie's abdomen, and rubbed the tiny body vigorously, front and back. He poked his little finger into the baby's mouth, scooped out mucoidal fluid, and rubbed her all over again. Finally, the baby's cry came in a hiccupping gulp and he heard Miss Bailey, behind him, release her own breath in a deep gasp of relief.

William passed the baby to his overjoyed assistant and turned his attention to the umbilical cord. When it stopped pulsating, he closed it off with two clamps, one near to the baby and one near to Jeannie. He picked his scissors off the bench and cut the cord between the clamps.

"Keep towelling the baby on the bench there, until her colour improves," he ordered.

William took the remaining section of the umbilical cord in one hand and pressed down firmly, massaging the bulge of Jeannie's belly above the cut.

"Come on," he growled to himself, exerting a steady, gentle pull on the cord.

"Aye!" he said in triumph as the flabby body tissue came away in his hands. He examined it closely to ensure it was complete. He looked up to see Miss Bailey staring at him, agape. William made an amused, mental note that delivery of the placenta should be included in future maternity first-aid classes.

"The placenta," he explained. "Mustn't leave any of it behind." He dropped the ugly, fleshy mass into a bowl on the side bench and turned back. He picked Jeannie's wrist up from the table and felt for her pulse.

"Take the bairn to Mrs Robertson now, and come straight back—don't touch anything out there."

William heard Annie's surprised pleasure, her quick inquiry after Jeannie and Miss Bailey's over-confident reassurance.

"Formalin pad," he ordered, as soon as his assistant returned.

William had never taken more care stitching a wound. At one point Jeannie stirred and he paused, needle and silver wire in mid-air.

"Chloroform," he whispered, afraid he would wake her. "Just a whiff, not too much, that's enough!" It was a major leap of faith, he thought, trusting Miss Bailey with the chloroform pad.

"Check her pulse," he instructed and Miss Bailey, with all the aplomb of an experienced nurse, obliged.

Jeannie's pulse was low, fibrillating. He worked as fast as he could.

~

"You've done a truly amazing job, Miss Bailey. Thank-you." William plunged his fingers into the water basin where he found the carbolic soap and rolled it against his palms. He shrugged himself out of his gown, and bundled it up with his gloves before throwing it in a metal bucket in the corner of the room.

"You do the same," he pointed to the wash basin.

While Miss Bailey scrubbed her hands and disrobed, William checked each of Jeannie's eyes, gently rolling her upper lid.

"Time to wake her up," he said, picking a small jar of smelling salts off the bench.

When he held the jar to Jeannie's nose she gagged and tried to move her head away. He held her shoulders firmly down on the table.

"Don't sit up," he said intently. "Lie still, take your time to wake. You're stitched across the belly."

"My back. Hurts," she whispered.

"That's good," he smiled, "it's meant to."

"The bairn?" Jeannie said a moment later, with more intent.

William gestured to Miss Bailey, who moved towards the door.

Annie came into the room carrying the baby, washed and wrapped in a colourful crocheted shawl. She had tears in her eyes as she held the newborn close to Jeannie's face.

Jeannie tried to reach out and her mother moved the baby to meet her unsteady hand. With one finger Jeannie stroked the baby's face.

"Hello sweetheart," she murmured, and William felt himself fall in love, all over again, but bigger.

IV

1893 - 1896

Chapter 13

Jeannie

Tuesday 26th December 1893

Her arm was numb. Jeannie's careful effort to pull it out from under William's head failed.

"Sorry," she apologised as he woke.

He grabbed at her and hugged her desperately. He was crying.

"Willie!" she exclaimed when he let her catch a breath. "Whatever's wrong?"

Her fever had reached 101.5° Fahrenheit. If her temperature had climbed to 102°; if her pulse had suddenly dropped or if four more hours had passed without her temperature falling below 99°, William told her, he would have had no choice but to re-open the caesarean incision, remove her uterus and try again, with almost no chance of success, to eliminate the infection.

"Where's the bairn?"

"She's with your mother."

"I want to see her." Jeannie realised, upon trying to move, that getting out of bed was going to be difficult. She also realised she didn't know what day it was.

"You've missed Christmas," William answered her question. "It's Boxing Day, and John and Bert are here."

Like Annie, John and Bert had endured an extraordinarily hot journey by train and paddle steamer from Melbourne. The temperature reached a record 109° in the shade on their first day on the river, and 100° on Christmas Day. John had declared, as they drove indirectly home through Section F and past the brown, tree-less fields on the outskirts of town, that he hadn't realised that William lived in hell. Bert, upon introduction to her comatose body, had said it would be surprising if Jeannie's temperature was anything *less* than 100°.

"You brought them in here to see me?" Jeannie was horrified.

"You woke. You talked to them," he consoled her.

"I don't remember."

Jeannie heard a wail, rising in volume, from the living room. She felt, with alarm, a rapid swelling in her breasts and a warm spurt that saturated the left-side of her nightie.

Her mother was at the door, carrying the baby, ushering William out.

"Left side first this time," Annie said matter-of-factly.

Jeannie remembered feeding the baby through the first day. She didn't remember her breasts feeling hard, or the milk spurting over the baby's face as she struggled to get her nipple inside the tiny, hungry mouth.

Her mother plumped extra pillows behind her back, then helped guide Jeannie's hands. The baby took hold of the nipple and sucked hard. Jeannie's breast ached sharply, and then came a luxurious flow of relief. She looked in amazement at the small face on her chest, eyes pinched closed, nose pressed so deeply into her skin that Jeannie wondered if the child might suffocate. As she pressed down on the top of her breast to make some breathing-space, her mother brought her blessed, cool relief with broad sweeps of a bamboo fan.

"Annie Calder Isabella Cameron," Jeannie recited the name she had chosen in honour of both grandmothers. "Did Willie tell you?"

"Aye. In your absence though, we've called her 'Nancy'. I didn't want to hear my name on her and 'Nancy' suits her well."

"Mine-Ancy," Jeanie crooned. "My spring-flower."

"Aye."

"Have I been feeding her properly?"

"She hasn't missed a meal."

"Is everything all right with her?"

"Perfect."

"Have you been sleeping in the nursery?" Jeannie realised she was lying in William's room.

"So that ye didn't disturb each other, and William has been in here with you mostly. Sleeping on his knees there, with his fingers on your wrist."

"I've ruined Christmas."

"Pff! It's hardly *your* fault, lass."

Jeannie hoped her mother was not implying it was William's fault.

"I'm thirsty."

The glass her mother held up to her was filled with a pale reddish-green water. Jeannie looked at it quizzically; sipped carefully and winced.

"Raspberry leaf tea, chilled and sweetened with honey. Drink it all."

"Raspberry leaf?"

"For healing."

"Dr Abramowski?"

"My suggestion. He agreed."

"Does Willie know?"

"He has nothing better to offer."

The raspberry leaf tea wasn't too bad after the first mouthful.

"Other side now," Annie instructed.

Her mother lifted and turned the baby, but Nancy was not keen to continue her feed. She looked up at Jeannie with one dark eye, and squirmed in protest when Jeannie tried to direct her onto the nipple. Annie repositioned the baby firmly, and in response Nancy sucked—resentfully, Jeannie thought, and not for long. When Nancy pulled away again, Annie lifted the baby up and walked around the room holding her in the burping position, patting her on the back.

Jeannie tried to sit herself up and felt a sharp pain in her lower abdomen. She explored her scar gingerly with her fingers, feeling the sharp spikes of more than a dozen stitches. She remembered the pain that attended a walk to the commode that sat in the corner of the bedroom.

"I need to go to the toilet," she told her mother with embarrassment. "Could you get Willie for me?"

~

Jeannie was sitting up, eating a breakfast of fruits her mother had prepared for her, when Miss Bailey knocked at the bedroom door.

"It's wonderful to see you normal, Mrs Cameron," Nora bent over and gave her a kiss on the forehead. "Doctor and I were so worried about you."

"You should call me 'Jeannie', Nora. I understand you've dealt with me in the most intimate circumstances."

Nora laughed and waved Jeannie's humiliation away. "Doctor says I'm to train as a nurse. He says I have the gift and he'll commend me to the hospital. He's very kind."

"He means it, Nora. He told me you were an excellent help during the operation."

"I was *terrified*!" Nora sat on the edge of the bed, talking animatedly. "Doctor was so *calm*, telling me exactly what to do. I thought I would faint when he used the scalpel to cut you, but he kept talking to me, calling for formalin pads; clamps;

forceps. And who would think that a man could *sew*! He was amazing. I've been telling everyone. If I should ever need an operation, call Dr Cameron to me."

"I expect he couldn't have done such good work without your help, so thank-you, and thank-you also for coming since, to nurse me and the bairn."

"Oh, but Nancy is lovely. I don't mind a bit, and it has helped me decide to become a nurse. This is excellent experience for me."

"Fortunate all round then." Jeannie finished the last slice of melon on her plate and wiped her hands on her napkin.

"Are you wanting a bath now?" Nora asked eagerly.

"Aye. I can't meet my husband's brothers smelling like a cow byre!"

~

Meeting John, in particular, was startling. He looked *so* much like William. Not quite as tall, but every bit the same gaunt frame; the same gait; the same manner. He looked at her with William's direct blue eyes, deeply set and moody, overhung by dark brown eyebrows. He had the same straight nose and that cleft in the centre of his clean-shaven chin. His pencil-thin upper lip underlined the moustache he smoothed with a long-fingered gesture that was intimately familiar to her and he spoke, at least to her first impression, in William's gravelly voice.

Robert had exactly the same Cameron features, but overall, the effect was different. He was rounder, more cheerful, less ominous. His skin glowed with a robust tan.

It was evident, seeing John and Robert standing next to each other, that John was not well. What was also suddenly, shockingly, evident to her, was that William was not well either.

John had been diagnosed with phthisis in August. His father had been quick, despite the extreme disappointment he felt in losing another son, to order John's immediate dispatch to Australia. Robert, aching for adventure and lacking ambition towards any of his father's aspirations, begged to be allowed to travel.

John Cameron Senior was not keen. Angus was running the sawmill in Perth. Alexander was ensconced in the bank. John, aged 27, had been running the Cameron Brothers shipping and warehousing business, ably assisted by James who was now 23. James would have to step up into the management role, and Robert, now 20, would have to become his assistant. Joseph, 17, was a disappointment. A madcap. A wild one. He was young, of course, but—Bert laughed and John looked grim as they told the story—the family was sure Joseph wouldn't amount to anything.

"Mind you," John added dryly, "now Bert has turned Da down, *Bert* won't amount to anything either."

They were sitting in the living room at The Nest, drinking ice lemon tea to which William, John and Bert had added heaps of sugar. The men were appreciatively eating scones, with raspberry jam and clotted cream, while Annie had supplied Jeannie and herself with plates of sliced fruit. Nancy was asleep on Jeannie's chest and, despite this inactivity, the baby had in her keeping much more of Jeannie's attention than did the Cameron brothers and their family tale.

"I don't want to manage a warehouse," Bert said with a good-natured smile. "I want to farm."

"I'm surprised Da let you go." William licked cream from his fingers.

"Ma ordered it," Bert replied. "She won't wait for the rest us to sicken. She'll send Joseph in a year, she says, when he's more sensible."

"That won't happen," John said dourly.

"Ma will have her way," William surmised.

"Aye, but Joseph won't be more sensible."

William and Bert laughed, and Jeannie was dismayed that William, who had barely spoken to her of Joseph, readily joined in this dismissive, unkind banter about his youngest brother.

"Tell me about your sisters," she redirected the conversation only to find, as the brothers told of marriages and births, that she struggled to keep up. She did fix in her mind the announcement that Margaret, the sister William had talked most about, was pregnant with her third child.

"They live in the Borders, don't they?"

"Peebles." William confirmed.

Jeannie knew Peebles. She called to mind green fields; massive shady oak trees; narrow roads between high hedgerows; mossy, stone arch bridges over cool, swiftly flowing streams. Margaret and Dr Clement Gunn, she imagined, led exactly the life she and William should have had. Jeannie blinked hard against the tears that stung her eyes. She was feeling unaccountably sorry for herself.

"Jeannie's tired. She needs rest." Her mother's voice cut authoritatively across Bert's ongoing disclosure of Cameron family news.

Jeannie did not object. She gave Nancy up to Annie and offered her hands to William so he could pull her from the chair.

John and Bert—well-mannered boys, she thought—jumped to their feet and nodded a polite farewell.

~

"It's normal," her mother said, "to feel sad."

They were sitting on the veranda in the cool night air. Nancy had finished her feed and was sleepily tucked into Jeannie's arm. Upon her mother's insistence, Jeannie was drinking a raspberry leaf tea, feeling envious of Annie's cup of their normal evening sustenance. William had taken his brothers in the jinker, returning them to their rented house for the night.

"I'm not sad, I'm happy. I'm blessed."

"Why tears then?"

"I don't know. Overwhelmed. Tired."

"Homesick."

Jeannie hummed.

"Your disappointments are crowding in on you. But it will pass. You'll get your energy back, and then you'll concentrate on the bairn."

"Did *you* feel sad after we were born?"

"Not with my first bairns, but with you, very much so."

Jeannie felt affronted. She couldn't cope, just now, with her mother's criticism.

"You weren't the cause. The sadness isn't disappointment in the bairn."

"Why then?"

Annie shrugged. "The sadness happens to most at one birthing or another, and if there be something for it to fix on, then it will. Our Johnnie drowned only months before, and after you were born my mind fixed on it, without mercy. Your grandma was ailing, in bed with the palsy down a side. She didn't know my face; she didn't acknowledge you as my new bairn. She died a month after you were born and I took it as the end of the world."

Jeannie was overawed. Her mother had never before spoken to her in this way. In comparison, her own concerns were suddenly trivial.

"I have ever felt a guilt on me," Annie continued, "that I didn't hold you close, in the early months. That I went far into the melancholia and took so long to come out. Your Aunt Agnes was by me those months. She held you for me and when I recovered, she returned you to me with such grace, trusting I could raise you after all. I owed her a child. To bear our William for her was the least I could do."

Annie drew a deep breath while Jeannie sat in dumb silence —glimpsing, for the first time, her mother's path from grief to strength.

"But the sadness was with me *first*, is what I say." Annie motioned towards Jeannie's cup, as a reminder that she must drink the bitter brew. "It's a sadness that's there because the birthing has taken your energy away, and left you without the strength you normally have, to deal with the losses you feel. You must think of the good things. You must think upwards, not down; forwards, not back, and it *will* pass."

*Thursday 1*st *February 1894*

"You are a Godsend, Nora Bailey," Jeannie called out from the bench seat on the back veranda, watching Nora hang the morning's batch of square cotton nappies on the line. Nora gave her a cheerfully dismissive wave in reply and Olga, who had been sniffing around a piece of iron laid beyond the end of the garden, took the sound of Jeannie's voice as a summons. The dog padded through the dust of the well-beaten path, up the back stairs and laid her head on Jeannie's lap. "You too, Olga," Jeannie murmured, fondling Olga's ears. "You're a great comfort."

It was the first day of February, and the sadness was still with her, though it didn't overwhelm her the way it had at first. She had become accustomed to sitting with it; wearing it like a shabby dressing gown at times when Nancy was asleep, and there was nothing for her to do. It would leave her, her mother had promised, in autumn, when she could get back into the garden and make herself busy again. Every day, despite the ongoing, suffocating heat, Jeannie walked a bit further, lifted something slightly heavier and added marginally to her self-sufficiency, but she still dreaded the thought of riding in the jinker, or bending over a shovel.

Her mother would be arriving at Struan, in Melbourne, today. There would be green grass and purple wisteria. There would be plump courgettes, running beans, and carrots ready to pull. Maybe Frank would stay for dinner. They would talk about how awful Annie thought Mildura; how she couldn't bear the heat. In the week prior to her sudden departure the mercury had passed 100°F on seven consecutive days and Annie had left, claiming Jeannie could cope without her, thanks be to Nora Bailey.

Frank and Annie would disparage the cracked-earth emptiness that stretched in all directions away from The Nest. They would, Jeannie knew, speculate on the poverty of Mildura's circumstances and bemoan the coarseness of its society. They would debate William's strange, antisocial behaviour and draw invalid conclusions.

There was no rift between herself and William. She understood that he preferred the company of his brothers to that of his mother-in-law. She understood that Annie had monopolised the baby, giving William the clear message that the care of Nancy and of Jeannie, was *her* domain. She understood that William felt thwarted, and had banished himself to John and Bert's farmstead rather than let his anger show. On many nights in January, he had not come home to sleep in the surgery waiting room, and how could she blame him?

For the last three nights, with his house restored to him, William had reclined comfortably on the sofa, with Nancy sprawled on his bare chest and a look of smug contentment on his face. Watching them, Jeannie felt her cloak of sadness replaced by the heavier burden of love. Love and fear of what she might lose. She had never felt more vulnerable. How could anything be this precious?

William was, however, behaving strangely. The rabbits were gone, thank goodness, but the box of test tubes was still in the corner by the stove and Jeannie—monitoring the box with horror—had observed that it disappeared with William, at times, into the surgery store room. He was continuing to cultivate tubercle bacilli, but to what end? She had learned not to quiz him about his research—it only led to gruff, insulting obfuscation. She wished he would be open with her. She supposed he was secretive because he didn't want to worry her, but that only made her worry more.

What worried her most was that he had unexpectedly closed the surgery a few times after a night at John and Bert's house. He had been unwell, he said, though he was showing no signs of the usual respiratory distress. Had he taken to drinking whisky with John and Bert? To the extent that he could not work the next day? How could she even think that of him?

John, like Annie, was blunt about Mildura's shortcomings. He hated the heat, he was not interested in horticulture or farming, and nothing in all the Antipodes could console him in his exile from Scotland. His vigorous intent to return home made Jeannie realise how far she and William had come, in accepting their life in Australia. William asserted vehemently that it was a mistake for John to think that the tubercles were defeated; there was no short-term cure for phthisis. William was on what struck Jeannie as a Messianic quest, to keep his brother in Mildura.

Meanwhile, Bert was on a quest to master the practicalities of horticulture, specifically fruit growing. He had borrowed Jeannie's books and newspaper cuttings, and had asked her many questions. Jeannie enjoyed his boyish enthusiasm, and she was looking forward to the day she would be able to climb up into the jinker and endure the stomach-jolting trip to Bert's block to see what he was up to.

The sound of Nancy's waking wail interrupted Jeannie's thoughts.

"Will I get her for you, Jeannie?" Nora stepped from the grass directly onto the veranda with an agility Jeannie envied.

"No, I can do it, thank-you." Jeannie positioned herself on the edge of the bench seat and pushed herself carefully upwards. She walked slowly into the room she now shared with Nancy, and lifted the small, grizzly bundle into her arms. She sniffed unhappily at the smell of Nancy's full nappy.

"I could change her for you."

"I'm alright, Nora, really," Jeannie dismissed the girl, who had anxiously shadowed her into the room. "I want to do it myself."

~

At the end of March, John booked a single ticket on *The Ellen* for Murray Bridge. From there he would travel by coach to Adelaide and pick up a steamer heading back to England.

Jeannie had thought William was not going to accompany his brothers to the wharf, but at the last moment he grabbed his hat from the hall stand and marched out the door towards the jinker.

John frowned after him, then turned back to Jeannie.

"I'm very glad to have met you," he said gently.

"Likewise," she held out her hand to him, and John grasped it in both hands, bowing over it instead of kissing her, as was his careful, hygienic habit.

"I wish it could be otherwise," he murmured.

"I understand. He may not have said it, but he will miss you terribly."

"I hope he won't stay angry with me for long."

"It's sorrow he's feeling, John. It's only an appearance of anger. Will you take word back to your family that I desperately wish I could meet them all? One day we *will* bring our family home to yours."

"I leave him the better brother." John nodded towards Bert, who was sitting in the driver's seat, watching them impatiently. "But don't you *ever* tell either of them I said so."

She laughed. "Away with you, and God bless."

Jeannie was not entirely sorry to see John go. She expected John's departure to lead to a reduction in William's anxiety; the strange intensity of his behaviour and the restlessness of his nights. She knew now what William had been up to because she had interrupted him, when she was walking the house, burping Nancy after a mid-night feed. She had seen that his bedroom was empty, and light was glowing dimly under the door to the surgery.

He had looked at her in guilty alarm, syringe balanced delicately inside his elbow. Then came defensive anger.

"Leave me!" he ordered, with such vehemence that she did, without comment.

The next morning, she insisted he explain himself.

He had described the intravenous formalin injections to her in such positively authoritative terms that she could have thought he was running a successful research project for the Berlin Institute. She knew her husband well enough, however, to see through his bravado to the extreme risk he was taking. She was furious with him—and terrified—which, he told her stiffly, was exactly why he had kept his self-treatment a secret.

He had to stop the disease, he said. He had so little time left, he said. For John. There was mania in the way he had stabbed his finger at his microscope.

"And for you?" she asked pointedly.

He had refused to say more.

Jeannie hoped William would regain his balance once John was gone. She was glad Bert had decided to stay, and she hoped William would be uplifted by his younger, healthier, more affable brother.

"Why would I go back?" Bert had said to her, a joke in his tone, as always. "There's nothing but servitude waiting at home for me—to James, if not to John. I can be my own man here."

When William and Bert came back to The Nest for their mid-day meal, having seen John onto the paddle steamer, William was in a more positive mood.

They had encountered George Chaffey at the wharf. The great man, William reported enthusiastically, was off to London, by way of San Francisco. Upon his return in six months, George would have 250,000-pounds worth of debentures with which to fund the recovery of the settlement.

With the money, William asserted, Chaffeys would move the intake for the town water.

They would concrete the base and banks of the irrigation channels, said Bert.

No, they would completely enclose the channels in pipes, William countered.

The agricultural college could finally be built, Bert enthused.

The sewage could be put underground, and pumped to a distant soak away field that would be planted with lucerne and used as a common for pasturing cows, William suggested.

Jeannie wondered if there would be any money left over to pay the staff at the hospital their long overdue wages.

~

Jeannie first gathered the courage to climb into the jinker not in order to visit Bert's place, but to ride to St Andrew's for Nancy's baptism in May. At the end of the slow, but none-theless uncomfortable trip, she handed her precious, firmly-wrapped bundle of baby to William, and tried to determine the easiest way to climb down.

Looking back to William for help, she found that he had already been surrounded by women who wanted to see Nancy, and it was Bert who arrived gallantly at the footstep of the jinker and lifted her down with a light, teasing flounce. Bert was much stronger, she realised with poignant surprise, than William.

William was showing off to the ladies. He had unfolded Nancy's wrap and was bouncing her in his arms, pulling faces, tickling her neck and trying to make her smile. Nancy was in a contrary state of mind. She was gracing the crowd with her hardest stare, on the precipice of a bawl rather than a laugh. At four months, Jeannie thought, Nancy was showing signs of having a wilful character. The blissful days of her lying peacefully on William's chest, easily roused to smiles and laughter by tickling games, were coming to an end. Jeannie had a growing suspicion that the bairn might take after her primary namesake.

"Annie Calder Isabella Cameron," the Reverend Matthew intoned as he splashed water in the shape of The Cross on Nancy's forehead.

Nancy issued a resounding howl, the congregation laughed, and William struggled to keep hold of the outraged child as she squirmed and reached out for her mother. Jeannie kept her hands firmly clasped in front of her skirt. She cast her eyes down in embarrassment rather than reverence as Nancy screamed all the way through the baptismal prayer.

"She *is* a feisty one!" Mary Shilliday said afterwards, leaning in for a close look into Nancy's wary eyes.

"A good pair of lungs!" said Ellen Findlay.

"A successful audition for the choir," joked Gilbert and he slapped William on the back with such force, that William had no choice but to thrust Nancy into Jeannie's arms while he turned, and stumbled away, coughing.

"Gilbert!" Ellen admonished her husband.

"Sorry," Gilbert apologised to Jeannie, "I forgot."

"How is he?" Ellen anxiously watched William as he isolated himself by the bushes that lined the side of the church.

"He's fine. He'll be alright," Jeannie reassured them.

But William was not fine. At night, while she was feeding Nancy, she could hear him struggling for breath, coughing, turning and struggling again. He did not share a bed with her, but nevertheless, she knew from the hugs she forced upon him that he was steadily losing weight. He avoided all manner of physical work and even so, she often witnessed him short of breath. The simple action of bending over was likely to cause him to reach for the support of a chair or a wall, swooning for lack of oxygen. His lungs, he had admitted to her, were beset with a permanent, fiery ache.

How was it then, she asked him impertinently, that he continued to smoke a pipe?

His response was that his pipe was one of his few pleasures in life. It had a beneficial effect in that it calmed his nerves. She was not to nag him about it.

Jeannie conceded, to herself, the importance of calming William's nerves. Since John's departure he had remained volatile. He could go from happily lying on the floor playing with Nancy in one moment, to yelling, in the next, with furious irrationality at Olga for something as trivial as entering the house with a bedraggled, dirty tail.

On occasion, as she provoked him for his feelings, he dropped fragments that she tried to piece together as if his psyche were a jigsaw.

When she asked why he monopolised Nancy, he retorted "Why complain of me? *You* have time in plenty for yourself!"

When she asked why he had such a vehement reaction to the report that Chaffeys' debenture issue had been undersubscribed, he growled "They're ruining the settlement. Your blocks won't be worth anything. They're all bloody fools!" When she told him, it didn't matter to her, he replied tersely. "It will!"

When he found her digging manure into her vegetable patch in order to plant her autumn seeds, he quite lost his head in anger.

"William," she replied sternly. "I am healed, and I am going to plant my garden!"

"*You* have an incision THIS wide," he demonstrated with the gap between his two index fingers, "*inside* your body. You may think your outer scar has healed but what of the one inside? Huh?"

She wavered under the strength of his tone. "I feel fine, Willie. I need to do just a little work here."

"No. NO." He took the shovel from her. "If those stitches break you will die. Understand? Who will there be to look after Nancy then?"

"Are you saying I can *never* work in my garden again?"

"Aye! Don't do it. Just don't do it!"

He stormed off, taking the shovel with him, leaving her agog.

He drove her to it, she told herself, with this sort of irrational behaviour. He needed her help, and she didn't know what else she could do.

One afternoon, while he was away on his rounds, she read through his exchange of letters with Dr Springthorpe, and she examined the entries in his red journal. She knew now that he was injecting himself with increasing doses of formalin and she knew that Dr Springthorpe had flagged mood disorder as one of the side effects found in experimental subjects in Britain. Some of the people treated had, after a lengthy battle with the menacing impact the anti-toxin had on their bodies and minds, successfully recovered. But there were many more who had not been so lucky.

Having invaded his privacy, and having informed herself as well as she could, Jeannie still had no idea what she could do to help.

She went to Abramowski's chemist shop on the pretext of buying paints and, finding the apothecary unoccupied, she invited him to talk to her about a home-nursing class that she wanted to run as an adjunct to the next series of first-aid classes, starting in August. It would be good, she told him, to help women understand what natural foods and remedies were beneficial for restoring health to the children and invalids in their care.

"I understood that William does not take stock in such remedies?" Abramowski queried.

"I have my own mind on the subject, Otto," she replied firmly.

Abramowski cheerfully set about a lengthy explanation of which nutritive foods and restorative herbs could be grown in Mildura. Jeannie left the chemist with a basket full of seed packs, fresh nuts, raisins, olives, and a small handful of tinctures.

She was going to build William back up again, and she knew it couldn't be done with the sugars and starches of which he was so fond.

She planted her seeds, and if William noticed her new garden patch, he was sensible enough not to comment. As for the nuts, raisins and olives she left in dishes in his surgery store room and on the mantlepiece ... they were eaten by the end of each day.

By July, in her estimation, William was much improved. His journal showed that, at the point where the number of tubercles per field (column 'TB/F') had begun to decline, he had marginally reduced the concentration of formalin ('CH20%'). He was injecting himself twice a week and recording his TB/F morning and night. There was a pattern of a reduction in the TB/F, 24 hours after his injection, followed by stable counts until the next injection.

He was watching her feed Nancy when she asked him, hoping for full disclosure, whether the formalin injections were working. He looked at her with a canny half-smile.

"What do *you* make of the results?"

She felt herself blushing, re-balanced Nancy against her breast and chose to act as if she had done nothing wrong. He had, after all, left the journal sitting in evidence on his desk. He must have wanted her to read it.

"It's good, isn't it? The reduction in the TB/F... is that the *dormant* tubercles leaving your bloodstream?"

"Aye."

"They'll be gone? They can't be reactivated?"

"*Those* ones are gone. Time will tell if others are seeded."

"You can't stop the injections?"

"I will stop, when no tubercles remain."

"I worry Willie, what the formalin does to you."

He shrugged.

"But I'd rather *know* how it's going."

"How is feeding me going?" He reached for the ever-present dish on the mantlepiece and emptied its contents into his hand.

"*You* tell me."

"I like walnuts better than almonds." He picked out an almond and offered it to her.

She shook her head. He dropped the almond back and tipped the entire mixed handful into his mouth.

~

With the arrival of spring, Jeannie insisted upon a day trip to see her block and Bert's. The horse was harnessed and Nancy was strapped into her basket, about to be secured onto the jinker seat when a buggy careered around the corner of 10th Street and pulled up at the surgery gate.

William looked at her apologetically.

"I'll go anyway," she said.

"No."

"Bert's expecting us."

The lad who had jumped from the buggy was calling 'Doctor!" and running for the surgery door.

"I don't have time for this," William said tersely. "Leave the horse till I come back." He strode into the house and a few moments later she watched the buggy carry him away.

She finished cross-strapping the baby basket onto the wooden plank that served as a seat. Satisfied that the basket could not move, and that Nancy could not escape, she picked up the reins and slapped them against the horse's sides.

Chronometer—named for his reliable, clockwork pace— turned his head, spying on her past the wide blinker on his bridle as if disbelieving her instruction to disobey their master.

She slapped the reins harder, demanding "Get on with you!", and Chronometer shuffled off, through the gate.

"You're late!" Bert greeted her at the gate to her block.

"Willie was called away at the last minute."

"She's asleep." Bert dropped his voice to a whisper when he looked into the basket Jeannie handed him.

"It's a wonder, isn't it? This jinker shakes the bones out of me, but sends *her* to sleep."

Bert tucked the basket under one arm and swung Jeannie off the jinker.

"Leave her here," Jeannie directed Bert to place the basket in a modest patch of shade under a young fig. They wouldn't walk far, or for long.

A stick-figure with sandy hair and bare, muddy feet approached them through the field.

"Hullo Missus. It's a right pleasure to see you here!"

She tried to see through the splashes of mud on his face, unsure which of her workers he was. Then she spotted the scars on his thin forearm.

"Ned," she smiled and pointed to his arm, which he raised for her to examine. "How is it going?"

"Much the better. Don't hurt no more."

She worried that he had worked too soon; he could have dirtied the burnt flesh that still needed to heal under its new covering of skin.

"Nah, it's good." He smacked his arm roughly to show her how good.

She winced for him. "What are you planting, Ned?"

"Melons by the channel. Tatties and turnips behind you there. It's been a Godsend for us Missus, you letting us grow food here."

"You're looking after the irrigation?"

"Aye, but it's hard when pumps don't bring us water enough."

"Has there not been enough water?" Jeannie looked to Bert.

"Barely," he confirmed.

Jeannie cast a critical eye across her stunted trees.

"A wet year will catch them up," Bert assured her.

"Ned," Jeannie pointed her sandalled foot towards the lush vegetation on the edge of the irrigation trench, "You must keep the weeds down. Your vegetables will grow better without competition."

"Aye Missus, we'll be weeding this week."

"They won't," Bert whispered into her ear as Ned returned to his melon patch. "What they do, is let their goats in here to graze."

Jeannie looked at him in alarm. "But the goats damage the trees!"

"Aye." Bert stepped up to a peach tree and pointed to the unmistakeable teeth marks in its thin trunk.

Jeannie sighed in frustration. It was of mutual benefit, allowing the clearing camp workers to grow their vegetables along the irrigation ditches while they tended to her orchard, and it was sensible that the goats which gave them milk, cheese and the occasional celebratory feast of meat could graze on the weeds. But the goats could not be allowed to damage the fruit trees.

"Tell them, Bert, they *must* have a herder watching the goats *all the time*!"

"I have. But I'm not here to watch *them* all the time."

"Pff!" She stared crossly at the weeds that were clogging the irrigation ditch, sure to limit the flow of water. "What can I do?"

"You're too kind to them."

"I can't be *unkind* to them."

"That's why they love *you*. They don't like William."

"What?" She was stunned by Bert's bald statement. "*He's* the one who repairs their wounds!"

"Aye, but they call him a snob. So do the blockers."

"Why are you telling me this?" she demanded.

"Well," he faltered, "it's the truth. That's what they say. And he is."

"You shouldn't speak that way about your brother."

"He's nowt but angry with me since John left. He patronises me." Having started, Bert let his dissatisfactions flow. "If you were to believe *him*, I'm not doing anything right. The wrong sprays, the wrong fertiliser, he always speaks to me as if he knows better."

Jeannie was lost for a reply. Bert ripped a long stalk of grass from the ground and chewed on it.

"He's always in The Mildura Club with his cronies—W.B. and such. That's why the blockers call him a snob."

"He has to spend time with them," Jeannie rose to William's defence. "It's just as well he has friends amongst the gentlemen of the town; they're the only ones who pay their bills!"

"That's not why he's there. He likes the status of the club."

"W.B. is a good man; a good friend."

"The blockers say the Chaffeys ripped them off."

"Well, you shouldn't believe their bitching."

Bert raised an eyebrow at her language. He laughed at the reddening of her cheeks.

"I've joined The Settlers' Club," he announced.

It was Jeannie's turn to raise an eyebrow. The Settlers' Club was a recent addition to Mildura's society. It was the equivalent of the professional men's Mildura Club, giving the blockers a place to meet, have a meal and be served wine and spirits. The Temperance Society was strongly critical of the increasing erosion of Mildura's moral virtue.

"You're drinking?" she queried, askance.

"Better there than at Pinkie Bend," he replied provocatively.

"You never!" She did not believe him. Pinkie Bend was where town workers met to consume illegal crates of 'the craythur', home-brewed whisky and spirit concoctions, brought across the river from Gol Gol.

"William drinks."

"A whisky after a meal sometimes."

"Wine with W.B."

"That's only polite."

"So, William drinks."

She was obliged to soften her tone, "Go to The Settlers' Club on occasion, but you're *not* to go to Pinkie Bend."

Bert laughed at her. "It's the one in the basket you should be mothering."

Jeannie, intent on her exchange with Bert, had been ignoring the grumbling coming from the baby basket. Now Nancy broke into a wail, demanding Jeannie's return.

"A feed or another ride in the cart?" Bert asked as Jeannie bent to the basket.

"Your field," Jeannie replied.

Bert lifted the basket, and skipped to the jinker, bouncing and jiggling Nancy in swirls that kept the bairn dumbstruck. Jeannie couldn't help but smile.

"You drive," he said, as she came to the passenger side behind him. Before she could answer he had clambered up onto the seat and was strapping the baby basket into place. "Quick! Before she starts crying again!"

In the early afternoon, when she drove back through the gate of The Nest, William stepped out onto the veranda. As she unbuckled the baby basket and brought it down from the jinker, he stayed there, leaning against a post; arms folded; lips tight.

Nancy woke immediately. The poor bairn was desperate for a feed and she let the neighbourhood know.

"I have to feed her," Jeannie murmured as she hurried inside.

"You'll put the horse away later?" William growled.

"Aye!" she retorted.

He changed his stance, however. As Nancy latched onto the nipple and the living room fell quiet, Jeannie heard the harness slapping, and the cart wheels scraping as William rolled the cart into the barn.

Replaying their angry exchange, inside her head, she was reminded of countless similar moments with Frank. It had always been Frank, giving her orders. And it had been Jim, airing the grievances he had against his older brother. She remembered her mother's words of advice. "You have a kind ear, Jeannie. Be mindful, Jim is spouting for your sympathy. There's nowt Jim wants you to do, other than that he thinks he can win the more of your love. Don't take sides."

She would say nothing to William, Jeannie decided, about what Bert had said to her. It would not help.

~

As December came and January went, Jeannie was very glad of her mother's vow to never again visit Mildura in summer. For days on end the temperature soared beyond 100°F, and while Jeannie was prostrate with the heat, Nancy was cruising. Up on her feet, balancing herself hand over hand along a piece of furniture, then launching herself at a tottering run in the hope of making it to the next possible support—solid or not. New bruises emerged daily on Nancy's forehead, elbows and shins. Jeannie had moved everything that could break onto high shelves, or into lockable cupboards. It was surprising how far Nancy's arms could reach. Nothing Jeannie put on the kitchen sideboard was safe. It would have been a disaster, had she accepted her mother's invitation to spend Christmas at Struan. Surely none of Annie Irvine Robertson's children behaved this badly?

"She's gorgeous!" William countered Jeannie's concerns. Bouncing Nancy on his knee; throwing her into the air; twirling her one arm and one leg outstretched in a circle while she squealed with delight. At the end of playtime, he would kiss Nancy on the head, wish her 'sweet dreams!' and disappear into his surgery, expecting the child to be peacefully asleep, and his dinner on the table within the hour.

Annie Irvine Robertson, Jeannie told her husband ruefully, had the benefit of a nursemaid, a scullery maid and a cook.

"Ask Nora to come back," William said airily, chewing a mouthful of rabbit-loaf and potato-bake.

"And pay her with what?"

"She wouldn't ask for money."

"She's working at the hospital."

"She doesn't get paid for that either."

"When is *anyone* in this town going to be paid, William?" Jeannie asked in desperation. "What does W.B. say?"

William hummed irritatingly.

"Meaning, it's not going well."

"Hmmm."

"The Shillidays are trading in promissory notes now. Can you believe it?"

"John's furious with Mary."

"She has no choice. No one has cash. They pass the notes from hand-to-hand promising credit from a bank that, as far as I can tell, no longer exists."

"True."

"That the bank no longer exists?" Jeannie challenged him, angered by his flippant replies.

"Hmmm." William diligently mopped the remaining gravy from his plate with a piece of bread.

"Do we have any money in the non-existing bank?"

"Fortunately, not."

"In your test tube box?"

"Fortunately, yes."

"Well, we also have a wad of promissory notes against the non-existing bank in the safe. I suppose you want me to use those now, to shop at Shillidays?"

"Yes."

"Mary will be very disappointed."

"We're all disappointed." He pushed his plate away.

"Meaning, you're disappointed in me?" She snatched his clean plate and her unfinished one, up from the table and marched them to the sink.

"No ..."

"Because people in your waiting room hear Nancy screaming like a banshee? Because your house is a wreck? Because your dinner is late and overcooked?" She was furiously tearful.

"Valid reasons for divorce!" He came up behind her, wrapped his arms around her waist and kissed her on the neck.

"What *is* so funny? *Why* are you in such a good mood?!"

"Come." He took her hand and pulled her into the surgery.

He opened his red journal and stood waiting for her to make sense of his entries.

"So ..." she stopped her left index finger on the last entry in the dosage column, and ran her right index finger down the

'TB/F' column. "It's thirty days since the last injection, and there are no tubercles."

"None."

"Willie ... can we believe this?" She looked up at him, tears of hope filling her eyes.

"Aye. Aye, we can."

She dissolved, crying and laughing, in his arms.

~

She thought he might be agreeable to starting another bairn.

There was a high risk of uterine prolapse, he told her, shaking his head resolutely. She must wait at least two years after Nancy's birth to be sure she was healed. He would absolutely not take the chance, and she would not trick him, not this time.

Chapter 14

William

Saturday 16th March 1895

William threw the letter down, frustrated even though he had known not to expect a reprieve. Springthorpe didn't know —no one could know—if new tubercles would appear next week, next spring or in five years. But in the letter, Springthorpe queried whether the improvement in William's health was due to the formalin or Mildura's extremely hot weather.

William was annoyed by this. There was a clear correlation in the data he had sent to Springthorpe, between the dates of the injections and the reduction in tubercles. The results could not, of course, be commended to medical peers. His 'research' had been an act of desperation; in no way a controlled testing regime. It was unnecessary for Springthorpe to remind him of that. William had made it clear in his letter that he was offering the data as a matter of interest; to support a proposal for a proper trial.

In reply, Springthorpe maintained his original position: that formalin was a poison known to induce severe illness. Its long-term effects were unknown, and William had taken an enormous risk. It was true, William acknowledged, that he had felt dreadful for weeks as his tolerance to the injections built. So ill that some days he had not been able to open his surgery, and some nights he had stayed at John and Bert's rather than let Jeannie see his dire condition. But the results proved it had been worth the risk. He was sure patients suffering from this debilitating, deadly disease would agree.

The evidence Springthorpe chose to focus on, in William's case, was that his brothers George and John had also contracted the disease. This supported Springthorpe's theory that 'while the root cause of phthisis is, without doubt, bacterial transmission, its prevalence is promoted by constitutional weakness and inherited vulnerability'. He wanted William to let him know if further relatives fell victim to phthisis, and he warned William that such constitutional weakness would, in all likelihood, be passed on to his offspring.

Words which greatly displeased William.

Springthorpe closed his letter with the 'strongest recommendation' that William not be tempted to leave the climate that was benefiting him so favourably.

There was much about Mildura, apart from the climate, that was *not* benefiting him favourably, William thought ruefully, shaking open the copy of *The Mildura Cultivator* that had been delivered with Springthorpe's letter. He had been promised a stipend from the hospital for his work, covering Dr Hill's absence in December and January, and it had come to him in the form of a promissory note. Which was better than the annual 'thank-you' he received as an assistant surgeon, but irritating, nonetheless.

Thanks to his friendship with W.B., Chaffey employees were sent to William when needing treatment, and initially the company had reliably paid in cash. Since the bank closed, however, payment had been by promissory note. William was disappointed in his hope that, when George Chaffey returned from his fundraising trip abroad, those notes would be converted to cash. The desperately needed loan had been written successfully, but the money was being used to line the irrigation channels with cement.

Could William's promissory notes be exchanged for cash?

"Not yet," W.B. had said, "regrettably."

The Shire Council had paid William's £2.50 December quarter wage with a promissory note. There had been a lengthy debate in chambers over amalgamating the roles of Public Health Officer and Inspector of Public Nuisances. William would *not*, he had assured the councillors, take on the job of investigating whose chickens had strayed into the school's vegetable patch. He would *not* be disciplining people who allowed the slurry from their pig pen to drain into the street. The extra responsibilities had instead gone to the Ranger, whose normal task was to gather and impound the bullocks and horses that frequently strayed through the settlement. William noted, with wry amusement, that there was an item in today's *Cultivator*, stating that the Ranger, that 'unfortunate employee', was 'altogether overworked and disgracefully underpaid'.

Council could do away with his own role, William thought angrily. Each month they accepted his reports, agreed to act upon them and did precisely nothing. Nine months ago, he had reported on the shocking state of sanitation in the town. Council's contractor was not satisfactorily disinfecting the sanitary pans, and his method of treating the excreta before resale as manure was grossly inadequate. The sanitation contractor had defended himself, saying he did the best he could, cleaning 1700 pans with the meagre payment Council gave him. William had won only a temporary ban on the use of the potentially infectious manure on the town's gardens and fields, while the contractor's method was investigated. William knew nothing would come of the investigation. Council's ineffective response infuriated him and he found the contractor's mercenary negligence deeply offensive.

He had pressed W.B. for funding to put the town's sewerage underground. A 'stellar idea', W.B. had said, but 'regrettably', unaffordable.

The Irrigation Company, encouraged by heavy December rains, had deferred the summer irrigation schedule. Why pay wages the company could not afford to pay? The irrigationists were ill-prepared for January's heatwave, and their trees and vines had suffered. What did they expect? *The Cultivator* mused. There were '1000 sturdy adult men to do the work'—they could have jumped-to and manned the pumps themselves, as volunteers. There was no excuse. All of Chaffeys' equipment was serviceable and available to them.

"It only needs organisation and management to make the settlement absolutely secure from the danger of a stoppage to the water supply," the editor of *The Cultivator* had written.

Organisation and management that must be supplied by the Irrigation Company, asserted W.B.

Organisation and management that had not yet been applied towards *any* improvement that William, as the town's Public Health Officer, had suggested.

He was totally fed up with Mildura's 'regrettable' impecunity and ineffective administration.

The next harvest was, as ever, held up as Mildura's saviour, but the same had been said before the last harvest. Mildura's 'best crop yet' had, in fact, proved *too* bountiful. The Mildura Fruit Preserving Company had operated their small establishment day and night, while the mouldy smell of rotting fruit wafted from the crates stacked tall along their common border-fence, across Jeannie's vegetable garden and into his surgery.

The last crop, William knew from Bert's dismal experience, was large, but not necessarily the 'best'. It had rained heavily over two separate weeks in December—an unprecedented total of five-and-a-quarter inches in the month, exactly when the apricots were ripening. There was more *bulk* in the crop than the year before—Bert's five acres had yielded 17.5 tons—but the rain had darkened the colour, which was unacceptable to the fresh fruit market. Recognising this, Bert paid to have his apricots dried before he despatched them on their long journey to Melbourne. By the time his produce reached the market, moth larvae had been detected in another batch of dried apricots and the price for all of Mildura's dried stone fruit had dropped by half. It would have been cheaper for Bert to plough his apricots into the ground.

Bert's peaches were a problem too, but for a different reason. The previous owner of his acres had been duped by a rogue traveling nurseryman who sold what turned out, upon bearing, to be 'mongrel peach' trees. This, William learnt belatedly, was the reason the previous owner had quit the colony, and readily completed the sale William had thought such a bargain. The market did not want 'mongrel peaches'—they were too small, the wrong shape, the wrong colour, good for nothing but jam and not much good, in William's opinion, for that either.

William preferred jams made from berries, especially raspberry. He also liked honey, and he was dismayed to read in *The Cultivator* that the heavy Christmas rain had ruined this year's harvest of honey from the redgums along the river front.

What next?

William slapped the paper down in disgust and glowered at his empty waiting room.

~

"Do we have any of the redgum honey left?" William could not see it on the shelves in the kitchen.

"It's there, right where you look." Jeannie tried to hand him his dinner plate, but he reached up instead to pick out the jar of honey and reorganise the jars of jam.

"Is this the only one?"

"Aye."

"There's no harvest this year on account of the rain in December," William cradled the now-precious only-jar.

"Then you'll have to ration it. Can you bring the gravy jug?"

Jeannie walked through to the dining table with both plates.

"You could put a sign on the surgery desk: 'Payment accepted in redgum honey'," she suggested when he joined her.

"Good idea."

"You had a letter from your mother?" Jeannie queried.

"Aye. It's on and on about the wedding."

His brother James had married Ethel Watson in January, in the great St Giles cathedral in Edinburgh. There were pages upon pages in Isabella's letter, about the bridal gown Ethel wore; the guests who attended; the presents they gave; the decorations in the church. It was exactly the sort of letter Jeannie loved to read.

"Any news of John?"

"No, only that he is steady at the helm of the company, and Da has time to concentrate on the parish council."

"Have you decided on becoming a councillor?" Jeannie asked.

Dr Hill was retiring from Council and had nominated William as his replacement.

"I have decided 'absolutely not'. I couldn't stand it. They get nothing done. Their ineffectiveness is surpassed only by the Irrigation Company."

"Aye," Jeannie agreed, "it's bad enough, your temper, after reporting to a meeting."

"Dr Hill is resigning from the bench. I'll consider that, though they do little but deliberate on petty debts."

"And prosecuting sly-groggers?"

Jeannie's question reminded William of something W.B. had said.

"Do you know if Bert drinks with the groggers at Pinkie Bend?"

"Bert's a member of The Settlers' Club," Jeannie replied.

"He was reported to Sergeant Carter, who told W.B., to tell me."

"Did you speak with Bert?"

"I'm asking you first, since you have his confidence."

"It's alright if he has a drink with a meal at Settlers, isn't it?"

William shrugged in reluctant assent. "He'll find himself before the bench if Carter nabs him at Pinkie's Bend."

"He's no reason to go there."

William was satisfied by her answer. Disciplining Bert was a disagreeable business, best avoided.

"Have you any money left for Bert?" Jeannie was referring to the funds his father had originally supplied.

"No. I gave the whole of it to him. Has he run it through?"

"He worries he can't afford the chemicals he needs. He doesn't want to be next with moths attacking his fruit."

"If he wants to beg Da for more money, he'll do it himself. There'll be no loan ..."

A wail came from Nancy's bedroom and they both froze, forks poised, listening. There was a grumbling, a shuffling and a kick to the nursery wall. A lesser wail, a creaking of the cot, then quiet. William looked at Jeannie with uncertain relief. She nodded with a wry smile, and they continued their meal in silence.

Saturday 21st September 1895

When news next came about John, it affected William deeply. John's tuberculosis had reactivated late in the summer. He was to over-winter in a sanatorium at Davos Platz in the Swiss Alps. The high, rarefied air would be good for him, the specialist advised.

William paced the house from hearth to surgery railing against God, doctors and medical researchers. It was ten years since his first diagnosis. Why had they achieved so little? He slammed doors and reopened them a moment later, storming through in the reverse direction. Fearful of the impact of his mood on Nancy, Jeannie opened the back door and ushered him into the fresh spring air of the garden.

William strode to the rabbit shed that was now Jeannie's potting shed. He glared at the garden tools stored higgledy-piggledy along the corrugated iron wall, falling at all angles to the dirt floor. How could she find anything in this mess? He organised the shed: spades, then forks, then hoes, then rakes; pots stacked by size and type under the bench on which the rabbit crates had stood; smaller tools hanging on hooks on the wall above. He swept the bench clean of its covering of plant propagation mix, garden twine, fragments of root, stem and leaf. Finally, he raked the litter off the floor, out of the door and onto the compost heap nearby. He surveyed his work with satisfaction, then tried, unsuccessfully, to close the door.

He kicked the obstinate rectangle of corrugated iron savagely, swearing until his breath ran ragged and he had to bend over, sucking air into his damaged lungs, wheezing like a pump run dry.

She was on the porch, Nancy on her hip. Mother and child watched him with the same thin-lipped, narrow-eyed, worried stare.

He waved to dismiss their concern. He repositioned the dented door on its hinges, lifting it so he could push the bolt home.

"I've made us tea, Willie," she called.

"Joseph's coming." Jeannie opened the conversation as she poured his tea.

He had read that, in his mother's letter, but his attention, overwhelmingly, had gone to John's situation.

"Your mother wants to be sure he's not the next with the trouble," Jeannie added.

"Da doesn't know what else to do with him."

"How old is he?"

"Nineteen. He's been dafty at quay. Dafty at mill. Now dafty at bank. Da's got nowhere else will have him."

"Is he like Alexander?"

"No." William munched on a coconut biscuit, considering his words. Jeannie disliked hearing criticism of her fellow man, and yet … she took the Bible literally. "Alex is intelligent. More sensitive than befits a man. Good at the bank. Nothing wrong with Alex. But he doesn't fit with the manners expected."

"He's one who will never marry."

William nodded, appreciating Jeannie's neat summation. "Joseph, though … he's not sensible in his head. No sense of proportion. Follows any wild idea. Forgets what he's asked to do. Needs a firm hand. The navy, Bert thinks."

"Your father's putting him on a ship to work his passage. Perhaps that will set him right?"

"Not likely."

They both looked towards the door, hearing the clatter of a buggy pulling up at the gate. Olga jumped to her feet with a sharp bark, and reared up at the window for a better view.

"Expecting anyone?" William asked.

Jeannie shook her head. William selected the last cookie from the plate on the table and prised himself from his comfortable chair. With the cookie jammed between his teeth, he donned his hat, then his coat, picked up his medical bag, and walked out the door.

The young English lieutenant was semi-comatose when William arrived at the hospital. Abramowski was already there, and William was quick to agree that the man had suffered a dislocation and fracture of the spine. There were strong spirits involved. A Mildura Club dance on Friday night, after which the lieutenant had met with young larrikins who partied until dawn. There had been rough play, daredevil acts, and not long after sun-up the alcohol-addled lieutenant had dived into the river from a height. He was pulled out of the water and taken to the Coffee Palace by his party-pals. There, it was ascertained that he could not move either his upper or lower limbs. He had been transferred to the hospital on a cart, and his condition was deteriorating.

Could anything be done? The case was so desperate that William suggested Abramowski send for Dr Hervey from Wentworth who had experience in spinal injuries.

Abramowski left the ward to dispatch a messenger and William remained, standing by the patient's bedside, looking at the young man's inert but otherwise handsome, well-formed body. Lieutenant Orr was 28, the same age as John. Before he had been such a fool as to dive into the river, the lieutenant had been in perfect health. It was an unspoiled body ruined; a life squandered. William felt the injustice tearing at him.

"Your Bert's gone for Dr Hervey," Abramowski reported.

William was surprised.

"He was at the river. More than keen to ride to Wentworth."

William clenched his teeth, keeping his thoughts in. Larrikins from Pinkie Bend or The Settlers' Club? It didn't make much difference; he must have the strongest possible words with Bert.

~

"Has Bert stopped his drinking?"

William was in the kitchen, watching Jeannie experiment with the crystallisation of fruit she had brought home from Bert's orchard. She had cut a recipe from a November edition of *The Cultivator*, and was following it, step by step. Satisfied that the dozen apricots in her tin colander were scalded to the perfect degree of softness, she was now focussed on attaining the ideal saturation of sugar syrup.

"Do you think that's 70 percent?" She held the glass mixing bowl up to his eye so he could read the Balling's saccharometer that floated on top of the mix.

"Your eyes are better than mine," he protested.

"I think I need more sugar." She added a teaspoonful and whisked again.

"Bert," William insisted. He had a strong suspicion that, despite the censure he had delivered regarding the circumstances of Lieutenant Orr's untimely death, Bert had not quit the company of his roughneck settler friends.

"Can't afford to drink," Jeannie responded testily.

"Crop not the best?"

"The crop *is* the best, but they say the drought will close the river by month's end. We won't get *any* fresh fruit to market. It will all have to be preserved or dried—or crystallised like they do in Germany." Jeannie peered at the saccharometer.

"Bert's rates are overdue."

She hummed, which annoyed him.

"It's in the paper. It's shameful." William spoke fiercely. "Our name in the debtors list. The whole town will see."

"With so *many* names," Jeannie conciliated. "Bert will settle his bills after he's sold his crop."

"He won't get paid until it gets to Melbourne. There's *fifteen hundred tons* of canned fruit in storage until the river opens in July."

Jeannie grimaced and sighed, surrendering the argument. William watched as she gently shook the apricots from the colander into an earthenware bowl and poured the sugar syrup over them. He liked the crystallised fruit he had occasionally eaten as a luxury imported from Germany. Hopefully this line of home production would work out well—it looked easy enough.

"What happens with this now?"

"I watch it for six weeks, and each time it starts to ferment I must heat it just to boiling. By that time, the sugar syrup will have replaced all the natural juice in the fruit."

"And then?" William picked up the glass bowl and smoothed his fingers around the inside of the rim, collecting the remnants of the syrup.

"Take out the fruit, rinse and dry it, dip it in a much thicker sugar syrup, and dry it in the ice box. The sugar will harden on the outside."

William sucked his sticky fingers. Not easy after all.

"But," Jeannie added, "the crystallised fruit will keep in *any* climate, and through *any* transport. This is something every orchardist could do at home."

"Bert needs a paying job," William declared, not for the first time.

"Mildura needs a railway line." Jeannie rebutted.

"Tell that to your friend the Shire President."

"I think Otto already knows," Jeannie said dryly. She removed the bowl from his hands and took it to the sink.

Otto Abramowski had been elected Shire President in August. Meanwhile the Minister for Railways, motivated by the parlous state of Victoria's finances, had decided Mildura didn't need a railway because river transport was so cheap and convenient. The Minister had also said that the government would not step in to 'save' Mildura because responsibility for the settlement lay with its private sponsors, the Chaffey Brothers.

The editor of *The Cultivator* had written that this drought could be the very thing to convince the government of the great merits of the irrigation settlement, while demonstrating the desperate need for a railway. There would always be enough water for irrigation, the editor maintained, but at harvest-time there was not enough water for paddle steamers.

William reckoned the government immune to such common-sense. He was anticipating an unhappy end to the situation.

He had asked Jeannie to stock up on supplies using only the promissory notes he knew would soon be useless. When she protested, citing Shilliday's rigorous 'CASH ONLY' policy, he insisted she must shop elsewhere.

He knew Jeannie understood the situation, because she obstinately refused to pay her maid with the promissory notes. It had offended him, though he could see the humour in it, when Jeannie pulled a sock from her drawer and tipped out her stash of coins. She sold her spare vegetables in the town and now, using her own cash, she afforded herself help with the cleaning and the daily wash. Jeannie would be in the garden 'any day', she had declared firmly, rather than the scullery.

The maid who had helped Jeannie for several months, was now heavily pregnant. Becca had, to William's mind, kept working for much too long, but Jeannie had stubbornly sided with the desperate girl because her family had no other income. William had a very low opinion of the ne'er-do-well who was Becca's husband. Whatever it took, he asserted to Jeannie, the man should get out and find work that would provide for his family. Jeannie's response was to remind him to be kind to his fellow brethren.

William admired her charitable nature, but he wished he could rouse her into proper argument. Some people did not deserve her kindness, and she was wrong to defend them. He would have liked her to hand the proceeds of her vegetable sales over to him. He would have preferred that she had *not* advertised for a maid to replace Becca. Did she not understand that they could not spare the money?

Tuesday 3rd December 1895

William read over his Public Health Report with a woebegone sense of déjà vu.

There were three typhoid cases near the 12th Street livery stables; four cases in the town overall. He had asked Council to remind the sanitation officer to scrupulously disinfect the sanitary pans. He had told them the irrigation channels were dangerously low and must be cleaned immediately. He had recommended that the 12th Street stables should be inspected due reports of putrescent odours, and also the 7th Street fowl yard, which was causing similar offence to its neighbourhood.

He knew, however, that there was no one acting as Inspector of Public Nuisances, and he remained determined that it would not be himself dressing up in rubber boots, gown and gloves to go into the mucky confines of the stables and the fowl yard to gather samples.

He closed the cover of his Public Health folder and shifted it to his left, replacing it with the stack of seven first-aid graduation certificates that were waiting for his signature. Abramowski, whose untidy scrawl was already affixed, had conducted the examination and his compliments were overly effusive. None of these girls was as good as Nora Bailey, but maybe it was just as well these candidates were not high achievers. Nora, like all the most promising girls, had left Mildura for Melbourne, where she would either further her career or find an eligible husband. This loss of girls to the city was one of the reasons Bert couldn't find a match. A suitable lass like Nora, William mused, would make the world of difference to Bert.

Jeannie burst through the door as William was addressing the certificate envelopes. Bert followed, carrying Nancy. Jeannie's face was flustered and there were damp trails through the dust on her cheeks as she presented herself in front of his desk.

"Chaffeys have liquidated!"

~

He hadn't known. Though, with hindsight, he realised that W.B. had hinted at the company's course of action. William had taken W.B.'s advice in using up as many of the promissory notes as possible; in keeping hold of his cash. His financial position, nonetheless, was tenuous and he knew that the situation for the wage and contract workers in the community was disastrous. All local payments by Chaffeys had been stopped, all 'unnecessary' work halted, and the promissory notes circulating in the town were now worthless.

Neither of the Chaffey brothers were in the settlement. Rumours abounded. Conspiracy theories spread. Mildura was ruined; the Chaffeys had run off with the settlement's money. William was certain W.B. would not have absconded, but he was wary about George. George, he knew, had taken the irrigationists' complaints about the settlement personally, affronted that his genius, and his efforts on behalf of the colony were so under-appreciated. George had threatened to quit Australia a number of times. W.B., however, had assured William that Mildura was his permanent home.

If W.B. left, William thought, their coterie of business friends would have no reason to stay. Within a few years, Mildura would again belong to the rabbits.

He had been in remission for 11 months. Could he take Jeannie and Nancy back to Melbourne? What an appealing idea that was!

He raised it with Jeannie.

"We *can't!*" she exclaimed.

He knew she was right.

The rumour, spread softly amongst W.B.'s supporters, did not take long to reach William's ears. It was said that, by declaring bankruptcy, W.B. had cleverly manipulated the government into the supportive action that Mildura needed most. Alfred Deakin, the minister who had originally championed Mildura's development, gave a rousing speech in Parliament in support of the irrigation colony, insisting that now Chaffey

Brothers had liquidated, the Victorian government must step in to support the settlement.

When W.B. returned to Rio Vista on Christmas Eve, the mood in the town brightened. George Chaffey returned on New Year's Eve after two years abroad. William and his friends at The Mildura Club, breathed a collective sigh of relief and hopefully raised their glasses to 1896.

Saturday 25th January 1896

"Where's Joseph?" Bert asked as William delved into the dresser and retrieved the bottle of Glenfiddich.

"God only knows," William retorted. He held the bottle up to the light and hummed with satisfaction to see it was three quarters full. More than enough to share with the Findlays and Campbells for their Burns night celebration at Craigieburn.

"He should be here by now," Bert insisted. "*The Glenhuntly* left Glasgow on 5th November."

"It docked in Albany ten days ago." William collected his tobacco pouch and his pipe from the mantlepiece, and pocketed them in his cream cotton pants.

"But you haven't heard from himself?"

"No."

"He should be here by now," Bert repeated.

"Who should be here?" Jeannie came into the room, carrying Nancy on one hip and a carry cot in her other hand. Bert sprang towards her, arms extended in an offer to take part of her load.

Nancy let go of Jeannie and swung herself precariously into space, meeting her uncle half way with a squeal of delight.

"Are we waiting for someone?" Jeannie rephrased her unanswered question.

"No, we're off!" William picked up the food basket, and led the way to the drive where Chronometer was waiting in harness and Moody, Bert's mount, was tied to the side of the jinker.

Jeannie tried to settle Nancy into the cot-basket, but the toddler fought back with howls of protest and stayed defiantly on her feet all the way to Craigieburn. On arrival, Jeannie gratefully handed her into the care of the younger Findlay and Campbell children, and disappeared into the kitchen to help Ellen prepare the dinner. William and Bert secured the horses, and joined Gilbert and Timothy Campbell on Craigieburn's wide veranda. The four men agreed that the Glenfiddich should be poured over ice.

It was slightly cooler this evening, but the day before, Gilbert confirmed, had been the hottest ever recorded in Mildura. 120°F in the shade. Cows had drunk the water troughs dry; melons had withered on the vine; the relatively cool hospital corridors had been full, but amazingly, none had died of heat-stroke. There would be typhoid, William reminded his companions morbidly. There always was after people had been cooling off in the irrigation channels, and gulping water from over-heated house tanks.

Mention of typhoid turned the conversation to the death, a few days earlier, of the young Congregational minister, Reverend Pepper. Gilbert wanted to know if the cause of death had been typhoid, tuberculosis or dropsy? Timothy pursued the gossip that there had been an argument between Doctors Abramowski and Cameron over Pepper's treatment. William demurred. The Reverend Pepper had been in the care of the Proudfoot family and he had simply been asked, by them, to look in on the man.

"Abramowski is furious!" Bert crowed. Gilbert and Timothy joined in the merriment, and William scowled at his brother.

"I heard Otto refused to treat Pepper, once you had 'looked in'," Timothy commented.

"That was between the Proudfoot misses and Abramowski. Not my doing." Which was true enough, William thought to himself. All *he* had done was give the good ladies his opinion on fruit and water fasting.

Sensing William's irritation, Gilbert changed the subject. "How is it 'on the bench', your honour?"

William gave a snort and sipped his whisky. His first sitting as a Justice of the Peace had been on 6th January, and every week since he had adjudicated an endless list of petty debt cases. His task was to listen to the competing claims of the parties and either dismiss the case or demand that payment be made. Cases brought to the Police Court were fully described in *The Cultivator*, keeping the townsfolk well acquainted with the pecuniary circumstances of their neighbours. Gossip about who owed who money occupied the men until Jeannie called them to dinner.

William would like to have stayed long into the night to help Gilbert, Timothy and Bert finish *his* bottle of whisky, but Jeannie was keen to take Nancy home to bed as soon as the meal finished. The child had enjoyed an exciting evening hunting garden fairies with Margaret Campbell and Jane Findlay. She was exhausted and belligerent as he strapped her cot onto the jinker. He pressed her face-down in the basket and patted her mercilessly on the back of her nappy. Jeannie started the jinker in the direction of home, and Nancy's cries de-escalated into weak gurgles, which soon ceased.

The moon was nearly full, which was a precondition for Jeannie driving at night. Even though Chronometer knew the way home and was sure to deliver them safely, Jeannie liked to be able to see where they were going. She also insisted, unnecessarily he thought, on taking the reins when he had been drinking.

William angled his legs sideways, out of the confined space of the jinker, and stretched his arms across the back-rest, lightly toying with the hair that had escaped Jeannie's bun. It was a calm, comfortably warm night, and now that Nancy had fallen silent, he could relax and gaze at the stars.

"Bert needs a girl of his own," he commented, apropos of nothing.

"So you've said before." Jeannie watched the moonlit road with nervous focus.

"He's waiting for me to die so he can take my place." William had been thinking this for many moons, but this was the first time he put it to words.

"Don't be silly." Jeannie replied crossly.

"I mean it."

"No. It's your whisky talking."

"He looks at you. I see it. Would be sensible. If only he made a success of himself. He's a right twat."

"You're not going to die. How often must I tell you?"

"Well, if I did." He pressed his fingers more firmly down her back, inside the loose collar of her light, summer dress.

"Bert is no twat. You're unkind to him."

He slipped her sleeve off her shoulder and brought his hand around to tease her breast.

"Willie! Let me concentrate!" She moved her hand quickly to halt his, and even though she dropped the reins, Chronometer neither paused nor deviated.

Jeannie wanted more children. The two years William had insisted were required for her complete healing, had passed. She was his eager bed companion, and William was greatly enjoying the change in their relationship.

Chapter 15

Jeannie

Friday 29th May 1896

She was bleeding again. The fifth month and the fifth, aching disappointment. Her cycle had cruelly stretched a few extra days this time, building her hopes, only to do her greater harm. Jeannie scrubbed her thin, precautionary cotton pad, turning one corner against the other, grinding her blood from the tightly curled fibre. She dipped the pad back into the wash bucket, squeezed the suds away and inspected it. Dissatisfied, she pressed it firmly over the yellow bar of hard soap and numbly scrubbed again.

Nancy was nearby, on the veranda by the scullery door, loudly enjoying herself with a stack of tin saucepans, a colander and a beaker of water. The result was a cacophony painful to the ears, but at least Jeannie knew exactly where the child was. Nancy liked to wander—usually with Olga for company, but Jeannie was not convinced that Olga could, reliably, bring her charge home. Not if Nancy had something else in her very independent, audacious mind.

In a paper bag on a high shelf in Nancy's room, was a doll Jeannie had made, together with a set of small clothes in a miniature leather suitcase. A present for Nancy when the next baby was due. That would be the right time, Jeannie thought, to soften the lass—to start her thinking about nurturing cuddles, sweet lullabies and delicately knitted clothes. As it was, Nancy was devoted to collecting stones, digging holes in the earth and filling them with water. Which was, Jeannie recognised, the child's version of her mother's daily behaviour.

Jeannie desperately wanted that to change. What could be wrong? She had fallen pregnant easily the first time. William was as confounded as she, but both of them, she knew, had the same unvoiced doubt. Had her operation, despite all William had promised her, somehow rendered her unable to have more children?

The Lord would decide, Jeannie counselled herself with less than her customary self-assurance. If it was the Lord's will, she would have another child. If not, she would have to make the best of the life He had given her.

The noise from the veranda had stopped.

Jeannie shook the pad out of its folds. She examined it again and, satisfied, dropped it into the nappy bucket. She dried her hands on her apron and checked the watch she kept tucked in the inner pocket of her dress. She had been slow. Her maid, Tess, should already be here to collect the washing.

Nancy and Olga had made it to the front gate, where Nancy had delayed Tess by excitedly telling her about the snake that had been seen yesterday, slithering across the drive. The three of them, Nancy, Tess and Olga were on a tour of inspection of the front garden, in case the serpent had returned.

"Would you like me to take her today, Mrs Cameron?" Tess called over her shoulder as Nancy towed her along the gravel path that circled behind the hibiscus towards the hawthorn hedge.

It had been Jeannie's intention to take Nancy with her to the orchard, but she changed her mind. She was too dispirited, and it would be much easier to accept Tess's offer. Bert would be disappointed, but Nancy would enjoy her day with Tess and could see Bert another time.

"If you would, Tess. I'll be spraying in the orchard today. Better she doesn't get mixed up in it."

"It's no worry, ma'am. I have another child today and they'll be right play mates."

Jeannie was relieved. She was keen for Nancy to have children to play with.

"Be quick on your way, then. If she sees B-E-R-T, she'll give you trouble."

Tess pulled Nancy to a halt and bent down to speak through the unkempt curls that covered the child's small ear. "We should look for the snake in the scullery," she whispered dramatically.

Nancy agreed enthusiastically and set off with a full-tilt, wobbling run.

Jeannie gratefully saw the pair off at the gate. Laundry basket balanced on the hood of the stroller, Nancy with her favourite teddy and her day-bag on her lap, and Tess cheerfully answering the child's insistent questions on the matters of why, when and where a snake might bite her.

~

Chronometer stopped, exuding boredom, at the front steps.

Jeannie lifted the pail of anti-fungal spray into the jinker's tray and set it down alongside Bert's head. He opened one eye and looked at her with a mischievous smile.

"I was asleep!"

"Very funny."

Bert had intended to tease Nancy with a horse and cart that arrived without a driver. He peeked over the sideboard, hoping to see the child before she saw him.

"Where is she?"

"Off with Tess to play with another child." Jeannie adjusted the lid on the pail, ensuring it would not leak.

"Oh." Bert sat up, disappointed. "And where's Himself?"

"Surgery at the hospital today."

Jeannie handed the spray can to Bert, and he laid it down between a shovel and the side of the tray. She retrieved her basket, containing her hat, secateurs, and gloves, from the step and positioned it in the tray so that it propped the pail into a corner.

"Ready to go?" Bert stepped over the wooden seat and took up the reins.

She took the hand he offered and climbed up beside him.

"He's busy then?" Bert asked as he coaxed Chronometer into a trot.

"Aye. With Dr Hill gone and Dr Abramowski performing duties for Council." Jeannie reached behind to steady the rocking pail. "This is his third day at the hospital this week."

"Abramowski is being paid as the head surgeon, but William is doing the work?"

Jeannie hummed, wondering if William had complained, or was Bert fishing for gossip?

"His is an honorary position, isn't it?" Bert persisted.

"In return for his work, he can give his patients a bed there."

"Hoo-bloody-ray!" Bert said sarcastically. "Does William earn *any* money?"

"That's impertinent, Bert," Jeannie snapped at him.

"He tells me *I'm* useless. I'd like to know what *he's* earning. Doesn't look any better to me."

"I don't know, and *you* should not care," Jeannie said firmly.

They drove in moody silence for a few minutes before Bert spoke again.

"Do you know he's the only JP in town who'll judge rate cases?"

Jeannie didn't know and couldn't guess why Bert thought it important.

"The other magistrates know the rates are unfair. They *know* we can't afford to pay. That's why they won't take the bench against a blockie who owes rates. They're *decent* men."

Now Jeannie understood the case Bert was making. She rounded on him in anger.

"William *knows* that if the Irrigation Company can't afford repairs the pumps will stop. He *knows* that if they can't afford to pay someone to clear the weeds from the channels the water won't *reach* your block. He *knows* that if the irrigation ditches aren't cleaned there will be another bout of typhoid. How do *you* think *any* of that can happen if the Irrigation Company isn't paid the rates that are owed? William's a *decent* man, and he's brave enough to do the right thing even if it makes him unpopular."

"The Chaffeys ..."

"Are insolvent. *Insolvent*, Bert. There's *no* money coming from them."

"Two hundred thousand acres ..."

"Which is *not* irrigated, *cannot* be sold and is now to be resumed by the crown. It's a baseless argument that Chaffeys should ever have paid rates on that land."

"The government has given us five thousand pounds."

"It's a *loan*—to buy firewood, pay wages and keep the pumps running *while* the backlog of overdue rates is addressed. Mildura *has to* get back on its feet and pay its way."

Bert, casting around for a fresh argument, spotted two rabbits break cover in the weeds alongside an irrigation ditch and race, single file, brown tails bobbing, through a tangle of tree roots into a burrow.

"They don't even keep the rabbits out!"

"Which 'they' are you complaining about now?"

"The Vermin Board."

"You're a good shot, Bert—stop complaining. Go after the rabbits yourself!"

He was silent, watching for movement in the irrigation ditch.

"Why are you cranky today?" she asked.

"I could say the same to you," he retorted.

They drove on in silence. It was because Nancy was not with them, Jeannie realised. Bert would not say such things if Nancy were listening. With Nancy, he was full of fun and endearment. It saddened her to think that this anger against William, this massive dissatisfaction with Mildura, was festering in him—and herself so little aware of it.

"Can you not pay your rates, Bert?" she eventually asked in a very different, gentle tone.

He shrugged, watching the fields and refusing to look at her.

A fungus had attacked Bert's oranges. There was a chalky-white scar on the skin, and the pulp within was, in parts, blackened and spoiled. Jeannie had persuaded Bert to try a Bordeaux Mixture on the affected trees. She had made a creamy whitewash of slaked lime. In a separate pail she had dissolved molasses and sulphur of copper in water. She mixed the two liquids together to form a saccharate of lime of a thin consistency, suitable for use in the spray can.

While Bert sprayed his orange trees, Jeannie pruned the apricots. It was a job that needed to be done after the trees dropped their leaves, and before the first frost. With her gardening gloves on, and her freshly sharpened secateurs in hand, she examined every branch for the best positioned fruiting spur and she cut, parallel to the branch and at 45 degrees to the top bud. If a green twig was too small to carry the weight of next season's apricot, she severed it neatly where it joined the main stem. She clicked her tongue crossly at evidence of earlier, inferior pruning, and neatly snipped off all dead wood. She stood back often and viewed the tree to ensure it had the height, shape and appearance she wanted.

Jeannie knew the workers on her block laughed at her for being a perfectionist. There was not the time, orchardists told her, to trouble over each individual tree. Bert was accustomed to her method. When he finished spraying, he pulled his secateurs from his pocket and started at the further end of the row of trees Jeannie was pruning. Meeting in the middle, Jeannie looked with suspicion at the tree he had just 'finished'.

"*Don't* you touch that tree!" he ordered with a smile.

"*This* is a thing of beauty." Jeannie framed her carefully crafted tree between her hands.

"And *this* is practical," Bert waved towards his own work. "We have fifteen trees to go."

They worked away from each other, and when they met on the third and final row of the patch selected for pruning, they were much closer to Jeannie's end than Bert's.

"I don't seem to have done very much," Jeannie observed.

"More than you would have done if Nancy were here."

"True."

"I wanted to ask," Bert called for her attention as she started towards the jinker. "There is talk of growing tobacco between the trees. What do you think?"

It was the latest topic among the orchardists. There was an 'expert' in town, talking-up the prospects of tobacco as the settlement's saviour. The irrigated fields of Mildura were ideal, the man asserted.

"Some say it's too flat here," Jeannie replied thoughtfully, "and the soil has too much clay."

"There's a strong market, and tobacco can be dried and transported without spoiling."

Jeannie inclined her head; these were important factors.

"Would you consider planting it on your block?"

Jeannie visualised her orchard: its young trees, perfectly shaped and armed with a modest array of fruit spurs ready for their first bearing next summer; the vegetables growing abundantly between the rows.

"No," she said resolutely. "I grow food. I *like* to grow food. I can't see the worth in tobacco."

"On my block then, for the money?"

"You'll have years of work before you know if it grows well; before you can be sure it doesn't attract insects that harm your trees; before you know how the market goes. You can't believe a man who is here to sell you tobacco plants. Can you afford to give him money?"

Bert shrugged.

"Well, neither can I, Bert, if that be your thinking."

Chronometer was resting in the scant shade of a tamarisk tree, his harness loosened and a large tub of water within reach. As they approached, he turned his head lazily to look at them past the chunky blinker on his bridle. Bert stroked the horse's face gently, then tightened the harness straps, making ready to leave.

"I'll be away for a few days," he announced as he climbed into the driver's seat and took the reins. "I'm going to Swan Hill to collect saltbush for Roberts' nursery."

"Saltbush?" Jeannie couldn't imagine why anyone would want saltbush.

"For the alkali affected soils. Saltbush will grow there. We can rehabilitate the soil. I've talked with Roberts and he's agreed to try it out. He's buying the plants, If I fetch them, then I can plant some where the salt is coming up."

Bert, Jeannie knew, read agricultural journals as assiduously as William read medical ones. She had no doubt he was well across the latest ideas.

"Won't you have to fix the drainage?"

"I will. I'll change the direction of the furrows and I'll make a sinkhole to remove the surface water."

"How long will it take to come right?"

Bert shrugged. "Three? Maybe five years? But it's something. I can't leave the land wasted."

Jeannie agreed. The sight of salt patches, shining powdery white under sickening fruit trees and vines in many of the settlement's fields, was deeply distressing. It was something she had never seen, never imagined, knowing only Scotland's rich, deep soils. The Chaffeys knew of it from their Californian experience, but there it had not caused such a problem. Yes, there was high evaporation, but the Ontario irrigation area enjoyed a greater slope, better drainage. Alkaline lands were emerging as a dire threat to Mildura's irrigationists, and they were desperate to find solutions.

"I'll drop off at my house," Bert continued, "and you can take the jinker home."

Bert's 'house' was a wattle and daub hut with an iron roof, a treacherous wooden floor and a narrow, rickety veranda. Terribly poor, Jeannie thought, in comparison with Cullalo, the imposing stone mansion the Cameron family owned in Newburgh. Bert's house was hardly better than the shacks the Aboriginal families occupied on Kulkyne Station, upriver. She hadn't been there, but she had seen photographs. Occasionally she would see a group of Aboriginals in town, collecting supplies, or floating down river in a canoe with their dogs, but she had never talked to them. She felt embarrassed; she sensed their dislike. Always, they went quietly on their way and left her wondering if their lives, which seemed so poor to her, were satisfactory to them.

She was certain that Bert's life did not feel satisfactory to him.

"What are you doing tonight, Bert? Don't you need Moody?" she asked as she shuffled across to the driver's seat.

Their arrangement, in sharing the two horses and the jinker, was that if Bert had Chronometer and the jinker, William had Moody to ride on his rounds.

"No, I won't go to Settlers tonight."

Probably, Jeannie thought sadly, because he had no money. She wondered if he had any food in his house.

"Come and eat with us then. You can stay, or Willie will drive you home."

Bert looked tempted. "I need to wash."

Jeannie thought of the rusty iron tub that Bert used as a bath. She thought of the tin-clad, spider infested toilet pit that squatted behind the house, next to the tub, and she assessed the urgency of her need to relieve herself.

"No, Bert, just get back on. I need to be home for Nancy, and you can bathe at ours."

"Fresh pants then."

Jeannie waited while he darted into his house and returned with a bundle of clothes.

~

Bert was soaking—luxuriously, Jeannie hoped—in the bath on the back veranda when Tess walked in the front door, carrying the laundry basket.

Nancy, trailing behind, was wearing an ill-fitting dress.

"She made herself very grubby, ma'am," Tess apologised.

"I can imagine," Jeannie lifted Nancy up for a hug and settled the child on her hip.

"Her clothes will be back in tomorrow's wash."

"Did you have a good day?" Jeannie asked Nancy.

Nancy gabbled unintelligibly about someone called 'Arty'. Jeannie looked to Tess for interpretation.

"Nancy has made a bonnie new friend—Martie—who is *five* years old." Tess showed Nancy five fingers to reinforce Nancy's understanding of how big a number 'five' was. "Martha Abramowski, ma'am. Mrs A. is having a difficult time settling her wee bairn."

Dr Abramowski had remarried, almost two years ago. His wife was a reclusive woman who, Mary Shilliday confided to her friends, had an imperfect relationship with the children born of Abramowski's previous marriage. Martie suffered most, Mary said, haphazardly raised by Abramowski to age three and, since the new baby was born, all but ignored by her step-mother. The poor lass had been tossed 'from pillar to post' by an array of carers, with the result that she was a particularly wild child.

Which was sure, Jeannie thought ruefully, to make her a great pal to Nancy.

After Tess had gone, Jeannie carried Nancy through to the kitchen where she was preparing dinner. She set the girl on the floor, handed her a slice of raw carrot, and started filling a pot with water.

It was at that moment that Bert, rather untunefully, launched into song.

Nancy threw a sharp, excited glance at her mother and ran to find her uncle.

When Jeannie caught up with her, she was clambering over the side of the tub. Bert, naked and acutely embarrassed, tried to hide himself with one hand, while fending Nancy off.

Jeannie laughed at the absurdity, made a show of shielding her eyes, and prised the half-sodden child away from him. Nancy protested her mother's interference with irate howls. As she secured Nancy on her hip, Jeannie realised that Bert's cowering attitude was not owed to her. She turned to see William standing in the doorway, arms tightly crossed, his whole-body glowering.

"What the devil is going on here?!" he demanded.

Jeannie felt his rage like a shock-wave. It rendered her unable to speak. It was obvious, wasn't it? She was getting Nancy out of Bert's bath. She wanted to defend Bert against his brother's misbegotten anger, but words failed her.

Nancy did not suffer the same incapacity. She yelled a final protest at her mother, wriggled to the floor and ran to her father, arms up in characteristic demand.

William ignored her and remained, stiffly awaiting an answer.

"Nancy tried to get in Bert's bath," Jeannie said, dismayed by the weakness in her tone.

"And why are you bathing here?" William addressed Bert with a contempt that made Bert wince.

"*I* invited him to dinner, and *I* invited him to bathe here!" Jeannie's anger took hold. She needed to leave, before she and William launched into full-blown fight; in front of Bert; in front of Nancy.

She gathered Nancy up, wrestling the child's wiry arms away from William's leg.

"It's *not* Bert's fault!" she hissed at him before stalking into the house.

She heard no words pass between the men behind her. William, she assumed, would be punishing poor Bert with his hardest, most cutting stare.

She was in the kitchen, preparing gravy, when Bert, fully dressed, looked in the door. "I'm going to go."

"No, you will *not*. You will have dinner."

"I ..."

"It's not for running away from, Bert," Jeannie interrupted firmly. "You will have dinner with us, and if there was *anything* he said to you, *he* will apologize."

"He didn't, really ..."

"There's a letter from your mother on the mantlepiece." Jeannie saw Bert's eyes light up and it made her even angrier that William had withheld this news from his brother. "Settle down to read, and dinner will be along in a few minutes. I haven't read it myself, but I'm sure it will give us something to talk about."

John had returned from his winter stay in the Swiss Alps in 'significantly' better condition, which made for a positive start to their dinner conversation. William was in no-way apologetic, but he was at least taking care to be civilised and put the incident on the veranda to the side. John's apparent reprieve brought William great relief. Jeannie knew he agonised constantly over John's welfare; deeply disturbed by the idea that a letter would, one day soon, bring news of his brother's death. Bert took this as evidence of William's greater affection for John, without understanding that William would—Jeannie was sure of it—be equally anxious about Bert were the positions reversed.

A bigger talking-point, however, was Isabella's news that she had received a letter from Joseph. 'Letter', William scoffed, was the wrong description. Joseph had sent a scrap of paper that said 'Arrived Albany. In gold fields. Js'. The envelope was postmarked Coolgardie, 4th February 1896.

"Coolgardie?!" Jeannie echoed in disbelief. "Is he stopped there or passing through?"

"Is Coolgardie near Norseman?" Bert asked.

William shrugged. "A day's drive north, maybe two." Norseman was the gold field that had tempted several of Mildura's impoverished settlers to make the hopeful (and Jeannie thought foolhardy) journey west in search of their fortunes. Some of the business men in the town had formed a share syndicate, the 'No. 4 Goldmining Company', around a prospector who had claimed 'The Great Mildura Lease'. William was closely following the news from Norseman, encouraged but not yet convinced by his friends at The Mildura Club, to take a stock holding.

"What's at Coolgardie?" Jeannie asked.

"Dirt with some gold lying around, I expect," William's tone was dismissive.

"Is there a town? A railway?" she persisted.

"It's a large town. The railway has just arrived from Perth."

"A railway!" Bert laced his tone with irony.

"More money in gold than fruit," William said dryly.

"Can you get a letter to him?" Jeannie asked.

"How?" William's question was rhetorical.

"No address," Bert elaborated unnecessarily. He was keen, Jeannie could see, to agree to everything William said.

"He's probably wearied of digging by now."

"Aye. Joseph wouldn't take to hard work."

"Then where is he?" Jeannie restated the question they had all been asking themselves for months. Where, indeed, was Joseph? He could walk in the door at any moment. Or he could be aboard a ship on the way back home. It was useless, but it was a speculation that saw them through dinner.

"Do you want to keep Moody here while I'm away?" Bert asked William nervously, when it was time for him to leave.

"Take Moody tonight," William said gruffly. "I'll collect her tomorrow."

Bert looked relieved that he was not going to spend more time, privately, with his vengeful brother. He nodded his fare-wells and stepped out into the night, leaving Jeannie and William looking grimly at each other in the doorway.

It was instantly clear they had nothing pleasant to say, and silence would be the better option. William picked his mother's letter up from the dining table and went into his surgery. Jeannie went into the kitchen to wash the dishes.

Later that night, Jeannie spent a long-time bathing, making up a new pad thick enough to cater for what was usually the heaviest night of her monthly. When she eventually returned, carrying her kerosene lamp, to the bedroom she intended to share with Nancy, she found William inside, cradling the sleeping child in his arms.

"She was restless," he said; defensive.

Jeannie looked closely. "Sound asleep now," she whispered.

"Are you alright?" he asked.

She fought off the sudden urge to cry.

"Are you alright?" he repeated.

She took Nancy from him and laid her gently in the cot.

"Are you bleeding?" he asked as she turned back to him.

She nodded and he took her into his arms. She could feel, in his ragged breathing, a disappointment that matched her own. Eventually they drew apart, their argument dissolved.

"I didn't ask about the surgery you did today?"

He shook his head despondently.

She sighed in sympathy. "Bad day then."

"Bad day," he agreed.

He took her hand and led her into his room.

Sunday 21ˢᵗ June 1896

Jeannie was by the fire, stitching a teddy-bear-size pair of khaki dungarees, when William gave a loud, snorting laugh of derision. She raised her eyebrows at him in inquiry.

He leant forward from his chair, holding his copy of *The Mildura Cultivator* towards her. The paper was folded and re-folded so that the editorial column was uppermost. Jeannie could see the sub-heading 'LIGHT AHEAD!'.

"Is this not the most avowedly optimistic newspaper on this planet?" It was a long sentence for William; he finished it with two short, throaty coughs.

"You read it for me," she said, thinking to test how his cough was going. He—being something of an optimist himself —had told her it was better. She continued to stitch instead of taking the paper, repetitively piercing the khaki fabric with her needle to join a leg-seam.

William cleared his throat and read.

"'It can at last be said'" (throat clearing) "'and with a fair measure of certainty,'" (throat clearing) "'that the clouds which have so long beset Mildura'" (throat clearing) "'are beginning to break.'"

His lungs were bad, Jeannie thought grimly. God would forgive them for staying indoors on this bone-chilling, winter day instead of going to church.

"'Those who have steadily hoped on and worked on now see a prospect of surmounting their troubles and of winning the reward they have striven to deserve. In every direction the horizon is brightening. Mildura's products are finding their way to many markets and their excellence is everywhere admitted. Many settlers who were in financial difficulties a year or so ago have been enabled to improve their position, and provided that they can be assured as to the water supply being satisfactorily maintained, all their doubts about the future would disappear.'"

William stopped reading and fished for his handkerchief. He bunched the large piece of cloth over his mouth and delivered a series of wracking coughs. He habitually checked the folds of cloth and then crammed them back into his pocket.

"You'd tell me, if you were troubled again?" she entreated him.

"I'm fine."

"You're finding nothing with the microscope?"

"Not a thing." He pointed the newspaper at her. "Goes on to say. The Royal Commission. Will make the government. Face up to its responsibilities. Do what settlers can't. Mildura doesn't depend on the Chaffeys. The Citrus Fair is conclusive proof. Mildura is worth the risk." He successfully cleared his throat and began reading again.

"'Our settlers should take heart and work with renewed energy. It has been proved that funk begets funk, just as confidence begets confidence. Once let the pessimistic wail be silenced, let everyone act on the conviction that the worst is over, and all the troubles and difficulties will be quickly left behind. Mildura is destined to be a great success.'"

"This, from a newspaper in liquidation." William concluded, slapping the paper onto the tea table beside his chair.

"Will *The Cultivator* close?" Jeannie asked anxiously.

William shrugged.

"Is the surgery secure?" Jeannie tied off her cotton in a tight knot. She wove the strand into hiding in the seam and snipped it off close to the fabric.

"It's fine," William was annoyed, she knew, that she had asked the question.

Jeannie suspected the surgery wasn't fine. She knew a ledger balance written in red ink did not bode well. She worried about the stress William was under and wished he would share his worries with her. Stress exacerbated his cough.

"I saw you brought in more of the diphtheria anti-toxin," she commented.

"It's expensive, but we must have it."

William had recently treated the Johnson child, a close neighbour to Tess on 12th Street, with the new Klein's anti-toxin recommended by Dr Springthorpe. The child, near to death before the injection, had made a remarkable recovery. The serum cost eight shillings per dose delivered to Mildura, but she knew William would give it freely, as he had done this first time, if a family could not afford it. Saving the Johnson child from the disease, he had told her, was the most affecting moment in his medical career to date. He would stake their entire worldly goods—such as was left of them—to save a child from diphtheria.

Conversely—perversely, Jeannie thought—he would not give a shilling to help Bert. Bert had to pay his debts. Bert had to make a man of himself. Bert must not rely on the charity of others. In the midst of an argument, earlier in the day, she had accused him of being too hard on his brother.

"I just want him to better himself," William countered.

"From *his* side," she replied sternly, "that looks indistinguishable from not loving him ... *as he is.*"

William frowned at her, and discontinued their discussion. She felt she had won the point.

She hoped, when Bert brought Nancy back from church, that William might show he had taken some note of her words. Perhaps the two men could talk together about Bert's dire financial situation; perhaps William would agree to seek more money from their father.

Jeannie knotted a length of cotton and started on the second seam. *"Clouds will break,"* she reflected on *The Cultivator's* literary reference. "Isn't that one of your favourites?"

William threw his right hand across his chest and spoke dramatically from memory:

> *"One who never turned his back but marched breast forward,*
> *Never doubted clouds would break.*
> *Never dreamed, though right were worsted, wrong would triumph,*
> *Held we fall to rise, are baffled to fight better ..."*

He started coughing; ripped his handkerchief out of his pocket and smothered his mouth.

Jeannie put her sewing down on her side table, stood and shook scraps of cotton from her apron.

"We'll *fight better*," she said, looking down on him, "if we've had our cup of tea before Bert and Nancy get back."

Half an hour later, Nancy arrived with a large piece of butcher's paper ingloriously smeared with multicolour paints blended to a brown splodge. Bert followed her in, carrying a small newspaper cutting. Nancy's paper, in the scrawled hand of the Sunday school teacher, proclaimed God's Church.

Bert's, in typeset, proclaimed Gold at Coolgardie, and it was Bert's offering that captured the whole of William's attention. He read it aloud and Jeannie strained to hear over Nancy's insistent chatter.

"'Messrs. Fieble & Cameron, prospectors, have made a discovery half a mile from the Golden Crest, near Dunsville, and they have, it is asserted, traced visible gold on a reef at the surface for 200 feet. This statement was brought in by a couple of prospectors in the employ of the Martin Syndicate, who have pegged on to the new find, north and south. They further state that the country has been pegged out for a distance of two miles.'"

"How do you know it's Joseph?" William probed.

"I don't. But Charles thinks so."

"Who is Charles?"

"A woodcutter. Left for Coolgardie last month. I asked him to look out for our Joseph."

"Has he actually spoken with Joseph?"

"This is all I've got. It's recent." Bert pointed to the top of the newsprint, "Coolgardie Miner, June 10."

William stared at the newspaper, as if plumbing the depth of its meaning.

"*Gold*, William."

Jeannie didn't like the tone in Bert's voice. She had heard it before; in Frank; in Jim. She had hoped never to hear it again.

Chapter 16

William

Wednesday 7th July 1896

Bert left a crate of his personal belongings in the back corner of the barn, behind the jinker. He gave Jeannie a note for William to give the Irrigation Company, promising to pay his outstanding rates as soon as he cashed in some gold.

William had seen many such notes submitted to cases he had judged over the last few months, but none had made him as angry as this one.

The note shook in his hand as he accused Jeannie of foreknowledge.

She denied it, and if there was one thing he knew about his wife, it was that it was impossible for her to lie.

Bert was on his way to Coolgardie with two similarly bankrupted blockies.

"What about his orchard?" William sputtered.

"He took a deposit of five pounds. He expects to get fifty pounds for the land and some shillings for the tools."

"It cost three times that!" William fumed. "What else did he say?"

Jeannie shook her head, implying either 'nothing' or, more likely, nothing she was prepared to tell him.

"Why did he not discuss this with me? Why did he not say goodbye to me?"

"You haven't been easily approached, Willie. He thinks you would call him dafty."

"I would!"

"There you have it. He didn't want to hear it."

William glowered at Jeannie and she looked down, wriggling Nancy's small arm to jolly the child. Nancy leaned into Jeannie's skirt, and peeked out in daunted silence at her uncommonly angry father. He felt the tightness in his chest increase its asthmatic grip. He exhaled carefully, and turned away.

It wasn't only indebted blockies like Bert who were departing the settlement for West Australia. A week earlier, William had joined a send-off for Henry Williams, a close friend and one of the town's most eminent original settlers, who was moving to Freemantle. During that gathering, Sharland, the architect who had designed not only The Nest, but Rio Vista, the Coffee Palace and many more of Mildura's best buildings, had confided that he too had plans to leave. There was money in Coolgardie, Sharland said with great conviction. A grand town was in-the-making, in desperate need of architects and builders. There was a shortage of all manner of professionals, including doctors. Especially surgeons. There was no need for men such as himself and William to pick up a shovel. Clients paid with gold nuggets.

Coolgardie was a frontier town, William countered. It was no place for women and children.

Which was why, Sharland argued, the settlers were strongly motivated to set up a congenial township, and they had the cash to make it happen.

The town was rife with typhoid, William contested.

All the more reason, Sharland responded with a wry smile, that they needed a good public health officer.

William had been studying Coolgardie, since learning of Joseph's supposed 'find'. He had garnered stories from those with personal experience—most of them troubling. He had ordered a subscription to the *Coolgardie Miner* from the post office, and had already read two editions from cover to cover. He was convinced that those departing for the gold fields, including Bert, were making a stupid mistake.

August passed without news from either Bert or Joseph. It passed without any improvement in Mildura's circumstances, despite the 'gashes' that *The Mildura Cultivator* claimed to see in the clouds that overshadowed the settlement. In a single sitting on the bench William gave verdicts against 37 water rate defaulters, excused two cases and, having run out of time on the day, deferred 11 more. It was important work, but endlessly tedious and it dragged on his morale. He would have preferred to bring down judgments against parents who refused to vaccinate their children against smallpox, but he had reluctantly handed those to fellow JPs because he could not be impartial.

Indeed, nothing made him more furious than people who failed to bring their children in for vaccination. There was no excuse. Vaccination, as he explained to every parent who entered his surgery, was not just an essential safeguard for their child, it was *the* public health measure that would, in the longer term, eradicate deadly diseases. The obstinate ignorance of many in the population confounded him; their willingness to believe misinformation. No, vaccination against smallpox did *not* cause diphtheria! No, the vaccine had *not* been drawn from the arms of people infected with syphilis. In his practice, William insisted on supplying only good quality calf lymph cultured in the method devised by Sydney Copeman. It was the method approved for the vaccination of the Royal Family. He had used it to vaccinate his own daughter.

What more could he say to convince people? It did not help that Otto Abramowski publicly argued—notwithstanding that vaccination was a legal requirement for all children—that a diet of fruits, vegetables and nuts with plenty of fresh water would render the body immune to all diseases, including smallpox. It was widely known in the settlement that Abramowski had stood by, a 'conscientious objector', while William had administered the vaccine to the Abramowski children.

It was also widely known that there had been a dispute between the two doctors over treatment of Mr Briggs, who had come into William's care after Abramowski's efforts to alleviate the man's suffering had failed. Nothing could be done to repair Briggs to health, but there were ways to alleviate his pain that Abramowski refused to contemplate. The Briggs family had come to William, via Gilbert Findlay, to consult on the matter. Abramowski, outraged, had declared he would not treat his patient further because he had been 'abruptly supplanted by another medical man'.

Her diet of fruit and nuts had not stopped Martha Abramowski from contracting Scarlet Fever, one of first children to fall victim to the contagion that caused the state school to close for three weeks. Martha had, before her symptoms were obvious, passed the infection on to Nancy who had given her parents an exceptionally trying week as the bumpy, red rash spread irritatingly over her body. Fortunately, given her youth and robust disposition, it was only a mild case and William had not been seriously concerned.

Jeannie, however, had been beside herself with worry. So much so that William's serious concern had been not for Nancy's health, but for Jeannie's state of mind. Why so inordinately anxious? William's conclusion was that Jeannie believed she would never have another child.

That disappointment sat heavily on them both. She blamed her body; her failure as a woman. He blamed the silver wire; his failure as a surgeon. They didn't speak of it.

William's moment of revelation was delivered by a sentence in a journal article on a German trial of formalin infusion in the treatment of tuberculosis. A single mention of infertility as a measurable side effect.

He sat on his stool in front of his microscope, his eyes fixed on his medicine bottles, while his thoughts churned and his stomach sickened.

He had resisted the idea of looking at his sperm under the microscope. He didn't want to know. He preferred any other possibility. But through the night the thought had circled him remorselessly. He needed to put an end to it and so, in candlelight before dawn, he had emptied himself into a glass beaker and prepared several slides.

There was not a living, moving spermatozoon to be seen.

It was worse, he sympathised with himself, than feeling he had failed as a surgeon. In his private thoughts, he had tempered the possibility of a misplaced stitch, by attributing blame to Jeannie's body. Now, he knew there was only himself at fault. The risk he had taken in treating himself with formalin; the shortcomings in his rushed, inadequate research. It hadn't occurred to him that *he* could become infertile. The self-congratulation that he had enjoyed, almost daily, for being in remission, deserted him. He wished himself a child again. He wished tears could flow.

How to tell Jeannie?

Would he tell Jeannie?

Could his sperm recover? He didn't know. Men rarely came forward for fertility testing. There was very little research data. There were remedies he had heard of—everything from aphrodisiac tonics to rigorous exercise regimes—but nothing scientifically proven.

William searched his memory for medical references to infertility, arriving at none. Eventually he carried his candle to his desk, shed its light into a drawer and pulled out a sheet of writing paper. He primed his pen with ink, smoothed it on the blotting pad and wrote the headings he customarily used on semi-official correspondence.

He paused before refreshing the ink.

Did he really want to admit this to Dr Springthorpe?

Perhaps a week of abstinence. A second test. To be absolutely sure.

~

Jeannie had thrown herself into fundraising for St Andrews. She was organising a Gipsy Encampment to be held in mid-September. It was a point of difference between them, though William was happy, in this instance, to let Jeannie have her way. To William, gipsies were an unsavoury nuisance. Homeless vagabonds; liars, thieves and mischievous peddlers of spurious health tonics. Jeannie not only sympathised with them; she found them entertaining. She enjoyed their musical abandon, rowdy theatrics and colourful clothes. It reminded her, William knew, of her childhood. Grandpa Calder had welcomed gipsies at Yetholm Mains; there was nothing the old man enjoyed more than a gipsy story-telling night around a bonfire; slow-cooked mutton with tatties and a round of whisky. In return for his generosity and his friendship, Jeannie said, the gipsies never stole from him. She remembered that when extra hands were needed to repair the barn roof, they had arrived *en masse* to help—and to party after the work was done.

The colonial gipsy troupe that Jeannie had invited to Mildura might disappoint her, William mused ruefully, but he had agreed to open the event at the Institute Hall.

Perhaps, in the speech he was trying to compose, he would harangue the gipsies about the importance of having their children vaccinated?

Jeannie would edit his speech, removing all such remonstrations. To avoid dispute, she had made for him a bullet point list of possible subjects: bonfire stories; slow-cooked mutton; barn roof repairs. She should give the speech herself, he thought crossly.

William reached into his drawer for a fresh piece of writing paper. His unwritten letter to Dr Springthorpe lay obstinately in the way.

Jeannie's monthly had come again. Her disappointment, her tears. This time his guilt felt different. Deeper, achingly personal. The guilt of someone who was, in full knowledge, doing the wrong thing. Even the idea of writing the letter to Dr Springthorpe was a procrastination. He had tested himself again, with the same result and the only thing that a response from Dr Springthorpe could do was to marginally add or subtract from the faint hope that he would, one day, recover sufficiently to father another child.

But he had to know, before he confessed to Jeannie, if there was hope.

He took the letter out of the drawer and laid it on his writing pad. He picked up his pen and chewed on its end.

His reward for resolutely carrying his letter into the post office and handing it over the counter, was to find that the postman had mail ready for him in return. To be more precise, the letter was addressed to 'Mrs Cameron', but it was from Bert and therefore William had no hesitation in opening it.

Bert had found Joseph, and lost him again.

"How can that happen?!" William railed at Jeannie as she stood, aproned, in the kitchen, tea-towel in hand, reading Bert's letter.

Joseph had staked out a claim with a man, Fieble, who had jumped ship with him at Albany. Near Dunsville, they had collected gold dust on the surface, indicating a reef of some 200 feet long, but further diggings had been disappointing. Joseph had bragged of the find to 'friends' and the very next day extensive claims had been made on the ground to the north and the south; grounds that were yielding better than the area Joseph and Fieble had staked out. Fieble blamed Joseph, and their relationship reached flashpoint shortly after Bert's arrival. Joseph had left Bert holding the shovel, literally, and headed north into the dry wilderness, sure that his reef would resurface in that direction.

Bert was worried. He had expected Joseph to return within a day or two. It had been two weeks, without any word.

"I should have gone to Coolgardie myself!" William declared.

"Surely Joseph didn't go into the bush alone?" Jeannie worried, reading on.

The existing claim was giving up a modest quantity of gold dust and small nuggets. Bert boasted that he had earned more money during his month in Coolgardie than the previous six months in Mildura. Fortunes were being made throughout the district. Everywhere there were signs that Coolgardie was destined for great things. It was certainly possible, Bert said, that he was just one shovel strike away from enormous riches, and despite his loneliness—now that Joseph had gone—that thought kept him going.

"He hasn't made any friends, Willie," Jeannie surmised sorrowfully. She sat at the kitchen table and started reading the short letter again, from the beginning.

If she noticed that Bert had addressed the letter to her, she did not comment.

"He'll be making friends over a bottle, mark me," William growled.

"Not the right kind."

William knew she meant a marriageable woman. "There aren't many of *them* in Coolgardie," he replied ambiguously.

"Willie, what are we going to do about Joseph?" She held the letter out to him.

"Nothing we *can* do about Joseph," William grunted. He took the letter and stalked into his surgery, pondering the real answer to her question.

~

William was saved from fawning on itinerant gipsies at the opening of the encampment on the evening of 15th September, because Reverend Matthew decided belatedly to make an appearance at the event and Jeannie changed tack. William must bid the Reverend farewell on the community's behalf.

Reverend Matthew was taking leave of Mildura for six months, returning to the 'old country'. William was exceedingly jealous. How he longed to be able to do the same, and he said as much in the opening of his speech. The blanketing snow. The grand hills. The wee burns. The smells of black earth, sheep manure and fermenting barley. Being surrounded by the family, friends and accents of Home. And yet ... the Reverend must promise them he would return to Mildura, because they would miss him so!

To that William added a few words about the desperate need St Andrews had for funds to make several new pews and to replace the window that had been shattered by an errant cockatoo—bless its misbegotten soul. At sixpence per entry, the Gipsy Encampment was sure to hold something that would entertain, mystify and bemuse all.

William left the stage and made his way to the back of the hall, where he had spotted Gilbert Findlay. After a smiling welcome and a derogatory joke about William's speech, Gilbert nodded his head towards the door and, with a conspiratorial air, asked William to step outside with him.

"Briggs," Gilbert said, by way of explanation.

"What of it?" William responded defensively.

"A rumour."

"Abramowski."

"That you over-supplied opium."

"We give opium, Gilbert. It's approved practice."

"Word is you killed him."

"And what's your view?"

"Don't be uppity. I'm just telling you the gossip."

"He pleaded, and his family agreed."

"I know it, I know it. Still, gossip."

"His kidneys failed, Gilbert." William said earnestly. "What drops of urine he was able to pass were purple. There was fluid encasing his heart." William cupped his hands and squeezed them together, and Gilbert winced in response. "He was in the *utmost* pain."

"If he were one of my cows, I'd have shot him months ago," Gilbert contributed with a sage nod of his head.

"Opium gives a more easeful death."

"You'll do the same for me should I need?" Gilbert asked seriously.

"Aye," William vowed. "I'd do the same for any man. A doctor does *not* walk away from his patient when *that* final need comes."

Gilbert hummed. "No love for Dr Otto, then?"

"Gilbert, I *can't* tell you how *angry* I am."

~

Jeannie was sure to have heard the gossip, but she had made no mention of it. Euthanasia, the recently coined term for the long-standing medical practice of easeful death, and the title of a seminal work published in 1888 by William Munk, was a subject on which they had long since agreed to differ. He had borrowed the book from Melbourne's medical library, which led to a discussion that was at first philosophical but soon became surprisingly heated. Jeannie believed that the Lord gave life and only the Lord should decide on the moment life would be taken away. She had not seen the pain William had seen. She had not heard the wretched pleas of dying men. She did not concede that sometimes, with the Lord otherwise occupied, it was up to doctors to exercise humanity. William was in no doubt about this. He knew what he wanted for himself, and what he would do for those he loved. He had a reserve of opium, secreted in his store room.

There was a chill between them. It might have been the Briggs case, but it could also be his recent ambivalence towards sex. There was a deepening despondency that they were failing to discuss.

The problem with avoiding an issue, William had realised after four years of marriage, was that your wife would, inevitably, ambush you with the central question on a bad night, when you desperately needed to go to sleep.

"Have you given up on another bairn, Willie?" she asked.

He didn't handle it well.

She was more upset, as far as he could reckon, by his admission that he had known for two months, than his admission of infertility.

"*Two cycles of despair!*"

He thought she was going to slap him, but physical blows didn't come. Instead, her acid tone cut him down.

"How long would you have let me go on? William! Month after month, I've been thinking myself a failure!"

"You're not ..."

"A *failure*, William."

"I wanted to be sure."

"No! You *didn't* want it to be true. When were you going to tell me?"

"I've written to Dr Springthorpe."

"What's he got to do with it?! You already knew!"

"If there's treatment. Hope."

"What hope is there for us if you aren't honest with me?!"

"I didn't mean to hurt you."

"Well, you *have* hurt me!" She pulled her arm out of his grasp. She fled, in angry tears, to the room she shared with Nancy.

Perhaps he should have followed her, to try to explain, but in all probability she had further, hysterical words to say. It would surely have woken the child.

William had remained in his bed, obsessively replaying her accusations, rehearsing replies that were better than the ones he had given. He had wanted to find the answer before worrying her with the problem—was that wrong? Was that not the best, most optimistic way forward? He could have been dead, instead of infertile. Would she feel better about that? Could she not sympathize with what he had been through? The risk he had taken, to stay alive *for her*?

By morning, William had decided Jeannie had not given his legitimate reasons enough consideration. She had not given him room to explain. She had been unfair and ought to apologize.

He ventured from his room after Nancy's early-morning noise had been replaced by silence. Jeannie was not in the kitchen making him breakfast. Neither was she in the surgery reception ready to receive patients.

Tess, returning from the out-house with a cleaning bucket in hand, told him Jeannie and Nancy had taken a lift into town with the Findlays.

William felt the intended sting deeply. He opened his surgery door, thoughts seething.

Two of his morning patients missed their appointment— which was not out of the ordinary, but the waste of his time stoked his temper. His third patient seemed more anxious than usual.

Mrs Haworth was an elderly Englishwoman, a lonely hypochondriac in William's view but, on the positive side, she had learnt of his fondness for coconut and usually brought him a plate of cookies to enjoy while he listened to her account of the week past. Today, her exposition dwindled into silence before he had finished his second cookie.

"There's something else troubling you, I think." William brushed crumbs from his moustache. "Best you speak of it."

She was smoothing her skirt unnecessarily; clasping and unclasping her hands, and having trouble looking at him.

"The talk, Doctor."

He hummed encouragingly.

"In town, you understand."

"What talk is that?"

"About Mr Briggs."

"And what are people in town saying about Mr Briggs?"

"That perhaps you made a mistake, Doctor. I can't believe it, Doctor, and I've told them so." Having started, the words came in a rush.

"You know I can't discuss matters involving another patient, Mrs Haworth," William said tersely.

"I can't bear to hear them, Doctor. You're a good, kind man."

"Thank-you. If you don't mind me asking, who is engaging in this talk?"

"The Catholics, Doctor. Never the Presbyterians, no. It's those in the Catholic congregation behind it, to be sure."

"Well, you know Mrs Briggs, don't you?" Mrs Haworth nodded, miserably. "Then you should get your information directly from her, and pay *no* attention to others in the meantime."

Mrs Haworth sniffed. "That poor woman. I don't want to interrupt her. In her grief, you understand. But I can't bear to hear them speak ill of you. I have to reply in your defence." She leant forward on his desk and looked at him imploringly.

"All you need to know," he replied earnestly, taking her hands in his, "is that I have acted, as always, in exact accordance with medical convention and with the law."

He replaced her hands on the desk and gave them a light pat before selecting another cookie. "These are delicious," he shook the cookie at her with a light, playful smile. "I *must* have a third."

William went on his afternoon rounds in a simmering state of anxiety, wondering who was talking about him, as he rode by. When the matter did come up, it was from a completely unexpected quarter.

As he was untying Moody from the hitching rail in Lime Avenue, a boy detached himself from a nearby tree and sauntered over, holding out an envelope.

"From Sergeant Carter, sir," was all the boy said before turning away.

The note politely requested his attendance at the police station after his rounds. It was ludicrous, he assured himself, but that did nothing to lighten his mood.

The sun was setting as he trudged across the wooden veranda into the police station. At the sound of the creaking floorboards, Sergeant Ambrose Carter appeared from a back room, waved him to a seat and moved past him to close and bolt the front door.

"A formality, William."

"Ridiculous," William replied.

"There are those who think this area needs to be regulated."

"*I* am the doctor. Who else is to judge? Will you have the Lord on the bench?"

"Maybe a second doctor should give witness."

"Abramowski? Really? Has he put you up to this?" William's voice stormed upwards.

"Steady, William."

"We would never get an agreement from him. People would be left to die in agony."

"An officer of the law then."

"Hah! With all respect Ambrose, what would *you* know?"

"It's *something*," Ambrose spoke firmly. "You take too much risk, deciding these things on your own. I know you'll say that's how it's always been done, but times are changing."

William clenched his teeth and looked around the small station building, eyes coming to rest on the tiny, empty lock-up.

"So, will you charge me?" he challenged, holding out his wrists.

"Don't be stupid! I just have to make inquiries, and I'm starting with you."

"Start with Mrs Briggs, why not! She'll tell you."

"I'll speak to her later. Who else, William?" Ambrose picked up his pen, dipped it in ink and held it expectantly above his note pad. "Someone to speak for you—a witness."

"Gilbert."

"Findlay?"

"Aye."

"And the opium, you *would* have purchased that from a legitimate medical supplier?"

William remained silent.

"Down the track, you might get asked for a receipt."

William acknowledged the inference with a nod.

"Do you have any thoughts of having a holiday away from the settlement?"

"Are you serious?!" William was incredulous.

"Till this ruddy thing is sorted."

"You want me to run as if I'm guilty of something?"

"You won't be found guilty of anything, unless *I* say so."

William was furious, and Ambrose was uncompromising, as they held each other's stare.

"I'm not going anywhere," William growled.

"Here's a suggestion. You have brothers in Coolgardie. You've been working for some time now, towards visiting them.

Like many others here—the gold fields are beckoning. Your ideas have already been discussed amongst your friends at The Mildura Club."

It was so nearly true. William sat absorbing Ambrose's words in confounded silence.

"Wouldn't do any harm for *some* people to realise how much you do for our community," Ambrose continued smoothly. "In my opinion, this would be a ruddy good time for you to make that point."

Instead of going home, William went to The Mildura Club for a meal, and a few drinks, with his friends.

In the morning Jeannie looked at him warily. She made his cup of tea, set it down on the table in front of him in silence, then walked away. Clearly, she had no sympathy for his sorry, whisky-induced condition. His inability to confide in her deepened.

"I'm going to Coolgardie," he announced at the dinner table, after Nancy had gone to bed and there was an opportunity to talk privately.

She raised an eyebrow.

"I leave tomorrow."

She gasped.

"I'll take *The Gem* down to Morgan, train to Adelaide, then S.S. *Bullara* arriving Albany on 2nd October," he hurried on, giving her his itinerary with all the indifference he could muster. "I should be in Coolgardie by the 4th or 5th."

"Willie, you said ..." she began her protest, aghast. He didn't want to hear it.

"I have to go and find Joseph. I can't leave it to Bert, he's useless. I have to see what's going on in Coolgardie for myself."

"Willie ... your patients ..." This time she was barely audible.

"I've sent a telegram requesting a locum. Month by month."

"How long?"

"I don't know. As long as it takes. I don't know."

"You're leaving us?!"

"I'll see what's going on in Coolgardie and if it's better for us, I'll come back and get you. I'm out of patience with Abramowski. I'm fed up with Mildura. There's no money here, and precious little appreciation."

"Willie … I'm sorry I was angry." Jeannie took his last justification personally, as he had at least partially intended it. "It was a shock for me … we need to talk about this."

"I've made up my mind."

"It's not the end of the world, we have Nancy."

"This is not about you and me. I've decided. It's up to me to find Joseph."

"I have *no* say in this?"

"No, you don't."

She fled the kitchen, leaving her dinner unfinished.

He sat staring at his plate, feeling sternly resolute and wretched, in equal parts.

~

He carried Nancy onto the wharf, taking her right up to *The Gem* and pointing out the paddle steamer's mooring lines, cargo nets and deck poles. He helped her walk, precariously, up the gangway and back down again while her mother watched on in grim silence. His active attention to Nancy papered-over the chasm that yawned between himself and Jeannie. When *The Gem* hooted its intention to depart, Nancy covered her ears with both hands and started to cry. He knew it was the loud noise that had upset her—she had no conception that she was not going to see him, as usual, at the end of his working day—but it felt as if she was sad, because he was overwhelmingly sad.

Jeannie didn't look as sad as he had expected; as upset as he would have liked. She had said very little to him since the night before. She didn't believe him, he knew. She didn't want to hear him lie, and had settled for a stony, resigned silence.

At the club it had been agreed that Sergeant Carter should not come to see William off—it could look like he was being run out of town. Instead W.B. arrived after the paddle steamer's second whistle. There was hand-shaking, back slapping and a publicly cheerful farewell.

To Nancy, but mainly for Jeannie's benefit, William spoke reassuringly. "I'll be back, as soon as I can."

Nancy clung to Jeannie, looking at him curiously; plumbing the distress that hung in the air between her parents. A moment ago, she had asked him for a paddle steamer story at bedtime. Now, he pressed her straggly blonde curls onto the top of her head with a kiss, then lent across her to peck Jeannie's cheek.

He looked back, from the top of the gangway, and saw that W.B. had put his arm comfortingly around Jeannie's shoulders. She looked slender, frail and uncertain, encased in the burly Canadian's supportive hug. William felt a stab of jealousy. He clutched at the reassurance that Jeannie's gaze remained intently on himself, as if W.B. were not even there. Nancy, meanwhile, had forgotten her father. She was laughing and tugging mercilessly on one side of W.B.'s abundant, drooping moustache.

Chapter 17

Jeannie

Wednesday 23rd September 1896

W.B. insisted on driving Jeannie and Nancy home in his buggy. One of his few remaining employees drove the jinker a respectful distance behind. While the man unharnessed Chronometer, W.B. admired Jeannie's garden.

"Can't grow a decent garden in Coolgardie, Jeannie!" He laughed, when Jeannie asked whether he would follow the gleam to the West. "I'm an orchardist, a wine-maker, not a gold-digger. I need to see a river from my window."

"Will you return to California then? Perhaps you also think to leave this ungrateful place behind."

Jeannie had seen a summary of the report handed down by the Royal Commission; the blame placed on the Chaffey Brothers for having insufficient funds to properly implement their irrigation scheme; the criticism of their failures in planning—the slope required for drainage; the seepage from unlined channels; the trust structure of the Irrigation Company. It was a lot of blame, she thought, to lay on the shoulders of men who had been invited to bring their bold vision to this desolate part of the world. What of the Victorian government's failures? What of the train line that had not been built? The banks that had closed their doors?

Jeannie did not know George Chaffey well. He had sped through every social function, his thoughts on his next task, his attention only briefly captured by William's enthusiasm for modern engineering. W.B., in contrast, had been generous with his time, showing her through the gardens of Rio Vista, introducing her to the tropical plants he was able to grow in the fabulous conservatorium behind the house. Unlike George, W.B. had always spoken to her as if he valued her opinion, as if she were more than an ornament in the room. She appreciated the difference. William did too. W.B. was a true friend, and Jeannie knew that if he left Mildura many of Mildura's finest citizens, including William, would leave as well.

"I'm not done yet, Jeannie," W.B. assured her. "I came here to build an irrigation scheme—to turn Mildura into a paradise— and I mean to succeed. I mean to see my vines mature. I mean to drink my wine. Hell ... I mean to sell my wine to the world! No, I'm not leaving, not till the last dog is gone and the rabbits have torn down the fence!"

She graced him with the laugh he was seeking.

"George speaks of leaving though," W.B. continued more seriously. "He's done here. He's looking for another grand scheme. Not in Australia—America, where there are others who have dreams and money enough to support him."

"I heard you were looking for a buyer for Rio Vista?"

W.B. nodded. "Sadly, yes. Did Hattie tell you?"

Jeannie shook her head. "Rumour."

"Not because we're leaving, you must understand. To pay debts. To keep the winery going. We're not leaving, But I can't afford to keep the house."

"It's such a beautiful place. Is there nothing else you can do?"

W.B. shrugged. "There may have to be, if none come forward with a reasonable offer. Meanwhile," W.B. gave a nod in the direction of his waiting employee, "I must go. Someone will call on you *every* day, Jeannie."

"That won't be necessary."

"He insisted, Jeannie. We made a pact, at the club."

Jeannie hummed.

"Don't scoff." W.B. put his arm around her shoulders and squeezed. She stood uncomfortably, enduring his grip. She knew it was his habit with his friends—men and women. His peculiar, overly-familiar American manner. "He'll be back soon. We have work to do, all of us. Your husband, Shilling, Bowring—even Risby. We're going to see Mildura through. One day ..." He took his arm from her shoulders and swept it over the top of her head, encompassing her fledgling garden and the dry, empty paddocks beyond. "All this will be a productive paradise. We will be the premier fruit and wine region, serving the *entire*, federated nation of Australia. That's my vision, and I'll make sure it happens in my lifetime!"

That was W.B., she thought admiringly as he strode away from her. He had such bold, enthusiastic determination. You couldn't help but believe him. You couldn't help but throw your lot in with him. She expected he had said similarly inspiring things to his friends at the club, and it encouraged her. William would come back soon. W.B. said so.

~

W.B.'s workman dropped in at 3.15 each weekday to ask if she needed anything. At first, he tied his horse to the gate post, walked up the drive and knocked on her door, but on his third visit he took to riding up the drive to the steps of the veranda and calling to her from horseback, where he was safe from Olga's boisterous welcome. Undaunted by Olga, the postmaster dropped in three times a week, hand-delivering the mail and newspapers, and taking away any letters she had ready to post. His visits were time-consuming, because he never failed to accept her polite offer of afternoon tea. She assured him she could collect her mail in town, but he insisted, with a bright smile and a disturbing wink, that he was acting on Doctor's orders.

Mornings were trying. Nancy woke with the dawn and required constant activity until her early afternoon nap. Jeannie needed to get the child out of the house and into the company of others. Twice weekly, they rode on the Findlays' early morning dairy run, into town and back again. On Wednesdays, Nancy had a regular playdate at The Nest with Elsie Shilliday, Mary's younger daughter. On other days they walked around the block with Olga, or all the way to the state school to see if they could spot Bessie Shilliday or Martha Abramowski playing in the yard at recess. This latter activity held the risk of a tantrum, because Nancy could not see why she was not allowed to go into the playground and join the bigger children.

Sunday was the most enjoyable day of the week. The dairy run delivered them to St Andrews for the morning church service, and Sunday School, which Nancy loved. Afterwards there would be an invitation to lunch, an afternoon spent amongst children at someone's house, and an exhausted, fractious child on her hands at the end of the day.

On his first visit, the postmaster, Mr Davis, carried away with him Jeannie's letter to her mother. The letter that suggested, in as off-hand a manner as Jeannie could compose, that this would be a convenient time for her mother to avail herself of the spare room at The Nest.

On his fourth visit, Davis handed over a telegram dated 2nd October that unsatisfyingly said, "Arrived Albany."

"Today?" Jeannie flipped the paper over, and back again, in the hope of further information.

"This *very* morning," Davis confirmed proudly, knowing he deserved his cup of tea for prompt, personal service.

The postmaster made an extra visit on Tuesday 6th October, and this time the telegram said, "Arrived Coolgardie."

As Jeannie brought their afternoon tea to the veranda table, Davis was in a hurry to impart further information.

"I mustn't forget. The Boss said to let you know that the locum, Dr Barnes, will be starting work on Friday morning."

"The Boss?"

"W.B.," he clarified. "Also, Mrs Irvine Robertson is on *The Ruby*. She arrives Thursday night, 7pm. He'll send his buggy to meet the boat and bring your mother here. You won't have to disturb the little one."

On Thursday, Jeannie was at the washing line unpegging the sheets she needed to make up her mother's bed, when Olga announced the postmaster's arrival. She allowed herself an exasperated sigh, bundled the sheets over her shoulder and hurried inside. As she passed Nancy's door, she heard the child, who had been blessedly over-sleeping, issue her habitual, escalating wake-up wail.

Her wish that Mr Davis would *not* come to her door so often, evaporated when she saw that the fat envelope he offered her, was written in William's tight, medical hand.

"The one you've been waiting for, Mrs Cameron," Davis said, with a wink.

"I must get Nancy," Jeannie countered, desperately hoping he would tip his hat to her and be on his way.

"Of course, of course." He waved her into the house, put his hat on the veranda table and settled into his customary chair.

~

Her mother's bed was made, there were flowers in vases throughout the house and Jeannie had a light tea-for-two ready in the kitchen by 6pm. Nancy, sensing that something was afoot, was resisting sleep, but Jeannie had resolutely closed the bedroom door and, by 7pm, she was trying to concentrate on William's long and descriptive letter to the sound of Nancy's waning outrage.

William had sent the letter from Albany, so there was no news yet of Bert or Joseph. Neither did it contain any words about himself; no feelings; no hint of the regret she hoped would beset him.

What William wrote about was the paddle steamer, the deck hands and his fellow travellers, the river below Renmark, the port of Adelaide, the S.S. *Bullara*, the steamship's menu, the passengers at his dining table and the rough weather at sea. For some reason beyond her comprehension, he wrote that he was 'particularly pleased to report' that he had suffered from sea sickness during the passage to Albany.

He closed with "I am well. Will write once established in Coolgardie. All my love, Willie."

She was re-reading the letter, searching for nuance in his descriptions, when Olga lifted her head, looked at the door and whined. Jeannie followed Olga to the window, parted the curtain and they both looked out to see the carriage lights of W.B.'s buggy shining at the gate. Olga decided the neighbourhood should know about this strange event. Jeannie dragged her into the kitchen, and Nancy's wails started up anew.

Jeannie met her mother at the door, with Nancy in her nightdress, dishevelled, red-faced and tear-streaked, clinging to her hip. Nancy howled at the sight of the macabre witch she thought she saw in the half-light of the doorway's kerosene lamp. She flung herself across Jeannie's chest, rendering a welcoming hug impossible.

"Oh my! Isn't she a one!" Annie responded.

Jeannie had half-expected that W.B. would bring Annie himself, but instead his workman brought her mother's suitcases to the door.

"The Boss invites you and Mrs Robertson to join him at the Vice-Regal banquet on Monday evening, ma'am."

"I said we would go," Annie called from the living room.

The banquet was in honour of the Governor of Victoria, Lord Brassey's visit to Mildura. As one of the settlement's 'prominent citizens', William had earlier been given two tickets to attend. Jeannie had not entertained the idea of going without him but now, pressured by her mother's acceptance, she drew a slow breath and met the workman's eyes. "Thank Mr Chaffey for me," she said evenly, "we are pleased to accept his invitation."

"I'll pick you up at 5, ma'am."

"That won't be necessary, I can drive us ..."

"Let him pick us up." Annie reappeared at her side.

"Mr Chaffey *said* I was to pick you up at 5, ma'am."

Jeannie resigned herself. "Very well. We'll be ready then."

"You right with them bags, ma'am?" The workman bent again towards the bags.

"Yes, she's fine, they're not heavy." Annie waved the man away and turned her attention to Nancy who had reared back in Jeannie's arms to take a better look at this stranger.

"Will you come to your grandma while maw brings the bags?" Annie held out her arms.

Nancy signalled her rejection of the offer by planting her face firmly into Jeannie's blouse.

~

Friday morning surgery began at 8am. Annie habitually required a cup of tea in bed at 9, and would not emerge from her bedroom before 10. She had not come, she informed Jeannie firmly, to babysit. If Jeannie was required in the surgery to familiarise the locum with William's patients, then she would need a nanny. Jeannie pointed out that with the locum taking all of the surgery's proceeds in William's absence, she could not afford a nanny. She had also been forced to let Tess go, she told her mother in an attempt at persuasion. Now, all the washing—including the surgery's dirty linen—fell to her.

Her mother clicked her tongue in disapproval. She did not, however, agree to change her morning routine. What she said was:

"Fine circumstances your husband has left you to!"

Jeannie had Nancy on one hip as she showed Dr Barnes the surgery waiting room, treatment room and supply room. She had spread paper and crayons on the waiting room floor, but Nancy was not about to be left alone with such a boring activity; not when there was a peculiar man on the premises.

Dr Barnes *was* peculiar, Jeanne thought. Untidy black hair, partially grown beard and unfortunately pocked skin. Clearly, he was no friend to children, making no move to introduce himself to Nancy or even disarm her with a smile. Nancy watched him with misgiving, digging herself into Jeannie's side whenever the distance between herself and Dr Barnes became too narrow for her liking.

Mrs Haworth was the first patient to arrive, plate of cookies in hand, and she was bitterly disappointed to find that there was an imposter in Dr Cameron's chair. Jeannie met her in the waiting room, sat her down and explained the situation out of Dr Barnes' earshot, but Mrs Haworth flatly refused to discuss her concerns with a 'stranger'.

"Dr Cameron was once a stranger to you, Mrs Haworth," Jeannie reminded her gently.

"It can wait till Dr Cameron returns," the elderly woman insisted, the distress in her tone belying her words.

"That will be some months."

Nancy left her drawing and stood, gazing sympathetically into Mrs Haworth's distraught face.

"Oh, child! How pretty you are. Would you like a cookie?"

Nancy nodded and watched with keen anticipation as Mrs Haworth teasingly drew the tea-towel away from the plate of cookies.

"Go on now, pick one out. They're your father's favourites."

Nancy knew perfectly well what the cookies were, she regularly ate the leftovers from Mrs Haworth's visits.

"Tank-ee," she said, selecting a cookie with her best grace.

"What charming manners. Now what is that you're drawing? Will you bring it to me?" Mrs Haworth, Jeannie observed as Nancy showed off her clumsy artworks, was making a wholesome recovery.

"Mrs Haworth, I note your appointments are usually early in the morning?"

"Oooh yes, Mrs Cameron, I'm an early bird."

"And you live near here?"

"Just across the way dear, on 11th."

"It would be a great help to me, and Dr Cameron while he is away, if you could look after Nancy here in my house between 8 and 10 each morning. Is that something you would consider?"

Mrs Haworth looked at Nancy closely, giving the matter serious thought. "I couldn't accept any money, Mrs Cameron, not after all Doctor has done for me," she said earnestly.

Jeannie smiled. "I would be very happy *not* to pay you anything."

"Well, let's try that shall we?" Mrs Haworth addressed her question to Nancy, who nodded enthusiastically and selected another cookie.

More than half of those who called in that morning discovered that their ailments were not serious enough to be attended to by Dr Barnes. Of those who did go into the surgery, many emerged to share with Jeannie their discontent and their hope that the 'real' doctor would return sooner rather than later. Doubtless the gold fields had a need for medical practitioners, but Dr Cameron belonged to Mildura! When she knew his address, Jeannie schemed, she would create a stack of business cards to keep on the reception desk. She would invite the disgruntled, to express their thoughts to Dr Cameron in writing.

One of the disgruntled who called into the surgery mid-morning, was Otto Abramowski.

"Just a word," he told Jeannie, hovering by her desk, "with the locum between patients. A minute only."

Through the closed door of the surgery, Jeannie heard Dr Barnes respond to Otto's request.

Dr Barnes would *not* undertake pro bono work. He was prepared to attend patients at the hospital in an emergency, but patients must pay any hospital costs plus his hourly rate.

Dr Abramowski returned to Jeannie; within the minute he had asked for.

"If I have upset your husband, Mrs Cameron, I *do* apologize. Please make him aware. We *need* his return."

"How do you mean, Otto?" Jeannie encouraged Abramowski to explain. "Why do you think you have upset him?"

"We *were* in disagreement about Mr Briggs, it's true. But I did not feed the talk in the town. It was those at The Settlers' Club who do not like your husband."

"Who would they be, Otto?" Jeannie was sceptical.

"Those he fines for the water rates. He is unpopular amongst them."

Jeannie grimaced. This much she knew, but she was insulted that Abramowski thought it would be reason enough for William to leave her. "My husband has not left Mildura because of the settlers' sharp tongues."

"I *did* question the source of the opium, because he did not buy from me, you understand. The Chinese ... their opium is impure. It is cheap, but we can't use this opium."

"Otto," she scowled at him, weighting her words, "have you brought a charge against William for the death of Mr Briggs?"

"Oh no, no, no, no. This will not happen. This is not my intention, not at all. You must let him know this."

"I think you should write to him yourself," Jeannie gave the miserably apologetic man her sternest glare. "You have been most unappreciative, Otto, of all the work William does here. Not least the help he has given you, *for years,* pro bono, at the hospital. That *must* change. I'll let you know his address when I have it. If you want him back you must tell him what is going to *change.*"

Abramowski twirled his hat through his tremoring hands. "Yes, yes of course Mrs Cameron. I will write him."

~

Jeannie knew Abramowski had approached Dr Barnes because he needed a stand-in for the hospital. As Shire President, Abramowski was committed over the next few days, to entertaining Lord and Lady Brassey and the Vice-Regal contingent, which included two ministers vitally important to Mildura's future: The Minister for Public Works and Agriculture, and the Postmaster General. Mr Davis was particularly excited about this visit from his ministerial superior, and had filled Jeannie in on every detail of the three-day schedule. This afternoon, Saturday, the school children would assemble and greet the Victorian Governor at the Coffee Palace by singing the National Anthem. In the evening, His Excellency would open the Rose Show at the Institute Hall, where Jeannie, Annie and Nancy had spent the previous afternoon, applying finishing touches to the displays. After that, a Masonic supper with Abramowski and other brethren.

On Sunday, after mass at the Catholic church, Mr Davis would be accompanying the Postmaster General on a day-long tour of the outer regions of the settlement. Lord and

Lady Brassey meanwhile, would attend the Anglican church, a sacred concert at the Institute Hall, and then a walking tour of the more advanced orchards close to the town centre.

On Monday the busy schedule continued with a drive around the settlement, inspecting the irrigation works and pausing for a luncheon at Red Cliffs that Mrs Abramowski and a number of ladies, all of whom Jeannie knew well, had meticulously planned. Jeannie herself was to contribute by baking two large vegetable flans early on Monday morning.

Of all these events, Jeannie would most like to have attended the concert, but she had hesitated, trying to make arrangements for Nancy, and the tickets had sold out. Tess had committed herself to minding the Abramowski children for the duration of the Vice Regal visit, and Jeannie had found herself at a loss for a baby-sitter. It had been a scramble, finding someone for the banquet on Monday night, but fortunately a young lass from the most recent first-aid class had agreed. There were two hours between Jeannie's departure on Monday evening and Nancy's bedtime. How, Jeannie worried, would that time pass between Nancy and a stranger?

"Hah!" her mother exclaimed, pulling on her long, ivory-satin gloves by the front door. "What right of opinion has the child?!"

Nancy made her opinion felt, gripping Jeannie by the neck and tearfully proclaiming she did not want her mother to leave. Annie intervened.

"Enough of that nonsense, child!" She prised Nancy's hands apart and swung the protesting toddler across to the waiting baby-sitter. "Out the door!" She placed a forceful arm across Jeannie's back and bustled her to the waiting carriage.

The dining room at the Coffee Palace was extravagantly decorated with flowers and baskets of Mildura's produce. The tables were beautifully laid and the food was excellent. The diners were well-dressed and gracious, but the speeches,

Jeannie thought and Annie concurred, were dreadfully tedious. Toasts to the Queen with congratulations for her very long reign, and vacuous pledges of allegiance that no doubt sounded better to the ears of the English than the Scots and Irish there present. Abramowski assured the guests that Lord Brassey had, over the preceding days, become well acquainted with the settlement, was convinced of Mildura's merits and would do all he could to advance its case.

Lord Brassey, in turn, spoke of his pride in representing the sovereign, bringing her message of goodwill to her subjects in this distant part of her great and glorious empire. He went on at length about the state of politics at Home, and the current crisis with the East which could, unfortunately, lead to war. He was glad, he said, of the many 'manifestations of loyalty and patriotism' the Home Government received from 'every corner of the empire'; he was proud all would 'fight to the last gasp for each other'.

What Lord Brassey meant by that, Jeannie could almost hear William growl, was that if England declared war on Turkey, Queen Victoria's loyal subjects in the Australian colonies would be expected to leap to Her aid.

"I pay no attention to such talk," Hattie Chaffey confided, as she and Jeannie set down their untouched glasses of champagne after the toast, "and neither should you. What *we* should talk about is school."

Jeannie raised an eyebrow and started on her entrée.

"The School Board of Advice."

Jeannie hummed.

"The election is to be held in November and at least two of the five members will not be standing again."

"And?"

"Our children will be starting school during the next term of the Board."

"You'll stand?" Jeannie was surprised to think that Hattie would contest a seat on a traditionally all-male board. Americans, she mused, were very bold.

"We need women on the board. *Two* of them."

Jeannie laughed and shook her head.

"You would be perfect. I intend," Hattie lowered her voice conspiratorially, "to persuade you."

The speeches droned on between courses.

Mr Burrows toasted the Ministry, apologising for bringing the topic down from the lofty aims of empire to the petty concerns of the local community before reminding the ministers present that Mildura was in desperate need of a railway, a better postal service and more cash than the government had agreed to advance.

The Postmaster General replied that the he hoped Mildura's good citizens recognised the generosity of the government; he promised that if gold was discovered a train line would swiftly follow, and as for complaints about the postal service ... his department had come to love the constant correspondence they received from all parts of the colony.

"Funny man," Hattie said sarcastically.

The Minister for Public Works and Agriculture informed his audience that the Royal Commission deserved the thanks not only of Mildura, but of Victoria and indeed the world for putting Mildura back on 'a sound footing'.

"Where did he spend the weekend?" Hattie muttered while her husband, along with the other men in the room, gratefully applauded.

The Chairman of the Irrigation Trust thanked the government for ensuring an abundant water supply throughout Mildura's troubles, the result of which was sure to be 'the heaviest and finest crop yet produced'.

"*More* fruit we can't get to market," Hattie growled.

Abramowski, in his closing remarks, declared, that if Mildura's people were just allowed 'fair play', they would not only bring about Mildura's success as a centre for intensive agriculture. Mildura would become the 'Queen city of the North' and it would deserve selection as the Federal Capital. He added that he hoped Lord Brassey would be able to ride the 'iron horse' to Mildura on his next visit.

Jeannie wondered what William would have made of all of this talk. She wondered where he was; what he was doing now.

Lord Brassey made his concluding speech after dessert had been taken. He was gracious, enthusiastic about Mildura's prospects but non-committal about government participation. He understood, he said, that the importance of the railway was second only to the water supply, and would assert to the premier that Mildura was worthy of further government assistance.

When W.B. stood to reply, the dining hall gave him a hearty ovation. Enough had been said, W.B. assured his devotees, he would not bore them. He simply wished to thank Lord and Lady Brassey, and the ministers for making the trip; he was glad that they could see—as he did—Mildura's grand potential.

"He really believes it," Annie said, in the carriage on the way home.

"Who?" Jeannie asked.

"W.B."

"Believes what?"

"That Mildura will become a grand city. Perhaps even the capital of the newly Federated States of Australia. The capital of a country that becomes independent of the Crown, in the style of America. I told him. It will *not* happen."

~

Due a busy morning surgery, it was afternoon before Jeannie saw her mother again, and by that time Annie was sitting primly at the dining table, dealing cards, with Nancy on her lap and Mrs Haworth sitting opposite. Nancy watched the cards attentively, her hands clasped in astonishing restraint, waiting for Annie to tell her what to do.

"We have the four and six of spades," Annie pointed out the cards in her hand. "Here on the table is the five of spades. Do we want that card?"

Nancy didn't know. She looked into her grandmother's face questioningly.

"Aye, we want that card." Annie picked up the card and positioned it in her hand. "See? Four, five and six all in a row. Will we put these three on the table now?"

Nancy hazarded "Yes?"

"No, not yet. Because Mrs Haworth might be able to build on them. We will keep them *secret* in our hand. Mrs Haworth might discard the three of spades, or the seven, and we will *snap* it up."

Despite the fact that Annie was announcing all her moves openly to Nancy, it appeared by the pegs in the cribbage board lying in the centre of the table, that Mrs Haworth was losing the overall competition.

It also appeared, from the dishes on the table, that they had already eaten. Jeannie gathered up the plates and took them into the kitchen where she was able to make and eat her lunch in peace.

That evening, Jeannie and her mother ate together at the kitchen table.

As soon as Annie had finished her meal, she broached the subject Jeannie had, with a mixture of dread and resolve, been anticipating. "Could it be, that Nancy will be the only grand-child I have the joy of entertaining?"

"I don't know. What of Frank and Jim?" Jeannie deflected the query.

"The one can't attract the interest of a lass, and the other attracts too many."

Jeannie didn't need to ask which was which. She had already heard that Frank was living a largely sedentary life, sitting in his office in South Melbourne, managing the affairs of Union Oil, six days a week. His only social outing was to accompany Annie to church on a Sunday when both of them were sufficiently fit and inclined—which was at best twice in a month. He had acquired an 'unhealthy girth', Annie said disparagingly.

Jim was of much finer figure—some even said 'handsome'—but he was, in Annie's view, a 'rascal'. She heard, regularly, of the disappointment he had been to one young lady or another, attending them briefly before absconding to the further reaches of the colony. He was, according to Frank, moderately successful at sales but abysmal at responsibility.

"Surely there will come a lass who will capture Jim's attention?" Jeannie suggested.

Annie folded her napkin fastidiously. "There is *one*, he has said, who is the reason he doesn't want any of the others."

"Really?" Jeannie was suddenly interested. "Who is she?"

"It's an unsuitable match."

Jeannie was unsurprised to hear her mother say this. She waited expectantly.

"Agnes Miller; the daughter of Janet, my younger sister."

"Our cousin? From Lancashire?"

"The family live in Kirkintilloch now. Agnes has come to Melbourne as governess in the employ of a Scottish family. She's something of an adventuress." Her mother's neutral tone left Jeannie unsure whether this label was criticism or compliment.

"You think her unsuitable because she's our first cousin?"

"I think *James* unsuitable because he is a dilettante, a vagabond and ten years her senior. Agnes is 21, an intelligent girl who does not have the years to be as bold as she is. Her mother has entrusted her to me. I will *not* have James flirting with her and leaving her reputation in ruins. She is of the stuff, when older, to make a very fine match elsewhere."

Jeannie mused that it was little wonder Jim seldom visited their mother.

"Do you think Lily will have more children?" Jeannie asked.

"She does not speak of it in her letters. I think her reconciled."

"Does she speak to you of visiting us?"

"No. And to you?"

"I think it beyond their means. As it is beyond ours, to go Home."

"Will you return to Melbourne? You have said William is recovered."

"We can't be certain. We know from the past that his trouble may come again in a colder, wetter climate."

"If he is to be in the West, you could as well be in Melbourne; you could rent this house."

"I have ties here. Friends. I am part of things."

"Pff!" Annie snorted. "You and Nancy have *family* in Melbourne, and no more family to be had here, I'm gathering."

Jeannie stood abruptly and collected their plates without looking at her mother.

"It can hardly help the matter for your husband to be a thousand mile apart!"

"*You* didn't want us to have children!" Jeannie dumped the plates by the sink and went to the range to collect the kettle.

"Well now you have the one, and she needs a *family*."

"It will be as the Lord wishes it," Jeannie said firmly. She grated flakes from her bar of yellow kitchen soap into the sink.

"Pff! A husband, *at home*, has much to do with it."

"You don't know what you speak," Jeannie poured hot water over the soap flakes and angrily whipped the dishwater till the flakes dissolved.

"Then tell me."

Jeannie leant on the sink, staring into the froth as cold water from the tap raised the waterline. She dipped her fingertips past the bubbles to test the temperature and turned off the tap.

"William's trouble," she said with deliberation, "has likely caused him to be unable to father more children. We pray he will recover his ability, but at this time he is unable. We are *very* fortunate to have Nancy, and if Nancy is the only child we have, then we accept that as the Lord's will."

Jeannie pushed a pile of cutlery into the sink and began the wash. Annie arrived beside her and pulled the tea-towel from its hook.

"I'm sorry, lass." The rare sympathy she heard in her mother's tone rendered Jeannie unable to reply. They washed and dried in silence.

~

William's letter, giving his Coolgardie address, arrived with the mail the following Thursday. While Annie discussed the Vice-Regal visit with Mr Davis on the veranda, and Nancy took Olga 'on a walk' around the garden, Jeannie devoured William's words. The opening paragraph frightened her.

He had arrived in Coolgardie on the 6th October, rented two ground floor rooms in a respectable boarding establishment, and immediately applied for registration with the West Australian medical board as a general practitioner. Unlike his experience in Melbourne, in Coolgardie acceptance of his qualifications had been instant.

Chilled by the implication of permanency, she read on.

Coolgardie was evidently a town on the improve. There were wide, densely populated streets like those in Melbourne.

Hotels, banks, public buildings and even some mansions were being built with brick. He had met with Sharland on his first night in the town, and the architect's business had never been better. Everywhere, and in all occupations, the mood was jubilant. There was a variety of entertainment in the town, with the streets brightly lit and bustling, and premises open throughout the night. Sharland had invited him into membership of a club exclusively for professionals, and he had already made the acquaintance of several men who were enthusiastic about the arrival of an Edinburgh trained surgeon.

Jeannie was impatient with William's news of Sharland. What of Bert and Joseph? She had to read to the third page before they were mentioned.

Bert had ridden into town to meet William on the morning he had written the letter. There was still no sign of Joseph. Not—she sensed the chagrin in William's tone—that Bert had been doing anything towards finding their younger brother. It would be up to him, William, to conduct the necessary inquiries. Bert had said he was faring well with proceeds from his prospecting, though he hardly looked the part in his dirty dungarees, rumpled hat and badly worn boots. There had been three tiny gold specks in the pouch Bert had shown William— each no bigger than a split peppercorn. Bert had been on his way to the bank to cash them, and agreed to meet William at the digger's club in the afternoon.

William had been surprised, on attending the Coolgardie post office to send his telegram to her, that there were already a number of letters waiting for him ... though none from her. W.B. had written, letting him know she and Nancy were well, and closely attended by town folk. More disturbingly, her brother Frank had written—a brief missive with a markedly abusive tone. William understood from that letter that by now her mother would be staying with her at The Nest. Perhaps

Jeannie could do him the favour of correcting whatever false impression she had given her family.

The frosty tone of his closing words stung her sharply.

Jeannie put the letter on her bedside table, pulled her handkerchief from under her pillow and wiped her eyes. She could hear Nancy's voice outside, chirping in conversation with the much quieter, interlacing voices of Annie and Mr Davis. Olga, meanwhile, had padded in through the bedroom door. The dog laid her big muzzle on the bed alongside Jeannie's skirt, and looked up at her with solemn, commiserating eyes.

~

William's letters from Coolgardie came a week apart, on Thursdays. The second letter was predominantly about Joseph.

William had eventually located Joseph in hospital in Kalgoorlie where he had been admitted, suffering from heat stroke, severe dehydration and memory loss. He was far from the only man on the ward in this all-too-common condition, but there were only three who matched the physical description William had sent to all the medical services on the gold fields. Given the suggestion, in accordance with William's telegraphed instruction, that his name was 'Joseph Cameron', some self-recognition had occurred. William hired a buggy and made the day-long return journey to Kalgoorlie to fetch him.

Joseph was hardly the boy William remembered. William was so uncertain, on seeing the straggly, unkempt youth, that he wished he had made the trip with Bert, to ensure a positive identification. Joseph, for his part, showed no recognition of William, and had been hostile to the idea that William was to take him out of the hospital. The boy did, however, speak in the accent and manners of the Cameron family, and he did select the photo of his childhood self from a line of five photographs William set before him. Over a substantial mid-day dinner at a nearby hotel, the two relaxed with each other and, in random anecdotes, some confirming references were made. Joseph recalled the time his mother, armed with her slipper, had chased a drunken wharf labourer from the house. He cited one of their father's favourite claims: that he and his brothers were 'as cautious as goats in a briar bush'.

William took Joseph back to his rooms in Coolgardie, and the next day they drove out to the claim Bert was now picking over with Fieble. On arrival, and much to Fieble's disgust, Joseph promptly remembered his share in the claim. The two picked up their argument from exactly the point, Bert said later, where they had left off weeks previously. Bert and William had been obliged to muscle Joseph back into the buggy, and drive into town where they convinced him to take a break from gold prospecting in favour of a job William had seen advertised at the livery stable. Joseph had always had a great affinity with, and a true love of horses. Bert insisted—the job was a natural fit.

Fortunately, the manager of the livery stable was none too particular about the intellectual state of his hires. He tasked Joseph with harnessing the stable's most difficult pair of horses to a dray and, having done that with ease, Joseph was sent on a delivery. William was much relieved when Joseph brought the horses and dray safely home.

"He is decidedly odd in his mental state," William's letter concluded. "I confess, I am unsure what to do with him."

As a postscript, William wrote that his medical practice was quickly becoming known.

"It's most pleasing," he added, "to be properly recompensed for my services!"

"Will William be returning now he has found his brother?" Annie asked, after Jeannie finished reading. "Will he bring the lad back with him?"

"I don't know. I've said to you all that was in the letter," Jeannie replied, cross with William for not supplying the answer.

"It would be all you need, to have a simpleton in the house with you."

Jeannie slid the folded letter back into its envelope and set it on her side table. She picked up her embroidery and busied herself.

"You will find yourself in a situation not to your liking, if you do not speak up, lass," Annie insisted.

"I trust William to make his decisions," Jeannie said firmly.

"I wouldn't if I were you," her mother retorted.

Jeannie was angry. It was time to turn the tables; step into territory that had never been breached.

"Did you not trust our father to make his decisions? Did you always tell *him* what to do?"

Annie looked at her evaluatively.

"Your father was a fine agriculturalist. He made his decisions in the field. The house and the children were my responsibility."

"And so it is, with William and myself." Jeannie hurried on in case her mother returned to the subject of William. "Why did you not marry again? You had ample opportunity."

"I had the means to keep my independence. Why would I give it away? Why would I take on another husband to nurse in illness or old age? Why would I risk my children to a father who was not their own? I have seen this go very poorly."

"Have you not been lonely?"

Annie considered the question for so long that Jeannie looked up, thinking no reply was forthcoming.

"It's a loneliness I welcome," Annie selected her words carefully. "I'm happy in my own company; my own way of living. The compromises that must be made in married life are grinding; miserable for a woman. I was fortunate to have the means of making an income. I'm fortunate to have Frank. I have not had to subject myself to another husband."

"Were you unhappy in your marriage?"

"No. I had the blessing of six children. That I lost one caused me great unhappiness, and the rest of you were weighty on my thoughts ... but so it is with all mothers."

"But did you love our father?" Jeannie persisted.

Annie pursed her lips, her temper waning. "Amongst men, he was a *good* man. I was glad of him."

"I *love* William, mother."

"*So* you've said, but from what *I* can see, that sentiment led you to an unfortunate choice. Are *you* unhappy in your marriage?"

"*I* am unhappy that William is not *here*. I want him here, with us."

"Then, it's for *you* to tell your husband what you want. Don't imagine a man can work out your mind for himself. Ask him home. Say you *won't* go to a shanty town in the desert. Say you *won't* take his simpleton brother into your house. The better way through marriage is to make your own needs plain. Saves you resenting *him* for reading you wrong."

Her final words on the matter said, Annie pushed herself up from her chair. Trying to take her first step, she grunted with pain and rubbed her left hip. Jeannie watched with concern.

"It's picking up that child of yours. Pains my hip," Annie growled and stumped unevenly towards her bedroom.

Her mother was right, up to a point, Jeannie reflected. She had encouraged others to tell William they missed him, handing one of her hand-decorated Coolgardie address cards to each patient who asked after him, but she had not told him herself. She had filled her letters with daily happenings; what was growing in the garden; Nancy's latest words. She had matched him, in letter-writing style, instead of opening her wishes to him at the risk of rejection.

Jeannie crossed the room to the writing desk that William had given her in Melbourne, only four years ago. She ran her fingers over the smooth mahogany finish, recalling her joy; her belief that he knew—exactly—what she most wanted. She had felt treasured by him, knowing the trouble he had taken while they were courting and in the early months of their marriage to understand her and support her. Where had that gone? Had she disappointed him? Had he become bored? Did she dare ask him?

The letter she sent, after many wasted pages of paper, confessed that she missed him terribly and wished him to come home as soon as possible. It said she hoped he did not see Coolgardie as a place where he could settle because, in all the accounts she had read, it would be impossible to raise a garden there and a garden, as he knew, was manna to her soul.

Their letters crossed, as letters do.

William's third letter expressed bemusement at the number of cards he had received from his patients. He could only imagine, he wrote, that the locum the Victorian Medical Board had arranged was poorly suited to the job. He was immensely gratified, she could tell.

He was also gratified—smug, she thought—that Abramowski had written to him, giving assurances that changes were to be put in place. William would be compensated for his work at the hospital.

W.B., he told her, had sent a very optimistic letter, saying that the spring irrigation was underway, funded by the government loan, and Mildura was heading for a bumper season. Investment was starting to flow. Did she know that Swallow and Ariell, the biscuit manufacturers, were investing in the three-fold expansion of the Proudfoot's preserving factory? (She did not, and was alarmed by the thought of the extra work going on next door; the three-fold traffic on the road). It was probable the government would agree to compensate workers who had lost wages through the Chaffey Brothers liquidation.

Those wages, with the new investments, would greatly boost the wider economy of the township and W.B. was certain Mildura's recovery was now assured.

Joseph was faring well in his job in the livery stable, and was recovering his memory though he remained odd, having not the least social grace. He had long had this tendency, Bert said, but it had dramatically worsened. Fieble, according to Bert, thought Joseph had been 'a *bampot*' all along, which begged the question, William wrote, as to why Fieble had made a partnership with Joseph in the first place.

To William's mind, the prospectors were all *bampots*. It was the thrill of finding a speck of gold that drove them on. There was next to no chance of an adequate financial reward for their dirty, heavy labour. They were risking their lives and most certainly ruining their health in the dusty, dangerous mining sites. When they chanced on a shred of 'the gleam', they spent their takings in bars and bordellos. The amorality of the town was shocking, church attendances were woeful, and every place was in need of the dignifying effect of gentlewomen. The careless filth in the district; the disregard for waste disposal and thereby water quality; the lack of concern for public health, infuriated him. Typhoid was already endemic, destined to get worse, and no public official would give him the time of day on the subject.

"There are very few children," William concluded his diatribe against Coolgardie, "which is fortunate, not only due the horrendous conditions but also due the misery that strikes me, whenever I see one and think of Nancy. I miss you both, so very much."

Jeannie smiled, pressed the letter to her chest and cried in relief.

The following Monday afternoon, Mr Davis arrived at the door earlier than usual. "Wonderful news, Mrs Cameron!" he beamed.

She ripped open the brown envelope. The telegram was stamped 2nd November. Nancy tugged at her sleeve, prompting Jeannie to read the words aloud.

"Departing Albany today. RMS *Ballarat*."

"I presume," Annie said drily, "that RMS *Ballarat* is sailing in *this* direction?"

Mr Davis looked nonplussed. Jeannie touched his shoulder with a reassuring hand and bent down to enclose Nancy in her arms.

"Daddy's coming home, sweetheart."

~

Two days later, William's explanatory letter, written on the eve of his departure from Coolgardie, caught up with the telegram.

He was glad of her letter, he said. It mirrored his feelings and helped him make the decision that his brothers must follow their own paths. Perhaps they would see sense and come to Mildura, but he would waste no more time trying to convince them. He would start for home the next day, and on the basis that his trip outwards had taken 13 days, she could expect him on Wednesday 11th November.

He asked her to give the locum, Dr Abramowski and (oddly, she thought) Sergeant Carter, personal notice of his return, and suggested she should send a note to *The Cultivator* to advise his patients.

"I'd like to let them know," he wrote, "that I very much appreciate the many warm letters I have received during my stay in the West. Tell them I have seen no place on my travels that I prefer to Mildura and I will not be tempted away again."

On Saturday, when Annie put down *The Cultivator* to begin her second cup of tea, Jeannie took the paper from the table and turned the pages to the personal column.

"*Never*," she said crossly, throwing the paper down, "do they print what I ask them to print."

Annie read the paragraph. "What have they missed?"

"His thanks for the letters people sent him. The date he'll be back in the surgery."

"What's this about the School's Board of Advice?" Annie's interest was provoked by the paragraph prior to the announcement of Dr Cameron's return.

"Well ... Dr Abramowski gave his word to William that he will surrender some of his duties. He has resigned from the School's Board, and has nominated me in his place."

"Did he resign or did you push?"

"I might not be elected," Jeannie demurred. "There are nine candidates for five seats."

"But you have Abramowski's backing." Annie hummed thoughtfully. "Did you ask William on this?"

"There was no need."

"How long is the term?"

"Three years."

Annie found the article she had originally been reading and smoothed the pages into place.

Jeannie thought the topic closed, but after another sip of tea her mother added, as if an afterthought, "Will be a great benefit to Nancy. To see you do something of import."

~

Jeannie drove with Nancy to meet William when he arrived on *The Gem*. She expected Nancy to run to him as he stepped off the gangway and held his arms wide, but the child stood still, partly wrapped in the wide folds of Jeannie's dress. Nancy spied on her father warily, so Jeannie stepped into his arms instead.

"You've been away too long," she teased, "your child has forgotten you."

"It will never happen again," William hugged her fiercely.

He scooped Nancy up, taking her by surprise with a quick swing of one arm, and drew her into the hug. She tapped at his beard.

"Och, that!" William laughed. "You don't like it?" Nancy shook her head. "I will take it off as soon as we get home."

~

Annie booked herself on *The Ruby* for Swan Hill on 14th November. She could stay, Jeannie offered, but Annie was determined. Her task was over. There was insufficient room at The Nest; Struan would be needing her attention.

William wanted to take photographs of the three generations: Annie, Jeannie and Nancy together. They dressed for the occasion: Annie and Jeannie in their calf-length black formal dresses; Nancy in her best white cotton dress and knitted white cardigan. Jeannie, like her mother, arranged her hair in a bun tightly pinned at the back of her head. Then she did battle with Nancy's thick, shoulder-length, blonde locks, combing them out while the child howled in protest; making a part on one side and tying a bow on the other. When the group posed with their morning tea on the veranda, Nancy was in a fiercely combative mood. She sat on Annie's lap; her skirts splayed over her grandmother's knee.

"Sit *very* still now child!" Annie hissed in Nancy's ear, squeezing her waist for emphasis.

As Annie kept her eyes fixed on Jeannie, and Jeannie gazed absently at the garden with a teacup in hand, Nancy scowled in *very* still fury at her father.

William allocated three more slides to the photo session. One more of the three at the tea-table with Jeannie holding Nancy. A portrait of Annie by herself and for the last slide he posed himself standing, balancing Nancy on his raised knee, his foot poised on a crate.

Jeannie was either too quick, or too slow to press the shutter. William's head was blurred. The exposure was poor, though she knew enough about photography by now to know that setting the exposure was William's responsibility, not hers. It wasn't a bad photo of Nancy. At least she didn't look angry.

The only photo William commended, was his portrait of Annie. He had positioned her in the corner of the living room, looking out of the window on her right. He lit the kerosene lamp on the mantle to give some illumination to the left-hand side of her face. He had taken so long setting up the photo that by the time he pressed the shutter she was staring out at the garden in boredom. He took the risk of not telling her when to pose. He had her in slightly soft focus, which he had not planned, but it pleased him as he watched the print develop. He pointed out to Jeannie that, unguarded, Annie looked reflective, a little sad, almost—dare he say—kind.

One day, William told Jeannie and Annie enthusiastically as they viewed his finished prints, photos such as these would be made in colour. Exact reproductions, he promised, of the scene.

Annie, not won over by photography, could not see the point of this advancement. "You can colour these easily enough," she declared.

Jeannie rose to the challenge. She mixed a little red pigment with a dash of orange. With a quill tip she delicately coloured the two tea cups, the sugar bowl and the milk jug. Using only the red she coloured Nancy's lips and gave some blush to the child's cheeks.

"Too strong," Annie criticised.

Jeannie added beige to the blush for her own cheeks, and mixed brown with a smidgeon of red for her hair.

"You're not as red as that," Annie complained.

When Jeannie dipped her brush in the blush again, Annie intervened firmly. "No more! Keep to china-painting."

1903, Friday 13th November

The Iron Horse

The arch across Deakin Avenue, outside The Workingman's Club, was ingenious. The columns were made of sweat boxes provided by the fruit preserving company, stacked high and decorated with palm fronds. On top of each column were drying trays, fanned out precariously, and tied between those trays, criss-crossing the road, were colourful banners and a large sign that read:

"Welcome to the Railway."

"What are the words underneath?" William asked Nancy.

Nancy squinted with her whole face: eyes, nose, cheeks and mouth concentrating hard.

"*Omnia vincit labor.*" She spelt out the words in phonetic chunks.

"And what does it mean?" William pressed.

"It's Latin, Pater," Nancy said condescendingly.

"It means 'Work conquers all'," he told her. "It means we have all worked very hard to overcome the difficulties and finally bring the railway to Mildura."

"What work did *you* do?" This was sardonic, Nancy knew that 'work' involved clearing mallee scrub, digging trenches and laying railway tracks.

"When men cut their hands off with a saw, I sewed them back together so they could get straight back to work."

"*Really,* daddy."

"Walk on," William directed.

There were more banners stretched across Deakin Avenue, and an impressive array of flags along the last block of Langtree, leading to an archway heralding the entrance to the railway station. 7th Street was lined, on the railway side, with station-ary buggies, their seats occupied by sight-seers. Between the fence and the railway line, and stretching well past the Coffee Palace, was a large, loose crowd standing idly, chatting.

"Not here yet," William surmised.

"Didn't need to hurry then," Jeannie retorted.

The first train—which Jeannie had not intended to meet—had been due at 8.50am; the second, carrying the Governor's party, at 9.30.

"Nancy! Nancy!" Elsie Shilliday had seen them through the crowd. The lass came running towards them, holding her straw hat to her head with one hand and lifting her skirts with the other. Nancy pulled her hand away from William's and ran to meet her friend.

Listening to Nancy and Elsie chatter excitedly, Jeannie re-gretfully pondered the colonialisation of Nancy's accent and idiom. At home, reciting Robbie Burns or singing songs from The Scottish Students' Songbook in concert with her father, she could produce the roundest Scottish vocalisations, but amongst her school friends she spoke with a deplorable Aus-tralian twang. She had also acquired a handful of swear words, though for this Jeannie suspected the old groom who had been employed by William to tend to the horses, and to milk their cow. Nancy relished the groom's colourful tales of bush-ranger robberies and river-smuggling. William countered with exaggerated accounts of the gipsies who pilfered stores from the Newburgh Quay, and the ghosts that haunted the ruins of Lindores abbey.

They were losing the battle, they had agreed ruefully, to grow Nancy into a Scottish lass.

Or even a true 'lass', Jeannie considered, because Nancy was a tom-boy; a thorough-going country child. She roamed the settlement with Olga, regularly heading out barefoot, and infuriating William by disobediently paddling in irrigation ditches. During the grape harvest, she would be in an orchard, gathering the fruit and eating it, or up on a dray, arranging the pickers' buckets into purpose-built trays. She would cajole a carter into letting her take the reins on the way to the processing plant, where she 'helped' dip perforated grape tins in the boiling, caustic solution that would split their skins and accelerate the drying process. No one but Jeannie, it seemed, minded her being underfoot.

"Private secondary college," Annie decided, observing Nancy's wayward developmental trajectory. "I've made a reservation with an excellent headmistress. Time with me in Melbourne will improve her."

Despite her irritation, Jeannie had accepted her mother's arrangements—there was no suitable college in Mildura. Nancy would go to college in Melbourne, but she would not be spending time with her grandmother.

It was still raw in Jeannie's thoughts; the telegram from Frank in June, her lonely dash by coach and train to Melbourne, the vigil with Frank and Jim by their mother's bedside, and the funeral in July. So much that had not been said. Understanding and forgiveness that went with her mother to the grave. More than anything else, Frank's immeasurable grief.

Frank and Jim had sold Struan, two years earlier, when Jim—against his mother's wishes—had married his long-time sweetheart, Agnes, and wanted money to buy his own family home.

Frank and Annie had settled into a smaller house in South Yarra, where he continued to care for her as her health failed. Jeannie worried about him now. Alone, bereft, overweight and in poor health. She hoped Jim would exceed his usual self, and take good care of their older brother.

Jim, she thought, had finally settled down. He and Agnes lived near to Frank, in South Yarra, with their baby girl, Sheila, born in January 1902. It had been a great consolation, during Jeannie's visit to Melbourne, to hold her niece for the first time; to see Jim as a father, and spend time coming to know Agnes.

In April 1901 Jeannie, William and Nancy travelled to Melbourne to attend Jim's wedding, and they had stayed to witness the federation celebrations held in the second week of May. They watched the Duke of Cornwall and York, son of the new King Edward VII, and his wife, the Duchess Mary, step ashore at the St Kilda Pier and travel along St Kida Road in an open carriage. The young Royals were magnificent, but Jeannie's heart was captured by the Earl of Hopetoun, then Governor of Victoria, who looked so gallant as he galloped past and wheeled his black charger to a halt, ready to greet the Duke and Duchess right in front of the spot where she, her mother, William and Nancy were standing, on the corner of Government House Drive.

On Tuesday evening, William took Nancy back to St Kilda Road to watch the Fire Brigades' Procession—a many miles-long parade that consisted, William reported, not just of Victoria's Fire Brigade bands and vehicles, but of every contraption on wheels from grocer and baker vans to the finest broughams and landaus. On Thursday morning, Frank managed to retain for them all a handy position near to the Commonwealth Arch, from which they were able to watch the spectacular military procession that accompanied the Heir Apparent to the Exhibition Building, where he was to open the first Federal

Parliament in the King's name. Surprisingly, William had been moved near to tears by the ceremony. He did not say he was proud to be Australian, but he *did* say he was immensely proud that federation had been achieved.

On Thursday evening, while William stayed home with Nancy, Jeannie escorted her mother to the State Concert at the Exhibition Building. Afterwards, their cab drove them through Melbourne's brilliantly illuminated and abundantly festooned streets on their way back to South Yarra. Her mother had been overcome by the pageantry and glamour. She had confessed to Jeannie, without reservation, that she was certain now that this new nation, Australia, would have a wonderful future. It was their last outing together, and it was a blessing, Jeannie thought, to have the gaiety of that Royal visit—of the concert and the carriage ride—to remember her mother by.

The sweat box construction outside The Workingman's Club paled in comparison with the Commonwealth Arch, but it was cheerful, and homely in a manner distinctly belonging to the irrigation settlement.

"Excuse me, Mrs Cameron," Martha Abramowski touched Jeannie lightly on the elbow. "Where is Nancy?"

"I've no idea, Martie. She went with Elsie towards the Coffee Palace," Jeannie pointed her finger to where she had last sighted the children. Mildura's big advantage over Melbourne, she thought to herself, was that she was content to have no idea about Nancy's whereabouts. Nancy would come home at the end of the day. Dirty, scraped and bruised no doubt, but safe.

Jeannie and William exchanged a nod of greeting with Dr and Mrs Abramowski, before the Abramowski family ambled on, with Martha skipping ahead in the direction Jeannie had indicated.

Dr Abramowski was still head surgeon at the hospital, and William still attended in an honorary capacity. The only thing that had changed, despite Abramowski's promises, was that William was allocated a private room in the surgery ward for his patients. Otto had kept his assurance that he would dedicate more of his time to the hospital. He had not made himself available for another term as Shire President and the stewardship of the Railway Construction committee had been taken up by W.B. In a recent Council meeting W.B. had, most fittingly in William and Jeannie's eyes, been elected Shire President. After the election, even William had taken to calling his friend 'The Boss', a deferential familiarity now adopted by most in the town.

William continued to argue in vain, as Mildura's Public Health Officer, for relocation of the intake pipe, flushing of the irrigation ditches, and proper sanitation in the town, and as a JP his hearings mostly concerned petty debt cases, but Jeannie had noticed that he was more equable about his work these days. He had grown accustomed to the ways of the settlement, more tolerant of the foibles of its people and its various managing bodies. He had been conscripted onto the committee of the Mildura branch of the Australian Natives Association, which Jeannie thought a strange choice since William regarded himself as anything but an 'Australian Native'.

Jeannie was on several committees herself: St John's Ambulance, the Schools' Advice Board, the Horticultural Society, the Floricultural Society, the Hospital Fete, St Andrew's church. She had fallen into the niche role of commander-in-chief of refreshment stalls and there was always something underway. In the month between now and Christmas there was the state school end of term outing to Red Cliffs; the Sunday School children's picnic at The Nest, Christmas carols at St Andrews and, of course, the ever-expanding First-Aid Graduates end-of-year party. Later today the Governor, Sir George Sydenham Clarke, would present certificates to the graduates of her latest first-aid class at the Municipal Chambers. Once again, she would have to step forward to curtsey, shake his hand and humbly accept his praise for her continued dedication to St John's.

There was to be a banquet tonight, but Jeannie had declined W.B.'s invitation. She had heard more than enough patriotic speeches; way too much about the Boer War and she had suffered too many jibes from W.B. because she would not drink his wine, even as a toast to the King. It was someone else's turn, she gracefully told W.B., because she and William had dined with His Excellency last year. Being no fan of what were overwhelmingly English formalities and reluctant, as always, to pay for the tickets, William had been more than ready to agree.

She and William *had* been intensely interested in news of the Boer War while Joseph and Bert were in South Africa, but thankfully both boys were now safely home in Scotland.

The pair abandoned Coolgardie and had come together to Mildura after news of their brother John's death, from a lung haemorrhage in March 1897. William had been inconsolable, raging against himself for letting John return to Scotland, lambasting doctors who entrusted consumptives to Swiss sanitoriums, voicing his guilt that John was dead, while he lived on. Deeply worried about William, Jeannie had written personally to Bert, asking him to return.

They were a happy family, together in Mildura, for the few months that Joseph's first job at the Findlays' dairy lasted. Unfortunately, when the Findlays' injured cow herder returned to work, they could find no suitable position tending horses or cows. Joseph tried cutting firewood; clearing mallee scrub; weeding irrigation ditches; hunting rabbits. But all his jobs led to complaints directed to William. The lad needed constant supervision; he was unable to make sensible, independent judgments; he had no concept of a time schedule and couldn't be trusted to carry out a set of instructions to the full. In very short order he became an insufferable embarrassment to William.

When Joseph told them he had enlisted with the Victorian Light Horse for South Africa, William was initially stunned, and then argumentative. On behalf of their father, William declared, he could not possibly let the lad go to a war that had naught to do with defending Scotland. It was Bert who took William aside and insisted, "Best thing for him!"

Joseph sailed from Melbourne on the *Medic* troop ship, in October 1899. Six months later, unable to make a living in Mildura, bored and at least partially caught up by the patriotic fervour, Bert followed and signed up in Durban as a volunteer with the South African Light Horse for Maritzburg. Joseph became a professional soldier, but six-months of heavy fighting was more than enough for Bert. He returned to Scotland after his unit disbanded, in January 1901.

Back home in Newburgh, Bert finally met the girl of his dreams and married. A son, Ian, had been born in July 1902, and his wife, Jane, was pregnant again. Unfortunately, Bert reported in his last letter, Jane was very close to her family, and she had made it clear she would not emigrate to Australia. He was now growing turnips and highland cattle, on a soggy patch of black soil in Perthshire, thinking fondly of endless sunshine, red earth and apricots.

Jeannie knew William missed Bert, every bit as much as she and Nancy did.

As the piercing whistle on His Excellency's train reverberated through the crowd, William checked his pocket watch.

"15 hours and 13 minutes." He snapped his watch closed and returned it to his pocket with a satisfied smile. "Wonderful."

"It will make such a difference," Jeannie mused, thinking of holidays in Melbourne and Nancy's trips to and from school.

The train eased majestically into the station, and as it came to a dignified halt the Mildura Rifle Club Band struck up the tune *'See the Conquering Hero Comes!'* The Governor appeared at the carriage door, the band launched into the National Anthem, and the crowd which had gathered into a tight knot at the station entrance, stood to respectful attention, lending hearty voices to *'God Save the King'*.

From his elevated place in the carriage doorway, the Governor thanked the crowd for their welcome and for their allegiance to the King. He was glad to have at last made this trip to Mildura on 'the iron horse'. Irrigation, he said, was 'an especial interest' of his, given that it would stimulate Victoria's agricultural production and 'make provision against future droughts.'

His Excellency moved then, along a pathway that opened for him in the cheering crowd, and climbed onto a drag positioned at the station entrance. In declaring the railway 'open' he further commented, to a roar of affirmation, that there had been no line in Victoria, so much needed as this one. He concluded by praising the good people of Mildura for keeping their faith in the settlement, and assured them that they deserved the prosperity that would now surely come.

As always, the Vice-Regal was treated to a drive around the settlement, but on this day the crowd's focus was on the two trains that sat in the station. As His Excellency and W.B. were driven away, the gathering swirled and reorganised itself into a new pattern with children, of all sizes, concentrated in a bulging semi-circle at the entrance to the station.

Jeannie stood on tiptoes, searching, but unable to distinguish one straw-hatted, white-dressed girl from another. She had no choice but to trust Nancy was amongst the throng.

"All aboard for Yatpool!" W.B.'s appointed train conductor boomed the order, and the children gleefully responded. What began as an orderly line, fragmented into a free for all as children at the rear skirted their minders and raced to the train carriages that had been appointed for them.

"There." William spotted Nancy, who was running for the rear, open carriage, amongst those who had broken rank.

Together they watched her climb into the carriage, with Martie, Elsie and Bessie Shilliday close behind.

"She's lost her hat," Jeannie said with flat resignation.

William hummed. "Someone will bring it home. Can we go now?"

Jeannie nodded and took his arm.

"Bonnie day," William commented, looking upwards as they passed under the railway entrance arch.

"Aye," Jeannie pulled in close, making him fall into step with her shorter stride. "Not a cloud in the sky."

1954, Spring

The Nest, Balaclava Rd, Caulfield, Melbourne

Jeannie found Peter in his favourite place—the train cubby at the rear of her garden. He was turning the wheel in his hands, pretending to be a train driver. On seeing her, he pulled at the rope hanging above the wheel, and the pipe on the roof of the cubby made a satisfyingly shrill whistle.

"Oi driver ..." Her call was interrupted by the phlegm in her throat and she stopped, arms across her waist and slightly bent, in the hope of coughing without hurting her ribs. It had been like this for months; nothing the doctors had been able to suggest.

"You're ailing," Willie's voice told her, when she coughed and wheezed uncomfortably in bed at night, and she customarily replied with "Pray the Lord; bring me Home to you soon."

"Don't take those," he instructed when she stood by her glass of water, pills in hand. But she wasn't as bold as him, she felt she must oblige her doctor by following orders.

William had been a terrible patient. He had flushed his pills, and when he could no longer make it unsupervised to the toilet, he had made a crevice in his mattress and stuffed the pills in there. He would not let the hospital keep him alive, he said. He had already outlived all his siblings except for Janet and Bert. 87 years was too long, he said. She had to stop praying and let him go.

"Oi driver!" she called with more success. "Your tea is ready."

Young Peter, who had turned five not long ago, did not hear any urgency in his great-grandmother's tone. He took the opportunity to climb up onto the roof of the train and look down on her.

She sat on the bench seat to rest, and cast a critical eye over her roses. The winter pruning had not been to her satisfaction. That was the trouble, now she could no longer do the work herself. Nevertheless, her garden was a boundless source of joy and comfort. She and William had made for themselves a wonderful garden during their 28 years in Mildura, but there was no question, the cooler, temperate climate here in Melbourne was much better for the Scottish flowers, shrubs and trees she could not help but love most.

"A walk through the Botanic Gardens, darling?" Willie's voice asked suggestively.

"I can barely make it from the back door to this seat," she objected.

"Are you tired, Grannie?" Peter's hands were cupped to either side of her chin. His head was cocked to one side as he looked into her face anxiously.

"Och, aye. Help me up, laddie. We'll go in for tea."

Jeannie made a show of leaning on Peter as he helpfully jostled her arm.

"Which is your favourite part of the garden, laddie?" she asked as they walked slowly towards the house.

"The train," Peter responded enthusiastically.

"Aye, but the garden itself. What do you like the most—the flowers or the trees?"

Peter looked around thoughtfully.

"I like roses, Grannie. The red ones. And the white ones. And I like the grass because it's so, so green."

"Och, aye. The *green*. Aye, it's lovely, isn't it, that it's so, *so* green."

End-Notes

[1] 'Perplext in faith, but pure in deeds,
   At last he beat his music out.
   There lives more faith in honest doubt,
  Believe me, than in half the creeds.'
(Alfred Lord Tennyson, In Memoriam, A.H.H.OBIIT MDCCCXXXIII: 96)

[2] 'The Impregnable Rock of Holy Scripture', a phrase often used by William Ewart Gladstone, 1809–1898.

[3] 'And said, Hitherto shalt thou come, but no further: and here shall thy proud waves be stayed? In your days, have you commanded the morning or assigned the dawn its place' (Job 38:11–12).

[4] 'Wherefore seeing we also are compassed about with so great a cloud of witnesses, let us lay aside every weight, and the sin which doth so easily beset us, and let us run with patience the race that is set before us, looking unto Jesus the author and finisher of our faith; who for the joy that was set before him endured the cross, despising the shame, and is set down at the right hand of the throne of God. For consider him that endured such contradiction of sinners against himself, lest ye be wearied and faint in your minds' (Hebrews 12:1-3, assumed by many to be written by Paul).

[5] Letter written by Isabella Cameron (1836–1909) to her son William, 18th March 1891. Minor editing for punctuation, capitalisation preserved as originally written.

[6] Ruth 1:16–17 full text: 'Entreat me not to leave you, Or to turn back from following after you; For wherever you go, I will go; And wherever you lodge, I will lodge; Your people shall be my people, And your God, my God. Where you die, I will die, And there will I be buried. The Lord do so to me, and more also, If anything but death parts you and me.'

Post-Script

Heritage

The February 1964 issue of Blackwood's Magazine, published by William Blackwood and Sons Ltd, Edinburgh and London, included a short story titled *Heritage* written by 'Isa Cameron', an Australian born in Mildura to Scottish emigrants.

My grandmother, Annie Calder Isabella Cameron, known as 'Nancy' to her friends and 'Gran' to me, showed me her copy of the magazine about 10 years after publication. Later, the original and considerably longer type-written and annotated manuscript came into my hands, along with Gran's personal diaries, William Cameron's photograph album, Jeannie Cameron's guest book from *'The Nest'* and other memorabilia related to the Cameron family.

From these writings and photos, and from the amazing resource that is the internet, I have put together a story with factual events, and real people, most of whom go by their real names, though I have necessarily imagined their personalities and interactions.

I do not know, as the prime example on which I must offer justification, whether William and Otto Abramowski were at odds, as I have described in my story. It seems obvious to me, given that their belief systems were distinctly opposed—the Scottish surgeon and the Prussian apothecary— that theirs could not have been a harmonious working relationship. What my grandmother recorded of Dr Abramowski was simply that he was 'a man far ahead of his day in his advocacy of sunshine, fresh fruit, fresh air and raw carrots.'

In 1907 Dr Abramowski, with the support of *The Mildura Cultivator*, published a book on his fruitarian diet: *Eating for Health: The Evolution of a Commonsense Conception of Disease and a Natural System of Its Prevention and Cure.* In 1910 his work was republished by Thomas C. Lothian under the title *Vitalism: The Art of Eating for Health.*

Otto Abramowski left Mildura in 1908, and established a 'Sun Sanitorium' in Cheltenham, Melbourne with the intention of bringing about 'a radical reform in habits of eating and living'. In support of the sanitorium he published a booklet '*A Doctors Raw Food Cure*', which can still be purchased via the internet today, in which he wrote:

> *'I ADVOCATE the simple and single natural foods of original man even for modern man, in spite of all the long centuries of mixed and cooked dietary of mankind. I feel strongly, very strongly, on this subject. And why? Firstly: because the natural uncooked food has saved my life, has rejuvenated my body and made out of an over-fed, old man, courting apoplexy and rushing blindly into a premature grave, a comparatively young, vigorous and healthy person, fit and willing to live another half century. And secondly: because it has, through my mediumship, saved many a valuable life threatened by disease, which would have succumbed under the unnatural modern diet and orthodox treatment.'*

That Dr Abramowski died less than two years later, aged 59, was not the best validation of the above claim, but it should be said that his daughter, my grandmother's friend Martie, lived to be 102. How closely she adhered to his dietary regime, I do not know.

Tuberculosis

Tuberculosis was not a reportable disease when William emigrated to Australia. There was, however, much fear and widely-spread misinformation about its causes and effects. Known consumptives were regarded as untouchables, and on this basis, it is incomprehensible that William could have operated as a child's specialist in Melbourne, and a GP in Mildura—indeed, he would not have been deemed a suitable husband—unless he hid his condition.

My grandmother's story tells that William, *after* marrying Jeannie, heard his death-sentence from a Melbourne specialist, pondered his future in Melbourne's Royal Botanic Gardens, and decided that he must investigate the option of settlement in Mildura. There is an interesting discrepancy here between Gran's story and the historical fact. William bought his land, and called for tenders to build their house in Mildura *before* their marriage. Did Jeannie know *before* they were married that she was to endure life in the outback? I have chosen the more romantic, more ethical option of her fiance's confession ... but it is not impossible that he deceived her and, left with no choice after tying the knot, she was obliged to follow him. That would have been a different and, I think, unhappier story. I can't reconcile it with the William Cameron my grandmother evidently adored.

Jeannie is quoted, by my grandmother, as saying that William's survival was due to 'hot air, formalin and prayer.' Formalin was, however, never adopted as an anti-toxin for tuberculosis; investigation into its use was brief and unfavourable and William's research, needless to say, went unheralded. Did intravenous injection of formalin cause him to become infertile? There are references to infertility in anti-toxin research results, but did he know? Did Jeannie? What I know is that Jeannie and William wanted many children, and only had one. My siblings and I did not think to ask why Gran was an only-child and, by virtue of the closely guarded privacy preserved by past generations, we were never told.

William lived to see the Bacillus Calmette-Guérin (BCG) vaccine introduced in Europe in 1921 and manufactured in Australia from 1945. Ever the optimist, at least in my characterisation, he would have believed in medicine's inevitable triumph, long ago, over tuberculosis and yet, according to the World Health Organisation, in 2019 some 10 million people worldwide became infected with tuberculosis. 1.4 million died, making tuberculosis one of the top ten causes of death. Approximately ¼ of the world's population have a TB infection. These people have a 5–10% chance of becoming ill and, while ill, transmitting the disease to others. The fight against multi-drug resistant tuberculosis is far from over.

Did William and Jeannie make the trip home to Scotland?

Yes. In April 1910, William and Jeannie took Nancy on a six-month journey 'home' on R.M.S. *Otway,* via the Suez to Naples, and then by train through Europe. Sadly, this was too late for William to be reunited with either of his parents. My 16-year-old grandmother was thrilled to visit the places in Scotland that were already familiar to her from the stories she had been told by her parents. She was dismayed when she was teased for her accent, and called a '*sassenach*' by her cousins. She brought back an album full of postcards from India, Egypt, Italy, Switzerland, Paris, London and Scotland. Jeannie brought back a collection of small jugs, and William brought back a motor car—arguably Mildura's first.

As she waved 'goodbye' to her Scottish family at Waverley Station, Nancy promised she would come back in five years "even if I have to come as a ship's stewardess." It was not five years; it was forty-five years. But that's another story.

Acknowledgements

The Latje Latje First Nations people

My story makes very little mention of the *Latje Latje*, the First Nations people who inhabited this part of the Murray River before the early settlers invaded their land and either killed or displaced them. I would have liked to delve into their story and find interconnections, but the sad fact is that there is no mention of Aboriginals in any of the personal accounts that I have, and no mention in the many editions of *The Mildura Cultivator* I have read that cover the time-span of this story. They were either absent from the settlement or, much more likely, the settlers rendered them invisible by not recording them.

I acknowledge the *Latje Latje's* custodianship and their continuing connection to the country in which my ancestor's story takes place.

Irene Cameron

My wonderful cousin, grand-daughter of Angus Cameron, who turns 100 in January 2023. Her memories of Angus, Cullalo and especially Joseph are built into this story.

Mildura and District Historical Society

What a great job they've done, and continue to do.

Trove

What an astonishing, free, online resource the National Library of Australia provides.

I'm sure my grandmother never imagined I would be able to sit at my desk, 125 years after the facts, and read the Wednesday and Saturday editions of *The Mildura Cultivator.*

Bibliography

Leaves From the Life of A Country Doctor, Clement Bryce Gunn; The Moray Press, Edinburgh and London, 1935

Lost Melbourne, Heather Chapman and Judith Stillman; Pavilion, London, 2015

Mildura Calling, Alice Lapthorne; The Sunnyland Press, Red Cliffs, Victoria, 1946

Orient Line Guide, Chapters for Travellers by Sea and By Land, Ed. W.J. Loftie; Sampson, Low, Marston, Searle & Rivington, London, 1888

The Australian Irrigation Colonies on The River Murray in Victoria and South Australia, Chaffey Bros 1888-1889; reproduced in 1983 by Sunraysia Multi-Cultural Education Committee (aka *"The Red Book"*)

The Book of Household Management, Isabella Beaton; Ogden, Smale and Co., Printers, Great Saffron Hill, New Edition 1869

The Oswald Album : The photographs of Ernest E. Oswald, Taken between 1889 and his death in 1892; Mildura and District Historical Society; reprinted 2015

Pansies, Oil on Wood by Jean
Emily Bolton Cameron

About the Author

Brenda Hall has degrees in philosophy and human rights. She has two daughters, three grandchildren, and lives by the Hawkesbury River in New South Wales. Clouds Will Break, Brenda's second novel, is the true story of her maternal great-grandparents who immigrated to Australia from Scotland in the 1880s.